The Resurrection File

"Craig Parshall is not only a brilliant lawyer...he is an excellent fiction writer. *The Resurrection File* is one of the most fascinating books I have read in years. It is powerful."

> **Tim LaHaye,** *coauthor of the bestselling* LEFT BEHIND® *series*

"Craig Parshall has written a gripping book that is a must-read."

> **Jay Alan Sekulow,** *Chief Counsel, The American Center for Law and Justice*

"Not a good book to start reading if you need sleep, because you won't get and...Very compelling."

> **Tim Wildmon,** *author, vice president of the American Family Association, and host of American Family Radio*

Custody of the State

"I simply couldn't put *Custody of the State* down! I can hardly wait for the next in the Chambers of Justice series. I'm addicted!"

> **Diane S. Passno,** *author and Executive Vice President, Focus on the Family*

"This is not only a great mystery, but also a deeply moving, redemptive book...Although few novels make it into Hollywood movies, this is one that deserves translation to the big screen. Bravo!"

> **Ted Baehr,** *Chairman of the Christian Film & Television Commission and publisher of* MOVIEGUIDE®

"Authentic characters and a believable story line make *Custody of the State* gripping and even unnerving reading."

Christian Library Journal

The Accused

"Grisham and Clancy...move over! Craig Parshall has truly arrived...*The Accused* [is] a super thriller—a masterful tale of suspense as well as romance...It could be a superb motion picture!"

Ken Wales, *Executive producer of the CBS television series* Christy *and veteran Hollywood filmmaker*

"I was riveted from the first page. Not only an excellent novel, it is also a highly accurate account of military justice and the covert world of special operations."

Lt. Col. Robert "Buzz" Patterson, USAF Retd., *former military aide to President Clinton and author of the bestselling book* Dereliction of Duty

Missing Witness

"A legal thriller wrapped inside a very poignant love story with a twist. Craig Parshall has the innate ability to provide fresh, compelling storytelling from a Judeo-Christian perspective but with enough grit to appeal to a mass secular audience. *Missing Witness*...delivers legal storytelling in its finest form."

Chris Carpenter, *producer,* CBN.com

The LAST JUDGMENT

CRAIG PARSHALL

HARVEST HOUSE PUBLISHERS

EUGENE, OREGON

Cover by Left Coast Design, Portland, Oregon

Cover photo © by Peter Steuart/The Image Bank/Getty Images

THE LAST JUDGMENT
The Chambers of Justice series
Copyright © 2005 by Craig Parshall
Published by Harvest House Publishers
Eugene, Oregon 97402
www.harvesthousepublishers.com

Library of Congress Cataloging-in-Publication Data

Parshall, Craig, 1950-

  The last judgment / Craig Parshall.

      p. cm. — (Chambers of justice ; bk. 5)

  ISBN 0-7369-1292-4 (pbk.)

1. Chambers, Will (Fictitious character)—Fiction. 2. Christian converts from Islam—Fiction. 3. Petroleum industry and trade—Fiction. 4. Muslims—Crimes against—Fiction. 5. Attorney and client—Fiction. 6. Billionaires—Fiction. 7. Terrorism—Fiction. 8. Jerusalem—Fiction. 9. Cults—Fiction. I. Title.

  PS3616.A77L37 2005

  813'.54—dc22

                                                                    2004015416

Printed in the United States of America

05 06 07 08 09 10 11 12 13 / BC-CF / 10 9 8 7 6 5 4 3 2 1

To Bob Kaminsky,
former Director of New Tribes Bible Institute
and lifelong missionary to South America,
who imparted the gospel of Jesus Christ to me
and introduced me to the hope of things to come.

Acknowledgments

As the last in the Chambers of Justice series, this novel has brought me full circle in a sense. Geographically, it begins in the pastoral landscape of Virginia—as did *The Resurrection File*, the first installment in the series—but ends, as did that first novel also, in the turbulent, evocative, inscrutable city of Jerusalem. Between those two distant points there were many miles…and many people who helped create this story along the way.

My thanks go to Rabbi Berel Wein in Jerusalem, noted Jewish historian and founder of The Destiny Foundation (and also a fellow lawyer). He took the time to share an intriguing insight about the Golden Gate in the Old City. Because the reader is not only taken on a side trip to Cairo, but also on a mini-exploration of a slice of Egyptian history, I appreciated the expertise I received from Dr. Walid el Batouty, Egyptologist and Cairo resident. Paul Gossard, once again, did a great job as my editor.

Michael Friedson (another lawyer!) and his wife, Felice, of TheMedia-Line.org, Americans transplanted to Jerusalem, have been a constant source of accurate Israeli information, Middle Eastern current events, geopolitical savvy, and wonderful friendship.

Amnon ("Nony") Shpak, in my humble estimation the best Israel tour guide of all, is owed so many thanks—of course for his personal excursions with my wife, Janet, and me—but also for the laughter we share when the three of us are together, as well as his generosity of heart. Eitan Sasson, of Unitours, has always been a first-rate friend and consummate travel connection between where our feet are and where our hearts always yearn to be.

But because this is also a story about how a trial lawyer and his wife navigate their way through an obstacle course of life's events, it couldn't have been told without my wife, Janet. She will recognize our travels—from the hazy mountain vistas of Virginia to driving the streets of Cairo, walking amid the ancient stones of Jerusalem, and even avoiding sniper fire in Gaza. But more than that, may she see that even a "legal thriller" is no match for the thrill of our life of love together.

1

In the Near Future

THE POLICE WERE RESTRAINING the tightly packed, screaming mass of people. There was a palpable feeling that something was about to give way. Like a flood tide stressing cement and steel, the undulating human wave was pressing against the police barricades. Nervous state and federal agents had their hands poised over their sidearms and nightsticks. Gas masks dangled from their belts. Behind them, a riot squad, armed with tear gas guns, stood rigid.

The small army of sheriff's deputies, state police, and federal agents had formed a protective ring around the angry, surging mob. But their line was being strained by hundreds of protestors. Many of them were screaming, red-faced, against "the bloody Butcher"—"the Sheikh of slaughter." Several of the women wore buttons bearing pictures of victims of the World Trade Center attack, as well as of the Wall Street bombing and the port and mall bombings that had followed in the years later.

The police had separated these protestors from the other group—the one with signs demanding "Tolerance for All Religions," and even-handedness and free speech for Arab–Americans, and calling for an investigation into "American War Crimes Against Muslims" and denouncing "U.S. and Israeli Atrocities."

The two separate knots of protestors and their law-enforcement restrainers were on the perimeter of the sprawling compound of the Islamic Center for Cultural Change, situated in northern Virginia about twenty miles off the Washington beltway. The shoving and pushing and the screaming of profanities and threats were going on at the fringe of the property, out near the highway.

Amid the confusion and anger, some of the deputies were still trying to figure it all out.

"I thought they weren't going to invite this sheikh bozo to come and speak..." one sheriff's deputy at the protest line shouted out to a fellow deputy.

"They weren't. They supposedly uninvited him."

"What happened?"

"He showed up anyway."

"How does a guy like that—somebody who says that Osama bin Laden was a hero, get into this country anyway? Why didn't INS stop that scumbucket at the border?"

But before his partner could respond, a protestor broke through the line and began running, an American flag flying behind, toward the Islamic Center buildings.

The two deputies lit out after him. He dodged. They chased. After a moment or two of head fakes, turns, and twists, and while one of the groups cheered him raucously, the man was tackled.

"Don't let the flag touch the ground!" someone in the protest group cried out.

The deputies held the man down and rapidly zipped his wrists together behind his back with heavy-duty nylon ties.

Fifty yards away, along the front doors of the Islamic Center— within the portico of the pink-stoned building, with its graceful Persian arches and the towering minaret in the background—a dozen private security personnel walked nervously back and forth, eyeing the mobs from a distance. They would pause occasionally listening through their earpieces to the proceedings taking place inside the cavernous auditorium.

Within the Great Hall of the Prophet, as it was called, every red velvet seat was taken.

In the upper deck, a hundred additional Muslim visitors were standing, straining to catch a glimpse of the notorious "glorious mufti."

Sheikh Mudahmid was at the podium. He was a man in his late sixties with a deeply lined face and a jet-black beard that reached down to mid-torso. He wore a gray-and-white robe with a white turban.

He had just finished his address. Now he was basking in the thunderous applause.

But here and there, in the pockets of shadow in the auditorium, there were a handful of voices. Questioning. Dissenting. They were whispering. But audible.

The sheikh surprised the audience by agreeing to take questions from the floor. When the Muslim clerics in the high-backed chairs behind him jumped to their feet and assured him this was not necessary, the sheikh waved them back to their seats with a slow, confident wave of his right hand. He turned back to the audience.

He was in absolute control. He feared nothing.

One cleric approached the floor microphone and asked a question that keyed into a statement the sheikh had made in his speech.

"Allah be praised," the man from the floor intoned quietly as he began. "I want to seek your wisdom. What you said, about the possibility of *jihad* regarding the 'American–Israeli Incest' as you called it—do you mean a *personal jihad* in our devotion to Allah and Muhammad his Prophet, and our personal war against the unrighteousness from the contamination of the infidels? Or do you mean an actual, corporate war of Muslims…a military gathering…a confrontation of Israel and the United States? I believe that the media has twisted your words in the past—there has been much misunderstanding."

"What I have said," the sheikh replied with a calm, pleasant smile, "I have said. There is nothing hidden. America is the beast of unrighteousness and Israel is its whore. What does the Quran say? What does it speak regarding such filth? Do we not have the instructions of the Prophet to rid the world of such abominations? Are we not the kin of the great warrior Saladin? Are we men— or are we little children?"

A loud murmur swept through the hall.

A second man, who looked about thirty, with closely cropped beard, short hair, and intense eyes, approached the microphone.

"Greetings, Sheikh Mudahmid."

The sheikh gave a half-nod, studying the young man carefully.

"I wish to return to the main theme of this conference," the man said. "Is it not 'The future of Islam'?"

The sheikh smiled broadly.

"I am heartened," he replied with his arms outstretched to the audience, "that our young cleric-to-be has at least learned how to read."

And with that, he turned and pointed to the large banner in back of him, bearing the words, *THE FUTURE OF ISLAM— ONE GOD, ONE PROPHET, ONE POWER.*

Laughter rippled through the great hall.

The young man smiled back. But he pressed on.

"The banner says 'one prophet.' And so you speak this day of Muhammad. But you speak *only* of Muhammad. What about Jesus? Doesn't the Quran also call Jesus a 'messenger' of Allah?"

The sheikh leaned forward. His smile had evaporated.

"Sura three, verses thirty-three through sixty. Yes, that is what it says. Go home and read it. But Muhammad is the last and the greatest of the prophets. Why do you bother me with such childish questions?"

"And yet," the young man retorted, "the true test of a prophet is whether what he speaks is shown to be the truth. Isn't that correct?"

The sheikh did not answer. His eyes narrowed as he cast a withering glance at the young man standing at the microphone.

"Those very same verses that you, Sheikh Mudahmid, just quoted to us—don't they also say that Jesus was, and I quote, 'created by God from the dust,' just like Adam? Which means that the Quran teaches that Jesus was only a mere mortal."

By now, several muftis and religious teachers in the audience had risen and begun commanding the young man to sit down.

But he was immovable, locked into place at the floor microphone. His shoulders were straight and his head rigid, as if he were fixed to some invisible scaffold.

And as he continued, his voice was becoming higher-pitched and more penetrating.

"But if what the Quran says is true, then Jesus is a liar. For Jesus tells us in His own words—not the words of the Quran hundreds of years later, but *His* own words, recorded by His apostles, His eyewitnesses, in the Bible—that 'before Abraham was, I AM.'"

The auditorium exploded. Half of the men in the audience were on their feet, yelling at the questioner.

"Sheikh, is it not true," the young man was now shouting to be heard, his eyes fixed on the sheikh, "that if the Quran is correct, then Jesus *cannot* be a prophet—He must be a blasphemous liar, worthy of death!"

Someone on the dais gave a sign to the security guards in black robes scattered along the walls of the auditorium.

Up on the stage, behind the podium, the sheikh could see the point coming. So he began to speak to drown out the approaching heresy—but not quickly enough.

"Unless…" the young man continued, his cries filling the great hall, cutting and sharp like broken glass, "unless Jesus was no mere human prophet—but was the Son of God. The second Person of the Godhead. Who shall come to judge the living and the dead. He is coming—coming very soon—and *that* is the future of Islam you have failed to discuss…the coming of the Lord Jesus Christ. And when He comes, then woe to you false teachers of the law…woe to you who lead millions upon millions astray…idolaters of religion, falsely so-called, vainly puffed up by your fleshly minds, taking delight in false humility and worship of angelic creatures—but failing to worship Jesus the Alpha and the Omega!"

The great hall now filled with a roar as the young man was dragged away from the microphone by the security guards.

"What is your name, infidel?" the sheikh bellowed from the stage.

The young man broke free and ran back to the microphone.

"I am Hassan Gilead Amahn...servant of the Lord Jesus Christ..."

"You are the enemy of Allah—and you are accursed!" the sheikh shouted back.

"There is no condemnation for me," the young man shouted as three security guards dragged him away by the arms, "nor for you, if you embrace Jesus the Messiah—His love is great enough even to save you, Sheikh Mudahmid..."

The audience poured into the main aisle like a rush of ocean surf, grabbing at the young man, slapping, shouting, and striking.

The three security guards had managed to drag their captive to within just a few yards of the exit, but the surging arms and fists of the angry crowd were pulling them down.

Hassan Gilead Amahn felt himself crushed to the floor under the human wave. As he tried to get up, fists flew at him from all sides, smashing into his jaw, his eye sockets, his forehead, pounding on his back.

He stumbled, dizzy and losing consciousness.

Then there was a face of a bearded man with a scarf wrapped around his head—he was wide shouldered, and strong. He grabbed Gilead by the neck, and pulling violently, launched him up and away from the floor and the crowd and yanked him safely through the doors.

For just an instant, Gilead's eyes focused, and he looked the bearded man in the face as he shoved Gilead through the front doors and out into the night air.

Then the man with the beard disappeared.

The law-enforcement agents were already running at a full sprint toward the great hall. A contingent of the protestors, seeing their opportunity, knocked down the barricades and surged forward onto the sprawling lawn that led to the front doors of the Islamic Center—where hundreds of screaming Muslims were pouring outside.

The police started swinging their night sticks and calling for the Muslims to go back into the building—and for the protestors to retreat.

But it didn't work.

Tear-gas canisters flew overhead, and bitter clouds swept over the yard. People covered their faces and fell to the ground.

Someone, somewhere, yelled to the police to arrest Gilead.

"He provoked it! He started a riot!"

Gilead was thrown to the ground, cuffed with thick nylon ties, and then led roughly to a squad car and pushed into the backseat—where he sat for close to an hour under the watchful gaze of two deputies standing outside.

Then one of them got in the front, looked over the seat at Gilead, and read Gilead his rights.

Then he asked, "Do you have a lawyer?"

Gilead looked back at the deputy but didn't respond.

"I said, do you have a lawyer?"

Gilead shook his head.

"Fine," the deputy replied.

Then, as he turned to his clipboard to retrieve the waiver of rights form, he muttered to himself, "Buddy, you're going to need one..."

2

THE ELEGANT HOTEL BANQUET HALL was filled with the sound of clinking coffee cups and after-dinner conversation. Waiters scurried quietly and deftly between tables, serving small plates with dessert. Hanging from the podium at the front of the banquet hall, a satin banner read, "INSTITUTE FOR FREEDOM."

At a table near the podium, lawyer Will Chambers tugged slightly at his starched tuxedo shirt. His wife, Fiona, in a sparkling black evening gown, bent over and adjusted his silk bow tie.

Looking nervously around the room, Will turned to Fiona.

"Okay. Len is still not here. How am I going to introduce our honored guest when he isn't here? Boy, this is awkward..."

Fiona glanced around the room, then looked back at her husband. She reached a slender, manicured hand to sweep one of her husband's long, unruly, silver hairs back into place. She smiled.

"Darling, you'll have to do what you've done so well for thirty years as a trial lawyer."

"What's that? Oh, you mean...*when in doubt, raise an objection?*"

Fiona giggled a little.

"No, that's not exactly what I was thinking about," she replied. "I was thinking of something else. What you told me after we had been married for a few years. You were preparing a case for a trial at the time. What you said really stuck with me."

"Oh, yeah," Will said with a smile. "That's it. Pump up my deflated male ego right before I walk up to that podium and start improvising like a bad stand-up comic..."

"Hey, I'm serious. You were preparing a case. And just to prove that I really do listen when you talk about the practice of law—you said that preparation for trial means preparing to handle the surprises you can't prepare for."

"It's interesting you should remember that statement," Will replied with a half-smile.

"Why?"

"Because I first learned it, years ago, from our honored guest."

The master of ceremonies appeared at the podium. He gave a short introduction of Will Chambers as the award presenter, reminding the audience of Will's career as a civil-liberties trial lawyer. And that Will had been the recipient of the Freedom Award the year before.

With that, Will took a last swig from his coffee cup and made his way to the podium.

The audience quieted. Will glanced quickly at his watch, and then gave the crowd an assured smile. For a moment, Will felt personally responsible for the nonappearance of his old friend, Professor Len Redgrove. Will couldn't help but think that he should have personally contacted Len about the banquet...perhaps even driving him to the banquet himself.

Len hadn't seemed like the same man over the last year or two. Ever since his wife had lapsed into Alzheimer's, and after retiring from his post at the University of Virginia Law School, Len Redgrove had not been just an absentminded professor. His brilliant mind and intellectual passion had apparently fallen into disrepair—even bizarre abstraction.

Will mused over his thirty-year relationship with Len. It had started in his law-school days, when he had first met Redgrove while he was a visiting professor at Georgetown Law School. Later, through Will's spiritual conversion and throughout much of Will's law career, Len had become both a professional and personal mentor. In Will's first criminal case before the International Criminal Court in The Hague in the Netherlands, Len Redgrove had been Will's co-counsel.

I should have picked him up and brought him here myself, Will thought to himself.

"I was asked to present the Award for Distinguished Service in the Field of Religious Liberties and Human Rights," Will said from the podium, still scanning the room for his old friend. "And this year's recipient, as we all know, is Professor Len Redgrove, retired professor of law at the University of Virginia Law School and former visiting professor at Georgetown Law. Professor Redgrove's long list of accomplishments is included in your banquet materials. And it would take me all night to detail each of them. He has not only been a professor of law, a scholar, and a trial advocate around the world in issues of human rights and religious freedom, he also possesses theological degrees. He has authored books on comparative religion. And he was an adjunct professor, teaching jurisprudence as well as 'The Christian Roots of Law' at the Blue Ridge Bible Seminary."

Will fingered the inscribed brass plaque honoring his mentor, which lay on the podium. And then he continued.

"And as a side note, I have the daunting responsibility, when I am not practicing law, of succeeding Professor Redgrove in that same position, in that same seminary. Now that I am teaching his classes, I am finding out exactly how immense his shoes really were, and how poorly they fit me."

A few chuckles swept over the audience.

Then Will looked to the back of the room, where a familiar figure swung open the doors of the banquet hall and then waved in his direction.

Will glanced down at Fiona, who was nodding in the direction of the back of the hall and smiling.

Will nodded back with relief.

"And I see our honored guest has just arrived...so let me be brief. I know of no other human being who deserves this award more than Professor Len Redgrove. Nor do I know of any other person who has so influenced my perspective on the law and the pursuit of justice. Ladies and gentlemen, please join me in giving a warm appreciation to this year's recipient of the Institute for Freedom Award—Professor Len Redgrove."

The audience broke into spontaneous and enthusiastic applause as they rose to their feet.

Redgrove made his way around the perimeter of the room and strode up to the podium. He was wearing a worn tweed jacket, khaki pants, a pair of tennis shoes, and no tie. He paused at the podium, extended both of his hands, and clasped Will's hands firmly.

The younger man turned to walk back to his table, but Redgrove reached out and touched his arm. "No, Will, don't bother going back to your seat. This won't take long."

It was then that Will noticed that his old mentor had what appeared to be a newspaper clipping grasped in his right hand between thumb and forefinger.

Redgrove adjusted the microphone and then spoke.

"Thank you for this award. There is nothing I can say to express my appreciation. But I must say, I will be brief...uncharacteristically brief."

He quickly glanced over at Will, and then down at Fiona at the table in the front row. Then he continued.

"My friends, the long night is coming. It's almost upon us. And the days are filled with evil—the son of perdition wants to sit...be enthroned in the temple. That is the focus of all my research and energy now, and the core of my concern. And I would suggest that it be yours as well. Events in the Middle East...and elsewhere around the world...make the conclusion absolutely unavoidable. So, we must redeem the time...redeem it for heaven's sake! May God grant us the grace to overcome—to be faithful to the end. And remember that the light will expose and make manifest the deeds that are done in darkness..."

The audience gave a hesitant and confused smattering of applause. Redgrove then walked over to Will.

"Sorry. Have to run," the professor said. "Give my love to Fiona. I would have liked to stay and talk..."

Then he began walking away toward the side door of the banquet hall.

Will followed. "Len, why don't you let me take you home—"

"No need. No need," Redgrove snapped. "I drove myself here. I can certainly take care of myself."

Will dashed up to the podium for the brass plaque, returned, and handed it to his old friend.

"Here's your award, Len. Don't forget that."

As Redgrove reached out to take the award, Will caught a glimpse of the headline of the news clipping that was still grasped in the other man's right hand: "FUROR OVER DEUTERONOMY FRAGMENT."

Turning away, Redgrove caught himself and turned back again.

"Oh, almost forgot—there's a nice couple I know...they'll be coming up to talk to you. A new case. I told them you might be able to help. God bless."

And with that, Redgrove stepped quickly over to the side exit and disappeared. As the master of ceremonies passed by Will, giving him a searching and troubled look, the attorney took his seat next to Fiona.

Suddenly Will was aware that a man had approached him from the side and was kneeling next to him.

"Excuse me, Mr. Chambers. I'm sorry to bother you. My name is Bill Collingwood. I'm here with my wife. Our son has gotten himself into some trouble. He has to appear in criminal court...he told us to contact Professor Redgrove. I guess he heard Professor Redgrove speak once. Professor Redgrove then suggested we talk to you."

Will fished in his pocket, pulled out a card, and handed it to the man.

"I'd be glad to talk to you about it. If you'd like to call my office, we'll make an appointment."

The man took the card, smiled, shook Will's hand, and quickly walked back to his table.

While the master of ceremonies wrapped up the evening. Fiona reached out and took Will's hand.

"What do you think about Len's comments?" Fiona whispered with a quizzical look.

Will shook his head.

There was a thought somewhere in his mind. Len's comments had a familiar ring. Will knew that as soon as he and Fiona had gotten home he would have to do some reading and check it out. He needed to satisfy his curiosity as to the source of Redgrove's cryptic comments. But beyond that, perhaps he just wanted to assure himself that the mind of his old friend and professional mentor was not unraveling because of old age, or grief, or even something else.

3

THERE WERE ONLY THREE MEN in the room. But their combined net worth could fund a small country.

The youngest of the three, the CEO of a multinational software and telecommunications conglomerate, was dressed in a golf shirt, casual pants, and sandals. He was twirling a complimentary pen from the El Dorado Hotel between his fingers.

Another, a middle-aged titan of international investment banking with a major share in several commercial airlines and three shipping lines, was pouring coffee for himself at the polished silver tea and coffee service at the end of the small room.

The third, a sixty-two-year-old media magnate who controlled two international cable news services, a dozen major newspapers, and three times as many radio and television stations—all in key markets—was finishing a conversation on his cell phone and furiously scribbling notes.

These three commercial giants knew exactly how extraordinary this meeting was. It was unique, in fact, since their personal assistants had been required to stay outside in the hallway.

The software CEO glanced at his watch and bobbed his foot nervously.

"Are we getting a late start here?" he asked. "When's the satellite broadcast going to start?"

The media magnate snapped his cell phone shut, tossed his notepad onto the burnished walnut table, and then glanced at his own gold, platinum, and diamond-studded watch.

"Three minutes and twenty seconds," he said. "Then Mullburn goes live on the bird…"

"I'm not sure if we've ever really addressed my question," the investment banker noted diplomatically as he carried his cup and saucer back to his button-tufted leather chair. "None of us refused to meet with Warren Mullburn personally in his little island kingdom. I was willing to take the time and make the flight—so were you two. So, why this satellite conference? I thought Mullburn was fanatical about secrecy."

"I don't see this satellite connection as a big deal. I really don't," the media magnate replied. "Time is money. This way Mullburn can say his piece, make his pitch, and in twenty minutes, forty-five minutes maybe, sixty minutes tops, he's in and out and done. Otherwise, we fly in—you know the routine—he's going to feel he has to wine us and dine us, show us around his Caribbean republic he's bought for himself."

"Yeah—Maretas. I had my assistant pull it up on a map. It's a chain of four—what—five islands? In the Caribbean," the software CEO added.

"The population is only just under a hundred and fifty thousand, even including the transients and tourists," the media magnate noted.

"Yes, and yet Mullburn's got this puppet president running the republic for him. And with a standing army of fifty thousand. And a private security and intelligence force that's soon going to rival the Mossad in Israel."

"Getting back to your question," the other man said, "about why Mullburn, with his history of legal problems and his desire for superconfidentiality, would want a meeting like this with satellite hook-up—maybe the fact is that now that the Justice Department has finally dropped its investigation of him…and Washington is no longer trying to extradite him…and he's got sovereign immunity anyway in his little island republic, especially with his position as Foreign Secretary—well, maybe the guy's feeling confident enough where he doesn't care about the interception of this broadcast."

"Well, call me paranoid," the software CEO retorted, "but I think there's something else going on. Maybe Mullburn wants us to believe he has nothing to hide. Or maybe he's deliberately trying to leak news of this conversation."

"That does sound a little paranoid," the other said with a chuckle.

"Well, as for me," the investment banker said, "I intend to ask Mr. Mullburn about the arrest of the Russian oil tycoon."

"You talking about Khodorkovsky?"

"Exactly," the banker replied. "He was on the verge of a major merger between his company, Yukos, and the smaller oil company in Siberia, the Sibneft. That merger would have made Khodorkovsky a major competitor in the world oil market. And his merged companies would have been somewhere around third- or fourth-largest private-sector oil producer in the world. But on the eve of this merger—and this goes all the way back to 2003—suddenly the Kremlin cracks down and arrests him on tax-evasion charges, and the merger falls apart."

"Well, of course Mullburn's assets are pretty oil-intensive," the media magnate said, "particularly with his Mexico expansion a few years ago…but what makes you think he's involved with the Russian thing?"

"I've got contacts in Rome," the banker said, lowering his voice. "A couple of other guys there are saying that there are rumors that Mullburn was pulling the strings to get the Kremlin to crack down on Khodorkovsky, to stop the merger, so that Mullburn's global oil position wouldn't be compromised. It's not rocket science. Seems to me that Mullburn—the world's richest man—is simply trying to get richer…"

"You really think Mullburn's got that kind of clout—that he can pull strings like that?" the media magnate asked.

His question was left unanswered because at that point the satellite video screen lit up with a test pattern. Then a moment later, Warren Mullburn appeared on the screen.

Mullburn was a man in his late seventies but tan, muscular, and possessing a strange form of vitality. Though he was balding, his face carried few wrinkles. He was smiling broadly as he sat in his silk flowered island shirt, comfortably positioned before the camera.

"Gentlemen, I'm very happy to speak with you today. I appreciate also your accommodating me by having this meeting limited to principals only. So, without further ado, let me first ask if any of you have any specific questions about the materials I sent to you regarding the need for these discussions."

"Well, let me start out," the software CEO said. "I was somewhat familiar with this United Nations trend. I was concerned initially when the UN unveiled the first document..."

"Yes. The UN called it the Global Compact. 1999. It was announced at the conference at Davos," Mullburn replied quickly and confidently. "And that was followed up by another document called the United Nations Norms. That was August of 2003. Adopted by the United Nations Subcommission on the Promotion and Protection of Human Rights. And if you look at the Norms, every one of us should be concerned about the implications for global free trade."

"Yes, I did examine those—and I share your concern, Mr. Mullburn," the investment banker said cautiously. "I do admit that I am somewhat troubled by the fact that the Norms recommend that the United Nations subject all of our international corporations to regular monitoring."

"Alright, here's my twenty-five-cents' worth," the software CEO began.

"I assume that your twenty-five cents reflects the current rate of inflation," the investment banker remarked wryly.

After a few chuckles the software CEO continued.

"Okay. Here's what I'm seeing. I don't particularly care for the UN's Norms. And I don't like their Global Compact. But isn't the intent behind these documents to force companies that do business in impoverished or oppressive countries to begin helping to enforce human rights for the local citizens, rather than just going in and making huge profits and ignoring the misery of the nationals—"

"So you *are* a bleeding heart—I'd always heard that," the media magnate said with a smile.

"It's just that I look at it differently," the CEO shot back. "I consider myself a corporate financier with a conscience. That's why I've set up all my foundations that help impoverished children, renovate urban ghettos—"

"Yes, we have all established foundations," Mullburn interjected. "I know the good work you gentlemen have done. And I'm sure you're familiar with the many philanthropic activities I've done around the planet. I'm sure each of you is familiar with the recent article in *Fortune* magazine where I'm listed as the creator of more nonprofit, charitable foundations than any other single person in the world. Which is why I am a fierce believer in the global free-market concept. I believe people will ultimately be bettered by the ability of companies to vigorously sell their products, render their services, and make their profits, free of this high-handed intrusion by the United Nations. And my sources indicate that the European Union is soon going to be backing these United Nations Norms with their own enforcement mechanism. That's why those of us with international corporate interests need to construct a solid front—a unified opposition."

After a pause, the investment banker spoke up.

"One unrelated question, Mr. Mullburn. But I would like an answer to it. My people would like to know whether you had any hand…directly or indirectly…in the arrest and imprisonment of Mikhail Khodorkovsky in Moscow. And please understand the question is not intended to impugn you. On the other hand, my people would appreciate a clear answer to that question."

Mullburn leaned forward toward the camera and smiled broadly.

"Surely, sir, you don't believe that I have either the intent or capacity to interfere with operations within the Kremlin? Besides, from what I know of Russian entrepreneurship, it is a complex, if not Byzantine, maze from which no soul that enters ever exits safely—or alive."

At that, the investment banker smiled, and the other two corporate giants chuckled.

For the rest of the video conference Mullburn smoothly guided the discussion toward a broadening of their coalition. To initiate the formation of a Global Economic Alliance—purportedly for the purpose of counterbalancing the attempt by the United Nations and the European Union to control the conduct of international corporate entities.

Yet each of the three attendees in the small conference room off the coast of California harbored their own suspicions. Concerns about Warren Mullburn's own private agenda.

At the conclusion of the conference the banker leaned forward, glanced down for an instant, then asked one final question.

"Mr. Mullburn, with all due respect, I don't believe that you directly answered my question. Did you have any role to play, in any way, in the arrest of Mr. Khodorkovsky in Russia and the stopping of his proposed oil merger?"

"Let me answer you directly," Mullburn said with a tinge of sarcasm. "I had nothing whatsoever to do with that event. I have no contacts within the Kremlin. I have no ability to dictate policy to the Russian Federation. Does that satisfy you?"

The investment banker smiled courteously and nodded.

When the satellite transmission was ended, Mullburn strolled over to his desk in his palatial Caribbean palace and pushed the intercom button.

"Ginny?" Mullburn said to his secretary.

"Yes, Mr. Mullburn?"

"Get me Secretary Lazenko. Try his private direct line at the Kremlin."

"Yes, Mr. Mullburn."

"Oh, and Ginny..."

"Yes, Mr. Mullburn?"

"Tell him it's important. I'm not in the mood to wait."

4

BILL COLLINGWOOD AND HIS WIFE, ESTHER, were waiting patiently in the lobby of the Will Chambers and Associates law office in Monroeville, Virginia. Bill was a middle-aged man, short and wiry, with a tan, creased face. He was wearing a faded blue denim shirt, work pants, and rubber, stable-mucking boots that came up nearly to his knees. He was twirling a baseball cap in his hands, staring at the ground.

Esther, though the same age, looked older. She was pale and slightly drawn. She was wearing a plain dress with a slightly faded flower pattern.

Hilda, Will's secretary, called them both into the inner office, where Will greeted them both with a warm handshake, seated them, and dove right in.

"Sorry I couldn't talk to you at the banquet."

"We understand, Mr. Chambers," Bill replied in a soft voice. "It's just that Professor Redgrove recommended you. Very highly. Said you were the best lawyer he ever knew. And told us about some of your cases. Around the country, even in different parts of the world. And also it was very important that we knew you walked with the Lord."

"I appreciate your confidence."

"Now, we're actually here about our son, Gilead. Esther and I have always called him Gil. His full name is Hassan Gilead Amahn. We adopted him. What was he...about ten years old then, dear?"

"Ten and a half," Esther answered quietly with a smile.

"You see," Bill continued in his plain, soft voice, "Gil's from Egypt. His mother was killed there. Right in front of him. It was a terrible thing. She had converted to Christ from Islam."

"Was that the reason she was killed?"

"Yes, sir. She was a martyr for the Lord Jesus. At first, when Jadeah—that was his mother's name—when she came to the Lord, well, it was an embarrassment, a great shame to her husband, Abul. His background was, unusually, Shiite Muslim—Shiites are a small minority in Egypt—though he was not particularly ardent or observant. But Gil's mother, Jadeah, after she got saved, was very open about the Lord. She shared her faith every chance she got. I tried to warn her to be a little more...more circumspect. But she was so excited...she just wanted to witness to every one of her Muslim friends."

"You sound like you knew the family. Were you over in Egypt?"

"Yes. Esther and I were missionaries with Sudan Gospel Mission. The target area of the mission was Northern Africa and the Middle Eastern countries. We were assigned to Egypt. As you probably know, the Islamic nations are closed to the gospel and to formal missionary work. So we were sent to Egypt with day jobs. I worked with an American manufacturing company in Cairo. That's where I met Abul—he also worked there. He was a foreman, and because I had an engineering degree, I was his supervisor. So, during the day, I worked at the plant as a production engineer, and Esther worked in the office as a secretary. At night we led small, very secret Bible studies. Jadeah was the first person to come to Christ in that group."

"How was she killed?" Will asked.

"I went over to visit that Saturday," Esther said, "and I arrived just after it happened. Abul wasn't there at the time. It was so brutal. Poor Jadeah. She was walking on her way to the market. She lived in a pretty traditional Shiite neighborhood in Old Cairo. There had been a number of threats against her...the *sharia* law of the Muslims—depending on which mufti you talk to—*sharia* law gives Muslims the right to kill those who leave the Islamic religion."

"Wasn't she still there in the street when you arrived?" Bill remarked.

"No," Esther replied. "Someone had dragged her body into her house by then. But she was already dead when I got there. A group had attacked her with rocks while she was on her way to the store. She was hit in the head. She fell to the ground apparently. Then one of them poured gasoline on her and lit her on fire."

There were a few seconds of silence as Will visualized the barbaric end of that unfortunate woman in Epypt.

"And her son—Gil—he saw the whole thing?"

Bill and Esther nodded solemnly.

Then Bill spoke up.

"Gil is why we're here. He's never been in any trouble before. Until now. But he was arrested the other night for starting that big riot with the Muslims—"

"Over at the Islamic Center?"

"Right. That's the one. Bless his heart, I just think he was there trying to share the gospel with those folks...but...well...you have to know Gil, I guess. He came to Jesus when he was eighteen. Now I call him our young Elijah—"

"Tell him about Abul, dear..." Esther added.

"Oh, yeah. Well, back about six months after Jadeah was killed, Abul had had enough of Cairo. He had an offer from a British company to work at one of their subsidiaries over here in the States—in fact, here in Virginia. Well, as the Lord planned it, Abul gets transferred and comes over here with Gil, and ends up only twenty miles away from where Esther and I were then living. See, shortly after Jadeah's death, Esther got real sick...malaria... she's been battling it for several years. So we left the mission field and came back here. Both of us are born and bred Virginians. I ended up working as a project manager for Roland and June Dupree, at their big horse stables. And I do engineering work every year for the Gold Cup—you know, the horse tournament—and doing some handyman projects, troubleshooting jobs, here and there. Well, Abul runs into us here in northern Virginia. We invite him to church with us. He ends up coming to the Lord...and we got pretty close. Good friends. Then he was killed in a car accident. And in his will he stated he wanted us to raise Gil. So we adopted him."

"Where is he now?" Will asked.

"They've got him down at the county jail. I was going to post bail for him. But the federal authorities are talking about holding him under some terrorist law—it's all Greek to me—but Mr. Chambers, our Gil is no terrorist. No way. If anyone deserves that label, it's that Muslim sheikh that Gil was preaching to, over at the Islamic Center...but certainly not Gilead."

"How old is Gilead?"

"Thirty. As of just three-and-a-half months ago," Esther answered.

"What has he been doing for the last few years?" Will continued.

"He graduated from Bible college. Then, I guess with a little prompting from us," Bill threw a knowing look at his wife, "he enrolled in the same mission school Esther and I trained in before going out on the field. And we thought that he was being led in the same direction—the mission field. But then...in the last semester, he just dropped out."

"Do you know why?"

"Not really," Bill said. "We tried to talk with him about it. He didn't say a lot. But after he dropped out, he did accept a position as an associate pastor in a small rural church in West Virginia."

"I was shocked," Esther said, "when we first visited the church. It was a Sunday that Gilead was scheduled to preach...the head pastor was out of town...it was a small church up in the mountains. In a very poor area. I just wondered to myself, *How in the world can they afford to pay two pastors?*"

"Did you ever get an answer to that?"

"Well...more or less." Esther gave a gentle laugh. "The fact is...I don't think they were paying him. There was a little apartment in the back of the church—a one-room affair. With a bed and a stove. And outside plumbing...had to pump water from a well. He was staying there rent-free. And folks in the church would take turns bringing him food every week."

"Maybe it was his growing up in the poor section of Cairo as a boy," Bill added, "but Gilead has never cared much for material things. He has always seemed content with very little."

"So...he continued working there at the church in West Virginia?" Will asked.

"Yes," Bill replied. "For a number of years. Until just before he showed up at that Islamic conference. I called the head pastor, Ralph Wyman, after Gilead had been arrested here in Virginia, and when all the news broke...I thought they should know, if they were looking for him. And Pastor Wyman said that Gilead had already given his notice and left the church, just before heading back here."

After jotting down a few more notes, Will glanced at his legal pad to see if there was anything else he needed to glean from the parents.

"Well. That gives me a good background. Is there anything else you think I need to know?"

There was a pause. Bill Collingwood threw his wife a quick glance. "Maybe it's nothing..." he finally volunteered. "But... well...the last few contacts we had with Gilead—"

"Yes?"

"He would say, quite a bit, *Dad—the time is short*. And so I would ask him what he meant. But he really didn't explain."

"That was it? He kept referring to that idea: *The time is short?*" Bill and Esther nodded.

"Do you have a guess as to what he meant?"

After a few seconds of silence, Bill answered.

"Just this...whenever he would talk like that—"

"Yes?"

"Well, I could just sense it—like he was carrying this invisible burden. You could just feel that something was troubling his soul."

Will studied the two parents as they sat there, hands folded in their laps.

He recognized the look on their faces. Will, now that he was a parent too, could understand it.

"When did you start to notice this change in Gilead?"

Esther spoke up after a moment. "I think it was after he came back from his trip last summer—don't you, Bill?"

Her husband nodded.

"What trip?" Will asked.

"Well...it was a short trip to the Middle East—Jordan, and Israel too, I think," Bill replied.

Will leaned forward with interest. "What did Gilead do while he was over there?"

After a moment, Bill answered, with a puzzled look.

"You know, we really never could get a straight answer on that..."

5

IN THE SMALL, DINGY APARTMENT in the eastern section of Jerusalem, three men were finishing their tea, sipping from small cups. One of them, an Arab, was serving his two associates from a corroded samovar.

A Frenchman with blond hair in his early thirties, one of the other two, was continuing to press his point in their discussion, in low, hushed tones. Now he was on his feet, quickly walking over to the window to look out, and then stepping back to his spot on the frayed sofa next to the coffee table.

"So the point is," the blond man said as he seated himself, "we don't know how closely we're being watched. I feel sometimes that there are eyes all around us here."

The third man was a young American, with long, dirty brown hair that hung to his shoulders. He wore glasses, which gave him an odd, scholarly look. His pants were army fatigues, and he wore a frayed plaid shirt.

"So, Yossin," the American said to the Arab man, "you're like the intelligence guy here. What's the deal?"

The Arab man paused. His wife, a delicate younger woman garbed in a dark brown burka, had quietly slipped into the room to check the samovar to see if it needed to be filled with more tea.

The Arab man nodded to her, and she bowed her head and retreated from the room. After she was gone, Yossin, the Arab man, answered.

"There is nothing new—nothing you haven't heard before. I keep a warm, open dialogue with the Christian groups. The Catholics, Greek Orthodox, the Coptic Christians…we talk. We share tea together. They invite me to some of their interfaith meetings. It's guarded, but friendly. I doubt any of them have any suspicions. Or concerns. I have no worries there…"

"And what about the Protestants? The evangelicals? I see them as a potential problem," the Frenchman said. "Because they are without hierarchy. Loosely organized—you never know what's going to happen there. Don't you think?"

Yossin was weighing the question, tilting his head slightly one way then the other, before he spoke.

"I do not share your concern. I've studied them—the evangelicals—yes, they are loosely organized. And sometimes…it seems…that they blow with the wind. But they have zeal. And their mobility of thought, sentiment—that can be to our advantage."

"So, you are now talking about—about *him?*" the Frenchman asked.

"Yeah," the American added, "you're thinking now about the appearing of the al-Hakim, right?"

Yossin threw the American a displeased look and raised his hand to silence him.

"My friend," Yossin said in a low whisper, "we must be cautious—very careful about *who* we talk about. And what we say."

"What about other groups?" the Frenchman asked. "Are there any…questions being asked?"

Yossin shook his head.

"I know of none…the Muslims, the Palestinians, they are preoccupied right now with this new peace plan and the statehood initiative. Now they're all focused on what they see as an imminent victory in obtaining eastern Jerusalem as their capital. And securing the Temple Mount. They pay no attention to us."

"And the Jews? What about them?" the Frenchman asked. As he did, he was on his feet again, heading over to the window.

"Yeah, like Israeli intelligence—the Mossad," the American added. "That's really the bottom line here, right? I'm kinda stressed about whether they've got some infiltrators in our group...tapping our phones."

"I'm not worried about the Mossad," the Arab man said. "Recently there have been...developments. I've made my own inroads. I am working with some people of great influence. And power. And wealth. I assure you, the Mossad will not be a problem."

The Frenchman was walking back from the window. His voice was tense, animated. He gestured vigorously with both hands.

"The timing is so critical. So monumental—a thousand years of waiting. And now we approach the consummation."

"And because the Great Appearing is almost upon us, we must be very careful," the Arab said with a sense of inner calm in his voice. He finished his tea and placed his small cup on the saucer. Then he stared at the American and continued.

"Which is why *you* must stop the frivolity. We do not want to be noticed—not until the very end."

"What are you talking about?" the American said, leaning back in his chair and tilting his head.

"I'm talking about the T-shirts. I've heard that you've worn them—with our name inscribed across the front. You must stop that kind of childishness right now."

"You're talking about one of these?" the American said with a big grin. He stood up and unbuttoned his plaid shirt to reveal a picture of a Latin cross on top of a hill with three pillars under the arch of the hill. And at the top of the T-shirt, across the chest, there were large block-printed letters: KNIGHTS OF THE TEMPLE MOUNT.

"That's exactly what I'm talking about," the Arab said. There was fierce rebuke in his eyes and in the tone of his voice. The American sheepishly buttoned his shirt and shrugged.

"Fine. I'll stop wearing it."

"Not good enough. I want you to get rid of them. Burn them. Every one of them. Do you understand?"

The American shrugged again and nodded.

"And so, we've prepared for the appearing of the last great Caliph." The Frenchman was barely able to believe what he had just said. He thought for a moment and added, "How can we know for sure? How can we know that *he* is truly the One?"

"We wait. And we observe. We all know the signs. The three of us will verify the fulfillment of the prophecy. Just like the turning of the constellations in the sky. If all the lights line up, then we will know. And then we will strike. We will make our move."

"Yeah. But just the same, it's got to be a bummer for you," the American said, "that you weren't picked to be the One."

"It's not a matter of being picked or not picked." The Arab's lips tightened ever so slightly, and then he continued. "The choice is not mine. My father, Caliph Omar Ali Khalid, made that clear. We were all with him at his death. He did not specifically name me—so, we must believe it will be another."

"Yeah, but still—"

But the Frenchman cut him off.

"So, we should stay here in Jerusalem? Rather than travel to the site of the First Appearing?"

"We stay here," the Arab said to the Frenchman, "but you will go to the appointed place. If he shows up—then we will know."

The Arab stretched back in his chair and eyed his two guests. Then he looked out through the dirty glass of the apartment window. He could see the spires and crowded limestone buildings of the Old City. Outside were the noises of passersby, children playing, and a few automobile horns far off in the distance where the traffic route circled Herod's Wall.

"And when that happens," the Arab man concluded, his face like stone, "we shall all know the end is near. Very near."

6

IN THE JAIL CONFERENCE ROOM, Will had just finished going over the facts with his new client, Gilead Amahn. Attorney and client were discussing what had occurred the night of the riot at the Islamic Center. Down the hall there were the usual jail noises—inmates yelling curses at one another and the echoing of heavy metal doors banging as guards moved from one cell block to another.

"What you need to understand, Gilead," Will said, "is that the misdemeanor charge of disorderly conduct is sort of a catchall—it's a broadly worded offense that means that you've caused an undue public disturbance through other than privileged conduct."

"And what do you mean by 'privileged'?" Gilead asked.

Will studied his client for a moment before he continued. Whatever he had expected before meeting Gilead, he had been utterly surprised. Gilead did not seem to fit the typical picture of the thundering prophet. Rather, he was a soft-spoken, courteous young man with a quick smile and a keen mind. He was deferential to Will's advice, and was an accurate, detailed historian of information in response to Will's questions. He seemed to fit more the part of a quiet young scholar than a riot-provoking extremist. And he seemed exceptionally out of place in a jail more typically populated by drug dealers and car thieves.

"In your case," Will replied, " 'privileged' has one application—that you were legally privileged—had a First Amendment right—to say what you said. Even though it ended up provoking a violent response."

"So, you think that my conduct was constitutionally protected?"

"I do," Will said. "I'm sure the Commonwealth attorney will argue that you were trespassing. But I don't think that's going to wash. You had a personal letter of recommendation from a Muslim teacher in Cairo, who knew your father before he converted. You came from a traditionally Islamic family, so your presence there was not a 'trespass.' Of course, there's still the question of whether your words were so inflammatory that they constituted 'fighting words.' In other words, that you should have anticipated your comments would cause a public disturbance."

Gilead nodded in acknowledgement.

"There is something else you need to know, however," Will added. "You know that your parents were willing to sign the recognizance bond for your bail. But the hold on you—the reason you're still in jail—really has little to do with the charges against you in the Commonwealth of Virginia state court. It's a hold placed on you by the federal authorities—the Department of Justice. They are apparently investigating your possible ties to a terrorist organization. Do you have any idea why the federal authorities are investigating you?"

Gilead shook his head vigorously.

"I have no idea. I mean...I'm an Arab—an Egyptian by descent—a former Muslim because my father was a Shiite Muslim. But I've been a Christian for a number of years, since I was eighteen years old. I reject terrorism in any form. And as a follower of the Lord Jesus Christ, I believe that the peacemakers should be blessed—not the war makers—not the murderers who kill innocent civilians in the name of religion. So to answer your question, I really have no idea why they're focusing on me."

Will studied his client. At that point, so very early in his representation, Will hesitated to draw any ultimate conclusion. But he was relatively certain about two things.

First, Gilead's recounting of the facts of the night of the incident at the Islamic Center was dead-on accurate. Will had reviewed the report from the sheriff's department, and Gilead's account of that night corresponded, point for point, with the version contained in the supplemental reports of the law-enforcement agencies.

Secondly, and perhaps even more importantly, although this was Gilead's first arrest and his maiden experience as a prisoner in jail, he showed extraordinary poise. Even a sense of calm. He seemed to exude a kind of inner peace.

The jailer who had walked Will to the interview room had confided in him that Gilead had been taking quite a bit of verbal abuse from some of the other prisoners. Gilead responded, the jailer explained, by merely smiling and telling them that Jesus loved them, and no matter what they had done in the past, His sacrifice on the cross could take care of it.

But there was one last, lingering question that Will had.

"Another question…your parents, when they met with me, said that on a number of occasions before the night of the incident at the Islamic Center, you said, 'The time is short.' Over and over—'The time is short.' What did you mean by that?"

As Gilead paused for an instant, an inmate from a neighboring cell yelled out a string of profanities. Gilead seemed unaffected— he shrugged, smiled, and then answered.

"The apostle Paul said that the time was short, didn't he? And the Lord Jesus said that He would be coming soon. That seems to say the same thing. That's all I was saying. If God tells me in His Word the time is short, then I believe it. That's all I was saying…"

"So you aren't implying that some kind of cataclysmic event— that something specific on the timeline was imminent?"

"Well, I do believe there are events that are impending. If I understand what you're talking about. The Christ is coming again. Before He does, certain world events are going to happen. They're happening right now."

"And is that what compels you to speak out the way you did at the Islamic Center?"

"I spoke the way I did because the Holy Spirit of God inside me told me to do so. I try to do what God wants me to do."

"I admire your zeal, Gilead," Will replied. "But I think it's important to temper your zeal to preach the gospel with advice and counsel from those whom God places in your path. Like your parents, for instance. They're seasoned missionaries. I think they've got a lot to offer you in terms of wisdom. Counsel. Advice. Just because Jesus said that *His message*—the gospel—may be an offense to a nonbelieving world, I don't think that gives *us* an excuse to be offensive—"

"Do you believe I was being offensive, Mr. Chambers?" Gilead asked.

Will studied his face. The question was an honest one. Gilead had the look of earnestly wanting to get an answer to his question, rather than simply making a point.

"All I know is that, personally, I would have used a little different approach," Will replied. "But to answer your question specifically—I'm not going to say that you blew it. And I'm certainly not going to say that you violated the law."

Gilead chuckled a bit. "Mr. Chambers, I don't mean to be disrespectful. But do you lawyers always talk like that? Fail to say exactly what you mean?"

Will replied with a smile, "We avoid sweeping generalizations. We try to define our terms. And we try to talk cautiously because words have power."

Will was preparing to conclude the interview. But one final thought had occurred to him.

"Something else," he asked in conclusion. "About the detainer being placed on you by the federal authorities because of this terrorism thing—I heard that you traveled to the Middle East last year. What was that all about?"

"My father was from Egypt. He had relatives in Jordan. I visited them summer before last."

"Where in the Middle East did you go?"

"Jerusalem for a while, mostly sightseeing. Then I crossed the border into Jordan. It was a very short trip—about a week or so."

"Where'd you get the money for the trip?"

Gilead studied Will carefully before he answered.

"It was donated to me."

When Will was finished, he shook hands with his client, assuring him he would do his very best to get him out of jail as soon as possible and would then start preparing for his trial in district court on the charge of disorderly conduct.

On the way back to his office, Will called the U.S. Attorney's Office in Washington, DC. He wanted to contact the assistant U.S. attorney assigned to the terrorism unit—the person responsible for placing the hold on Hassan Gilead Amahn.

After making a few phone calls, he left a message for a Susan Kastone. A few minutes later she called him back, while he was still en route.

After introducing himself as Gilead's attorney, Will quickly addressed the hold issue.

"When are you going to lift the federal detention order on my client? There's no question that he's not only not a terrorist, but has never had anything to do with any terrorist organizations," Will said firmly.

But Assistant U.S. Attorney Kastone was unimpressed.

"I'm not sure when—or if—we're going to be lifting the hold," she replied. "When it happens, we'll let you know."

"Well, with all due respect, Ms. Kastone, that's not acceptable. My client has to prepare for his misdemeanor trial. He's entitled to bail. But for the federal interference by your office, he would have had his parents sign the recognizance bond and he'd be out already. You can't hold somebody indefinitely on vague, unfounded suspicions—"

"What makes you think they're unfounded?"

"All right—convince me," Will replied. "What reasonable suspicion do you have that Hassan Gilead Amahn has any ties to any terrorist organization or activity? I'd like to hear the evidence.

Actually—I would like to hear one single scintilla of evidence. One scrap of information."

"We're not required to tell you that," Kastone said. "And as a result, it would be inappropriate for me to comment. An investigation is underway. As we get closer to a decision on whether or not we're going to file charges against Mr. Amahn, we will advise you accordingly. We have your contact numbers. We'll be in touch."

After this conversation, Will could see only two alternatives as a possible explanation for the mysterious hold placed on Gilead.

First, Gilead's Middle Eastern background, coupled with his presence at the controversial lecture given by Sheikh Mudahmid at the Islamic Center and his recent travel to the Middle East, had caused the FBI and the U.S. Attorney's Office to be over-cautious in making sure that he had no terrorist ties.

But the second alternative troubled Will even more. He knew there was a possibility that Gilead—as honest and unassuming as he appeared to be—had not told Will everything about his background, his travels to the Middle East, or his plans for the future.

After talking to Attorney Kastone, he had the lingering impression that in representing Gilead Amahn he might have stumbled over something much more malevolent than an isolated fracas at a Muslim center.

7

WILL AND FIONA WERE AT THE KITCHEN TABLE finishing breakfast. Andrew, their eleven-year-old son, was thundering down the stairs of their large log house. He dashed into the kitchen lugging his backpack and sports bag.

"Got to go!" Andrew shouted to his parents.

Andrew was a good-looking boy of medium height, with a sinewy body and bright eyes.

"You haven't eaten breakfast—" Fiona said.

"Mom, I did."

"Really?" she said probing.

"Yes."

"And is Mrs. Jankowski okay with our switching the car-pool dates—her driving today and me taking you guys tomorrow?" Fiona asked.

"Yes. Now I've got to go—really, Mom. 'Bye…"

And with the last word Andrew was already dashing through the front door.

"Gee, it's just the two of us," Fiona said with a smile. "Can you stick around for another cup of coffee?"

"I'd love to," Will said reluctantly, "but I've got to get to the office. The district court trial of Gilead Amahn is coming up in just a matter of days. I've got to start putting stuff together."

"How's he doing?"

"He's finally out of jail. The feds released him from that hold. Very strange. They never gave me any explanation. Say," Will changed subjects, "you're here at the recording studio today, right?"

Fiona nodded as she stood up and began to clear the dishes off the kitchen table.

"Right," she said, on her way to the sink. "We're going to do a little bit of work today to help finish at least one of the numbers for the next album. What a blessing it is to have a studio right here on our property! I remember the old days—having to go down to Nashville for days on end...or up to New York."

"Well, you know I wanted to get your studio built as soon as we could manage it—for selfish reasons, of course. I love having you around and not having to travel as much."

Fiona smiled and turned from the sink, wiping her hands on a dishtowel.

"Now, if I could just get you to stay put and stop traveling around the world on those high-stress international cases..."

"Well, to be accurate, it's been a while since I've done any globe-trotting," Will pointed out. "Maybe I'm just getting old. But I'm enjoying settling down...doing that part-time teaching at the seminary. And my work at the Institute for Freedom has been very important to me. You know, for the first time in a long time I'm enjoying the feeling of some stability in our lives. Predictability."

"I think that's a good thing," Fiona said. "You know, maybe it's starting to dawn on you, my dear, that you don't personally have to take on all the David-and-Goliath legal battles on the planet."

"Oh, I never thought that," Will said, his voice trailing off.

"Oh?" Fiona said with a chuckle. "Let's see—there's the Sudan case. Then there was the case before the International Criminal Court in The Hague. With side trips to investigate that one...let's see...you were—oh, that's right—spending time in the jungles of the Yucatán getting shot at. Gee, I almost forgot."

Will got up from the kitchen table with his plate and coffee cup in his hand. He put them on the counter next to the sink and wrapped his arms around his wife.

"I think those days are over," Will said. "I'm very content with the quiet life of a country lawyer in Monroeville, Virginia...here in the scenic shadows of the Blue Ridge Mountains…with my lovely gospel-singing wife at my side…"

Will had a bit of a smirk on his face as he started sounding like a cheesy TV ad.

"I can always tell when you're being sarcastic," Fiona said. "You get that nasty little twinkle in your eye. You get the same look that Andrew does when he's trying to weasel out of some of his chores on the weekend."

"Oh—I meant to ask you, when are you going to talk to Angus next?" Will asked.

"Actually, I was going to stop about five today and head over to the care center to see Da, which means that I won't be around for dinner. Want me to pick something up?"

"No, don't worry about it. I'll get something on the way home tonight."

Mentioning Fiona's dad brought something to Will's mind.

"You know, with the news about this Deuteronomy Fragment and all the discussion in the media about whether it's authentic— what it means for the geopolitics of the Middle East, all the interviews with the archaeologists on TV—I just wish your dad could be more aware of what's going on. If things were different, I would love to see him take this one on."

"You know, before his stroke and heart attack, Da chased the rumors about the Deuteronomy Fragment for years. In Israel. Into Jordan and Egypt. He was looking at the possibility of traveling up into Syria. He really wanted to be the person to expose it…because he had this feeling it was going to be another example of fraudulent archaeology. I appreciate your not talking to Da about it, though. I really don't want to get him overexcited."

"Yeah—and he'd sure get excited about what Len said at the Institute for Freedom banquet the other night. One of his cryptic remarks from the podium."

"Which one? There were several."

"The one about the Temple. The business about the 'son of perdition.' You remember it?"

"Yes. How could I forget? Dear Len, bless his heart…have you talked with him since then?"

"I did try to call him the next day. I feel a little guilty that we haven't had much contact lately. I wanted to take him out to lunch. Catch up on things. But he's not answering his voice mail. You know he's up there in the mountains, in that cabin—alone. I'm hearing all kinds of things about him. He's pretty much abandoned any work in the legal field. He's not writing any more law-review articles. Not publishing any legal treatises. Not teaching at the law school anymore."

"What about the Temple?" Fiona prompted.

"It took me a while, but I found the reference. Len was talking about the 'son of perdition'—that he would be 'sitting in the temple of God'—that's what I wanted to check on. I had read it before. I knew it was somewhere in the New Testament. I thought to myself, *Book of Revelation?* No. Then I remembered that it was in the epistles of Paul."

"So, what was the verse?"

"Let me read it to you," Will said. He walked over to a Bible that was on an end table next to the couch in the great room. "Here it is. Second Thessalonians, chapter two, verses three through five. Paul is talking about the second coming of Jesus Christ…and the signs of the times—

> Let no one deceive you by any means; for that Day will not come until the falling away comes first, and the man of sin is revealed, the son of perdition, who opposes and exalts himself above all that is called God or that is worshiped, so that he sits as God in the temple of God, showing himself that he is God.

For a moment, there was awkward silence between Will and Fiona.

Will's eyes were looking out the window, to the misty blue ribbon of mountains in the distance. But Fiona's eyes were on her husband.

"Do me a favor, darling, will you?" Fiona asked gently.

That broke Will's fascination with the horizon, and he looked at his wife and smiled.

"Sure. What is it?"

"Before you take on any more death-defying cases...before you get involved in something that might put you into the middle of another nest of terrorists...that might bring another attack against this house, or on our family...just do me a favor."

"Anything."

"Talk to your wife first. Talk to *me*, darling."

Will could see something in her face. An expression he couldn't remember seeing before.

"Fiona, honey, what's the matter?"

She shook her head and turned away, trying to minimize her own undefined fears.

"Some people call it woman's intuition. I call it a discerning spirit. But whatever it's called, I've learned to listen to it. Just be careful, will you?"

Will stepped over to her and wrapped his arms around her from behind. He kissed her on the back of the neck and on the cheek, whispering his undying love to her.

And Fiona believed it. And she was comforted. But there still was something else—something that could not be measured or quantified. Nothing she could point to. But a chill reality swept over the surface of her skin. A foreboding...but of what, she could not begin to guess.

8

WARREN MULLBURN WAS IN THE WORKING OFFICE of his Caribbean palace. He could hear the approaching footsteps of his visitor echoing on the marble floor. Mr. Himlet, his personal assistant, had been cleared through security. Now he was knocking and entering the room.

Himlet was a tall, square-shouldered man wearing dark horn-rimmed glasses, with a titanium briefcase and a no-nonsense look about him. And he was bearing an urgent message.

"He's done it, sir," Himlet said in his usual monotone voice.

"Done what?" Mullburn snapped.

"The code-breaking system."

"The encryption code?"

"Yes, sir."

"Quantum encryption?"

"Yes, sir."

"This person has devised a way to break into a quantum encryption system?"

"Exactly, sir."

Mullburn leaned back in his chair, pondering the implications of Himlet's message. Then he asked a question.

"What did you say this man's name was?"

"Putrie. Orville Putrie."

"What kind of a name is that?" Mullburn asked sarcastically. "His parents must have wanted to torture the lad."

"I've got a complete curriculum vitae and background check on Mr. Putrie," Himlet said, tapping his metal briefcase. "MIT.

One of the highest entrance scores in the history of the engineering school. But he was asked to leave the school for threatening a professor. Somewhat unstable personality. Worked for a number of years as a technical operations person for a drug dealer in the barrier islands off the coast of North Carolina. He was forced to flee the authorities there—ended up in the Virgin Islands for a while, and then I met him here, on the island."

"Is he a plant?"

"There's virtually no chance of that," Himlet said. "I've triple-checked all of the possibilities of his being an informant. All the time since his disappearance from the United States, there have been some outstanding warrants for him. I believe we've got a tremendous amount of leverage with Mr. Putrie. But I must say that his work on quantum encryption is revolutionary...even startling, it is so brilliant."

"At last," Mullburn said with a smile, "I've got somebody working for me who's almost as smart as I am."

"Yes, sir," Himlet said matter-of-factly.

"All right. Get him to work immediately on the encryption platform for Israeli intelligence. Get him into their computers. Find out who they're looking at—you know the particular groups I'm talking about. Find out if the Israelis are targeting them."

Himlet nodded obediently.

"Also, I read your report, Himlet, on our global alliance. Looks good. How are we doing with the merger with Petroléos Mexicanos?"

"Happened as of a few hours ago," Himlet replied. "We're calling the newly merged parent company Aztec Petroleum. So that, I think, finalizes your control over the offshore oil exploration project for Mexico."

"Where are we with the Russians?"

"Now that the Kremlin has taken Khodorkovsky out of the picture, I believe we are assured of capturing the Russian oil market as well."

"Alright, now it's time to contact the Saudis. You know who to call. I want to arrange a meeting. I've kept my part of the bargain. Now it's time for them to put up or shut up."

"I understand," Himlet replied. But before he turned to leave he added a final comment.

"On an unrelated matter, when I was in touch with the Russian Federation on the oil issues...the official I was dealing with said he remembered you."

"Oh?"

"Yes. He recalled that, about twenty years ago, he was in the audience during your chess match with Alexei Andropov."

Mullburn smiled.

"The Russian said he remembers you putting Andropov into checkmate in thirteen moves."

Then Himlet added one more thing. It came as close as anything he had ever said on a personal basis—as opposed to business—in his dealings with Warren Mullburn.

"If you don't mind my asking, sir, have you ever thought about getting back into chess competition?"

But the oil tycoon simply shook his head and dismissed his assistant from the room.

Warren Mullburn knew he had never retired from the game of chess. Not in any real sense.

Now, though, the chess pieces were bigger. Global corporations, parliaments, and kings.

And the squares on the board were the nation–states of the world.

9

THE ARCHAEOLOGICAL CONFERENCE in Tel Aviv had been underway for several hours. But now, the panel discussion was approaching the most controversial issue of the day.

The moderator stood at a podium off to the left side of the dais. Four archaeological scholars were assembled at the table, a microphone in front of each.

The atmosphere in the hotel auditorium was electric among the several hundred Egyptologists, archaeologists, experts in ancient linguistics, theologians, and epigraphers.

The moderator was setting up the question for the panelists.

"This brings us to the sensational reports regarding the discovery of the so-called Deuteronomy Fragment. We want to address two issues. First, the very narrow question regarding the level of certainty we can have that this fragment is authentic. And then the broader question, of course—and this is the one that has probably attracted the press and media attention to this conference—that is, to what extent can we archaeologists ensure that our work achieves the highest degree of scientific credibility? And how can we ensure that we will remain free of political bias—particularly when some of our discoveries, such as the Deuteronomy Fragment, have such explosive, cataclysmic political implications?"

The moderator then called on the British scholar on the panel to respond first.

"Well, taking this artifact at face value, the Deuteronomy Fragment purports to be a missing part of the thirty-fourth chapter of the Old Testament book of Deuteronomy, at the current location of verse four. Of course, textually, it changes everything. The traditional Jewish Scriptures indicate that God gives the land of Israel to the Jews through Abraham, Isaac, and Jacob—but now we have this Deuteronomy Fragment, which purports to be of greater antiquity than the oldest copies of the Old Testament extant today. And its text clearly says that God gave the land to Ishmael, whom the Arabs claim as their progenitor. So we have a seismic shift—a massive theological, political, and textual change."

"Well, and then I have my concerns," the Swedish scholar interjected, "about the radiocarbon dating of this Deuteronomy Fragment. I have read the protocols relating to the carbon dating. Frankly, I see some anomalies—they are minor, but they are there, nevertheless. Raising questions about the antiquity of the fragment. Is it actually older than the Dead Sea Scrolls?"

That is when the Egyptian archaeologist jumped in, his voice animated, his face close to the microphone as he spoke.

"The Dead Sea Scrolls—yes—let's talk about that. No one has yet raised the issue. Can't you see? What do the scrolls tell us? In the Dead Sea version of Deuteronomy chapter 34, in the oldest monographs of the book of Deuteronomy—excluding for a moment the Deuteronomy Fragment itself—what do they show?

"That section in the Dead Sea Scrolls is *missing*," the Egyptian continued. "Damaged beyond repair. So, we are unable to say with any certainty what the original manuscript of the Dead Sea version of Deuteronomy 34 really said. That leaves open, entirely, the possibility that this Deuteronomy Fragment may have had it right—and the traditional Jewish scriptures had it wrong."

The moderator stepped into the discussion.

"Thank you, Doctor. All of this does raise the question—the most explosive and perhaps most intriguing question of all. The second part of the question being posed to this panel, in this conference."

With that, the moderator faced the panelists again and paused briefly. Then he continued.

"And that question is this—how can we ensure that our scientific work is free from political bias when the political implications of what we do, particularly here in Israel, are so omnipresent?"

Then the moderator pulled a newspaper report from the file that lay on the podium.

"By way of background, many of you may have seen this article in the *Jerusalem Post*. A similar one appeared in *Harretz*. It refers to a poll taken among Israeli citizens immediately after the publicity surrounding the discovery of the Deuteronomy Fragment. It shows a substantial shift in the minds of moderate Israelis regarding the Israeli–Palestinian peace plan. The poll indicates that the majority of Israeli moderates now favor the proposed plan that gives the Palestinians some control in East Jerusalem along the proposed borders, as their capital. Now of course, the Orthodox Jews show almost no discernible change in their position regarding that issue. But again, the moderates are retreating from many of their historical positions, in some great measure perhaps because of an archaeological discovery. So let's return to my question. How can we ensure scientific objectivity in the midst of such a highly charged political climate?"

In the back of the hall, one audience member—a Saudi national—did not wait to hear the answer. He rose quietly from the second-to-last table and slipped out.

Walking through the large lobby of the hotel, he found a quiet corner, he took out his cell phone, and punched in a number. He waited for the call to connect to his contact in Saudi Arabia.

When the phone was answered, the Saudi man began to speak excitedly.

"This is Kali. I'm calling from the conference."

"Is it over?"

"No, they're still discussing—now, the political issues. But I waited long enough to get a good feel for the consensus."

"And? Is it as we had hoped?"

"Yes. There are no surprises. The arguments—for and against—seem to be along the lines we anticipated."

"Will any of those arguments destroy the vitality of the Deuteronomy Fragment…in its practical application?"

"No, definitely not," the Saudi man answered. "The moderator just referred to the newspaper articles. The ones about the poll taken among Israeli citizens."

"So you can say," the man at the other end of the telephone continued, "that the Deuteronomy Fragment is still a powerful tool. Just as has been represented to us?"

"Oh yes. Very much so…" The Saudi looked around quickly to make sure he was still alone.

"Just so you understand," the official said solemnly, "much relies on the value of the Deuteronomy Fragment to us. This weighs very heavily on our decisions."

"Of course, I understand that. And I will stay through the rest of the conference. I'll give you another report at the end. I'm going to circulate. Speak to as many of the prominent scholars as I can. But I can tell you that, as far as the opening session is concerned, they are taking this Deuteronomy Fragment very seriously. Public sentiment here in Israel is getting very soft now, and very accommodating—you know, on the Palestinian issue, and on Jerusalem."

After the man finished his call, he slipped his cell phone into the pocket of his robe and returned to the conference hall.

In Saudi Arabia, the official—a Saudi sheikh—hung up the phone. Then one of his assistants entered the room, announced himself, and bowed.

"Sorry to disturb you, but there is a call from an assistant of Mr. Warren Mullburn. A Mr. Himlet. He wishes to speak to you."

The sheikh paused for a moment.

"Tell him—I will take his call."

As the assistant turned to leave, the sheikh added something.

"Tell him that I have carefully weighed and considered Mr. Mullburn's contribution to the field of ancient religious artifacts. And now, there is much to discuss."

10

As USUAL, BILL COLLINGWOOD ROSE at five and was out the door at six in the morning. His wife, Esther, though ill with malaria, had managed to get up and make breakfast. Their small cottage in the Virginia countryside was on the grounds of the one-hundred-and-fifty-acre Arabian horse farm of Roland Dupree and his wife, June. As manager of operations, Bill's responsibilities included everything from overseeing the stables and the horse groomers and trainers, to making sure that the horse transport vehicles were in good operating condition and the electric fence and security systems on the property were in functioning order.

Bill had a small office in the main stable. That morning he was reviewing the shipping documents relating to the anticipated arrival of a new Arabian.

But he was finding it difficult to concentrate. His eyes wandered to the small window over his desk, gazing out at the bright blue sky that outlined the Blue Ridge Mountains in the distance. He was disturbed that Gilead, who was such a God-fearing young man, had gotten himself into trouble with the law.

As a life-long missionary, Bill Collingwood understood his son's zeal to evangelize Muslims—particularly in view of his background. But Bill's philosophy was the classic missionary strategy. Patience and a loving approach to cross-cultural evangelism, with painstaking groundwork in planting seeds and building bridges.

By contrast, Gilead's incendiary oratory at the Islamic Center seemed to contain too much fiery prophecy and not enough of the gentle proclamation of the gospel.

Something distracted Bill, and he glanced over to the door leading to his office. Standing there was Dakkar, the senior horse trainer for the stables.

Born in Bahrain of Saudi parents, Dakkar had met the Collingwoods in Cairo through a mutual friend. Though he had always been a zealous Muslim, he had developed a casual friendship with the Collingwoods. Before leaving Cairo for the United States when Esther's health problems increased, the American couple had invited him to look them up in the States.

Then two years previous, Dakkar had come to the United States to pursue graduate school. But he had dropped out and asked the Collingwoods for a job. Bill had recommended him to Roland Dupree, knowing that the young Arab had had experience training and riding Arabians for a Saudi family—and later, for a wealthy family in Egypt.

Now Dakkar stood in the doorway, staring at Bill.

"You look like you've got something on your mind," his boss said with a smile. He pushed himself back from the old wooden desk.

"What is it?" Bill asked, probing.

"Mr. Collingwood—I had a talk with Mr. Dupree yesterday. I'm very worried...about my job...you think that I'm doing a good job, right?"

Collingwood nodded. "Sure. I do. I'm a little concerned that sometimes you show up late and leave early. You know—you and I had a talk about your hours—"

"Right. Absolutely," Dakkar added quickly. "And I've been trying to do better. Much better. But Mr. Dupree, he says he's thinking about firing me. Says he is tired of my not doing the right hours. Coming in at the perfect time. I had told him I couldn't work one Saturday...and I didn't think he'd been too upset about that. But now he says he doesn't know if he wants to keep me. Is there something—please, sir—that you can do?"

Bill Collingwood paused for a moment.

"I'll tell you what I'll do. I'll talk to Mr. Dupree for you. I'll put in a good word."

The younger man's face brightened.

"Okay, thank you. Thank you so much, Mr. Collingwood," he said with relief.

Then he disappeared from the doorway.

Collingwood turned back to his paperwork, but he still couldn't focus. He was thinking about the implications for Gilead if he ended up being convicted of a criminal offense, even if it was a misdemeanor. A conviction would likely mean he would be disqualified from finishing at the mission school. Gilead had completed the first year before he'd dropped out and taken the position as pastor in West Virginia. Bill had been secretly hoping and praying that Gilead would complete his missionary training, and then return to the Middle East with the same missionary organization through which Collingwood and his wife had worked for more than two decades.

Though Gilead had spoken little of returning to mission school and completing his training, Bill had hoped it would be so. But now, with the criminal charges...

At least, the veteran missionary thought to himself, *Will Chambers agreed to take the case. That was a blessing. But whether he can win the case remains to be seen.*

11

Virginia District Court was in session in the courtroom of Judge Lawton Hadfeld, where testimony in the criminal misdemeanor trial of Gilead Amahn had taken up most of the morning.

In his early forties, Hadfeld had been a judge for nearly a decade. His approach to the law was not particularly elegant, though it was thoroughly practical—having been shaped by general practice of law in Virginia, followed by his years on the district court bench. His court heard the mundane stuff of real life rather than the deeper mysteries of constitutional law—single welfare mothers being evicted, busy executives going eighty-five in a sixty-five-mile-per-hour zone on I-95, homeowners violating the brush-burning ordinances.

Hadfeld was leaning back in his judge's chair, rubbing his eyes.

The prosecution case had started with the testimony of the "imam," who supervised the worship in the Islamic Center Mosque, and of the "mufti," who was also in attendance at the Islamic Center at the time of the riot. The Commonwealth attorney had also called as a witness an attendee at the conference, a professor at a Florida university who had suffered a broken arm in the melee. His injury, according to the testimony, was likely to leave him with a small percentage of permanent disability.

Now the prosecution was wrapping up its case with testimony from the arresting officer who had obtained a statement from Gilead.

The prosecutor led the thirty-year veteran of the sheriff's department through a description of his presence at the Islamic Center that day. The deputy described the tensions with the two groups of protestors outside the Center. Then he said that a mob of angry Muslims had burst out the front door of the Center chasing after Gilead Amahn, whom he then identified as the man sitting at the defense counsel table next to Will Chambers.

Then the Commonwealth attorney went to the heart of the matter.

"And you arrested Gilead Amahn?"

"Yes, sir, that's correct. Then I placed him in the patrol car. And then after that, I proceeded to read him his rights, after which time he gave me a free, voluntary statement concerning his side of the incident."

"Now tell the Court," the prosecutor said, "exactly what Gilead Amahn told you in the patrol car after he was arrested."

The deputy paused for a minute and turned to squarely face Judge Hadfeld.

"Mr. Amahn told me," the deputy said in a slow, clear voice, "and this is his statement verbatim…'I knew they would react—I was not afraid of violence.'"

"And after Mr. Amahn told you that he knew the audience in the Islamic Center would react to his speech, and that he was not afraid of their violent reaction, what did you do?"

Will Chambers quickly rose to his feet.

"Objection, Your Honor," Will said "The Commonwealth attorney is misstating the deputy's testimony."

"Oh, I suppose Mr. Amahn's confession was fudged a little by the Commonwealth attorney," Judge Hadfeld said, glancing at his notepad in front of him, "but this is not a jury trial. The Court is not misled. I'll instruct the Commonwealth attorney to be a little more careful in restating the testimony. Now let's get on with this."

The prosecutor smiled and restated his question.

"After Mr. Amahn confessed to me he knew the audience would react," the deputy said, "and that he wasn't afraid of violence, I informed him that I was taking him to a magistrate for the setting of bail, and that he would be charged with a criminal offense of disorderly conduct."

"Your witness," the Commonwealth attorney said to Will, and then sat down with an air of satisfaction.

Will was back on his feet but without any notes in his hand.

"Did you read something to refresh your memory before testifying today—so that you could memorize Gilead Amahn's statement word for word?"

"I'm not sure what you mean," the deputy said, hedging a bit.

"Let me approach this from a different angle," Will said in a casual tone. "As a deputy, you wrote out a formal incident report on this event, did you not?"

"Yes, I did."

"And in your formal report you quoted Gilead Amahn exactly, word for word, as you recited in court today. Correct?"

The officer nodded.

"That's right. Word for word."

"So my question is this," Will continued. "Did you have with you that day, the day of the incident, a memo book?"

"You'll have to specify—"

"I mean a daybook. A notebook—a personal log that you keep, as most officers do, to write down events, statements, and observations on the scene. Then when you get back to the station, you use your log or memo book to reconstruct the information you then put in your formal report. Isn't that the way it's done?"

The deputy paused for a moment and smiled.

"Yes. I do have a logbook. If that's what you mean."

"And you made entries that day—the day of the incident where you encountered Gilead Amahn at the Islamic Center?"

"I'm not sure."

"Do you have that logbook with you today?"

"Yes, I do."

"Please pull it out, Deputy," Will said.

The deputy reached down into the small briefcase he had with him at the stand and retrieved a spiral-bound memo book. He flipped through the pages, glanced at a few of them for a moment, and then resumed his testimony.

"I do have a few entries here, if that's what you mean," the deputy replied.

Will asked that the deputy hand the memo book to him, and the officer reluctantly complied. As Will walked back to the counsel table, the Commonwealth attorney swept up to his position and stared over his shoulder, reading the pages as Will examined them.

After a few moments, the other man shook his head a little, smiled, and resumed his position at the prosecution table.

But Will continued staring at the memo book, absorbed in something that he was reading there.

"All right, Mr. Chambers, let's get this show on the road," Judge Hadfeld remarked.

Unperturbed, Will smiled, nodded, and resumed his cross-examination.

"Deputy, let's take the first of Gilead's statements—the statement 'I knew they would react.'"

Will was holding up the memo book in his right hand for emphasis.

"Would you agree with me," Will continued, "that, according to your notes in your memo book, you asked Gilead Amahn this question: 'You knew the audience would react'? And when you asked Mr. Amahn that, he simply replied that he knew there was a chance that the audience might react to what he had to say. Right?"

The deputy shrugged and said he couldn't say for sure without reading his notes again. So Will handed the memo book back, open to the appropriate page, to the deputy. After a moment he replied.

"I suppose that's one way to interpret my notes...they're a little sketchy..."

"You would agree that what I just said is the most reasonable interpretation of your notes? The most accurate interpretation of your notes?"

"I suppose so."

"And as to the second statement by Gilead Amahn—the statement 'I was not afraid of violence.' That was a statement prompted by your question, as indicated in your memo book. You asked Gilead Amahn this: 'When the riot broke out, were you afraid of the violence occurring around you?' To which Mr. Amahn replied, 'No, I was not afraid of the violence directed at me as I was being beaten and then chased out of the building.'"

The deputy paused for a moment and then answered.

"Mr. Amahn told me he was not afraid of violence. That's what he said, and that's what I put in my report."

"Prompted by a question, put to Mr. Amahn by you, as to whether he was afraid of the violence that was directed at him after the riot had already broken out."

"According to my memo book...that's correct."

"And your memo book contains your notes written at the time of the arrest, at the time of your encounter with Mr. Amahn, when the matters you're testifying about today were the freshest in your memory, correct?"

The deputy paused one last time before answering.

"I've testified to what I recall happened that day. Not everything I observed or heard was recorded in my memo book."

"But the fact is," Will said, his voice rising now with a sense of finality, "that Gilead Amahn's statement about not being afraid of violence was *not* in response to any questions by you about his intentions to create a violent episode, or a riot—but in fact had to do with his feelings while he was being beaten and pursued by the crowd. Correct?"

"I guess so."

"Deputy—can you point out any entry you made in this memo book, on the day in question, where you record any statement from Gilead Amahn in which he indicates his sharing his religious beliefs with the attendees of the Islamic conference was intended in any way to provoke, instigate, or incite a riot or a public disturbance?"

"I don't believe so. I don't believe there's anything in my memo book that says that," the deputy answered.

"But Gilead Amahn did tell you in the squad car that the reason he felt compelled to share his faith in the midst of such a hostile environment was that he was a former Muslim himself. That his mother had been a former Muslim. And that his mother had been killed for her faith over in Cairo, Egypt. Is this all correct?"

The Commonwealth attorney leaped to his feet and objected to the multiple form of the question.

Judge Hadfeld sustained the objection with a growing sense of impatience.

Will asked the question again, this time breaking it down into several parts, but with increasing emphasis in his voice.

"Yes," the deputy answered quietly. "Mr. Amahn did say some of those things."

Will rested his cross-examination, and the prosecutor presented no redirect and rested his case. Will then began arguing his motion for dismissal based on grounds of free speech and free exercise of religion. But Judge Hadfeld quickly cut him off.

"Counsel, I'm not going to grant your motion. But you can renew these arguments again in detail after the close of all the testimony. Now let's hear the defense case."

Will nodded, then bent down to Gilead Amahn, who had been sitting quietly and patiently next to him at counsel table.

"This is it," he whispered to his client. "Are you ready? If you'd like me to ask the Court to start this after lunch, I could probably make a pitch that way…"

"No," Gilead replied confidently, "I would like to testify now. Let's go."

He quickly made his way to the stand, raised his right hand with his left hand on the Bible, and swore to tell the truth, the whole truth, and nothing but the truth, so help him God. And then he sat down.

Will looked at Gilead, ready to commence his direct examination—but noticed something in his client's expression.

His eyes were not on Will or anything else in the courtroom, but somewhere else. Nor did he appear nervous. His face was relaxed, with a slight smile. It was as if Gilead Amahn, while waiting to testify in his own criminal case, was actually harboring a secret that had little to do with the legal proceedings in the District Court of the Commonwealth of Virginia.

Will had thoroughly prepared his client for the trial, conducting a painstaking review of the sheriff's department's incident reports. However, he had been unsuccessful in his attempt to get the reports of the federal agents and the Department of Justice relating to their initial temporary detention of Gilead Amahn.

If his client was hiding something, Will wondered whether it, like some concealed detonation device, would be inadvertently tripped during the trial.

12

"GILEAD, TO REVIEW, THESE ARE THE REASONS that you went to the conference at the Islamic Center that day: to preach Jesus Christ to those Muslim attendees, to honor the memory of your dead mother, who gave her life for her Christian faith, and to obey what you described as the command of the Great Commission—to preach the gospel to the whole world?"

"Yes, Mr. Chambers. That is why."

"Did you deliberately seek to incite a violent reaction?"

"Of course not. That would be wrong."

"What desire did you have to cause injury or harm to the attendees?"

"None whatsoever. I was very distressed that one of those in the audience—that professor fellow from Florida—got injured."

"Did you make any threatening gestures while delivering your comments in the auditorium?"

"No."

"Did you threaten to commit any act of violence yourself?"

"No."

"What is the best description you can give of the nature of your comments that day at the Islamic Center?"

"Evangelistic. I was doing evangelism. Delivering the message of the Lord Jesus Christ."

Will rested his direct examination. The Commonwealth attorney stood up slowly and confidently.

"Mr. Amahn. You said you were being an evangelist—is that what you said?'"

"Yes, sir."

"Well, I've been to some real hell-fire-and-brimstone church services—but no evangelist I know gives a sermon with the intent that folks start throwing punches and get broken arms. Now, are you saying that you believed—as an *evangelist*—that you were somehow above the law?"

"Oh no. I never believed that."

"But you *knew* that the whole auditorium of die-hard, fundamentalist-type Muslims—when you got through having your say—that they would set on you like a swarm of angry hornets out of a nest that had just gotten whacked. Right? You knew that, didn't you, Mr. Amahn?"

"I thought it might happen—"

"You told the deputy, in fact, that *you knew that they would react.* Those were your very words—your words to the deputy when he arrested you and put you in the squad car. Those were your *exact words.*"

Gilead was silent, considering the question.

"Speak up there, Mr. Amahn. Those were *your words*—admit it."

"Yes."

"I don't know about you, Mr. Amahn, but I can't think of any Christian men in the preaching ministry that give a sermon knowing it might cause a riot..."

"I can."

"Oh? You can? You really can?"

"Yes."

"Name one."

"The apostle Paul. The riot that broke out in Ephesus. Book of Acts, chapter nineteen."

The prosecutor waved his hands to signal a different tack in his questions, but not before Gilead added one more comment.

"Verses twenty-two to the end of the chapter, I believe."

"You are comparing yourself to the apostle Paul—to Saint Paul himself, now are you?"

"Oh no."

"And even Jesus said, 'Blessed are the peacemakers'—didn't He?" the prosecutor asked with a hint of sarcasm in his voice.

"Yes."

But before his questioner could change the subject, Gilead continued.

"But you see," Gilead added softly, "Jesus, in His sermons, said He was many different things. Some were very beautiful and pleasant—He called Himself a shepherd...a door...waters of eternal life. Others were not so pleasant. Jesus also said that he came as a *sword*."

"Are you saying that you were a sword, Mr. Amahn? Is that what you were, over there at the Islamic Center? A sword that would cut into the hearts of those people—who don't share your religious beliefs—prompting them to explode in a natural expression of anger at your insults—"

"I did not insult them—"

"Oh? You didn't?" the prosecutor said, his voice rising to almost a falsetto.

"'You false teachers of the law...woe to you who lead millions upon millions astray'—if I am not mistaken, those were your exact words spoken at the microphone in the Islamic Center, isn't that correct?"

"Yes, but—"

"'Idolaters of religion, falsely so-called, vainly puffed up by your fleshly minds, taking delight in false humility and worship of angelic creatures'—those were also your words. Weren't they, Mr. Amahn?"

"I do admit I said that—"

"And you don't think that your words were insulting?"

Gilead was silent.

"You don't think that a bunch of fundamentalist Muslim clerics wouldn't be outraged by such epithets being hurled at them?"

When Gilead still did not respond, the prosecutor snorted, then told the judge he didn't need to hear the answer. He rested his cross-examination.

Will Chambers rose to his feet slowly. He was unperturbed.

"Gilead."

"Yes, Mr. Chambers."

"Those words you spoke at the microphone. Before the riot broke out. You said that these Islamic teachers were 'vainly puffed up by your fleshly minds, taking delight in false humility.' Right?"

"Yes, sir."

"Where did you get those phrases—those words?"

"From the Bible."

"The New Testament?"

"That's right."

"As a matter of fact, you were quoting, more or less, from the book of Colossians, chapter two, verse eighteen—isn't that right?"

"Exactly right."

"Why?"

"Because in that part of Colossians, Paul is attacking the idea of false religion."

"What kind of false religion?"

"The kind that imposes impossible, man-made standards of conduct as a condition of salvation. Paul calls them 'self-imposed religion'—in contrast to God's truth revealed in the gospel."

"And why did you pick that message to deliver that day?"

"Because I felt that, as a former Muslim myself, I wanted them to understand that grace and freedom and salvation comes only in one way—and not in some self-imposed rituals or command-ments."

Will paused a moment before his last series of questions.

"Gilead, can the message of Christ sometimes be like a door—and also at the same time, be like a sword—depending on the atti-tude of the hearer of that message?"

"Absolutely. To the seeker with an open heart, Jesus is the doorway leading to eternal life."

"And how about the person with a closed heart?"

"I suppose to that person, the message I gave...was like a sword."

"So," Will concluded, "whether the person sees a door or feels the cold steel of a piercing sword—that's really up to them, isn't it?"

"Yes, Mr. Chambers. It is."

Will sat down.

The Commonwealth attorney rose for his final recross.

"A sword?"

"Yes. That's what I said," Gilead answered.

"So you are the almighty 'sword of the Lord'—is that it?"

"I didn't exactly say that—"

"But Jesus said He was the sword, didn't He?"

"Yes. At one point in the Scriptures, He does say that."

The prosecutor narrowed his eyes and studied the defendant sitting calmly in the witness chair. Several seconds went by in silence as the prosecutor allowed the thought of Christian terrorism to sink into the judge's deliberations. Then he asked his last question.

"You consider yourself some kind of messiah, Mr. Amahn?"

Instinctively, Will Chambers was on his feet, objecting to the question on the grounds that it was argumentative.

The judge sustained it and instructed Gilead not to answer.

With that, the prosecutor, confident in the effect created by his interrogation, leaned back comfortably in his chair.

But somewhere—just outside the regions of the trial-lawyer part of Will Chambers' brain—something was telling him that it was too bad he had had to object to that last question.

To Will, Gilead's quiet, impervious calm up there in the witness stand...and the mysterious smile that said little but seemed to conceal much...had raised more questions than answers, despite the orthodoxy of his testimony.

For reasons that could only be assigned to intuition, or some spiritual experience of the numinous that had made the hair rise a little on the back of his neck, Will Chambers could only wonder how his client would have answered that question.

13

"SO YOU THINK THIS WHOLE CASE boils down to this question—whether Gilead Amahn's comments at the Islamic Center constituted 'fighting words.' Is that your position, Mr. Chambers?"

Judge Hadfeld had been sitting quietly, listening to Will Chambers' final arguments for dismissal of the criminal charges against his client. But now the judge interrupted to get to the bottom line.

"That's it exactly," Will replied. "The free-speech clause of the First Amendment protects Mr. Amahn's comments from prosecution, with only one exception—if this Court finds that the prosecution has made a case that his comments constituted fighting words under the rule of *Chaplinsky v. New Hampshire*."

"Now, give me the legal definition of 'fighting words' again…I know it's in your brief somewhere. But, Mr. Chambers, just tell me how the Supreme Court defined that."

"Certainly, Your Honor. In *Chaplinsky*—and more recently, in *Virginia v. Black,* the cross-burning case of a number of years ago—the Supreme Court said that 'fighting words' are those words 'which by their very utterance inflict injury or tend to incite an immediate breach of the peace.' In other words, in order to convict Gilead Amahn, this Court would have to conclude that the statements my client made at the Islamic Center were so outrageous, so injurious to the listeners, that ordinary persons would have to conclude they were likely to provoke an immediate riot. And the mere fact that a riot ensued is not the test."

Judge Hadfeld was rocking back and forth in his chair. Then the rocking stopped and he leaned forward.

"Mr. Chambers, I've already told you I am not going to dismiss these charges on the grounds that Mr. Amahn had a First Amendment freedom-of-religion right to say what he did at that time and place. I just can't accept your argument on that. But on this fighting words–free speech issue, I'm closer to the fence on that. But I am going to tell you this—I'm no expert on Islam, but from what I know about the people gathered at that event that day, they were what you might describe as your more fundamentalist-type Muslims. Seems to me that anybody coming in and preaching a Bible-thumping, Jesus-is-here-to-save-you type of a message to that kind of Muslim group has to wonder whether a riot will break out. Just common sense."

"Well, by applying that standard," Will immediately countered, "you create a heckler's veto. You put the power in the hands of fundamentalist Muslims everywhere to silence those who would preach a different message, merely because they have a reputation for violence against those who are, in their eyes, infidels—"

"Well, that's the reality today," the judge continued, his arms sweeping wide in an athletic gesture. "You can't just say anything you want to without accountability or responsibility for what can happen. We live in a violent world, Mr. Chambers—"

"Admittedly," Will interjected. "But the duty with which this Court is burdened is to draw constitutional lines of protection around the free-speech and free-exercise-of-religion rights of every citizen—so that our fear of violence doesn't act as a gag order on the ability of people like my client to preach the gospel of Jesus Christ to unwelcoming ears—"

"You're not hearing me, Mr. Chambers," Judge Hadfeld countered, cutting off the dialogue. "We've got threats of terrorism every day in our country. Every day we check the sliding scale of colors on our TV news reports to find out our level of terrorist risk. There's constant war in the Middle East. We have rampant terrorism throughout the world. If I had my way, I'd do everything I could to try to minimize the violence that can happen as a result of the kind of religious preaching demonstrated by your client."

The judge took only a short breath before he continued his comments to Will.

"Mr. Chambers, do you realize how lucky your client is?" Judge Hadfeld asked, his hands held up. "It's regrettable that the professor who was in attendance had a serious injury to his arm as a result of that riot. But listen, people could have been killed. Shots could have been fired. This could have been really tragic…"

Then Judge Hadfeld lowered his hands and placed them on the desk. He paused a moment and then continued, his face revealing an inner moral conflict.

"I sure hope your client gets the message right now, and right here. Because he's a bit of a loose cannon—he just may walk into a situation and ignite a powder keg. I don't want to read that in some other place your client has triggered some kind of holy war…"

And then the judge turned slightly to face Gilead Amahn, seemingly deep in thought, and then concluded his ruling.

"On the other hand, your counsel has raised some good points. This is a close case—and because the burden is on the prosecution and the benefit of the doubt goes to the defense, I am—reluctantly—going to find you not guilty."

The judge gaveled the proceedings to an end, rose, and disappeared into his chambers. The Commonwealth attorney gathered his files and quickly left the courtroom.

After Gilead had thanked Will enthusiastically, the attorney asked what his plans were.

"I have some places to go. The path is now set before me. And I have to start as soon as possible."

"What kind of path are you talking about?"

But Gilead was extending his hand to shake Will's and appeared unwilling to discuss it any further—except for one final oblique and mysterious interchange.

As the two left the courtroom, Gilead asked one last question.

"Mr. Chambers, tell me this—do you believe in divine destiny? That God has a destiny and a plan for each one of us?"

Will searched the face of the young man standing in front of him. He was struggling to decode his client—as if deciphering a map where the place names were all written in a foreign tongue. Where was his client heading? And why was he so evasive about it?

After a moment's reflection, Will answered the only way he could—with the truth.

"Yes. I believe that God has a divine design for each of our lives."

"God bless you," Gilead said, shaking his hand and thanking him once more. Then he turned and quickly walked away.

As he did, Will Chambers was wondering about Gilead Amahn's undisclosed destination.

But he also was reflecting on Judge Hadfeld's somber warnings to his client, which were now ringing in the back of Will's mind like a bell tolling in the night.

14

In the west wing of the White House, Secretary of State Thomas Linton, Deputy Secretary of State in Charge of Middle Eastern Affairs Bob Fuller, and Special Middle East Envoy Howard Kamura were preparing for their meeting with the president, who was expecting them in thirty minutes.

The trio of State Department officials had spent several days preparing for this. That they would be meeting with President Harriet Corbin Landow rather than her predecessor was almost as extraordinary as the subject matter of their anticipated discussion.

A year into his term, her predecessor, President Theodore Warren, had suffered a debilitating stroke. For the last three weeks he had been at the Bethesda Naval Medical Center. The extent of his recovery was still in doubt.

President Warren's chief White House counsel had transmitted to the President Pro Tempore of the Senate and the Speaker of the House of Representatives a written declaration that the president was unable to discharge the powers and duties of his office.

As a result, Vice President Harriet Landow became acting president. In the next week she was expected to name a vice president, subject to approval of both houses of Congress.

However, President Landow had her eye on another, even larger issue.

Just prior to his falling ill, President Warren had received an urgent message indicating that both Israel and the Palestinian Authority appeared to be at a critical point where a historic peace agreement seemed possible.

Entering the Oval Office at that critical juncture, President Landow now had her own personal aspirations. She suddenly found herself in the position of a potential candidate for a Nobel Peace Prize, should a permanent agreement between the Palestinian Authority and Israel be forged. The chances of her election to a second presidential term in her own right would be catapulted considerably.

Secretary Linton was now leading off in the final discussion with his deputies.

"I know we've been through the drill before, but this is our last opportunity to remind you, Howard, of the scope of your charge in the preliminary negotiations between the Palestinian prime minister and the Israeli prime minister. If things move from the preliminary stage toward the framework we're anticipating, then the president and I are going to be involved, in the background, on an hour-by-hour basis. And of course, if it looks like the pieces are beginning to fall together, then we will arrange to bring the Israeli prime minister and the Palestinian prime minister back here to the States—preferably for a series of photo-op meetings— you know, the handshake and signings at the Connecticut White House with her family gathered around."

Fuller and Kamura nodded.

"Now, as to the general outline," Deputy Secretary Fuller interjected, "just remember the basics, Howard. The president wants her personal sign-off on the basic elements. Gaza to the Palestinians, with a guaranteed safe travel corridor between Gaza and the West Bank. The West Bank—and you know how we're defining that, all the charts and maps will document it—and have them with you—the West Bank to the Palestinians. Jerusalem is a hard sell for Israel, but we think we may be able to create a special transitional status for that area, with it ultimately going to the

Palestinians—again, using the green line as the starting point—West Jerusalem to the Israelis…"

"Let me just put in something here," Special Envoy Kamura said. "I think language is key. I'm concerned about the semantics. I thought I had a pretty good feel for President Warren's use of terms, his personal linguistics on the diplomatic situation over there in the Middle East. But not so much with President Landow. For instance, Bob, you're using 'East Jerusalem' and 'West Jerusalem'…you know the old saw brought up by the Zionists. They yell and scream that there isn't any real East Jerusalem and West Jerusalem. There's only one Jerusalem, and they try to nail me every time I make some kind of public statement, saying I ought to talk about *eastern* Jerusalem, as a point of geography rather than a distinct municipal segment."

"Good point," Fuller noted. "You should sensitize the president to those terms in case she gets caught in the cross fire during some press conference on it while you're engaged in your initial discussions with the folks over there in Ramallah and Jerusalem. But on the other hand, you've got to remind the president that this doesn't amount to a hill of beans. Just use the argument—you know, that everybody knows what we're talking about when we talk about East Jerusalem—it's not exactly a state secret—and that we have to get beyond the war of words to the substance of the real peacekeeping mission. That kind of thing.

"I do believe you need to be prepared for the president to try to nail you on some of the counterarguments," Fuller continued. "She is working her way through this issue, playing catch-up. This wasn't her strong suit during the campaign. And she has a real strong desire to become an instant expert on this. She's going to want to address some of the counterarguments and how you're going to defuse them."

"You're talking in particular about the East and West Jerusalem thing?" Kamura asked.

Linton and Fuller both nodded at that.

"I think one of the best arguments that the Zionists and the right-wing Israelis have is, you know, the fact that in so-called East Jerusalem, which is always touted in our negotiating position as the 'Palestinian-populated area of Jerusalem'—in fact, the demographics don't always bear that out."

"You're talking about the total numbers-type thing, right?" Secretary of State Linton asked.

Kamura nodded vigorously.

"Exactly," he said. "That presents us with a problem...to call it Palestinian Eastern Jerusalem is not exactly accurate, demographically. It only becomes accurate—"

"It only becomes accurate," Deputy Fuller interrupted vigorously, "if, by Palestinian East Jerusalem, we mean that the *political reality* is that we're giving it to them *regardless* of the demographics."

"I don't mean to get us off track," Secretary Linton added, "but did you see the discussion by one of the talking heads last night—I think it may have been *Crossfire* or *Hardball.* Congressman Littleton has now come out and calls himself a full-fledged Christian Zionist. Anyway, he's making this point that our talking about giving Eastern Jerusalem over to the Palestinians because of the sheer numbers of them living there is like saying if you come home at night and find your house has been taken over by gypsies, then the more gypsies that keep moving in, the more you really ought to presume that they have a legal right to stay there."

There was a pause for a few seconds while the trio considered the implications.

All three of them knew full well that the proposal to divide Jerusalem was really not based on demographics—or even any sense of history. It was an arbitrary division created by political expedience and imposed upon Israel as a matter of pure political will.

"You know, we've left something out," Howard Kamura noted.

Secretary Linton and Deputy Fuller glanced at him. And then both spoke the same thing at the same time.

"The Temple Mount."

"It always seems to get down to that," Linton added.

Kamura nodded his head.

"Well, the framework we're using," Linton noted, "is reserving the Temple Mount as the last bargaining chip in the process. But, ultimately—we all know it's got to go to the Palestinians. Or to state it conversely, it can't possibly be given to the Israelis."

"Look," Fuller added, "when the president wants to go over that Temple Mount issue, just give her the *Cliffs Notes* version. After all, with the al-Aqsa Mosque being used by millions of Muslims every year for worship, the only claim of the Jews is some obscure legal technicality about still owning the sides of the Temple Mount because of the 'Wailing Wall' representing part of the wall of the original Temple, where they still pray to this day…you know the drill."

"Yes," Secretary of State Linton noted somberly. "The Temple Mount. That's always the problem, isn't it? To the orthodox, its not a legal technicality. It's a mandate of biblical proportions."

"I really don't know," Fuller added, trying to find some optimism. "You know we've got an atmosphere of change over there in Israel. Sure, you got the hard-liners still screaming for the Temple Mount—the ultra-orthodox, the super-Zionists. But then you've got a very significant change among a lot of Israeli moderates, with waning support for a claim to the Mount. And you've got the Deuteronomy Fragment discovery, which raises the possibility that the original religious writings may have said that God was giving the land to Ishmael of the Arabs, not to the Jews. Without going into the details, because there's a lot of controversy about that discovery, you could just let the president know that the Israelis are scared to death about the alternative to a peace plan."

"You're talking about the one-state solution?" Kamura asked.

Fuller nodded his head emphatically.

"The Jews know that if the Palestinians are forced to be part of an Israeli state, with their burgeoning population and their birthrates much higher than the Israelis', in a matter of years the Palestinians will actually be running the nation of Israel from the inside out. That's the Israelis' worst nightmare. So, faced with that alternative, they know they have to make a plan. They've got to cut a deal."

Suddenly Fuller and Kamura noticed that the Secretary of State had been notably silent for a while.

Both turned to him questioningly. Then he spoke up.

"Gentlemen, don't hit too hard on that Deuteronomy thing. On the archaeological discovery. In fact, I wouldn't mention it at all."

There was a stunned silence.

"I don't know about that, Tom," Fuller rejoined. "I think it's a strong argument for the fact that we've got the Israelis on the run, and we've got the opportunity for a cram-down of a peace plan."

"Let me repeat again," Linton said, "don't hit on the Deuteronomy Fragment."

"Do you know something I don't know?" Fuller inquired.

Linton sorted mentally through the protocols of propriety, legality, and confidentiality.

"Let me just tell you that we've got some intelligence reports that raise some questions about that discovery. You don't want to base a major diplomatic pitch on a piece of science or archaeology, as the case may be, that may be subject to some very troubling questions. Let's just leave it at that."

With that, the three stood and shook hands, and Fuller and Kamura stepped out for a minute before the walk over to meet the president. The Secretary of State hung back, gazing out the windows overlooking the outer perimeter of the Rose Garden. He was not thinking of the president or the meeting they would be having with her in a matter of minutes.

Instead, he was thinking back to a classified report he had received from the Israel field office of the Central Intelligence Agency, casting doubt on the Deuteronomy Fragment.

Certainly, his Middle East experience had taught Thomas Linton one thing. He knew that when it came to the geopolitics of Jerusalem, even the most brilliant diplomacy must always be strapped, inexorably, to the great grinding stones of history and theology.

15

Fiona Chambers was calling from the bottom of the stairs for her son, Andrew.

"Andrew, will you please come down—Dad and I are leaving in a few moments...please!"

"I think I'll go up and get him," Will said, squeezing her hand and heading for the stairs.

Fiona glanced nervously at her watch.

"It's just that I promised Da we would be there by no later than eleven. He really counts on these visits..."

As Will climbed the stairs, he gave his wife a gesture of assurance.

"We're going to be okay, honey. We've got time. We'll be there by eleven."

Just then Andrew came thundering down the stairs and met his dad halfway.

"I just got off the phone with Danny. His parents are coming over in a couple of minutes and we're going to go go-cart racing."

"Oh, Andy, I don't know..." Fiona said.

"Mom," Andrew pleaded, "his parents are going to be there with us. And the people who run the go-cart track never let you do crazy stuff. In fact, they make you go so slow that it's almost boring. Can I go, please? Can I go?"

Will reached out and squeezed Andrew's shoulder.

"You can go. But you've got to be safe. And only if Danny's parents are with you. And remember this is go-carting—not bumper cars."

"Great!" Andrew said, and turned to run back upstairs.

"While you're up there," Fiona called to him, "I never got a good look at the badge you won last night in the contest. Could you please show it to your mother before we leave?"

Andrew sprinted up the stairs and then came bounding down again, holding a small object over the railing so his mother could reach up and grab it.

Fiona beamed as she looked it over, proud that Andrew had won the Regional Christian Church Bible Memorization Contest. She handed it to Will.

It was a heavy brass badge with a clothing pin on the back. It was in the shape of a shield, and at the top, the words "Shield of Faith" were inscribed. And at the bottom, it read,

> Taking the shield of faith.
> —Ephesians 6:16

Will smiled as he read the inscription. Before he could give it back to Andrew, he had scampered back up the stairs.

"Do you remember where Dad and I are going?" Fiona said, calling up the stairs after him as Will laid the badge down on one of the side tables in the great room.

"Yeah," Andrew's voice responded from his room. "You're going to visit Grandpa Angus."

"We'll be back this afternoon," Fiona added, "so please be home by supper time. That means no later than six!"

Will and Fiona drove to the care center, arriving ten minutes after eleven. Angus MacCameron had already been wheeled out to the day room to wait for their arrival. The elderly Scottish man had never quite recovered from his series of heart attacks and strokes, and his worn and ruddy good looks had now been reduced to pallidness, his face saggy and shallow. His eyes, once fiery and brilliant with insight, were now sunken and circled.

"Hello, Da," Fiona said, kissing her father multiple times on the forehead and holding his wrinkled face in her two hands.

MacCameron, a former pastor and editor of a small biblical archaeology magazine, may have been greatly weakened, but he still retained much of his acerbic wit.

"So, *I'm* the old one here, right?"

"What do you mean, Da?" Fiona asked.

"*I'm* the one who can't remember things?"

"What are you talking about?" Fiona asked with puzzlement.

Angus MacCameron turned slowly to glance at the large brown wall clock that now read eleven minutes after eleven.

"You're both too busy to keep track of time?"

"Angus, you can blame me," Will said with a smile. "Fiona was trying to get this show on the road. She did her part."

Angus MacCameron looked up from beneath his bushy, iron-gray tangle of eyebrows with a slight grin. "Chivalry is not dead. Always the knight in shining armor."

Fiona smiled and glanced at Will. "Yes, that's just about right."

Will walked around behind Angus' wheelchair, and he and Fiona began rolling him out to the outside grounds with their tall trees and well-kept gardens.

"So, Da, how are you?" Fiona asked.

"The food here is terrible. Did I tell you that?" Angus growled.

"Yes. You told me that the last time I was here. And the time before."

"I really preferred the other place…the other place where I was staying."

"No, not really." Fiona threw her husband a helpless look. "In fact, you hated the last place, and when we first moved you here you said you loved it."

"What?"

"I said, when you first got here you told us you loved it."

"That must have been my twin brother…because I never would have made such an asinine statement."

Fiona gave her husband a fatigued look as they strolled around the grounds.

Then Will noticed a rolled-up magazine tucked into the side of the wheelchair.

"What are you reading?" Will asked him.

Angus gave him a slightly befuddled look, then reached down and unfurled the magazine. The cover article dealt with the Deuteronomy Fragment controversy.

Suddenly, Will and Fiona regretted the question.

Angus pointed with an unsteady index finger at the cover of the news magazine.

"Why didn't you tell me about this?"

"Da, it was all over the news…what do you mean?"

"You know exactly what I mean," Angus said with a combination of hurt and anger. "I spent years tracking this…following the rumors…trying to find out whether it really existed—and you don't even tell me that it's been discovered."

Will explained reluctantly. "Frankly, Angus, Fiona and I didn't want to upset you. We didn't want you to get excited. Fiona asked that I keep it quiet when we visited you, so I did."

"So," Angus said, eyeing Will, "do you always do what my daughter tells you to do?"

"Only when she's right," Will said with a smile. "Which is most of the time."

By mid-afternoon, Will and Fiona both noticed that Angus was getting fatigued and a little incoherent.

They called for the aide to help him back into bed, but he waved her away testily and looked at Fiona.

"You're my wee bairn," Angus said. "And take care of that lad of yours…what's his name?"

"Andrew," Fiona said gently.

Then Angus turned to Will. In his expression Will saw a man who had much more to say than his limited capacity would permit.

"And you," Angus said looking Will in the eye. "Like my own son…and remember…as Paul before Agrippa, so you'll be."

Then Angus's shoulders slumped slightly, and his head bobbed with fatigue, his eyes half-closing.

"I'll get him into bed. He looks tired," the aide said.

Fiona kissed her father on the cheek, and Will grasped one of his father-in-law's limp hands in both of his, squeezed it, and then whispered in his ear, "I love you, Angus."

There was silence for a while as Will and Fiona drove home. Then Fiona broke the quiet.

"I've heard that before."

"What?"

"What Da said to you. He told me that once before."

"You mean the business about Paul and Agrippa?"

"You were down in Mexico. During discovery for your case before the International Criminal Court. I went to visit Da. He was still in his apartment then. He told me the same thing. He said something about your standing trial like the apostle Paul stood before King Agrippa."

She gazed over at Will who, while driving, was beginning to chew on what his wife had just told him.

"What are you thinking?" she asked, her voice higher than normal.

"Book of Acts. Paul in chains before King Agrippa. He was one of the Herods, I believe. I think it was around chapter twenty-four or twenty-five. Just thinking about that..."

"When Da said that the first time, back in his apartment, he was starting to get a little confused—"

"I know," Will said with a reassuring smile.

He glanced over at his wife. But the look on her face, just then, told Will that she had not been reassured.

16

Gᴉʟᴇᴀᴅ Aᴍᴀʜɴ ᴡᴀs ᴀsʟᴇᴇᴘ for the last leg of the trans-Atlantic flight. He awakened as the Egyptian Air pilot announced they were preparing to land at Cairo International Airport.

Gilead rubbed his eyes and glanced out the window. As the plane neared the airport, Gilead surveyed the outstretched Egyptian metropolis that housed some seventeen million inhabitants.

After the plane landed, he pulled down his single piece of luggage from overhead, shuffled slowly behind the passengers down the aisle of the jumbo jet, and finally, descended the metal staircase to the tarmac. He knew the significance of that moment.

It was the first time he had set foot on Egyptian soil since he was a boy. Since the time his father had moved him to the United States, he had never returned to Egypt. Until now.

For Hassan Gilead Amahn, his appearance in Cairo, Egypt, at this time and under these circumstances was slowly becoming an overwhelming, even staggering reality.

He knew what it meant. He hoped that his appearing, at that time and place, would be like the first spark that is set to dry kindling.

Gilead hailed a cab. He was picked up by a dented, older-model yellow Mercedes. It dodged in and out of the horn-blasting, weaving, and bobbing mass of vehicles that were passing through the downtown of Cairo. He drove past sights that had been long forgotten, but that were now rekindling old memories.

Past the blocks of five-story-high square, unadorned red-brick apartment buildings, separated from each other by streets full of rubble, trash, and refuse. Children were playing amid the broken concrete between the buildings. They occasionally passed carts pulled by donkeys, which were piled high with alfalfa or onions.

Gilead gazed through the dirty cab window at the streets of crowded shops selling raw meat and vegetables hanging from hooks, baskets, and trinkets. Some of the shops had small, makeshift hibachis constructed out of metal buckets, with burning coals in them.

And everywhere he saw the robed adherents of Islam. The men in their fezzes and headscarves, and the women—a few in modern dress and driving vehicles—but many, if not most, walking like human silhouettes along the roadside, draped in the black burkas of traditional Muslim dress.

This was Cairo. It had been his home. And it had also been the scene of his mother's cruel murder.

And now, at last, he was here again. This was the beginning.

Gilead asked the driver to take him to the Citadel, in the Islamic quarter of Old Cairo.

"You wish me to take you to the front gate...for the tourist's trip?"

"No, not there," Gilead replied. "Take me beyond, to the Salah ad-Din Square. Just outside the Citadel. Drop me off there."

The Citadel, a mighty fortress of Islamic power, with its domed top, huge mosque, and two towering spires on each side, surrounded by battlements and walls from the thirteenth century, had initially been constructed by Salah ad-Din, known to Westerners as "Saladin."

Saladin, Sultan of Egypt, had left Cairo with his Muslim army and attacked Jerusalem in the fall of the year 1187. His goal was to drive the Crusaders of Christendom out of Jerusalem forever. After an eighty-eight year occupation by the Crusaders, on October 2, 1187, Saladin's forces finally breached St. Stephen's Gate in the outer wall of Old Jerusalem, invaded the city, vanquished the Crusaders, and broke their grip on Jerusalem and the Holy Land.

The cabbie pulled the dented yellow Mercedes to a stop at the curb at the perimeter of the Salah ad-Din Square, and turned around, reaching out his hand.

Gilead paid him fifty Egyptian pounds, grabbed his bag, and exited the taxi.

In the open square leading to the mammoth Citadel, Gilead surveyed the army of pedestrians. Tourists from Europe, pilgrims from Africa, Muslim worshipers from around the world swarming to the Citadel—a symbol of ancient Islamic domination.

Gilead walked approximately thirty yards into the square, then put down his bag and zipped it open. He grabbed a handful of small pamphlets. Then he closed his eyes, lifting his hands to the sky, and said a silent prayer.

Then the young man opened his eyes. With his hands still outstretched, and in a voice loud enough for passersby to hear, he said,

> You prepare a table before me in the presence of my enemies;
> You anoint my head with oil...

17

"Do you speak English?"

"I do some," the Swedish tourist replied. He was standing with his wife in front of Gilead Amahn, in the Great Square of Salah ad-Din.

"Do you come to see the Great Citadel? And the mosques?" Gilead asked.

The Swedish man and his wife nodded.

"Have you read about the great Salah ad-Din, the Muslim warrior who built the Citadel?"

The man nodded again.

"The great Salah ad-Din, the Sultan of Egypt, followed one whom he believed was greater than he. He followed the Prophet Muhammad," Gilead continued.

As Gilead was conversing with the tourist couple, an older man, sporting a bushy moustache and wearing a long black robe and red fez on his head, passed through the tourists, business-people, and Muslim worshipers in the square and stopped a few feet short of Gilead, staring at him intently.

Gilead ignored him and pressed on.

"But there's One whose coming has been foretold. There is One greater than Salah ad-Din. And greater than Muhammad. He shall establish a new kingdom and shall rule the world with a rod of iron."

"What are you saying?" the man in the fez asked in Egyptian Arabic.

Gilead quickly turned to the man and answered him in the same dialect.

"I am preaching the coming of God's Anointed One. The One who is greater than Muhammad. One whose coming has been prophesied from age to age…the One whom you have rejected…the One who is *not* worshiped in all your great Islamic mosques. The One whom the Quran has spoken about…but both it and you have not understood. You hear, but you do not listen. You see but you are still blind…"

The man in the fez threw his arms out in a frantic plea.

"It is forbidden! You must not say these things…you defile this holy place!"

Gilead turned from the man in the fez back to the wide-eyed Swedish couple and handed them a pamphlet. Its cover read,

THE ONE WHO IS
GREATER THAN MUHAMMAD.

The Egyptian man continued to yell. Then he bent down, snatched off his sandals, and began striking Gilead in the head with the heels.

"You are accursed!" He continued to strike Gilead in the face and on the head.

Within moments several worshipers, a few local businessmen, and an imam of the local mosque had gathered around Gilead. After learning of his "blasphemy," they too removed their sandals and began slapping, punching, and kicking him with the heels of their shoes.

Tourists and passersby quickly fled the ever-increasing ring of angry Muslims.

And in the middle was Gilead, covering his head as he was pummeled.

Soon, Muslim worshipers from the el Azhar, Bab Zuweila, and Emir Khair Bey Mosques nearby—and from as far as the El Hakim Mosque, a full three kilometers away—were streaming into the streets and running toward the Square across from the imposing fortress walls of the Citadel.

Three Egyptian squad cars and several blue-jacketed Egyptian police on foot arrived at the scene and began swinging their batons at the crowd to break it up. The commanding officer at the scene, using a bullhorn, instructed the crowd to disperse immediately.

But without waiting for a response, one of the officers lobbed a tear-gas canister into the mob. Robed men collapsed to the ground coughing and gagging.

The captain with the bullhorn set it down, put on his gas mask, and waded into the crowd swinging his baton left and right, hitting heads and torsos. When he came to the vortex of the mob, where Gilead Amahn had fallen to the ground bleeding from the nose and blinded by the tear gas, coughing and gagging, the captain grabbed him by the neck and dragged him out of the center of the now disorganized crowd, off to a curbside.

When Gilead tried to sit up, he was struck on the back with the officer's baton and collapsed down to the ground again. In a few minutes, after the tear gas had begun clearing, the captain removed his gas mask, wiped the sweat from his face, and then knelt down next to his captive.

"What is your name?" The officer was rifling Gilead's pants pockets and removing his wallet.

"Hassan Gilead Amahn," Gilead gasped out.

"So, you speak Egyptian Arabic. Are you Egyptian?" the officer asked.

Gilead nodded.

"Are you a Coptic Christian?"

Gilead shook his head no. The officer studied Gilead's passport and driver's license as he was still recovering.

"You live in America?"

"Yes. From the time that I was a boy," Gilead said, clearing his throat.

"Why did you leave Egypt?"

"My father took me. He got a job in America. I went to school there."

"You're not a Muslim. You're not a Coptic. What are you?"

Gilead lifted up his right hand. It was wrapped around a small pocket Bible. He handed it to the officer, who glanced at it.

"What you've done is forbidden," he snapped. "You are a fool. Now lie down on your stomach. Face down. Arms at your sides. Stay in that position until I tell you to get up."

The officer rose to his feet and flipped on his walkie-talkie.

"And if you move," he warned Gilead, "then you will die a fool's death."

18

GILEAD HAD BEEN DRAGGED in handcuffs to the Egyptian police station and finally to the small cement-block interrogation room. He was seated in a metal chair that had been bolted to the cement floor. While he waited for his interrogator to appear, one of the jailers brought him his wallet.

Gilead opened it and, not surprisingly, found that the small number of Egyptian pounds that had been left there had been removed.

After five minutes a captain of the Egyptian police nonchalantly strolled into the room, a man in his early forties with a well-trimmed moustache and carefully combed hair, which had been dyed black to cover the gray.

He wore the black Egyptian police department uniform with gold epaulets at the shoulders. His coat was unbuttoned in the front, revealing his black police tie and white shirt. He was wetting a finger and applying it to a small coffee stain on his shirt.

Sauntering over to a metal desk, he wheeled the small chair from behind the desk to a position immediately in front of Gilead. Then he sat down and lit a cigarette.

After taking a long draw and blowing it up into the air, he held out his pack to Gilead.

"Cigarette?"

"No, thank you."

"Do you know why you're here? Do you know why you were arrested?"

"I'm not sure—"

"Because you committed the crime of contempt of religion. You slandered the heavenly religion. Under Egyptian law that is a serious offense. You should know that. You are an Egyptian also. Is that not true?"

Gilead nodded.

"Your passport shows you are an American. Why are you here in Cairo?"

"I'm here as a messenger of God," Gilead said quietly in Egyptian Arabic.

The captain leaned back in his chair and took another long draw from his cigarette. He blew several smoke rings, and then waited until they dissipated before he continued.

"Messenger of God. Yes. Cairo sees many of those. The caliphs and the muftis. But there is only one great messenger of God. There is only one true prophet. His name is Muhammad. And you have come here to Cairo to insult him. In front of the Great Citadel. In the square named after our hero, Salah ad-Din. You came to that sacred place to insult us?"

"I came to insult no one," Gilead replied.

"But you're not a Muslim?"

"No."

"And you're not a Coptic Christian?"

"I am not a Coptic."

"Well," the captain said, picking something from his teeth with his fingernail, "ninety percent of us, as you know, are Muslims here in Egypt. The other ten percent are Coptics. That doesn't leave much room for outside prophets like yourself."

Gilead studied the captain but did not reply.

"Do you believe you're a prophet?"

Again silence.

The captain rolled his chair up so that he was only a few inches from Gilead's face. The captain placed the heels of both of his patrol shoes down onto the toes of his prisoner's feet and began to press down hard.

"I asked you a question. I need to know whether you are a prophet."

"You have said it," Gilead replied cryptically.

"On the other hand," the captain continued, "you don't come out of the desert into the city like most of the prophets—you come from America to Cairo. Tell me...what did you do in America?"

"I was an assistant pastor in a Christian church. In West Virginia..."

"Tell me about this West Virginia—what kind of place is it?"

"It was a small church. In a very remote, rural part of West Virginia."

"Wilderness? Would you say that it was wilderness?"

"You could say that," Gilead said cautiously.

"So, perhaps you *do* think you are a prophet. Out of the wilderness of West Virginia and into Cairo—preaching like an infidel—or maybe you're just an agitator. Are you an agitator?"

Gilead was silent.

"Tell me right now. Who were you meeting with here in Cairo?"

"I am not meeting with anyone. I came alone."

"What are the names of your groups? What terrorist network are you part of?"

"I am not a terrorist. I don't know what you're talking about."

The Egyptian police captain slowly rolled his chair back and stood up. He took a few more puffs on his cigarette and then threw it to the ground, crushing it with his boot.

"I know all about you. Surely you know that. All about the death of your mother. Jadeah. Obviously not an Arabic name. It was not her given name. Excuse me for saying it, but she was a very misguided woman. I know about your father taking you to the United States. And many other things...are you going to be truthful with me now?"

"I told you the truth. And you've rejected the truth—"

"So. You want to play the part of a prophet. But you know how they all end up. I'm sure you've visited the tombs of the pharoahs in Giza. You will end up like them. You know the old Egyptian saying? You're Egyptian too—surely you remember it. 'The sun rises in the east so that it may die in the west.' But you've turned things around…"

Gilead looked at his captor with curiosity.

"The sun may rise in the east so that it can die in the west— but you've come from the west, apparently, with the desire to die in the east."

And with that the Egyptian police captain chuckled to himself, which turned into a coughing spell.

When the coughing stopped, he walked up to the American, stepping again with the heels of his boots on his toes.

"Tell me, do you know Muhammad Wafa?"

Gilead shook his head no.

"How about Tarek Dahab?"

"No," Gilead said, wincing with pain.

"How about Hisham Ghani or Tarek al-Ashkar?"

"I know none of these men," Gilead said through gritted teeth.

The Egyptian police captain studied his face and then, after a few more moments of twisting his heels back and forth, grinding down, he took a step backward.

"Just wondering…because these four men—the human-rights agitators talk all the time about these four men. Most unfortunate. Some people say they were tortured after they were arrested and then killed while in our custody. I, of course, know nothing about this. Truly a shame…just wondering if you knew them…"

Then the captain lowered his face down close to Gilead's. And with breath that stank of cigarette smoke, he gave his last warning.

"Mr. Amahn, I would suggest that you answer all of our questions. And give us as much information as you know. Because, if you do not—things could be very uncomfortable for you."

With that, the police captain turned, buttoned his jacket, and strode out of the room. After a few moments a jailer entered the room and escorted Gilead to his cell. On the way Gilead asked whether he could make a phone call.

The man laughed but did not answer.

"How much for a phone call?" Gilead asked.

The jailer stopped, looked down to both ends of the corridor, and then whispered, "One hundred pounds. Egyptian."

Gilead rolled back the cuff of his pants, opened the seam, and pulled out a one-hundred-pound note.

The jailer smiled through his bushy moustache and stained teeth.

"You get a bargain today," the guard said, laughing. Then he added, "Tomorrow, the price goes up—to two hundred pounds."

19

WILL HAD BEEN IN HIS OFFICE for only half an hour that morning when Hilda, his secretary, buzzed him on the intercom.

"Will, you've got a call. Overseas. It's from Egypt. And it's collect."

"Who is it?"

"Gilead Amahn," she said. "He said he has only a few moments to talk."

Will had the call immediately transferred to his desk.

"Gilead, what are you doing in Egypt?"

"It would take too long to explain," the young man said in a rushed whisper. "I've been arrested. I'm in the Egyptian police department. In the station nearest the Citadel. Just remember that it's the Egyptian police building over in the Islamic quarter—"

"What did they arrest you for?"

"I think they call it 'contempt of religion.' Something like that..."

This is déjà vu all over again, Will thought to himself.

"Have you been formally charged?"

"That's not the issue here—it's not a matter of a formal trial. The point is, if you don't intervene, I think it will probably be too late."

"I'll make some phone calls immediately," Will assured him. "You're still an American citizen...we may have to use diplomatic channels."

"Have to go," Gilead said hurriedly and then the phone hung up.

Will burst out his door and into the office of Jacki Johnson, his senior legal associate. She was knee-deep in research for a motions hearing scheduled for the next day.

Will sat down in the chair opposite Jacki's desk. Jacki was an attractive black woman in her late thirties. She had been married to her husband, Howard, for a number of years and was now four months pregnant with their first child. As she eyed Will, she knew the frenzied, obsessed look. She had seen it before—during all the years she had worked with him in and out of courtrooms around the country and the world.

"So it's not a matter of *whether* it's an emergency," Jacki observed sardonically. "It's a matter of whether Jacki is going to jump into the fray alongside Will Chambers, hero of the oppressed and the underdog. Do I have it about right?"

"Oh, I suppose so," Will replied. "Here's the deal. You remember Gilead Amahn. He's the disorderly conduct guy who was arrested for preaching at the Islamic Center and sparking a riot…"

Jacki was already nodding that she remembered the case.

"He's over in Egypt," Will explained. "Arrested by the Cairo police. Apparently he has offended the Muslims over there as well. I don't know the details…what I've explained to you is about as much as I know. But I need your help. I think that we both have to start working the system together. I'm going to start making calls to the State Department. Amahn is an American citizen. He was naturalized a number of years after he came here as a young boy. I'll do what I can to get the State Department to intercede and ensure that we can get him legal representation…or maybe I need to make arrangements to go over there. Or get local counsel for him. I'll figure that out later. Meanwhile, I'd like you to call the Egyptian embassy here and start making a fuss about the conditions of his arrest. Tell them we want a full investigation—you know that Egypt has a bad record with some of their detainees. They have a habit of disappearing, or being tortured, or ending up dead."

Jacki nodded solemnly. But after a moment's reflection she felt compelled to add something.

"Didn't that kid learn anything in that trial that you had in district court here in Virginia? Did he really think that he could go over there to Cairo and pull the same thing?"

"Well, with all due respect, I don't agree with your characterization. I think it's more complicated than that."

"Look, Will, I'm just being a pragmatist," Jacki added. "You can't go into a Muslim country and start preaching the Christian religion and then act surprised when you end up being roughed up—"

Will was back on his feet and halfway to the door when he turned around. He was about to say something, but stopped.

Jacki studied Will's face.

"All right, counselor, what are you thinking right now?"

"Something Gilead told me before he left the United States. At the end of his case. I didn't know where he was heading. But he kept acting as if he had some kind of divinely orchestrated appointment. Next thing I know he calls me from Egypt. I wonder what's going on."

Jacki took it in, and then remembered something.

"Wasn't Gilead Amahn the one," she said, thinking back, "who was detained by the feds for a while? The idea was that maybe he was a suspected terrorist. And then suddenly they dissolved the detainer and let him go. That was before his trial, right?"

Will nodded.

"Yeah. And I never got to the bottom of that. I made a fuss, made some demands for information. But I ended up getting stonewalled by the Justice Department."

Will lingered in the doorway for a moment.

"And don't think that the federal detainer, and the terrorist suspicions, haven't weighed on my mind."

"You think there's something to it?" Jacki asked.

"I guess it's really easy for me to say no. The kid has great parents. And he's a straight shooter. He told me point-blank he had no terrorist associations or affiliations. I see nothing in his background to indicate anything different. But there's something that I can't put my finger on…I don't know what it is."

Will changed mental gears and added, "So contact the Egyptian embassy ASAP. And let's put our heads together within the hour and compare notes. Okay?"

Jacki nodded, and Will stepped down the hall, waving off several messages from Hilda, and disappeared into his office.

He put a phone call through to the State Department, scrolling through his electronic memo pad until he came up with the direct line for Deputy Secretary of State Bob Fuller. He had contact with Fuller a number of years previous because of a civil suit that Will had brought against the Sudanese government. The State Department had cooperated with him, and Will and Fuller had developed a cordial, though limited, acquaintance.

But Will was able to contact only Fuller's secretary, who assured him she would have him return the call at his earliest convenience.

Next, Will placed a call to his old friend Len Redgrove. He had wanted an excuse to get in touch with his friend and mentor, and this was the perfect opportunity.

But when Will called Redgrove's cabin in the Blue Ridge Mountains, he received only his voice mail.

Will decided to leave a lengthy message. It ended with a few of the basic facts surrounding the case.

"…so I do need to talk to you, Len. This Gilead Amahn is the same one I represented who was charged with starting a riot at the Islamic Center. Next thing I know he shows up in Cairo, Egypt. Apparently he's caused an uproar over there—I presume by doing some more preaching. Because he told me he was being held by the Egyptian police in Cairo on a charge of contempt of religion. So that's all I know…obviously, I need your help on this. I'd love your insights into the Egyptian court system. And also, old friend, I sure would like to catch up with you. We haven't talked since the banquet...so, give me a call as soon as you can. Fiona sends her love."

But Will Chambers could not have known that Len Redgrove was seated in his living room, staring at the answering machine and listening to the message, word for word, as Will spoke it. The professor had his hands folded in a posture of intense contemplation as he sat as immovable as a stone sphinx.

20

Forty-eight hours into his incarceration in the Cairo police building, a jailer appeared in Gilead's cell.

"You must have big friends. Very big friends…"

"What do you mean?"

"Somebody called from the American embassy. Very concerned about you. So—you're out today…isn't that good?"

Gilead stood up from his cot and stretched.

"Are you sure? I'm being released today?"

The guard nodded and smiled a wide grin, showing his stained teeth.

"You have been well-treated, yes? We have not caused you any problem…you have not been hurt at all, right?"

"No. You haven't hurt me."

The guard led Gilead to a clerk at a desk. His bag was sitting there, and next to it was a clipboard with a document attached.

"Look through the bag. Everything is there. Sign this piece of paper."

The American looked inside. Everything was there except the pile of religious tracts he had been passing out across from the Citadel.

"Where are my pamphlets?"

"Everything's there—do you understand? Everything is there," the clerk said emphatically.

Gilead looked at the clerk, then glanced over at the jailer, who was smiling and nodding.

He slowly signed his name. The clerk shoved his bag toward him, and after Gilead picked it up, he was escorted by the jailer down several hallways, past the front desk, and out onto the street.

"We would very much like you to leave Cairo…and please do not return. Have a nice day, Mr. Amahn!"

With that, the guard gave a somewhat silly little wave, smiling broadly with his dingy teeth. He lifted his brimmed cap slightly in a semi-salute, then turned and vanished into the police station.

Gilead began to walk down the al-Sadd al-Barrani toward the Nile River, in the direction of the shops and markets. It would be a long walk. He would have preferred to take the Metro, but he had paid his last Egyptian pound in order to call Will Chambers.

As he walked, Gilead looked across to the other side of the avenue. There was an old man dressed in a long, drab robe with a dirty turban. He had a switch in his hand and was occasionally touching the hindquarters of a donkey that was pulling a cart. Over its top was a burlap bag stretched over the load and tied down with rope. The old man stared at Gilead, and after a few seconds, he nodded and smiled in his direction.

After walking nearly half an hour, Gilead glanced around and noticed that a blond European-looking man was walking behind him about a hundred feet back. Gilead turned around again and looked. There was something familiar about him. Gilead thought that perhaps he had seen the man's face in the crowd at Salah ad-Din Square, mingling with the passersby before the man in the fez began arguing with him.

Gilead glanced back again. Now the blond man was picking up speed, his walk turning into a jog. As he approached, he gave a short wave and flashed a smile.

"Hello. Do I know you?" Gilead asked, extending his hand and shaking the hand of his follower.

"No. I do not believe so," the man said in a thick French accent. "But I know you."

"Oh?"

"Are you heading into downtown?"

"Well, I am, right now, without funds. And so—"

"Then I am here to help."

"You said you knew me," Gilead replied. "Have we met before?"

"I saw you at the Square. Preaching. Very brave, but—as some might say— perhaps even foolish. What brought you to Cairo to preach?"

"I felt that it was the leading of the Lord…"

Now the Frenchman was nodding and eyeing Gilead intently.

"I'm Gilead Amahn," Gilead said, reaching out his hand again to shake hands with the Frenchman.

"Are you from America?"

"Yes, though originally from Egypt here. Native-born. But I went to America with my father as a boy."

The two continued to chat as they walked along the side of the avenue.

"And you were the one involved in a court case in Virginia? You were saying some controversial remarks at a conference at the Islamic Center there?"

"Yes. That's right. How do you know so much about me?" Gilead asked with surprise.

"Oh…I spend much time on the Internet—there were some newspaper articles about your case on the Web."

"What brings you here to Cairo?"

"Actually, like you, I was born in one country—France—but transplanted to another. Actually, I have a little apartment in Jerusalem."

"So, what are you doing in Egypt? Sightseeing?"

"Not exactly," the Frenchman said. "I have a deep interest in the things of God. And also in the history of the religions of the world. There is much religious history here in Cairo. The ancient religions."

"Then you and I may have some things in common," Gilead said with a smile. "I also have an interest in the things of

God...which, I suppose, you already know, having seen what happened in the Square."

Both of the men laughed a little.

"So, do you come to Cairo to study?"

"In a manner of speaking," the man said. "For instance, on one of my trips here I studied the ancient Egyptian calendar system. I wanted to get some information about that. And also about one of the pharaohs. Amenhotep IV—he was also called Akhenaton. He ruled around 1400 BC."

"What is your interest in him?"

"Just this." Gilead's companion studied him closely. "Akhenaton was the only pharaoh in a long line of polytheistic pharaohs who broke with that religious tradition. He was the pharaoh who declared that Egypt should worship the one true God. In his words, the God who was not in the sun, but the God who actually had made the sun."

"You know, though I was raised here in Egypt, it's been a long time since I studied Egyptian history. But now I recall Akhenaton. In fact, wasn't he the one whose life may have intersected with the life of Moses? He may have even been the pharaoh the Old Testament refers to in the book of Exodus. If so, that might explain the source of his monotheism. He may have broken with the polytheism of the other pharaohs because he was able to see firsthand the display of the power of the God of Moses..."

"Yes. Very interesting. You are a fascinating man, Gilead. I have come to the East in search of truth. I think, perhaps, that there is much—very much I can learn from you."

Gilead smiled.

"So, you said you have no money. May I impose upon you with a suggestion?" the Frenchman asked. "I do have some money. I was going to hire a driver to take me back to—but that's a little presumptuous of me. Where were you heading next?"

Walking along, Gilead paused a minute before he answered.

"Actually...I was bound for Jerusalem. That is my destination."

The other man stopped in his tracks. Gilead halted in surprise and looked closely at his new acquaintance.

He was smiling and staring through Gilead, as it were.

"Then it is settled." The Frenchman extended both hands to take Gilead's, and squeezed them. "I will hire a driver. We will go to Jerusalem. Are your passport and visa in order?"

Gilead nodded.

"Wonderful!" his companion said as they resumed their walk. "The driver will take us to the border station outside Elat. Once we get through the Egyptian border guards, we'll pick up a taxi in Elat by one of the hotels. There are many of them. We'll take the Dead Sea route and head to Jerusalem that way."

The Frenchman reached into his backpack and retrieved a candy bar.

"You hungry?"

"Famished. I haven't really eaten in the last two days."

The man handed it to Gilead.

"When we get closer to the downtown, before hiring our driver, I'll make sure you get a good meal. You have to keep up your strength. I have a feeling that, looking back, we'll realize how this day was the beginning of something quite significant—who knows, perhaps even prophetic!"

Gilead nodded, busy devouring the candy bar. But the Frenchman was studying his every move as they walked.

Up ahead, the old man in the robe was gently touching the hindquarters of the donkey with his whip. The donkey was tired and refusing to pick up the pace. So the old man reached into his robe and pulled out a carrot, tied it onto the whip, and then put the end of the whip in front of the face of the donkey, the carrot dangling just inches from its mouth. The donkey brought up its head instinctively, and then picked up its pace.

21

I<small>N THE PRIVATE PALACE OF</small> W<small>ARREN</small> M<small>ULLBURN</small> on the island republic of Maretas, Orville Putrie was being escorted by two armed guards up the spiral marble staircase.

Putrie was a man in his late thirties, but his face had a worn look that made him look much older. His body was frail and slightly hunched over. His head had a rectangular look to it, with a tuft of unkempt hair. He had thick glasses of an almost telescopic optical quality and a small mouth that seemed always to be set in a twisted grimace.

When Putrie and the guards reached the main portico of the second floor, they were greeted by two other guards, who then led the visitor into the inner offices where Warren Mullburn's personal assistant sat behind a large, ornate, hand-carved desk.

Putrie announced himself and the woman nodded, then rang Mullburn and asked if he wished to see Mr. Putrie.

The meeting between Mullburn and Putrie was, admittedly, an extraordinary one. Mullburn met with few subordinates—and almost never met with those who were destined for what he euphemistically described as "direct action."

Even the deferential Mr. Himlet had soberly advised against Mullburn meeting personally with his newest chief of computer-intelligence research.

Mullburn had listened patiently to Himlet's advice, but then had abruptly rejected it.

He had not felt the need, of course, to explain himself.

Putrie was led by the armed security detail into Mullburn's spacious office, the one used for private receptions and informal meetings.

He took a few steps toward the billionaire after the guards had retreated behind closed doors and reached out his hand to shake Mullburn's.

"It's an honor…great honor…to meet you…" Putrie stuttered.

Mullburn glanced down at Putrie's extended hand but did not shake it. Instead, he simply smiled politely and invited his guest to join him on the outside veranda, which overlooked the crystal blue of the Caribbean.

"I was very interested in your work on breaking into quantum encryption," Mullburn began.

Putrie nodded enthusiastically.

"I'm so glad you are interested, Mr. Mullburn. I know you have an engineering background yourself…"

"Yes. Like you, I'm an MIT man. Though I was there many years before you were."

Putrie glanced down sheepishly. "I did attend MIT…but…I must tell you that I did not finish my work there. I didn't exactly graduate—"

"A mere formality," Mullburn said with a broad smile. "Yes, I'm familiar with some of the problems you had with a particular professor there. And I do know they considered your comments to him to be of a threatening nature. It's apparent your professor had no sense of humor."

Putrie laughed nervously. Mullburn smiled.

"If you'd be interested," Putrie blurted out, "in going through the schematics I've worked out on exactly how we can break through the quantum encryption system, I'd be glad to show you. My drawings—I don't have them with me. But, well…let me just say, what I did was, I worked on the principle of what I like to call the reflective cipher system—a kind of mirror reflection of the code-carrying photons. Actually, it's not too far from the old computer cookie idea…I just created a reverse-image algorithm—"

"Orville, there's really no need to go into the details. I've reviewed all of this. So have my computer people. And my management team. And do you know what?"

Putrie was staring at Mullburn, slightly slack-jawed. He shook his head no and waited for the answer.

"The fact is, Orville, we really think you can do this. And we'd like to have you prove your theory. We need you to gain access into a very complicated quantum-encryption process used by another government. Now, as you know, the Republic of Maretas, your employer, has legitimate security concerns. Your work will help ensure the safety of this island nation—and perhaps even other nations of the world. Do you realize how important you are, Orville?"

"I had no idea," Putrie stammered.

"Of course you didn't."

Then Mullburn stood abruptly and told Orville Putrie that their meeting was over.

As the billionaire walked his visitor to the door, he added, "You will get your further instructions from my Chief of International Security."

Putrie nodded dutifully, then extended his right hand again. But again, Mullburn simply glanced down at it, but did not shake it.

As Putrie was turning to leave, Mullburn scanned his clothing: scuffed dress shoes with a black lace on the left and a brown one on the right, wrinkled khaki pants, and a blue dress shirt that was missing a button.

"Oh, and Putrie..."

"Yes, sir?"

"On your way out, talk to my assistant at the desk. Give her your pants, shoe, and shirt sizes. We're going to dress you appropriately."

The computer genius gave a nervous laugh and a twisted smile, and then hunched his way through the doors, which he closed behind him.

The intercom buzzed.

"Yes," Mullburn snapped.

"I'm sorry to bother you. President La Rouge wondered if he could schedule a meeting with you. It is about picking a new ambassador to the UN."

"I don't have the time," Mullburn said brusquely. "Tell him I'll authorize the Assistant Foreign Minister to meet with him in my stead. I'll convey my thoughts on the matter through him."

The oil tycoon had grown increasingly impatient with Mandu La Rouge, the figurehead president of the Republic of Maretas. Mullburn had originally bailed out the bankrupt Caribbean republic in return for the position of permanent foreign minister. He had thought, back then, that he and La Rouge had arrived at a good working relationship.

But these constant interruptions, Mullburn thought to himself, *have to stop.*

"Oh, and one other thing," he said into the intercom.

"Yes, Mr. Mullburn?"

"Tell my chef I want the crusted sea bass for lunch. And make sure you tell that hack he has to sear the fish at the appropriate heat this time."

22

WILL CHAMBERS WAS EVENTUALLY ABLE to contact Bob Fuller in the State Department. They had a short and cordial conversation. But Fuller seemed guarded and noncommittal.

At the same time, Jacki tried to open a dialogue with the Egyptian Embassy. Unfortunately, she got nowhere.

Yet despite Fuller's initial hesitation, the State Department apparently did contact Cairo. Will discovered this when he hired an Egyptian translator to set up a conference call with the police department in the capital city. Will, to his surprise, was informed that Gilead Amahn had been released from the jail. His destination after release, they explained, was unknown.

Will then contacted Gilead's parents, Bill and Esther Collingwood, and brought them up to date with his limited information. That Gilead had been arrested in Cairo, apparently for illegal preaching. He had been detained for two days but then released. And no one seemed to know where he was heading.

Collingwood told Will that Gilead had mailed them a letter the day before he left for Cairo and shared a few of his son's comments. After he heard it, Will could no longer dismiss the growing concerns he had about Gilead Amahn.

Later, after Will had wrapped up things at the office for the day, he decided to pick up dinner for everybody. Today was a recording day for Fiona, so he stopped by a carry-out deli called Blue Ridge Grub-to-Go.

When Will arrived home, he turned at the "Y" in the driveway and took the route to the recording studio. The two-story, log, barn-shaped structure was some two hundred feet away, connected to the house by both a separate driveway and a stone path. Per Fiona's specifications, it had two state-of-the-art recording studios and a full sound board.

As Will parked his Corvette, he saw Fiona's Saab convertible and the two cars belonging to the sound engineer and her recording manager.

Will plucked the large plastic bag of food from the passenger's seat and took it in through the front entrance. The recording light was on, so he quietly moved into the sound booth, where he waved hello to the board operator and the sound engineer. Both had headphones on, and they smiled and waved to Will as he laid the food on the table.

Fiona was at an overhead microphone on the other side of the glass, and she waved and threw several kisses to Will when she saw him.

He leaned over and flipped on the intercom switch.

"Hey, darling, I brought some grub. I'll go over and eat with Andrew."

"Stick around for my next number. You haven't heard this one before—I'd love to get your take on it later," Fiona said.

Will agreed, and he settled back in one of the comfortable chairs in the studio as the background orchestration began playing.

Fiona's soprano voice was soft and ethereal as the song began, accompanied by the recorded strings.

> Are there shadows
> all around you?
>
> Does the night fall
> hard and cruel?
>
> Is your heart a
> thirsty desert...

Has your past
caught up with you?

Then the orchestration broke into a pounding, jubilant beat as Fiona sang,

*GO TO
THE WELL SO NEAR YOU*

*TO THE WELL
HE'S WAITING THERE*

*HE WILL TELL YOU
ALL YOU'VE EVER DONE*

*AND THE GRACE
THAT WAITS FOR YOU...*

Will rose from his seat, and as he passed by the sound engineer, he patted him on the back. The engineer lifted a headphone from one ear.

"Tell Fiona it's terrific. I just love it."

He waved through the glass as Fiona continued to sing, walked out through the lobby of the recording studio, quietly closed the front door behind him, and drove his Corvette over to the house.

Andrew was already sitting at the kitchen table with a pad of paper, a pen, and a book in front of him.

His father caught him staring out into space as he walked through the front door.

"Hard at work—that's my man!" Will said to his son.

"Hi, Dad."

Then his eyes lit up when he saw the bag.

"All right! Blue Ridge Grub-to-Go! Did you get me the ribs and shrimp?"

"Do I know you, or do I know you?" Will replied with a smile.

Andrew shoved his homework aside and quickly poured drinks for himself and his dad.

After he sat down Will asked him to say grace.

"Mom's still over at the studio?" Andrew asked as he began athletically separating the barbecued ribs.

"Yeah. I think she'll be there for a while. She's working on a new song..."

For a moment there was only the sound of a father and his son noisily licking their fingers and gobbling Blue Ridge Grub-to-Go's famous spareribs.

Then Andrew broke the silence.

"Can I ask you something?"

"Anything. Shoot."

"It's about the Sunday school lesson we had at church."

"What was it about?"

"Abraham. Isaac."

"Which part?"

"How the dad was going to sacrifice Isaac."

"Oh, that one," Will said in a quiet voice. "That's a tough one, isn't it?"

"Yeah."

After a few seconds of silence, Andrew continued. "So I'm wondering..."

"Yes?"

"If God told you to sacrifice me...would you?"

Will stopped eating. He glanced over at his son. At his soft, young face. His bright eyes and the swatch of uncombed hair, with a small cowlick in the back.

"So...Dad...would you?"

"I'm going to give you a lawyer's answer," Will said with a smile.

"Awww—that's no fair!" Andrew said, laughing a little.

"All right, here's the deal," Will began. "For me...it's one of the toughest parts of Scripture. Every time I read it—that story— I ask myself that question."

Andrew's eyes widened as he listened intently.

"All right," Will continued. "Here's my point. You asked me whether, if God ever asked me to sacrifice you, would I do it. But here's the fact. That story happened in Genesis, and it was between Abraham and his son Isaac for a specific reason. It was the only time ever in Scripture where God asked someone else to offer his own son up on the altar. And God stopped Abraham's hand at the last moment. And I bet you know why…"

"Yeah," Andrew answered. "Because God wanted to provide the sacrifice. Because the only time that a son would ever have to be offered by a father was when God gave up His Son, Jesus, for a sacrifice on the cross. Right?"

"Bingo. A-plus-plus-plus."

"But I still don't understand."

"What?"

"Would you or wouldn't you?"

"God wouldn't ask me that question. He wouldn't ask me to do that."

Will could see that his son was not satisfied with the answer, but he relented and returned to his spareribs and shrimp.

After a few more moments elapsed, Will added something.

"But I will give you one answer."

"What's that?" Andrew asked, dipping his last fried shrimp in the cocktail sauce.

"I'll say this—that if I ever had to, I wouldn't hesitate to give my life for you."

Andrew paused before he dropped the last shrimp in his mouth. He looked at his dad and simply said, "Huh." And then he smiled and gobbled his shrimp down.

After a few more moments, Andrew spoke up.

"Sarah Tompkins got sick at school—she threw up all over her desk. I thought that was so gross."

"Poor kid. That had to be really embarrassing for her."

"Yeah. I guess so…" Andrew said thoughtfully.

After he finished his homework, he and Will watched the last few innings of the ball game. Then Andrew went to bed.

His dad showed up in his bedroom to tuck him in. The two talked for a few moments, discussing their schedule for the next day. Then they said prayers together, and Will bent down and gathered his son in his arms, giving him a near bone-crushing hug—so tight that Andrew had to say, "Give," before he let go. Then Will bent down and kissed his son on the forehead, reminded him that he loved him, and said, "Good night."

As Will came down the stairs, he looked through the large windows of the great room of their log house, casting his eyes along the ridge leading to the recording studio. The lights were still burning brightly there.

Will settled into one of the leather chairs in front of the immense fieldstone fireplace. He pulled something out of his briefcase. It was a copy of the letter that Gilead had mailed to his parents as he was leaving for Egypt. Bill Collingwood had faxed it to Will after their phone conversation. He had thought that Will ought to see it.

As Will read it, the house was very quiet, except for the mournful evening song of a whip-poor-will somewhere out in the woods. Will studied the letter, and as he did, his mind was troubled.

At the end, Gilead had signed off by writing,

> The Spirit of the LORD is upon Me,
> Because He has anointed Me
> To preach the gospel to the poor;
> He has sent Me to heal the brokenhearted,
> To proclaim liberty to the captives
> And recovery of sight to the blind,
> To set at liberty those who are oppressed;
> To proclaim the acceptable year of the LORD.

Will Chambers recognized those verses as from the Gospel of Luke, fourth chapter. It was Jesus' announcement of His Messianic mission at the beginning of His ministry.

Will was haunted by two things about Gilead Amahn.

First, he could no longer ignore his misgivings about what appeared to be Gilead's apparent delusions of grandeur. It had now gone far beyond mere evangelistic zeal. His headlong rush into theological conflict might be, Will thought, a symptom of a larger problem. Had Gilead assumed a self-appointed role as a martyr? And was that, in some way, connected to his mother's brutal death?

But there was also a second concern. Will knew what had happened in the latter part of chapter four of the Gospel of Luke, after the proclamation by Jesus in the synagogue.

Will picked up the Bible lying on the end table and flipped it open to verses twenty-eight and twenty-nine of Luke four. The rest of the story was that the people who had heard the proclamation of Jesus

> were filled with wrath, and rose up and thrust Him out of the city; and they led Him to the brow of the hill on which their city was built, that they might throw Him down over the cliff.

23

THOUGH IT WAS ALMOST MIDNIGHT, the meeting was still going on.

In an empty second-level store above the corner café, less than a half-block from the Damascus Gate of the Old City section of Jerusalem, several dozen people had crowded into the room. Most were sitting cross-legged on the floor while a thin outer circle of onlookers stood against the walls of the empty room. Most were young—under forty, some as young as eighteen or nineteen. They were there because they had been recruited or solicited quietly in the markets of the Old City, in the bistros and coffee shops, and among the backpacking travelers strolling among the shops and sidewalk cafés of Ben Yehuda Street.

One young man who was sitting cross-legged in the middle of the floor was debating with Gilead Amahn, who was standing and leaning against the wall.

"So tell me," the young man sitting on the floor asked, "you talk about the future events. You talk about the fulfillment of the Bible. But on the other hand, you and your religion have been waiting for two thousand years. Nothing has happened."

"Look around you," Gilead said. "Where are you now? You're in the state of Israel. And you don't think that shows the fulfillment of the events prophesied by God's Holy Word?"

"All right," the young man countered, "maybe yes, maybe no. But the creation of the state of Israel—that's a political act. The

UN. The community of nations getting together and deciding that the nation should be created."

"The hand of God," Gilead replied. "We see immediate causes and effects on the stage of current events. But we fail to see God's providential hand behind the scenery."

"And how long do you wait?" the man said, persisting. "After two millennia you're still waiting?"

"With God," Gilead answered, "a thousand years is like a day—and a day is like a thousand years. If He has delayed it's because He is giving the world, and each of you, every opportunity to understand the choice you have, and the decision you must make. God is merciful. It is not His will that anybody should perish…"

A young woman with a backpack and long straggly blonde hair, leaning against the wall at the opposite end of the room, raised her hand and began talking energetically.

"I'm not quite sure why I came here. But I heard about it…I was interested because for years my family—they're Orthodox—they fed me the Torah. We were observant. But now, I just can't accept that anymore. I respect my parents. I respect their beliefs. But I really don't care about the Torah. I don't care about what you'd call the Old Testament. So if I don't care about the Old Testament of my parents' religion, then why should I care about both the Old Testament and the New Testament of your religion?"

Gilead smiled and paused a minute. And then he answered.

"If it was a matter of my religion, I wouldn't blame you for not wanting to take on something that seems even more burdensome than the religion that you've already rejected. But it's not my religion. It is either God's revealed message, shared to you in a written communication that bears the personal autograph of His mercy and love, or it's not. And it's not about a burden. Or regulations. It's about God's grace. And let me venture an opinion about something else…"

The girl now had her arms crossed in front of her and was tilting her head with a combination of suspicion and curiosity.

"I believe that you're here tonight because of a reason—not coincidence. You're here because God moved the circumstances of your life to bring you here. He wanted you to hear the message. He wants you to make a decision. God says now...today is the day of salvation. Not yesterday, which is come and gone—you can do nothing about it. Nor is it tomorrow, because tomorrow may be too late. You do not know what tomorrow holds. But you do know where you are today. And I believe today you are here because God has set eternity in each of our hearts. If that eternal place in our hearts is not filled with God, then it will be a hollow and empty place. It will continue to haunt us—like the sound of the wind whistling through the desert."

In the corner of the room, by the doorway, Yossin, the Arab leader of the Knights of the Temple Mount, gestured subtly to the blond Frenchman, who was sitting shoulder to shoulder with the crowd on the floor next to him.

Yossin discreetly slipped through the doorway, followed by the Frenchman. They walked down the narrow stairway and exited past a small grove of white plastic tables and chairs where some of the local inhabitants were conversing, drinking tea, and eating dessert.

"What do you think?" the Frenchman asked.

"It is as I had expected," Yossin answered.

"But I spent time with him in Cairo and on the trip up to Jerusalem," the Frenchman said. "I didn't want to press it too much, but we did a lot of talking. I listened to him tonight. It's the same thing. I've described it as...how could I say this... traditional orthodoxy. You know, the same old evangelical or fundamentalist Christian–type theology. So, I just have to ask myself—"

"Whether he is the real al-Hakim?"

"Well, yes."

"And you doubt my judgment?"

"No, that's not it," the Frenchman said, slight irritation in his voice. "It's just that I think we have to be absolutely sure. So much depends on this…"

"You saw the audience we had today, didn't you?" Yossin asked calmly. "Secular, nonobservant Jews. Some former members of Greek Orthodox churches. I think there is also a handful of secret Muslims up there. The point is, that I am not surprised at his approach. Remember, my mother was a Jew and my father was an Arab. And they were both practicing members of the Druze religion. There has to be some syncretism—some bringing together of people with diverse backgrounds. All this is expected."

"And when do we put the question to him…you know, about who he is—who he *really* is?"

"We don't. We don't force the question. I believe he is the one. I've told you that. And it will be revealed by him at the perfect time. He will give us the signal. You will see—that's the mistake the zealots made when they dealt with Jesus. Remember what we've studied and read? If the zealots would have worked on Jesus' timetable, rather than forcing Him to work on their political timetable, the kingdom could have arrived back then. But instead, the world has to wait for the appearing of the Great Caliph al-Hakim. And that time is now."

"And how about the other things—you know—the preparations we were talking about?"

"Oh, those are continuing. I've made several contacts. And we are in the final stages of the great event. I'll bring you into it when you need to know. Not until then."

The blond Frenchman nodded, taking in what Yossin had just told him.

"Meanwhile, let's go upstairs. When the meeting breaks up I'm going to do a follow-up with the girl with the backpack against the wall. I want you to zero in on the young man on the floor who was asking the other questions. I think we should be able to reap a number of good prospects from this group."

Yossin motioned for them to start back up the stairway.

"Just make sure you report back to me," Yossin added as they mounted the stairs. "I want names, contact numbers, addresses. Employment background. Family connections. You know what we need. Remember the significance of what we're doing here. We're building the new army of light. The righteous ones. The rulers of the new kingdom..."

24

THE CENTER FOR COMPUTER-INTELLIGENCE RESEARCH for the Republic of Maretas had been built specially for Orville Putrie. It was a room with walls lined with lead, and no windows or access to the outside world. Within the gray room, there were two walls filled from floor to ceiling with state-of-the-art computer and satellite equipment.

Putrie was seated before the massive computer console, facing three oversized computer screens. He had set up the menus and was ready for his demonstration. Now all he could do was wait.

He ran his hands through his hair nervously, spun three-hundred-sixty degrees in his console chair, then put his hands on both sides of the keypad and began madly drumming his fingers on the computer desk.

Then he heard a sound at the door.

Outside, Mr. Himlet had inserted the index fingers of both his right and left hand into the fingerprint identification ports. After a second, the screen flashed "Identification Secured," and the electric door opened slowly. Himlet walked in with, as always, his titanium briefcase. And, as always, he was wearing a black suit, black tie, and white shirt.

And he brought with him, predictably, his usual no-nonsense expression. He adjusted his glasses and pulled a chair up to the computer console.

"Mr. Putrie, I'd like you to begin."

"Yes, sir. Okay, okay," the computer expert said. "Here's my first menu..."

And with a few keystrokes on the keyboard, the screen flashed with a box that read "RCS," and under that the words "Reflective Cipher System."

Orville tapped in the address for the site he had already run successfully on his own.

After twenty seconds the screen downloaded a page of text in Hebrew. And at the top of the page, on the right-hand side, there was a replica of the Israeli national flag.

He then keyed in his text-translator program, and in a matter of seconds, the Hebrew text disappeared, and English text appeared in its place.

Now, at the top of the page, across from the Israeli national flag, it read, "THE INSTITUTE FOR INTELLIGENCE AND SPECIAL TASKS," and under that, "MOSSAD."

Himlet bent forward, his eyes scanning the computer screen.

He turned to Orville and remarked simply, "Good. Very good, Mr. Putrie. Continue."

Putrie then typed in the key words "INTELLIGENCE BRANCH—TERRORIST ORGANIZATIONS—MONTHLY MONITOR REPORTS—DOMESTIC UNIT."

Himlet smiled.

Putrie paused for a minute to expand on his own achievement.

"No one understands..." Putrie explained in a nervous titter. "You know, everyone is so interested in breaking quantum encryption...but they don't understand that first, you have to do a really good...I'm talking, a really sweet hacking job...to even get into the system. And you have to get into the system in a way that you're not going to be detected. So you don't send up a lot of flares and warnings, and trip a lot of the traps."

"Please continue," Himlet said.

Putrie tapped in the address for the subject index for the intelligence department reports and waited.

"Come to Papa...come to Papa...oh yeah, come to Papa," he muttered as he waited for the text to emerge.

After fifteen seconds, there it was. Following the instructions given by Himlet, Putrie had broken the quantum encryption record of the Mossad internal intelligence reports. He selected, pursuant to Himlet's lead, those reports which described the monitoring of known or suspected terrorist organizations.

The English list began with the "A's": al-Aqsa Brigade...al-Aqsa Jihad...

Putrie scanned down slowly, glancing nervously at Himlet, who gestured for him to continue scrolling down.

Then they reached the "H's." Hamas...Hezbollah...and then the "K's."

At the "K's" a name appeared on the screen, and Himlet reached over and grasped Putrie's wrist so firmly that he cried out.

"Stop right there..." Himlet said. And then he pointed to the name of an organization under the "K's."

The screen read, "Knights of the Temple Mount."

"I want you to access that," Himlet said, reaching a long index finger to the computer screen and touching the words.

Putrie clicked his cursor onto the organization's name, and then onto the monthly reports, ending with the latest one. At the side of the screen there was a box, and next to it the text "Digest of Daily Reports."

"Click on that," Himlet commanded.

Putrie complied, and a terse memorandum appeared on the screen:

AGENT: JKA

TERR. ORG.—KNIGHTS OF THE TEMPLE MOUNT

SUSPECTED LEADER YOSSIN ALI KHALID

IDEOL.—SUBSECT OF DRUZE RELIGION. APO-
CAL., SYNCR., ISLAM + CHRIST. MYST. + JUD.
CULTIC

OPERATIONS—DATA NOT COMPLETE

"Good. Very good, Mr. Putrie." Himlet rose from his chair and leaned down over the computer desk, his face only inches from the computer screen. He pointed to the last entry, where it indicated "DATA NOT COMPLETE."

"I will, of course, be reporting this to Mr. Mullburn. I'm sure he will be quite pleased."

Putrie's face beamed.

"Now, for the next phase," Himlet said, placing his hand on Putrie's shoulder. "That is going to be perhaps even more challenging."

"What are we talking here?" Putrie squinted through the thick lenses of his glasses.

"I need you to rearrange this data a bit. Take out a line of text. And then imbed another line of text. Without leaving a trace. Without leaving a clue behind."

Putrie paused for a moment, considering Himlet's directive. He smiled, removed his thick-lensed glasses, and wiped them on his shirt.

"I assume this project is very important…this is critical information…Mr. Mullburn told me how important I was in our meeting together."

"And your point is?"

"A little financial incentive…some bonus action." Putrie started rambling. "If I'm able to complete this project exactly the way that you described it. I would expect that there would be some really big-time, juicy remuneration for me."

But Himlet was already halfway across the room, heading for the door.

He spun on his heels and made one last comment.

"That next project needs to be completed in seventy-two hours. And then after that…we'll talk about one additional, much different computer application...also a rush. Good day, Mr. Putrie."

Himlet activated the entry, slipped through it, and then the massive electronically operated door slid shut behind him.

Putrie was rocking gently in his chair in front of the computer console. He was half-talking and half-singing to himself now. And smiling as he did.

25

IT WAS VERY LATE. Andrew, Will, and Fiona were asleep.

Fiona was dreaming—but what it was about, she could not later remember.

Then she was aware that the telephone on the nightstand next to her head was ringing. Getting her bearings and separating dream from reality, she reached for the phone, knocking the receiver off the base.

She then turned on the nightstand light, grabbed the receiver, and put it to her ear.

"Mrs. Chambers? Fiona Chambers?"

"Yes," Fiona answered slowly, still emerging from sleep.

"I'm very sorry, Mrs. Chambers—"

"What?"

"I'm very sorry, Mrs. Chambers, to tell you. But your father, Angus MacCameron, has just passed away…around three AM. I'm so very sorry…but he did go very peacefully."

Fiona sat on the edge of the bed in stunned silence.

"What…what did you say…how did he die?"

"He died in his sleep, Mrs. Chambers. Very peacefully."

Fiona began sobbing gently, and she said in a very quiet voice, "Oh, Da…Da…you're with the Lord now…"

By now Will was awake, sitting upright in the bed next to her. He jumped out of bed, circled around, and gathered his wife in his arms while he gently took the telephone from her.

With the night-shift nurse, he discussed the strangely mundane and bureaucratic details of the body, the funeral home, and the other arrangements.

After he hung up the phone he gathered Fiona in his arms and held her for a long time while she cried, and tried to talk, and cried some more.

Will knew that he had to be strong for Fiona. But it was hard. He choked back his own tears as he held her, thinking how Angus had been a kind of second father to him.

After a while, Will walked downstairs to the great room with Fiona. He fixed some tea, and they talked and drank tea, and hugged and cried until the first gray light of dawn broke through the windows. And they stayed there until the piercing light of the sunrise appeared over the mountain range they could see from the front windows.

They heard some movement upstairs and went up to Andrew's bedroom. He was awake. Somehow he had sensed that some important—some very difficult event had just happened. They lovingly told him that Grandpa Angus had just died in his sleep.

Now, they said, he and his wife, Helen, who had died some years before, were rejoined in the splendor and the glorious hope that Angus had always preached and had so intensely trusted in.

Five days later, the funeral was held. Angus was buried next to Helen. A bagpiper played and a gospel singer, a friend of Fiona, sang a contemporary version of "A Mighty Fortress Is Our God."

There was a large turnout. Not only members of Angus's current church, but also a few members of the church that he had pastored in Pennsylvania many years before. And of course, there were scores who came because they had been ardent subscribers to Angus's Bible archaeology magazine, *Digging for Truth*. They were also joined by the staff of Will's law firm, as well as many of Fiona's friends and music collaborators.

Dr. Len Redgrove did not attend the funeral. Instead, he sent a simple sympathy card.

The most surprising attendee at the funeral was Jack Hornby, the Washington, DC–based reporter who had covered the original legal case that had first brought Angus MacCameron, his daughter, Fiona, and Will Chambers together.

Hornby respectfully expressed his condolences to Fiona, then shook hands with Will. And just before turning to leave, he said something quietly, as an aside, to Will.

"This is not the time, but I've been meaning to get ahold of you. I need to talk to you about something. I'll give you a call at your office in a couple of days. Is that all right?"

Will nodded.

Will's aunt, Georgia Chambers, was there also, having driven up from North Carolina. Her husband, Bull, was too ill to join her.

After the funeral, friends and family members gathered at Will and Fiona's great log house. Georgia Chambers took Andrew aside and hugged and kissed him, and took the opportunity to reminisce about his birth. How he had been born at the end of a summer vacation when Will and Fiona had come down to Cape Hatteras and stayed in the small ocean cabin next to Georgia's. She went over, again, the strange and exciting story of the circumstances of his birth. How, just days after his birth in a hospital on the Outer Banks of North Carolina, his father, Will Chambers, became engaged in a life-and-death struggle with a man who, to Georgia's way of thinking, "was just about the total personification of evil."

Of course, Andrew loved to hear the story of how Will had handled and won a bizarre legal case down near Cape Hatteras, only to become embroiled in a modern-day encounter with piracy, buried treasure, and drug-smuggling villains.

Andrew and Georgia sat on the swing on the front porch of the house, looking at the mountains. The boy sat mesmerized, hearing again the real-life adventure story where his father was the hero.

Until the last visitor left, Fiona kept herself busy serving food and greeting everyone. But when the house was empty except for her and Will, and Andrew had gone to bed, Will could see the fatigue on her face. He came up behind her at the kitchen sink and wrapped his arms around her.

"Don't do the dishes, honey. I'm going to do them. I want you to stretch out on the couch. Want me to make a fire for you?"

Fiona simply shook her head and kept working on the dishes. She had a vacant and tearful look on her face.

So Will chipped in, working next to her as they rinsed the dishes and stacked the dishwasher full.

Fiona said she didn't want to go to bed—that she couldn't—and it was well after midnight when, at her request, Will finally did make a fire in the fireplace, even though the night air was quite balmy.

They didn't say much. They sat next to each other on the couch in the great room, Will holding his wife tight. They fell asleep that way. But before they did, Fiona wiped the tears from her face and said something to Will.

"Stay with me. Please don't leave me…"

Will pulled her closer. And he reassured her that nothing in the world could separate them.

26

In the little café on Topis Island, the second largest island in the Republic of Maretas, Orville Putrie was looking at the real estate closing statement. He was shaking his head and muttering obscenities to himself.

Across the table, his real estate agent—middle-aged, decked out in white linen pants, a flamingo pink shirt, and an ocean-blue tie—was sucking on a cigarette and smiling from behind his Ray-Ban sunglasses.

"Look, let's hurry this up," the agent said. He waved a waiter off. "I don't have time to eat here. I've got to catch a plane out of this tropical dump. Eat later I guess—come on, Putrie..."

"This can't be right..." the other man muttered. Suddenly he noticed something.

"What is this...this $10,000 charge for 'additional risk services'?" Putrie whined.

"Just what it says. I risked a lot taking care of your beach house back in North Carolina—you know, buying it out of foreclosure for you after you took off with the cops after you...and then getting a very pretty profit for you out of it. It's all part of the cost of doing business—"

"You're supposed to be my real estate agent, not a rip-off artist."

"Buddy boy, there are still arrest warrants out for you back in North Carolina. Get real. I'm running a big risk even flying down here to pay you off. Just be glad I was able to salvage something for you—especially after you vanished into thin air with the cops trying to hook you into the drug running stuff."

"You can't do this to me." Putrie's face was screwed up into a knotted expression of internal rage.

"I can't do it? I can't? Who are you to talk to me like that, you twisted little bug? So what are you going to do about it? How about this—how about, when I get to Miami, I make an anonymous call to the feds...or maybe to the district attorney down in Cape Hatteras when I get back home...and tell them I know where you are. How about that?"

Putrie was silent in his mental agony.

Then the agent got up and tossed an envelope onto the table.

"Don't be an idiot, Putrie." He threw his cigarette onto the ground, crushed it, and walked away.

Orville Putrie took the envelope, looked into it, and counted the money.

"$10,000 short," he muttered.

He trudged over to his house on Topis Island. After a few minutes of stewing on his couch, he looked at his watch. Then he strolled into his little greenhouse in the back. He looked at some of the plants and trimmed off a few of the leaves. Then he strolled among his plant collection, misting it with his water sprayer. Now his mind was calmer.

A few hours later, the real estate agent checked out of his motel room. A taxi was waiting for him. And Putrie was in his car, a hundred feet away, watching.

The man he was following was dropped off at a little restaurant next to the airport. He strolled in and was shown to a table. Putrie parked, then walked to the back of the restaurant. Outside, next to the dumpster, one of the cooks, in a dirty apron and a T-shirt, was taking a cigarette break.

Putrie greeted him and made small talk.

At his table, the agent ordered the seafood salad with lime-juice-mango dressing and a martini.

Three hours later, his plane was cruising high over the Atlantic, en route to Miami. Suddenly, the flight attendants alerted the pilots about a medical emergency.

The crew radioed ahead. One of the passengers had gone into respiratory distress—followed by convulsions and frothing at the mouth.

Twenty minutes later, the real estate agent was dead.

27

THERE WAS A NEARLY ELECTRIC MOOD of anticipation in the Old City section of Jerusalem. For the last three days Gilead Amahn had been preaching, almost nonstop, on street corners, in front of sidewalk cafés, and along the rows of shops frequented by both tourists and locals.

And on each occasion, the Knights of the Temple Mount made sure that a dozen of their secret contingent were there, creating an enthusiastic semicircle around Gilead whenever he spoke.

The group would create a useful magnet for drawing a larger group of onlookers. But in addition, the Knights, who never identified themselves by dress or even gesture, understood they were there for another purpose—to provide security in the event of any attack on their prophet.

That morning Yossin had met with the other two members of leadership of the Knights—the Frenchman and the American. He told them that he had been fasting and praying. That he believed this was, indeed, the day.

This would be, he told them, the beginning of both the grand horror and the divine unveiling.

And so they led Gilead through the Old City to a designated spot.

The American was given the task by Yossin, of guiding Gilead down the Via Dolorosa with a large group of disciples of the Knights of the Temple Mount close behind. Along the winding, narrow streets, through the tunnel-like labyrinth lined with stone façade, and under the shadows of the canvas awnings stretched over door openings, Gilead was smiling and greeting people they passed.

The group, with Gilead and the American at the lead, passed beneath the Ecce Homo Arch, the remnant of the first-century structure within which Pontius Pilate, Roman governor, had displayed a broken and bruised Jesus of Nazareth, and then said, *Ecce homo—Behold the man.*

The contingent paused as Gilead looked up at the two-thousand-year-old stones of the arch.

Tourists, local merchants, and shoppers filled the Via Dolorosa. Now they were having to squeeze past the large group encircling the young preacher.

As if on cue, the American whispered something to another in his group, a few gestures were quietly made, and then, with seeming spontaneity, the group began singing its own medieval-sounding hymn:

> *THE KINGDOM IS COMING,*
> *THE KINGDOM IS COMING.*
> *CLEAR THE STONES,*
> *PREPARE THE WAY.*
> *WE ARE HIS CHILDREN,*
> *THE CHILDREN OF LIGHT.*

The procession of disciples now gathering a larger entourage, was slowly making its way closer to the Temple Mount.

One of the onlookers, a member of the Knights, yelled out:

"Tell us, Gilead…about the end of the age. The coming of the Promised One."

The Knights had been careful to plan each sermon so it would begin with a seemingly random question and answer.

And so Gilead began to preach.

He said there would be both wars and rumors of wars.

Nations would rise up against other nations, and kingdoms against kingdoms.

He spoke of famines and earthquakes.

"Don't be afraid," he said to the crowd in a powerful voice, his words echoing off the ancient stone walls around him. "All of these things are simply the beginning of birth pangs—"

"What will happen to us? What can we expect? Will we be persecuted?" one of the secret followers of the Knights yelled out.

"Yes, of course," Gilead responded. "They will come and deliver you up to tribulation. And some of you they will kill. And you will be hated by all nations. And you must be on your watch because many will fall away and will turn one another into the authorities. And hate one another. Because lawlessness is going to increase. The love of human beings toward one another will grow dim…slowly…turned down like the heat on a stove—until finally, the love in the hearts of many will grow cold and dead."

As Gilead addressed the crowd below, up on top of the Temple Mount platform—that one-million-square-foot plateau of peaceful columns and trees and walkways and mosques—hundreds of Muslim faithful were gathering in the al-Aqsa Mosque for worship. They entered, removed their shoes, and then knelt in unison, bowing and worshiping.

Down at street level, Gilead's preaching had caught the attention of several Israeli police. A male and female police officer, glancing at each other and gesturing, both hurried over to the gathering crowd to disperse them. There were now nearly a hundred onlookers. Several had now appeared in opposition and had worked their way to the front and were arguing with Gilead.

But the preacher seemed unperturbed. He responded to the volley of questions with poise and confidence.

In the very back of the outer ring of humanity, Yossin and the Frenchman stood shoulder to shoulder, listening and watching intently.

One of the Knights shouted out a question, louder than the others.

"What about the Temple Mount? What are the signs? How can the Temple be built when the Muslims control the area? Doesn't Holy Scripture say that the Temple must be rebuilt?"

"Listen to the words of Scripture," Gilead shouted. "'Therefore when you see the "abomination of desolation," spoken of by Daniel the prophet, standing in the holy place'—"

He now stepped away from the crowd and pointed directly at the Temple Mount and the shining golden dome atop the plateau.

"That is where the holy place should be," he said in a voice that boomed and echoed.

The Israeli police were working their way through the crowd, trying to disperse them and get to Gilead, who was in the very center.

"The man of lawlessness shall be revealed. Before the very end, before the final coming of the Kingdom of God, he shall take his seat in the Temple of God, displaying himself as if he were God. In what temple? It is in that Temple—" he shouted, gesturing. "The Temple yet to be rebuilt from the ruins of the one that now lies within the ground of the Temple Mount. But it will be resurrected...the stones will come to life. It will be rebuilt. So all of the stones you see—and the buildings you now see atop the Mount—what will become of them? Can there be any question that God Himself must remove them first?"

Yossin whirled to face the Frenchman and grabbed the lapels of his shirt with both hands.

"The sign! The sign!" he shouted.

The Frenchman, half-dazed, blinked, nodded his head, and smiled.

And then the realization hit both of them. It would now begin. Yossin looked at his watch, grabbed the Frenchman and whispered something in his ear, and then sprinted from the group to a white van a block away and climbed in.

Meanwhile, the Frenchman ran in the opposite direction to an old rusted VW bus parked about two hundred feet away. He unlocked the door and got in.

Each man retrieved, from under the front seat, a black control box with a small keyboard, wireless antenna, and control switch.

It took them only thirty seconds to boot up the minicomputers. Then they set the coordinates. Each man looked at his watch. When the second hands slowly moved to bring the minute hands to exactly noon, then they would act simultaneously.

Each of them in their separate vehicles rested an index finger on the ENTER button on his keyboard.

By now the American had scrambled out of the crowd and waved down a taxicab driver—also a member of the Knights of the Temple Mount—and had given him the signal to exit when his human cargo arrived.

But neither the American nor the Frenchman nor Yossin, the Arab leader of the Knights of the Temple Mount, were able to hear their prophet's final admonitions.

"But be warned!" Gilead shouted. "Jesus the Lord has said, 'Many will come in My name, saying "I am the Christ," and will deceive many'—and He warned that many false prophets would arise and mislead many."

"But you are the Promised One!" one of the supporters of the Knights yelled out.

Gilead parted his lips to answer. He smiled, raising his hands high so all of the onlookers could see. By now the two police officers were breaking through the final ring of humanity and were almost to Gilead's position.

But before Gilead could speak, Yossin in the white van, and the Frenchman in the rusted VW bus, checked their watches—and then each simultaneously pushed down hard on the ENTER button of his keyboard.

A bright, blinding light exploded from the top of the Temple Mount. There was an awful rumble that shook the city of Jerusalem at the epicenter and then all the way to the suburbs from the two simultaneous, bone-jarring blasts. Windows of shops and office buildings throughout Jerusalem shattered.

The white stones of the al-Aqsa Mosque, and glass and trees, and the bodies of the Muslim worshipers and visitors atop the

Temple Mount and the Dome of the Rock were blown up into the air and scattered across the Old City of Jerusalem.

Great blocks of stone were hurled down onto the Jews at the Western Wall, as they stared up in shock and then ran in panic across the great plaza, trying to avoid the hurtling rock and stone that was raining down. The Knights of the Temple Mount and the onlookers screamed and ran in all directions.

The American grabbed Gilead, frantically pushing and pulling him to the waiting taxi. He stuffed him in and the driver sped off, through and around the traffic that was now bottlenecked by the debris that had rained down on the street in the Kidron Valley, which separates the Old Wall of Jerusalem from the Mount of Olives on the opposite side. Lurching the car off the street, over the curb, and onto the sloping hill that led around the Old Wall of the city, he drove wildly until he slammed to a stop in front of the dual walled-up arches of the Golden Gate—arches that had been closed for a thousand years.

Sirens could be heard all over the city as Israeli defense forces, ambulances, and police rushed into the Old City. The Palestinian police began shooting randomly at any suspicious person near the entrances of the Mughrabi Gate, which led to the steps ascending to the Temple Mount.

The taxi driver looked at his watch. It was exactly three minutes after twelve. He leaned down to a keyboard on the floor of his taxi and pushed the ENTER button.

The two walled-up stone arches of the ancient Golden Gate into Old Jerusalem exploded in a shower of stone.

One large rock hurtled through the left front window of the taxi, killing the driver instantly and rolling the vehicle over with the force of the blow.

Dazed, Gilead climbed out through the broken window of the passenger door of the taxi, which was now teetering on its side.

Suddenly he was aware of shots. Down the avenue, Israeli defense forces were firing on his position. Gilead wiped his face—

there was something liquid there—and realized he was bleeding from his nose.

With bullets whizzing by him, he scrambled over the rubble in the now wide-open Golden Gate of the Old Wall of the city of Jerusalem.

As Gilead stumbled through the opening, he saw screaming, running people crowding the streets, and others fleeing from what remained of the plateau of the Temple Mount above.

Gilead staggered and realized he could hear very little, except the once-distant sound of sirens—now getting very close. When the sirens seemed almost upon him, he looked up into the sky.

It was bright blue and serene. That was the last thing he saw before his knees buckled and he dropped to the ground unconscious.

28

Three Months Later

IN HIS LAW CHAMBERS IN LONDON, ENGLAND, Barrister Nigel Newhouse was holding a press conference. The room was packed with foreign press and television cameras.

The prominent human rights lawyer, a man in his mid-fifties with neatly trimmed gray hair and wire-rimmed reading glasses, strode to a podium with a sheet of notes for his public statement.

The barrister glanced down, adjusted his reading glasses, and then addressed the small army of reporters.

"The day before yesterday I met in Ramallah with my client, Hassan Gilead Amahn. As you know, Mr. Amahn is in detention pursuant to a multinational arrest resulting from the investigation into the bombing of the Temple Mount."

Newhouse paused for a moment, and then continued with what he knew would probably be the top news story of the day.

"Regrettably, I then advised Mr. Amahn that I must withdraw as his legal counsel."

Amid the noises of cameras, several dozen pens, as if in an orchestrated ballet, began scratching wildly on notepads.

"Mr. Amahn consents to my withdrawal under the unique circumstances in which I find myself. As some of you may know, I have been, for some time, legal counsel to Mr. Corin Mambassa, a newspaper editor. Mr. Mambassa was recently indicted by the

International War Crimes Tribunal of the United Nations, which is investigating war crimes committed in Sierra Leone. I have been, and continue to be, convinced of Mr. Mambassa's innocence of any human rights violations or war crimes."

Newhouse glanced again at the paper in front of him, then removed a newspaper clipping from his suit coat pocket and placed it in front of him.

"Unfortunately, Mr. Mambassa also wrote an editorial in his newspaper revealing the fact that his nephew was an active member of the Knights of the Temple Mount—the religious organization that is the target of the investigation into the Temple Mount catastrophe. Mr. Mambassa, in his editorial, lamented the death of his nephew, who was apparently caught in the cross fire between Palestinian police and Israeli defense forces following the explosion. He went on to say some rather nasty things about the Knights of the Temple Mount, and Gilead Amahn in particular.

"Now I was unaware," Newhouse continued, "when I accepted the case of Hassan Gilead Amahn, that my other client, Mr. Mambassa, had written these remarks. And while I do not believe this involves a direct conflict of interest, I am satisfied that I cannot, in good conscience, continue to represent Mr. Amahn at the same time I represent Corin Mambassa. Accordingly, with consent of Mr. Amahn, I am withdrawing from his representation so I can zealously, and with singleness of purpose, continue my representation and defense of Mr. Mambassa."

Newhouse looked up from his notes and scanned the room.

"I will continue as Mr. Amahn's counsel for only such period of time as is necessary for him to secure a new trial attorney. I will be glad to entertain any questions…"

Newhouse recognized a reporter from CNN.

"Do you have any idea who will be taking over the defense of Mr. Amahn's case? We've heard rumors that a number of high-profile American defense lawyers have offered their services…in fact, there was an article on the Internet earlier today indicating that a member of last decade's O.J. Simpson dream team has come to the forefront."

Newhouse chuckled.

"No, I don't know anything about that. I can say this—and my client has authorized me to make this clear. Mr. Amahn is very selective about who is going to represent him in this case. He originally wanted representation by an American lawyer but was unable to secure his representation—"

"Who is the lawyer? And why didn't he take the case originally?" another reporter bulleted out.

"The lawyer's name is Will Chambers—"

"Do you know why Mr. Chambers didn't take the case?"

"First off," Newhouse said, "I know Mr. Chambers only through a casual professional acquaintance. He has a reputation as a fine trial lawyer who has had experience in international human-rights cases. He successfully represented a former American military officer before the International Criminal Court in The Hague a few years ago. But as to Mr. Chambers' reason for declining representation of Mr. Amahn..."

Newhouse considered his words carefully.

"All I know is that Mr. Chambers said he had personal and family responsibilities that conflicted with his taking up the defense of Mr. Amahn."

"One of the wire services reported today," a Fox News reporter said, "that a court-appointed counsel has been provided to Mr. Amahn by the Palestinian Criminal Tribunal. Is that true?"

"Yes, I believe it is," Newhouse answered. "When the UN and the European Union, aided by the United States and Great Britain, helped to create the Palestinian International Criminal Tribunal specifically for the purpose of trying those responsible for the attack on the Temple Mount, that was one of the agreed-to items in the protocols for the tribunal. That is, the provision of a court-appointed defense amicus curiae for each person charged with criminal complicity in the Temple Mount bombings if they lacked the funds for their own counsel or if, for some other reason, they declined legal representation."

"Do you know anything about the attorney who is going to be provided for Mr. Amahn?"

"I heard today, just within an hour of my speaking to you, that the Palestinian Criminal Tribunal has appointed a Ms. Mira Ashwan to act as amicus curiae counsel for Mr. Amahn."

"Why was this Ms. Ashwan selected for representation?" a *Newsweek* reporter followed up.

"As I understand it," Newhouse explained, "the tribunal considered Ms. Ashwan as someone who has several points of commonality with Mr. Amahn. First of all, Ms. Ashwan is Egyptian-born. As you know, Mr. Amahn himself was born and raised in Cairo. Also, Ms. Ashwan is a Coptic Christian Arab. And Mr. Amahn is of Arab descent and professes to be an evangelical Christian. So those, among other reasons, I suppose, provide the background for the selection of Ms. Ashwan. Though I suspect Mr. Amahn is still desirous of obtaining his own personal defense counsel."

"What are the charges that are going to be brought against Mr. Amahn by the tribunal?"

"You have to understand, no charges have yet been filed. But I have also been informed by the prosecutor for the Palestinian International Criminal Tribunal that they are going to be utilizing a specific substantive criminal offense, formulated somewhat on American antiterrorism laws. I understand Mr. Amahn will be charged with multiple counts of causing the murder of others through the providing of material support for a terrorist organization."

"The Knights of the Temple Mount? That's the terrorist organization?" another reporter yelled out.

"Presumably, yes. I suppose that the tribunal will, as they have promised, name the Knights of the Temple Mount as the terrorist organization and will charge Mr. Amahn as being its spiritual and tactical leader."

"Can you tell us anything about Mr. Amahn's condition in detention?"

"I can say this," Newhouse replied. "Mr. Amahn is in remarkably good spirits. As far as I can see, he is being treated humanely in the Palestinian detention facility at Ramallah, where he is presently imprisoned."

Newhouse surveyed the flurry of hands and identified one final reporter.

"One last question," he noted, glancing at his watch.

"Is there any chance this American lawyer—this Will Chambers—will change his mind regarding representation of Amahn?"

Newhouse paused.

"I can't speak for Mr. Chambers. You'll have to ask him."

29

THAT DAY WILL CHAMBERS HAD a morning hearing in federal court in Washington, DC. So when Jack Hornby, Senior Bureau Chief for American Press International, made good on his comment to Will that he wanted a meeting, the two decided on lunch not far from the Federal Court Building on Constitution Avenue.

Hornby suggested Old Ebbets Grill. It was one of those Washington eateries full of etched glass, mahogany, and brass—an institution among the Capitol Hill crowd. For Will, it held a lot of memories—most of them not good—from back when he was an out-of-control drinker. On more than one occasion the proprietor had had to politely ask him to leave.

When Will got there at twelve-thirty, Hornby was already seated in a booth, checking his voice mail from his cell phone.

"Counselor," the newspaperman said with a grin, extending his hand to shake Will's. "Thanks for meeting with me. And, just so you know, lunch is on me..."

"Of course," Will said with a smile, "that's why I came."

"Now you can't take that for granted," Hornby replied. "Back when I was a reporter for the *Washington Herald,* they gave us almost no expense account for that kind of thing."

"Even for Pulitzer Prize–winning reporters like you?" Will replied nonchalantly, nodding his thanks to the waitress who was filling his water glass.

"Yes, I did win one of those, didn't I?" Hornby said sardonically. "I'm glad somebody around this town remembers that. But that was a long time ago. A lot of water has gone under the bridge since then…"

. After Will had ordered a Caesar salad and Hornby had asked for the mahi mahi special, he opened the door to what was really on the bureau chief's mind.

"I appreciate you coming to my father-in-law's funeral. That was very thoughtful of you. I know Fiona was touched."

"Don't mention it. And don't think I attended just because I wanted an opportunity to get a story out of you…"

"I appreciate that," Will said with a smile.

"Which is interesting, because it leads me to the reason you and I are sitting here having this friendly little chat. Of course, before your Resurrection Fragment case—if I can call it that—I knew you a little bit from some of your civil-liberties cases. But when I dove into the *Reichstad v. MacCameron* lawsuit and your defense of Angus MacCameron, it was my first up-close and personal with you. And also it was my first introduction to a guy who, at first, I considered a bit player in your legal drama."

"Oh?"

"Yeah. He was there, sort of lurking in the background. He was the odd man out. A celebrity oddity, admittedly, but an oddity nevertheless. And then the more I dug into the background, the more I realized this guy was cut from a whole different piece of cloth. In other words, I decided that—continuing with my fabric metaphor—he was a whole bizarre tapestry himself…"

"Who are you talking about?" Will suspected where Hornby was heading.

"The world's filthiest-rich man," Hornby said with a sardonic smile. "I never really got a chance to do a feature piece on Warren Mullburn back then. But I kept my notes. Every good newspaperman does. And so I've followed him. I've watched him. Not just the stuff on the news—I've continued to do my own spadework on the guy over the years."

Hornby finished the martini he'd ordered and put the glass down on the table with a flourish.

"You see, some people collect things. Stamps. Antiques. My mother had this little ceramic bunny rabbit collection. I don't know what they were called. Little rabbits in those cute little poses with coats and hats on—that kind of thing."

"And you?"

"I collect information on Warren Mullburn. In addition to the work I do at API, they let me do freelance writing on the side. I've been hired to do a cover piece on Mullburn for *Vanity Fair*. And I'm not talking about just a puff piece—I want to blow the roof off. Literally. I think you know what I mean..."

"So where do I fit in?" Will asked, as the waitress set down their plates on the starched white-linen tablecloth.

Hornby smiled at the waitress but waited until she had left before he resumed.

"So here's the skinny on all this," Hornby said in a hushed but intense voice.

Then he paused, took his notepad out, and pulled out a blank piece of paper. In the middle he drew a circle. Then he drew an arrow from the edge of the paper, pointing toward the circle.

"This arrow," he continued, "this is point number one. It takes us back...way back to your handling of the lawsuit of Dr. Albert Reichstad against Angus MacCameron and his archaeological magazine, *Digging for Truth*. Warren Mullburn was funding Reichstad's research center and was therefore—at least indirectly—behind the so-called discovery of the Resurrection Papyrus. Obviously, if that two-thousand-year-old fragment had actually disproved the resurrection of Christ, it would have been of immense value to the Muslims. But what I later found out was that Mullburn's ultimate goal was to make inroads into OPEC and bolster his own oil interests.

"So, that's the first arrow here." Then, taking a few bites of his mahi mahi, he quickly launched into his next point.

"Okay, so you defend Angus MacCameron against the defamation suit Reichstad filed and in the process debunk Reichstad's theories—but also in the process you stumble onto the seamy side of Warren Mullburn's dealings."

Hornby then drew a second arrow from a different edge of the paper, pointing, like the other, directly toward the empty circle in the middle.

"So this brings us to our second point—the second arrow here. I was getting some bits and pieces of data to the effect that Mullburn had used his wealth and influence to push the White House to broker a large arms deal with several Arab countries. My guess is that Undersecretary of State Kenneth Sharptin was working on the inside with Mullburn to illegally force the arms deal. But something happened...I figure it was when you were interviewed by the FBI and told them what you'd discovered about Mullburn. So, bingo, a grand-jury investigation—and when that hits the fan, Sharptin decides to drink a highball laced with Seconal and ends up sleeping the Big Sleep."

Hornby then drew a third arrow pointing to the empty circle.

"Now, point number three. In the grand jury investigation, Mullburn is not listed as an official target. But the Justice Department still issues a witness subpoena for him to testify. Mullburn hightails it out of town, vacating his massive Nevada desert compound, leaving behind very little except the empty mansion and the dead body of his personal bodyguard."

"All this history," Will said, "is very interesting, Jack. And you and I have gone over this before. But I'm not quite sure what this has to do with me now—"

"Hold on now," Hornby replied, bringing his hands up in the air like a referee in a boxing match. "Don't get ahead of me here. Stick with me—which brings us to our fourth arrow."

And with that Hornby drew yet another arrow.

"So the Department of Justice tries to extradite Mullburn from Switzerland. However, some very reliable sources have told me that Mullburn had an accomplice on Capitol Hill who was keeping an eye on DOJ's legal steps for him. Now I ask you, who might his contact have been?"

Will shook his head. "I have no idea."

"Does 'Senator Jason Bell Purdy' ring a bell?"

Now Will stopped eating. He put down his fork, folded his hands in front of him, and leaned over the table.

"As you know…I have some history with Purdy. At least before he got kicked out of the Senate. But what you're telling me about his connection with Mullburn is new information…"

"Of course it is," Hornby said with glee. "You may be a great trial lawyer, but what kind of news reporter would I be if I didn't have the real scoop on all the nasty dealings here in Washington, DC?"

And with that, Hornby toasted himself with his glass.

30

"LIKE YOU SAY," JACK HORNBY CONTINUED, "you had a history with Jason Bell Purdy. I know all about your case down in Georgia, where you exposed his corrupt financial dealings. But that's not the end of it..."

Hornby then drew a fifth arrow pointing to the circle in the middle of the piece of paper.

"Purdy leaves the Peachtree State and goes to Washington, DC as a new senator, all right. Just about that time a decorated Marine colonel, a United States special-ops guy by the name of Caleb Marlowe, leads an ill-fated attack on terrorists down in the jungles of Mexico. You defend Marlowe against war-crimes charges—first in a court-martial. But then, in a weird twist of fate, end up being subpoenaed to appear before that dog-and-pony-show excuse of a subcommittee of Senator Purdy."

"Yeah," Will said. "I did not find that hearing a pleasant experience."

"No, I suppose not," Hornby replied with a sarcastic chuckle. "But I have to tell you that you did a whole lot better against Purdy than you had any idea—in fact, in my humble opinion, you made mincemeat out of him.

"That brings us to our sixth arrow here," he said, and drew his last arrow pointing to the circle.

"By then, Mullburn is quickly escalating from oil magnate to mega oil titan with his new petroleum exploration project in Mexico. He wants to capitalize on dwindling oil resources versus the increased petroleum demand that has just been reported by the Energy Department. The way I see it, Mullburn figures that when Mexico files its complaint against America's military hero, Colonel Marlowe, relating to that Mexican jungle incident, useful pressure could be brought to bear against the United States."

"Fine. But…you know we won the Marlowe case before the International Criminal Court at The Hague." Will said. "So isn't all that moot?"

"Au contraire," Hornby retorted enthusiastically. "I put to you the question of the hour—what interest did Mullburn have in those proceedings before the International Criminal Court? I've just told you my theory that he wanted to capitalize on American embarrassment in the eyes of the international community and create tension over whether Mexico was going to export oil to the United States and bail us out. So I figure that Mullburn had a motivation to delay your case and drive up the international embarrassment factor against the U.S., wanting to build as much pressure and speculation among American oil interests as he could. In that way he was driving up the price of oil so that when he and his Mexican cartel finally did decide to sell it to the U.S— which they ultimately did—they could force a top-dollar price."

Then Hornby got a serious look on his face, tilted his head a bit, and continued in an even more hushed voice than before.

"Alright…so—I had this conversation, see—with a former economic consultant on Mullburn's team. This guy swears up and down that Mullburn not only knew about your case, but was watching it very closely. *Very, very closely,* if you get my drift. So I asked this guy, aside from wanting to help Mexico to embarrass the United States through the ICC, did Mullburn actually involve himself in your case?"

Will's eyes were riveted on the newsman.

Then Hornby gave a little smile.

"So do you know, Counselor, whether anybody was trying to delay the ICC case while you were handling it?"

Will studied Hornby's diagram for more than a minute. There was silence. The waitress came by and asked if they wanted dessert, but Hornby waved her off as the attorney continued to stare down at the piece of paper on the starched tablecloth.

"The French prosecutor handling the case," Will said in a distant voice, "she wanted it handled on a fast track. So the Court granted a pretty quick trial date, but…there was something else…"

"Like what?" Hornby asked, fully engaging his reporter's radar.

"Shortly after our first hearing in The Hague," Will continued, "when the tribunal decided that the case was going to be put on the fast track and that there would be no delays…something did happen."

"Like what?" Hornby could see a growing anguish on Will's face, which the lawyer was struggling to cover up.

"I hate to press—but like what, Will?"

"Shortly after the Court set the fast trial date…my house was attacked…there was a break-in…and…Fiona, my wife…"

Hornby didn't press further. He knew better than that. His eyes were wide open, and he was waiting for Will to finish.

"Fiona…well, I almost lost her," Will said in a voice barely audible. "As you can imagine, it's still hard for me to repeat all of that."

"I'm so sorry," Hornby said. "Will, I never knew anything about that—"

"Well…it was just a good thing that a private investigator I'd hired, a friend of mine by the name of Tiny Heftland, was on duty that night."

"Heftland. I know that guy. You used him in some of your other cases—big fella?"

"Yeah, he's the one. I had some very uncomfortable feelings about leaving Fiona alone when I left for the trial in The Hague. So I had Tiny do round-the-clock surveillance on the house while I was gone. He was there—when it happened, he pumped a round into the intruder…we never did find out for sure who sent the guy or what his plan was…"

There were a few seconds of silence between the two men.

"Look, Will," Hornby said, trying to put a coda on their discussion, "I obviously didn't bring you here just to give you a free lunch. Why am I telling you all of this? I'm not going to bore you with the most recent information I've got on Mullburn. The global business alliance he's establishing. Or even the fact he's now got his fingers in the Middle East peace-negotiation process— but let me just bring it down to this."

Hornby picked up the piece of paper containing his drawing and held it up.

"Tell me, Will, what do you see on this picture?"

"A bunch of arrows pointing to an empty circle. But then, I know you're fond of drawing pictures."

Hornby laughed at that.

"Here's why I wanted to meet with you, Will. As I plod, and climb, and claw my way through information and interviews and notes, filling notepad after notepad, do you know what I keep coming up with?"

Will shrugged.

"I come up with one constant, inescapable, and common link throughout everything I've shared with you. One thing smack-dab in the middle of this empty circle here, with all of these arrows pointing at it."

"And what's that?" Will asked, trying to figure out the other man's ramblings.

Hornby pulled back the piece of paper, took out his pen, and wrote something in the middle of the circle. Then he held the paper out to Will again.

Will stared at it. In the middle of the circle Hornby had written two words:

WILL CHAMBERS

"You see, Will," Hornby went on, "I just came back from the Middle East. I've been following what happened at the Temple Mount. Of course, everybody in the world is looking into that mess. At first I felt that there was no connection—but then, when

Mullburn started touting himself as a peace mediator in his phony-baloney capacity as the foreign minister of that Caribbean republic he bought for himself at a fire sale—I started thinking. Thinking real hard."

"And?" Will didn't know whether he really wanted to hear the answer.

"Then right out of the blue," Hornby said, "I'm listening to this press conference yesterday with the English lawyer who was representing Gilead Amahn. He withdraws as Amahn's lawyer. And I hear that you had initially been approached by Amahn to represent him—but you declined to take his case. So…can you tell me why?"

"It's personal."

"So? Everything's personal, isn't it? It's really a question of how much you trust me with something that might be sensitive. Do you trust me?"

"That's a funny question coming from someone in a profession that makes headlines out of excruciatingly sensitive information about people's lives."

"So—do you trust me?" Hornby asked again.

Will paused a minute. He thought back over the years. About his relationship with the newspaperman. He had always been a straight shooter. He had provided information to Will that had actually helped him on some of his cases. And there was never a sense of betrayal…he had never broken his word. Ever.

"Okay. Here it is…and this is off the record…which, I know, is a contradiction in terms when you're talking to someone in the media…but the fact is…well, the Temple Mount incident and Gilead Amahn's arrest over there all happened about the same time as the death of Fiona's dad…thanks for coming to the funeral, by the way. So, anyway, I decided I needed to be with Fiona. The death of her dad has been rough for her."

Will's eyes were now off Hornby, gazing on some faraway landscape.

"What are you thinking about, Counselor?" Hornby asked softly.

"Something you said," Will replied. "I hadn't heard it before… the fact that Mullburn had been closely monitoring the ICC trial. And how he would have wanted a delay in our case. And the next thing you know…some assassin attacks our house and my wife. If the attack had been successful, I obviously would have jumped off the case in a heartbeat. And that would have delayed things… and achieved Mullburn's objective."

Then Will's gaze shifted back to Jack Hornby. The two men locked eyes.

"And it doesn't get much more personal than that," Will said sternly.

Hornby paused a moment before he spoke again. He studied the look on Will's face, then gave his credit card to the waitress as she stopped by the tableside.

"I'm looking at the expression on your face right now," Hornby said as the waitress left. "It reminds me of something. When I was a kid. The circus used to come into town. Not just a carnival, but a real, live circus. And there was this guy—he'd go into a ring. He'd actually wrestle this huge grizzly bear. Now the guy was pretty well put-together—strong guy. But the grizzly bear was huge. I'm talking titanic. And what they did is they put a leather strap around its mouth so it couldn't open it. And they tied some kind of leather bag around each of its paws so the bear couldn't use its claws. So all the bear had was brute strength. And here's this guy—this wrestler—he runs into the ring like no bear is going to get in his way, you know, and the bear comes charging at him, and this guy actually, in two or three moves, he knocks the bear off balance. And the next thing you know, he's around on top of that bear, hanging on and riding him like a Brahma bull."

Will waited for the punch line. But he could see it coming.

"Let me tell you something, my friend," Hornby said. "The expression on your face right now is practically the same crazy look that wrestler had, going into the ring with that bear. Only there's one big difference."

"And what is that?"

"Warren Mullburn is no trained circus animal. As far as I can see, there is nothing restraining him. He's got claws. He's got jaws. And he will devour anything, and everyone, that gets in his way."

"Why are you giving *me* that advice?" Will asked, studying his own hands, which were now resting on the table in front of him.

"I dunno," Hornby replied. "Just thought you needed to be reminded. In case you plan on taking on Mullburn. I guess I'd hate to see you get ripped apart by a man-eating grizzly."

31

IN THE CORNER OF THE GREAT ROOM of their log house, Fiona was seated at the grand piano. It was Saturday, and usually she was running errands, or doing housecleaning, or pleading with Will to accompany her to some of the spectacular weekend craft fairs in the Blue Ridge Mountains.

Instead, her slender fingers were gently and softly playing Beethoven's *Für Elise*.

Will came into the kitchen wiping the grease off his hands. He had been working on the engine of his prized 1957 Corvette. Now that they were a three-person family, he was driving the Corvette less. The two-seater coupe was spending more time in the garage under a tarp. Now, most of their driving was done in their SUV, which transported not only the three of them, but also Andrew's baseball teammates, wrestling team, members of his drama club, and friends from church.

Attracted by the music, Will finished wiping his hands and strolled into the living room.

He pulled up a chair to the piano and listened until Fiona finished.

When she did, she turned to him, leaning her cheek into her hand, and said nothing.

"How you doing today?" he asked.

"Okay," she said. But her face and the fatigue in her posture contradicted her answer.

"It's a process…" Will said gently.

"I know," Fiona said with a slight edge in her voice. "I know that. I learned it when my mother died. And I'm surprised it's not any easier with Da…"

"Darling, why don't you let me take you to a craft fair today…I'm sure there's one around somewhere in the mountains…"

"So…you're going for the husband-of-the-year award," Fiona said with a faint smile.

"No, I'm serious, babe. I've got the 'Vette tuned up. I'll take the tarp off. It's a beautiful day. Let me take you for a spin in the mountains—along Skyline Drive."

"What time was Andrew going to be home tonight?"

"He's at the church retreat this weekend, remember? He'll be back tomorrow."

"Oh. That's right," she said with a flicker of embarrassment.

"It's alright," Will said in a reassuring voice. "You've always been the person who's tuned in. You always remember birthdays, anniversaries, exactly what Andrew has on his schedule. You're the master control center for this family. But life just came up and smacked you on the side of the head. You're allowed to forget some things…"

She gave him a smile, and he rose, stepped over, and wrapped her in his arms. He kissed her gently on the cheek and neck.

"Just tell me what I can do for you today. I'd love to do something for you…"

"Really?"

"Yes. Absolutely."

"Alright. You can finish the conversation you were having with me in bed last night."

"Which one?"

"You know—the one we were having. You were telling me about some things at your office—and then you fell asleep in mid-sentence."

Will burst out laughing.

"Boy, I'm really sorry. Yeah, I guess I did."

"So. You were telling me about the English lawyer. What was his name?"

"Newhouse. Nigel Newhouse. He's a barrister in London. He and I had met a couple of years ago at an international conference on religious freedom. We've exchanged e-mails a few times since then. He had a question once about International Criminal Court law. And then I asked him a couple things about some international treaties, an issue involving one of my cases. That sort of thing."

"You've met him only once?"

"Yeah. At that conference. Although at the time I met him, I asked him if we had ever met before. He said no. I just thought there was something that seemed very familiar about him. About his name...but anyway...yeah, that was the only time I've ever met him in person. But we've kept in contact. And then he called me on Friday. First thing in the morning our time—end of the day London time."

"What did he want?"

Will hesitated.

"Well...Newhouse is the lawyer for Gilead Amahn. At least, was for the last few months. Earlier this week he withdrew as his counsel. Remember, Gilead is still in jail over there in Ramallah. They're holding him until they file formal charges."

Fiona was silent. But Will could read a thousand-word essay in her eyes.

"So...he called me about Gilead's case."

Fiona remained silent. Then she tilted her head slightly to the side with an expression that showed she suspected more than she knew.

"And this barrister said he withdrew as Gilead's counsel?"

"Yes. It was all over the news this week."

"I haven't been watching very much news lately. In case you haven't noticed."

"I know that," Will said gently.

"So Newhouse called you. Because he's withdrawn as Gilead's lawyer. And now Gilead is looking for a lawyer. And so the barrister was calling you to ask whether you would reconsider representing him. Do I have it about right?"

"Yes. I think that just about sums it up."

"And you told this English lawyer...what?"

"He had met with Gilead in jail in Ramallah. And when he told him he had to withdraw, Gilead immediately asked him to pass a message on to me. That Gilead still wants me to be his defense counsel. I told Newhouse I'd declined originally. He had some idea why, but I didn't go into the details."

"How did you leave it?"

"I told Newhouse I'd think it over. And I'd get word back to Gilead about my decision."

Another dead silence.

"Did I ever thank you," Fiona began, "for deciding not to take on that case in the first place? It all happened right around Da's death...and I've really needed you desperately. I've needed you to be with me...like never before. I appreciated your decision."

"Thank you," Will said quietly.

"And you want my take on all this?"

"Of course."

"I really want to beg you," Fiona's eyes began to fill with tears, "not to take this case. Gilead Amahn is not going to have any problem getting a lawyer. Every lawyer in the world wants to take that case. Make international headlines for himself—"

"There you're right," Will said. "There are criminal defense attorneys from all over the world coming out of the woodwork..."

"I want you to pray about this," Fiona said, pleading. "And then after you've prayed about it, and I've prayed about it, I want you to please, please—*please*—not take this case on."

"I know Angus's death really blew a hole in your sail," Will said. "You're going through some really tough times."

"Well... I stopped my work on my new CD...I'm on the verge of breaching my contract. I've cancelled several concerts. It's hard to get up in the morning. And I don't want to go to bed at night. I can't concentrate…I can't focus…I spend time on my knees, asking that the Lord would give me some peace about Da's death. But it doesn't come."

After she had wiped her eyes, Fiona continued.

"I had a dream last night…"

"Oh?"

"Yes. About the babies. Both of them. And all I remember, through the whole dream, is trying to find out where the hospital had put my two babies. You know…I started feeling like I was getting over the first miscarriage. But when the second one came, and they told me I couldn't have any more babies…I don't know how to describe it…it was like a door just shut. And bolted. Part of my life was being closed up. A place where only dust, and bad memories, and broken dreams would collect. I can't explain it. It makes no sense. Because I thank God every day for Andrew. He's so precious. And he is so wonderful. And now I'm dreaming about those two babies. And Da being dead…and it all seems to be mixed in together…and I simply can't figure it out…"

Will gathered Fiona into his arms and just held her while she sobbed.

He knew that, though there were many questions, he had no answers. He only knew, in that one moment, he had to provide shelter and security for his wife.

32

It was six-thirty am. Bill Collingwood had driven the short distance in the rolling Virginia countryside from his house to the office and main stables of Roland and June Dupree.

Climbing out of his car, Collingwood was surprised to see Dakkar, the horse trainer, already there at the stables.

"You're early," he noted.

"I've been trying to get to work quite early," Dakkar replied with a big smile on his face. "Do good work for the Duprees. Keep on schedule...but I also wanted to meet you this morning to thank you."

"Oh?"

"Oh, yes, Mr. Collingwood," the young man replied happily. "Yesterday Mr. Dupree had a talk with me. He'd had worries about me. But he told me you'd vouched for me. You'd given him the word I was a good man and he should give me another chance—so I think he's going to keep me."

Collingwood smiled and told Dakkar how pleased he was.

"I owe you so much. Please, Mr. Collingwood...if there's anything I can do for you. You name the thing—anything to pay you back for your kindness..."

"Just do the kind of job I know you can for Mr. Dupree, and that will be enough."

Dakkar thanked him again and left to groom some of the horses.

In the stable office, Collingwood started up the small coffeepot, then sat down to review his paperwork and the statement he prepared for Roland Dupree each month. Then he drove to the back acreage to fix a broken gate. By the time he returned to his office, it was eight-thirty. He wanted to call Will Chambers and figured the lawyer was in his office by then.

Bill Collingwood was pretty good at compartmentalizing his life. And he had managed, with some measure of success, not to become obsessed with the dire situation of his son, Gilead.

But now, as he sat at his old wooden desk with his hand poised over the phone, the sense of dread became overwhelming. His hand was shaking, so he spent a moment praying, but felt no relief. He buried his face in his hands for a moment and wept.

Then after wiping his eyes, he took a deep breath, picked up the receiver, and punched in the number. His purpose in calling would be simple. He wanted to plead for Will to help Gilead. In light of the fact that his adopted son was accused of being responsible for a mass murder, where else could he turn?

When the call came in, Will had just breezed into his office.

Hilda, his secretary, let him know that it was Bill Collingwood on the line. Will knew exactly what the call would be about.

He closed his office door, took a deep breath, then picked up the phone.

Collingwood got right to the point.

"Mr. Chambers, I know you considered Gilead's request to have you represent him. I know you had good reasons for deciding not to a few months ago. But I'm sure you've heard about the English lawyer having to withdraw..."

"Yes," Will replied, "I have."

"My son is not a mass murderer. And yet the whole world thinks that he instigated this massacre on the Temple Mount. It's awful...it's beyond my ability to describe to you how I feel as his father."

"I'd like to say I know how you feel," Will said quietly, "but I really can't. Your burden must be horrendous right now."

"A couple of weeks ago I flew over and visited him in that Palestinian jail. He's really in pretty bad shape, Mr. Chambers. But

I'm coming to you on my hands and knees, Mr. Chambers…you must do this thing for me. You must represent Gilead in this case. He said he wouldn't take anyone else. We've got to show his innocence. I'm begging you as Gilead's father to please reconsider. Please defend him in this case…"

Bill Collingwood's voice started to quiver. Will knew he was struggling to hold back the floodtide of emotion and sorrow that was threatening to breach the walls of a father's heart.

Will hesitated slightly.

"I'm struggling with this decision. I'm being as honest as I can. I'm going to need a little more time…I'll get back to you as soon as I can."

After he hung up, Will stood up, stretched, and walked slowly over to the window that faced the main street in Monroeville. Through it he saw the tall steeple of St. Andrew's, the eighteenth-century church that had sounded its chimes when the news of Washington's victory at Trenton, New Jersey, had spread throughout the American colonies during the Revolutionary War.

Will knew of the places in Monroeville marked by little historical plaques. The places where the wives and mothers of Founding Fathers and Revolutionary War generals had spent the long war years on their knees, praying for the future of the country and the safety of their loved ones.

Somehow, the ghosts of those sacrifices and the echo of those church bells seemed almost palpable to the trial lawyer.

In every battle, Will thought to himself, *there is a moment of decision*. To attack or to retreat. To throw yourself, as a potential sacrifice, into the conflict…or to preserve, protect, and to wait.

Burdening Will's mind more than anything was his love for and sense of duty to his wife. A woman of great strength, Fiona had been dealt a disabling blow by the death of her father. That loss seemed to have uprooted her like a tree in a tornado. And Will knew that to defend Gilead Amahn now would be not only his own personal sacrifice of time and energy—it would also mean placing his wife, in her current emotional turmoil, on the altar of sacrifice as well.

And yet, with equal certainty, Will Chambers believed that at the darkest and most obscure core of Gilead's case, he might find an opportunity to wreak justice upon Warren Mullburn…whose past criminal attacks against Will and his family were, at least to Will, matters of dead certainty.

Perhaps Jack Hornby was right, he thought, that like it or not, Will Chambers was in the dead center of the circle on that piece of paper. And if that were so, then perhaps that was the way it had to be. Somehow, he would have to reconcile that with his loyalty to Fiona.

But for Will, it would also mean something else. That he might have to climb into the cage with a creature who—though he wore a suit and spoke in the erudite abstractions of a genius— would still prove to be a man-eating brute.

33

WILL CHAMBERS WAS SITTING in his favorite brown leather chair in the great room of his house. He had come home early from the office that afternoon and was now sitting down just in time to see the sun dying in bright fantastic splashes of crimson, pink, and orange, outlining the gray contours of the mountains.

He heard a door slam and a car drive off. It was Andrew's car pool. In a moment, Andrew, lugging his backpack, charged through the front door.

He greeted his dad and walked over to the chair. He studied his father's face for a minute.

"Dad, you look all stressed out. What's going on?"

"How could you tell?"

"Because whenever you start working on something in your mind and start worrying about something, your eyebrows get all...like...scrunched up."

Will laughed.

"Andy, that's one of the things I love about you."

"Oh, yeah?"

"You call it the way you see it."

"Where's Mom?"

"She left a message on the kitchen table that she was running some errands. Said she was bringing home dinner. So I suppose she'll be home before too long."

Andrew gave his father a high-five, grabbed a snack from the kitchen, and made his way up to his bedroom.

Will didn't notice. His eyes were on the waning sunset. There was still a thin red line of light rimming two of the mountain peaks in the distance when he noticed Fiona's Saab making its way up the long driveway.

Will greeted her on the porch, grabbed the groceries she was carrying, and gave her a kiss. As he put the groceries away and Fiona started making dinner, they exchanged the news about their day. But Will made a conscious choice not to tell his wife about the conversation with Bill Collingwood…at least not then.

"So I came to a decision today," Fiona said, slicing up chunks of beef for her Scottish stew.

"What kind of decision?"

"I called my manager. I said 'Look, Kevin, I don't feel like I have what it takes to finish these recording sessions. But regardless of how I feel…I'm just going to have to push my way through this. I've got an obligation to fulfill my obligations…and so I need to do it.' So…"

"So…what did you decide?"

"He's pulling the recording team together and they're coming by tomorrow. I'm going to try to put in at least a couple of hours in the studio."

"Gee, that's great." He walked over and kissed her gently on the back of the neck. "I'm glad."

"Pray for me," she said, transferring the beef from the cutting board to a frying pan.

"I always do," Will said.

He watched as she expertly peeled and sliced the potatoes.

"You want my help?"

"No. You can just stay here and talk with me. What's on your mind?" she added.

"Why is it that everyone in this family can read my mind?" Will asked.

"Good question," Fiona remarked. "I've seen you in court. You have a perfect poker face. But, somehow—and I think it's a blessing—when you're around the people you love, your face can't hide a thing."

Will let a few minutes go by, and then he decided to walk out onto dangerous ground.

"You made a decision today…about recording…"

"Yes."

"So…I made a decision too."

Fiona suddenly stopped slicing the potatoes, put the knife down, folded her arms, and stared at him.

"Look, honey," he said, "you can keep working on dinner. I'm not going anywhere."

But Fiona didn't blink.

"You made a decision about what?"

"I got a call today."

"Oh?"

"Yes. From Bill Collingwood. The guy was in tears. Now that I'm a father, I guess I understand what he's going through. Somewhat. He said Gilead won't take any legal representation unless it's me. Which means that the only lawyer he's going to have at his trial is this Egyptian court-appointed counsel."

"I'm still waiting…"

"So I'm listening to Bill talk. And I told you about my conversation with the English lawyer…Newhouse…who called me last Friday."

"That's old news," Fiona said. "Will, please tell me. You said you'd come to a decision…"

"I think I need to represent Gilead Amahn. I know this is a very bad time. But what I think I'll do is see if I can get local counsel there in Ramallah to do a lot of the initial work for me. I'll do as much as I can from home, here in Virginia. Put together our team from over here. We don't have to be separated, at least not until we get closer to trial."

"I thought we discussed this," Fiona said. "I really don't make a lot of demands, Will. I really don't. But when your wife looks you in the eye and says she feels like her life is falling apart, well…

And for some reason, at this point in time, I am struggling from day to day. And I need you desperately."

"Look, I need your feedback on this. We need to talk this out—"

"What's there to talk about?" Fiona's eyes filled with tears and her voice rose in agitation. "You say you made your decision. I know how you operate. When your mind locks into this decision-making—that's it. No matter what your mouth says, your mind goes into a launch sequence. The rocket is there on the launch pad. I can see the smoke coming out. I can hear the clock ticking down…you're in the space capsule, and I'm down on the ground waving. For all I know, it could end in total disaster…"

"Hey, there's no disaster here," Will said, walking over to try to reassure her. "I have no idea where you're getting that idea."

"Don't," Fiona said, pulling back. "I can see it in your face and your eyes. You feel the same thing I do. Don't deny it. We both have a feeling about this case. I'm not stupid. I know what's going on over there in the Middle East. I know that people are getting killed. I remember what Len Redgrove said about the Temple… the look on his face. And what Da said. His prediction about you—"

"Fiona, let's be reasonable. Let's be logical."

"Sure. Analytical. Objective. And dead." Fiona backed away from him. "I know you—and there's no language I can use… there's no translation between what I'm feeling and what you've decided, nothing that's going to change your mind. The launch sequence has begun—have a nice trip. Just do me a favor…please don't get blown up."

By now Fiona was no longer teary-eyed. Her face was expressionless. She washed her hands, walked by Will, and quietly made her way up the stairs and into the bedroom, where she closed the door behind her.

Will quietly took over the final details of dinner, alone in the kitchen.

He knew he had hurt her deeply. Probably very deeply.

And by now, they had been married long enough for him to know what Fiona did to protect her heart. When she sensed the deepest wounds, the most crushing and bruising assaults on her heart, she would often slip into a silent and unnerving detachment from Will.

But this time there was something beyond the normal struggles of married life to overcome.

Now, as Will worked in the kitchen, he couldn't shake the sensation that his decision about Gilead's case might extract a terrible price...beyond anything he would be willing to pay.

34

GREAT PAINS HAD BEEN TAKEN to ensure the secrecy of the meeting. There had been a handful of press reports that Warren Mullburn, in his capacity as foreign minister for the Republic of Maretas, was attempting to make an impact on the Middle East peace process. But only a handful of people in the world knew that Mullburn would be meeting in Cairo with a representative of the Arab League, the Palestinian foreign minister, and a special envoy from the president of Egypt, who was hosting the meeting.

The billionaire was attended only by his chief of staff and a bevy of plainclothes security agents, who were patiently waiting in the hallway outside the meeting room.

In the corner of the room, seated quietly in his white robes and turban, was Sheikh Mudahmid. Prior to his controversial appearance at the Islamic Center conference in northern Virginia, he had been labeled as a mufti who promoted terrorism and *jihad.* However, since the Temple Mount attack, the media had begun to focus on some of his earlier sermons predicting such an assault.

Over the months following the massacre, Mudahmid had been given airplay on several television talk shows and even permitted to make an address at an international peace conference hosted by the European Union.

Some Middle East pundits, however, viewed the sheikh's diplomatic philosophy a little differently...that he was using the slaughter of Arabs at the Temple Mount as the basis for a full-court press on a major carve-out of the state of Israel for the benefit of the Palestinians and, eventually, for all of the Arab League.

As host of the meeting, the Egyptian envoy made a few preliminary comments after introducing each of the attendees. He noted that, while Warren Mullburn was a newcomer to the field of international diplomacy and specifically negotiations in the Middle East, he came to the meeting as a potential mediator with the highest recommendation of the Arab League. In particular, he explained, Mullburn had the blessings of the Saudi family.

At that, the representative of the Arab League nodded enthusiastically.

"Exactly what interest," broke in the foreign minister for the Palestinian Authority, "does your Republic of Maretas in the Caribbean have in the events here in the Middle East?"

Mullburn smiled and nodded.

"First, let me say," he began, "that peace is, or at least should be, everyone's business. As I have proposed in my speeches and writings for many years, we need to look at the peace process in *any* part of the world from a global standpoint because it always affects *every* part of the world. Either we act as a community of nations, or we will be merely a collection of nations at war."

"So you would deny any connection between your position as a would-be peace mediator regarding the Temple Mount and the need for a Palestinian state and your...how shall I call them... aspirations regarding your worldwide oil interests?"

"Let me set the record straight," Mullburn said firmly. "There will be a vote in OPEC this month. I hope that, as we have lobbied, the Republic of Maretas is permitted entrance into OPEC. There has been some criticism because our island republic itself does not have any oil-producing sites. Yet, if you will check the ownership of my Mexico oil project, it has been transferred entirely to the Republic of Maretas. As such, Maretas has the right to be considered an oil-producing nation like any other. But to answer your specific question—why should my motives be questioned because of oil, any more than the Arab League's involvement in the peace process should be questioned because of their vast oil interests?"

With that Mullburn smiled and glanced over at the representative of the Arab League.

"Point well taken," the representative said. "And of course, while not a precondition to negotiations, it is certainly helpful that you profess to follow Islam..."

Mullburn nodded and smiled politely.

The Egyptian envoy then joined in.

"Just one technical question regarding that," the envoy said. "I do not question the honor of your profession of faith in Allah. And I do know that you have transferred all of your ownership interests in several Las Vegas casinos following your public announcement several years ago that you had converted to Islam. But there have been some unkind stories...articles in magazines...suggesting that the transfer was only to several straw men who were actually still employed by you, and that you were still exercising control.

"And of course, there were other complaints from some clerics—" and with that he threw a quick glance over at Sheikh Mudahmid. "About your adherence to the corrupt ideas of the German philosopher Hegel. But we need not belabor any of these points—we are very pleased to have you in our midst today. We just bring these things out...to place them on the table so that there will be nothing hidden. Nothing concealed. Our welcome to you as a potential mediator is a genuine one. And with that, perhaps we could discuss the matters on the official agenda that each of you has been given."

The Palestinian minister led off.

"As a matter of protocol," the minister stated, addressing Mullburn and shaking his head with concern, "I note that on your agenda for a peace agreement regarding the Palestinian state, you've listed the trial of that murderer, Hassan Gilead Amahn. I'm not sure that should be part of our discussions today..."

"Tell me your thoughts on that," Mullburn responded diplomatically.

"The Palestinian Authority has worked very hard—night and day for the last few months since the Temple Mount massacre." The minister continued, "The United Nations was pushing very hard to create a separate international tribunal under its auspices, like the ones for Bosnia and Rwanda—and of course, they would control it. That was totally unacceptable to us. We consider the massacre to have taken place on Palestinian soil—with the blood of Muslims, both Palestinians and other Arabs, shed there on top of the Mount. Besides, the UN would never support a tribunal that would permit a death sentence.

"For these reasons—and many, many others—we have worked very hard to make sure that the international tribunal we have created is deemed to be a *Palestinian* tribunal, though it's made up of an international array of three judges. Now of course, Israel has been making demands for the extradition of Mr. Amahn. They give out their cry about deaths of a few of their Jews at the Western Wall who were hit by some of the flying debris.

"We have fought very hard to control the legal process. And we have accomplished that. But now that that has been done, you can trust that the Palestinian Authority will see that justice is done. The full weight of the law. But at least publicly, there can be no official assurances of a result in the trial of Mr. Amahn that can in any way be tied in to the peace negotiations between Israel and the Palestinian Authority."

"And it might even be argued," the Egyptian envoy noted, "that both Israel and the Palestinian Authority have one common interest regarding this Mr. Amahn. His guilt, as the spiritual and tactical leader of this apocalyptic group, seems to be beyond any question. Therefore, I think that Israel and the Palestinian Authority both want Mr. Amahn tried, convicted, and sentenced to death. So, in that sense, I don't see the Palestinian tribunal issue, or the trial of Mr. Amahn, as being something that ought to hold up—or even be part of—the formal peace negotiation process.

How could it be? What would we say? That Mr. Amahn's conviction and execution is a prerequisite for a suitable peace agreement?"

"Let me just say," Mullburn commented with a smile, "that I propose to use all information, all techniques, and all advantages available to me to secure Israel's accommodation of the demands of the Palestinian Authority—as long, of course, as the Palestinian Authority's demands are reasonable. Which I have no doubt they will be."

The representative from the Arab League raised both hands in the air to indicate a question.

"So where does this leave us? Where are we going? It appears that there is a consensus among us that the trial of Gilead Amahn cannot be a formal part of the negotiation process. Perhaps it is the event that has actually forced Israel to its knees…although I am not sure. There are many among those in our League who believe that Israel was behind the bombing. That they secretly used the Knights of the Temple Mount and Gilead Amahn simply as pawns to accomplish what they did not want to do in the open. But of course, we have no proof of that—yet."

After a silence, the Egyptian envoy turned to Sheikh Mudahmid.

"Sheikh Mudahmid," he said graciously, "you've been very quiet. What are your ideas on this?"

The sheikh rose slowly from his seat in the corner of the room and walked to the wall of the conference room, where there was a large reproduction of an ancient Egyptian mural. In the center was a large scale, and from each end of its balance beam hung a plate. To the left of the scale was a figure of a standing man with the head of a jackal. On the right side was a figure of a man with the head of a hawk.

After studying the familiar picture for a moment, the sheikh turned to the group.

"Many of you have seen, as I know I have," the sheikh began, "these scales in the marketplace. But have you ever looked closely?

At the point where the balance beam swivels, there is a small screw. I've seen them myself. Almost invisible to the eye. A small thing, really…but very important. If the tiny little screw is tightened this way, or that, it can affect the ultimate balance…it can tip the scales one way or the other."

Then the sheikh put his hands behind his back and walked slowly along the conference table, behind the attendees, as he spoke.

"In the same way, I believe that the trial of Hassan Gilead Amahn is such a screw. It controls the scales. If he receives the just reward for his blasphemous, treacherous act—an act not only against Muslims, but against Allah himself—it can be said that justice is truly done. And then land can be divided up…and a Palestinian state can be created…and Israel can be made to accommodate the demands we have been making for generations and generations. But if justice is *not* done—then how can there be talk of peace? For such a peace would be a foolish peace. Of course, there will always be blood shed. But let it be their blood shed…not ours."

"You are a much honored mufti," the Palestinian minister said deferentially, "and we greatly respect you, Sheikh Mudahmid. But I know of no way that Mr. Mullburn, if he is to be the mediator and negotiator, can openly tell the Israelis that they must help us to convict and execute Mr. Amahn as part of this negotiation—"

"May I remind all of you," the sheikh continued, "that I am the only one in this room who has met this man—this Mr. Amahn. At the Islamic conference in Virginia in America. I met him face-to-face. I heard his Christian rantings…and I beheld his arrogant presumption of himself as a self-appointed messiah. We have waited a thousand years since the Salah ad-Din to recapture Jerusalem for Islam and for Allah. There can be no victory if Hassan Gilead Amahn goes free. No victory. There can be no peace if Amahn is not put to death for his crimes against Islam and against Arabs everywhere. And know this—that if this blasphemer is not put to death as the murderer that he is, then I will call upon each of you, and all of those in the Arab League, to participate in a worldwide *jihad* that will make the 9/11 attack in New York look like child's play."

With that, the sheikh gave a modest bow to the group, walked gravely back to his place in the corner, and sat down. As he calmly folded his hands in his lap, his gaze was on only one person.

The sheikh was staring at Warren Mullburn.

It was now clear to the billionaire in which direction the tiny screw in the scales must be turned.

35

THE DOOR TO WILL CHAMBERS' OFFICE was open. He had come to work early for the past few mornings. Looking up from his work, he noticed Jacki, his senior associate, standing in the doorway. She was wearing a loose-fitting dress to accommodate her seven-and-a-half-month pregnancy.

"Good morning," she said with an expression that told Will she had something on her mind.

"How are you?"

"So, I was driving to work this morning," Jacki began, "and I had the radio on. Top of the hour, usual stuff—weather—traffic report. And then I got the headline news."

"Oh?" Will said somewhat sheepishly.

"And you'll never guess what I heard."

"I *may* have a guess."

"I find out, not from you—but from the hourly news, weather, and traffic report—that alleged mass murderer Hassan Gilead Amahn, currently being held in a Palestinian jail for the massacre in Jerusalem, is going to be represented by Virginia lawyer Will Chambers."

"I was meaning to tell you…"

"When?" Jacki asked wryly.

"At our office meeting this morning."

"How convenient," Jacki snapped back sarcastically.

"Really, I was," Will replied. "And I know what you're thinking."

"Oh, you do?"

"Yes. You're going to be taking maternity leave in a few weeks, going to half time. And then, of course, when you have your baby you're going to be off indefinitely. And you're worrying about who is going to take over your workload while you're gone, because if I start usurping Todd Furgeson's schedule with this mammoth case in the Middle East, then who is going to pick up the slack from your cases? How's that?"

"You know, you and I go back many, many years," Jacki said. "And one thing I now have to admit. You're getting to be a better listener—specifically when it comes to women. So—are you going to usurp Todd's time? Are you going to enlist him to help you with this titanic case?"

"I'm going to respect the agreement we made about Todd helping you out during your pregnancy. I'm not going to change that."

"Well," Jacki noted, "that leaves only our newbie, Jeff. And young Mr. Holden is only two years out of law school. So what are you going to do, counselor? Are you handling this case entirely on your own? Or are you single-handedly going to redefine the term 'burnout'?"

"I'm working on it," Will said. "I'm going to figure out something."

"So let me be a bit nosy. Maybe it's none of my business. No, I take that back—it *is* my business. I consider you and Fiona very close friends. And I consider Fiona a very wonderful, precious woman. And I remember back…I think it was at the last Christmas party we had here at the office. She and I were just chatting. And she commented to me how nice it was that the two of you—and Andrew, specifically, now that he's getting older—were settling into regular family life. That your schedules were normal. Life seemed to be good. 'Normality'—that's the word I'm thinking of. She said she was really enjoying the normality of your lives together. And she seemed so happy.

"Now I do know what it's like to lose a parent. But for some reason, just talking to Fiona at the funeral of her dad—and I've spoken with her twice since then—I think your wife really got socked hard in the gut by this."

"I won't deny that. It's been rough," Will said reluctantly.

"You know, I've given you advice about Fiona over the years," Jacki plowed on. "Can I give you some more?"

"If I said no, would it stop you?" Will inquired with a smile. "Besides, you've got me cornered. I couldn't sneak out of the room anyway…with your profile you've got the doorway fully blocked."

Jacki tried not to laugh, but was unsuccessful. Then she added, "I don't know how this is going down with Fiona. But I can guess. This is going to be a strain on the office here. It's going to be a huge strain on you. But it's also going to be a super stress on your wife. Just some advice for you, Mr. Don Quixote…"

An hour later, in the office meeting, Will explained to the two other lawyers in his office his decision to take up the defense of Gilead Amahn. He told them the basics, although he didn't share with anyone, including Jacki, the most fundamental catalyst for his taking up the case—the chance to expose Warren Mullburn. Nor did he discuss his deepest fears—neither his vague sense of foreboding nor the fact that a wrong move in the defense of Gilead could bring catastrophic consequences.

He told Todd Furgeson that he would not be relying heavily on him. He told the youngest lawyer, Jeff Holden, that he would be using him for some background research and peripheral work. But somehow, Will had to figure out how he could put together a defense team adequate to the task, considering the immensity of the case.

When he got back to his desk after the meeting, Will immediately thought about contacting Len Redgrove. Len had served Will extremely well as co-counsel in the case they had handled jointly before the International Criminal Court several years before. But that had been a while ago, and especially since his wife's illness, Len's legal abilities had seemed to lose their edge. And then there was his strange behavior at the banquet.

Will put the possibility of contacting Len on hold while he did some preliminary research.

He accessed, through the Web site of the Palestinian International Tribunal, a copy of the indictment that had been filed just the day before Will's announcement that he would represent Gilead Amahn. It reviewed the provisions of the criminal code of the Palestinian Authority, which defined the crime with which Gilead Amahn was charged. Will could only shake his head at the irony of it.

The law was entitled "The Provision of Material Support to Terrorists Involved in Mass Murder, War Crimes, or Crimes Against Humanity." It had been passed by the Palestinian Authority a year before the Temple Mount bombing, and closely followed the language of antiterrorism legislation adopted in the United States. Will was aware that, in the years following the World Trade Center attack, the Department of Justice and the State Department had strongly encouraged other nations around the world to adopt antiterrorism criminal codes similar to those in the United States.

The language of the Palestinian antiterrorism provision law prohibited

> providing material support, encouragement or resources... knowing or intending that they are to be used in preparation for, or the carrying out of, acts of terrorism involving mass murder, war crimes, or crimes against humanity.

Did that provide an exception for Gilead Amahn's conduct? Will was unsure.

As he read the indictment against his client, one thing was clear. Gilead was charged with being not only the spiritual but also the tactical leader of the Knights of the Temple Mount. He was alleged to have encouraged them to orchestrate the devastating attack on the Temple Mount in order to fulfill their cultic religious prophecies. The indictment went on to allege that the Knights were a breakaway religious subsect of the Druze religion. That Gilead Amahn was viewed by the Knights—and in fact, viewed himself—as the promised messiah who would destroy the impediments to the rebuilding of the Jewish Temple that had been destroyed in AD 70 during the Roman conquest of Jerusalem.

The document then described the Druze religion as a combination of Judaism, Islam, and Christian mysticism. The Knights of the Temple Mount, as a religious subgroup had developed their own particular brand of apocalyptic theology, according to the indictment.

That got Will thinking. Back to the banquet, when Redgrove had delivered his brief and catastrophic vision of the immediate future.

He picked up the phone and dialed Len Redgrove's number, wondering what Len had been doing lately up in his mountain cabin. He hadn't been answering the phone or responding to contacts from friends.

The phone rang. It continued to ring. At the tenth ring, Will was ready to hang up. But just then, a voice at the other end answered.

"Hello."

"Len? Is that you?"

"Yes."

"This is Will Chambers. Len, how have you been?"

There was a pause.

"Will, I got your message some time ago…I guess it was a number of months ago…about this Gilead Amahn fellow. The one you represented in that misdemeanor case in Virginia…"

"Well, frankly, that's old news now, Len," Will replied. "At the time I called, I was trying to help Gilead out of a situation. He had been arrested in Cairo for preaching there. But we made some phone calls. The Egyptian police released him. And then shortly after that…well, I'm sure you've been reading the news.

You know what happened at the Temple Mount. And everything after that."

"Yes. I'm well aware of that."

"I thought perhaps I could talk to you about Gilead Amahn's case. I've decided to undertake his defense—"

"You must be kidding," Len said gloomily.

"No. I'm absolutely serious."

"I'm sorry to hear that."

"You know, Len, you and everybody else I've been talking with seem to have the same reaction. But I do want to pick your brain…"

"Is it about this case? The Temple Mount? Gilead Amahn?"

"Yes—"

"Then I want to talk in person, not on the phone. You know where my place is up here?"

"Yes. I've been up there a couple of times. I think I can find my way."

"I want you to come meet me today. I've got some time. But come alone."

"Alone?" Will asked with confusion in his voice.

"Yes. I'd prefer that," Len said.

Will had never heard his old professor sound quite so paranoid. Or so mysterious. After quickly finishing the phone call, he grabbed the file on Gilead Amahn, stuffed it into his briefcase, and breezed by Hilda's desk in the front lobby.

"I'm going out," he said without turning back.

"You know when you're coming back?" Hilda called after him.

"I have no idea," Will yelled as he walked out.

36

EN ROUTE TO PROFESSOR LEN REDGROVE'S CABIN, which was tucked away in the higher elevations of the Blue Ridge Mountains, Will made a quick call to his private investigator, Tiny Heftland so he could connect before he got out of roaming range.

The big private investigator picked up after only a few rings.

"Man alive, great to hear from you, counselor. Hey, real sorry about Fiona's dad. I sent some flowers and a card. I hope she got them."

"She did," Will replied. "I know she was touched by that."

"Look, I was up in Canada at the time of the funeral. Heard about it thirdhand. I was doing a surveillance for a former member of the Canadian parliament. Guy's a little paranoid...thinks he's being followed. Thinks people are after him. Of course, I can't blame him too much...he got a letter laced with ricin. So, all things considered, I suppose that would make anybody's nerves go a little jingle-jangle."

"Don't worry about it. I'm sure Fiona understands. The real reason I called, Tiny, is that I've got a new case I want to get you involved in."

"That's sweet news to me," the PI boomed. "What has it been, more than a year since the last time?"

"That's about right. I've been limiting my practice a little. Trying to ease back and spend more time with Fiona and Andy. And I'm doing some part-time teaching at a seminary. I replaced

Len Redgrove. You remember him? He was co-counsel with me on that International Criminal Court case in The Hague."

"Redgrove? Oh yeah, yeah. He's that brainiac law professor. Nice guy. But, as I remember him, just a little squirrely...head in the clouds. Like he's been hanging around places where the air's too thin. The couple of times I met with him when you were preparing for that trial, he was always talking about the 'big picture' this or the 'big picture' that."

"Well, as a matter of fact," Will said, "I'm on my way to see him right now."

"You going to use him on this case?"

"Probably not. He's getting on in years. He hasn't been doing too well since his wife's been going downhill with Alzheimer's. But I do want to bounce a couple of ideas off him. He's been a very special friend to me. Kind of a mentor."

"Well, I mean...I didn't mean any disrespect..."

"No. That's alright. Anyway, here's the case. Hold onto your hat. I'm representing Gilead Amahn."

"Counselor! In all the hot ones you've handled, I don't think you could have picked a hotter one," Tiny exclaimed. "Geez, if you don't mind my saying so, everything I see on TV about that religious group really makes them look like a bunch of wackos. How are you going to defend this guy?"

"I'm working on it," Will said. "But one of the first things we have to do is factual investigation over there in Jerusalem. About the group. About the circumstances of the bombing. We have to pick up some intelligence off the ground about the rumors that were floating around about this group and my client shortly before the incident. Tiny, are you up for some international travel?"

"Sure. Of course. And, uh, I don't mean to be indelicate, Will boy. You and I go back a long way. But there's always the issue of filthy lucre..."

"Don't worry about that," Will replied. "The client's family paid me the retainer through an organization that's supporting the defense. Some group called the Holy Land Institute for the Word.

I'm not familiar with it. But the retainer check has already come in. Your expenses and time—at your usual rate—will be more than taken care of."

"I know I can always count on you," Tiny said enthusiastically.

"I'll get you some background information by e-mail tomorrow...forward a copy of the indictment. I'll give you a page or two of some of my initial impressions. And then maybe a page of bullet points about areas for your investigation there. Names. Contacts. Some things to start you off."

Tiny signed off just in time. Will's Corvette was winding its way up the mountain passes toward the higher elevations of the Blue Ridge Mountains, where his cell-phone reception would disappear.

It was a clear, warm day, and Will had the top down and was enjoying the rush of the air through his hair and past his face.

He exited off the main highway onto a smaller road that took a steep incline up the mountain. After about two miles a small gravel road branched off at a bend. He recognized the intersection and turned onto the narrow drive that wound through the sparse trees, and finally to a small wood-shingled cabin nearly at the top of the mountain.

Will grabbed his briefcase, and as he stepped out of his car, he turned around to look at the vista of mountaintops spreading out in all directions. There was a haze hanging over the valleys below and a mild breeze blowing. As he turned toward the cabin, he spotted Redgrove's familiar Land Rover parked off to the side, so he figured he was home as he promised he would be.

After three knocks on the screen door he heard his old friend's voice calling for him to come on in.

Redgrove was pouring himself some tea. He was dressed in wrinkled khaki pants, a denim work shirt, and hiking boots. His thinning white hair was uncombed.

He finished pouring his cup of tea, put the teapot down, and then turned fully around to look at Will. Then a broad smile swept across his face, and he took a few slow steps toward Will and extended his right hand. As the men shook hands, Redgrove moved closer and put a hand on each of Will's shoulders.

"It's good to see you, Will. It really is."

The two sat down while Redgrove sipped his tea slowly. The older man said his wife had been having a particularly bad time of it on the day of Angus MacCameron's funeral. He had decided to stay with her rather than attend.

"So, what did you think when you got my voice mail about Gilead Amahn?" Will finally asked.

"Well," Redgrove replied somberly, "as a matter of fact, I was sitting right here in this chair. Listening to your message as it came in over the answering machine. I chose not to pick up the phone."

Will studied Redgrove carefully, trying to figure out his response.

"The fact is," the older man took another sip of tea, "that day I had just come back from visiting Anne at the full-care center. You know she's been slipping really fast. But that was the first day...that very day...the first time she didn't recognize me. She looked at me with this blank look. I was a complete stranger to her.

"I can't tell you how devastating that was. I just...was having a very difficult day. And wasn't up to taking your call."

"Perfectly understandable," Will said reassuringly. "Don't worry about it a bit, Len."

"But, well...there was another reason..."

"What do you mean?"

"I didn't want to pick up the phone and give you some snap response about Gilead Amahn...just off the top of my head. I had to be very careful—very cautious about what I was going to tell you."

Will searched for some explanation in his old friend's expression.

"I'm not sure I understand..."

"You know that Bill Collingwood and his wife initially contacted me. You remember that? They came to me about Gilead's situation. Described the riot over at the Islamic Center. I referred them to you. Now I wish I'd never had that conversation…"

"Why?"

"How much do you know about this Gilead Amahn?"

"I represented him in that case. Met with him a number of times. Met with his parents. He seemed like a credible person to me."

"Did he?"

"Yeah—Len, what are you getting at?"

"Did you ever talk to the head pastor of the church where Gilead had been working…over in West Virginia?"

"No. I didn't have any need to."

"Well, this pastor was at a conference where I was giving a talk. Maybe five months ago. He came up to me afterward. This was just after the first news came out about the riot over there at the Islamic Center. Bill Collingwood had called over to the pastor to let him know that Gilead was in Virginia, under arrest for the incident. Did Bill ever tell you what he and the pastor talked about?"

"No, not specifically…"

"Well, the pastor told me. He got me alone after the lecture. He told me Gilead was acting strange."

"In what way?"

"He didn't give me a lot of detail. But he did say Gilead had recently given his notice and left the church. And before that, he had taken an unexplained leave…"

"Why?"

"The pastor didn't know the specifics. But Gilead had told some members of the church that he was going into the mountains with a backpack and a sleeping bag. He was going to spend forty days and forty nights in the wilderness. Does that sound familiar?"

"Yes and no. Maybe he's an outdoors buff. Maybe he likes camping…"

"Tell me something, Will," Len said with a serious look on his face, "how old was Gilead Amahn when he walked into the Islamic Center and began his public preaching campaign?"

Will thought for only a few seconds.

"He was thirty years old."

"And how old was Jesus when He began His public ministry?"

Will chuckled a little and shook his head.

"That's a little far-fetched, Len, isn't it?"

"Jesus was thirty years old. Jesus went into the wilderness for forty days and forty nights. Then He appeared at the inauguration of His public preaching. Your client does the same thing. And something else…"

"What?"

"When Jesus began His preaching, where did He go? He went to His own people. To the nation of Israel. He preached in the synagogues. Where He was rejected and His life was threatened. Where does Gilead Amahn go? As a former Muslim, he goes to the largest conclave of Islamic clerics in North America. And he preaches to them. And he's not only rejected, but his life is threatened as well."

"Look, Len, you know how much respect I have for you. You know what a huge impact you've had on my life. After my life was falling apart, my drinking problem, when Audra was murdered…I'm dealing with the death of my wife…and then I came to faith—all along you encouraged me. You and Angus Mac-Cameron established some indispensable building blocks in my walk with the Lord. And I don't know if I ever thanked you sufficiently for that…"

"I know that, Will." Redgrove had a sympathetic look, but his voice conveyed a sense of hidden intentions.

"I'm here because I need your wisdom. About Gilead Amahn's defense…"

"You've probably noticed," Len noted, "that I don't teach law anymore or write on legal issues. The fact is…world events are telescoping very rapidly. I feel the leading from God to be an observer, a recorder, and an interpreter of some of those events. I know you probably thought my comments were a bit strange at the banquet earlier this year—"

"To be honest, I did. I was confused. And I didn't really understand your point. Of course, you're a brilliant man. So I had to figure there were some things you understood that I didn't..."

"You really want to know what I think?"

"Of course, I do," Will replied.

"Then you need to listen to me. You know I've been following the situation in the Middle East for years. Originally, just because I was doing a lot of international law teaching. But soon I saw a pattern. I saw things escalating. I know there are always wars, skirmishes, and negotiations going on over there. And at any given time there's always some problem. That's not new. But what was new was what I saw on the horizon. Something clear was beginning to emerge. It started with the Deuteronomy Fragment. A massive attack on the psyche of the Israeli people. An assault against the foundational Old Testament guarantee that the land of Israel would belong to the Jews. And then it became clear, as I continued to read and study, that the center of all of this was going to be the Temple Mount. It had to be. I don't know how much time you spend in prophetic Scripture in your Bible study..."

"I don't think you and I are very far apart," Will said. "I think your interpretation of prophecy and mine are pretty much the same. But I look at it from a practical standpoint. We don't know when God is going to wrap up history. We don't know when the Second Coming of Jesus Christ is going to occur. Scripture guarantees that. So, if we can't know, then let's emphasize applying our faith in a practical way for the present. And not speculating on the future."

"I figured that you'd say that," Len said with a smile. "But what happens when the future is suddenly dead center in the vortex of the present? What happens when thousands of years of prophetic promises suddenly start coming to be? Do you ignore them? Do you close your eyes and say, 'I'm just living for today'?

The point is this—there is no question, given a correct interpretation of the Gospel of Matthew, Paul's second epistle to the Thessalonians, and the book of Revelation, that Herod's Temple must be rebuilt at the Temple Mount location for Scripture prophecy to be fulfilled. The Temple has to be rebuilt. The animal sacrifice in Old Testament Judaism will be reinaugurated, and then a shadowy and metaphysically evil personage is going to defile that Temple and declare himself God."

"You aren't seriously thinking that this case—or Gilead Amahn—has anything to do—"

"I'm telling you—I wish you wouldn't have taken on this case. I fear for you. I tremble that neither of us may really understand the nature of the man you're representing...or be able to appreciate the implications of the maelstrom you're walking into. You can take every controversial, explosive, gut-wrenching case you've ever handled in your long legal career. And you can put them all together on one side of the scale, and I believe that this one case you are now undertaking, outweighs those by an exponent too immense to calculate."

Will fumbled mentally for a handle to grasp in this conversation that was spiraling into abstraction.

"I was actually only hoping, Len, that you could give me some guidance on the defense of this fellow."

Len leaned back. For several seconds he said nothing. Then he asked a question.

"Do you have the indictment from the international tribunal with you? The charge against Amahn?"

Will quickly fished in his briefcase, retrieved it, and handed it to Redgrove, who studied it carefully for several minutes.

"This corresponds to what I have heard in the news," the older man said quietly. "The Knights of the Temple Mount group was a sect, a cultic breakaway from the Druze religion. You need to get someone who has credentials. Someone who's an expert in Middle Eastern cultic groups like this. And an expert in this group in particular. There aren't many people in the world who have that kind of information."

"Good point," Will replied. "Any suggestions?"

Redgrove was thinking. After a few seconds of reflection he continued.

"There was a professor. Don't remember what his name was. I met him when I was in the Middle East several years ago. I was working on a book on comparative religions at the time. Something tells me that he taught at the University of Cairo—a professor in what he called 'esoteric religions.' I can fish around in my papers. See if I have his card. Or his name and address. He might be a good person to contact."

Then Redgrove rose abruptly and extended his hand to Will.

"I'll pray for you. My soul is troubled that you are entangled in this. Be on your guard. And if you see any opportunity to withdraw from representing Gilead Amahn…I would counsel you to carefully consider it."

With that warning, Will turned to leave. As he reached the screen door, his old friend asked him one more question.

"Since the Temple Mount bombing, have you had the chance to meet with Gilead Amahn face-to-face?"

"No. I'm sending my investigator, Tiny Heftland, over there to do some field work for me. But before too long, I'm going to have to go over there and have a sit-down with Gilead myself. Why do you ask?"

Redgrove began closing the door behind Will, but paused to add one final comment.

"When you meet with him, you ask him something—ask him point-blank, 'Do you believe you are a messiah?' You ask him that. Or better yet—ask whether he's the Antichrist."

Will's old professor gave him a quick nod, and then closed the door tightly behind him.

37

AFTER HIS INITIAL SUCCESSFUL OVERTURES to the Arab delegation in Cairo, Warren Mullburn returned to Maretas and at once directed the captain of his three-hundred-foot yacht, dubbed *Epiphany,* to prepare for a three-day cruise.

As the massive yacht sailed over the brilliant turquoise of the Carribean, Mullburn was in the stateroom when his butler tapped gently on the varnished mahogany door and entered.

"Sorry to disturb you, sir, but Mr. Theos Petropolos has just landed on the heliport. He's on his way down to see you."

A few minutes later a tall man, thirty years old, with dark hair, strikingly dark eyes, and chiseled good looks entered the suite, dressed casually in a silk island shirt, shorts, and deck shoes.

Mullburn, who was finishing lunch, rose to his feet, flashed a smile at his guest, and strode over to shake his hand.

"Theos," Mullburn said with a smile. "Very good to see you. Want me to order you some lunch?"

"Not necessary," the other man replied. "I grabbed some lunch before I got in the chopper."

Mullburn sat down at his private table, and his visitor stretched out on a couch set below a row of windows overlooking the ocean.

"Now that we're face-to-face," Mullburn said, "I need to thank you for handling that Middle East assignment. A job well-done. Executed flawlessly. Excellent work on the multiple firewalls between you and the direct actors, particularly regarding the grand finale."

"Thanks," Theos said. "That's certainly one thing I've learned working closely with you over these last five years. Protect yourself—immunize yourself—always work on a pyramid basis. You at the top. Limited direct access. And delegation that cannot be traced."

"I'm glad to see you appreciate your apprenticeship." Mullburn grinned. "You've been a good student."

Petropolos was casually lounging on the couch with his legs stretched out to full length. Not the usual position for a man in the presence of the Warren Mullburn empire.

"And I still consider you a great teacher. Even a mentor," he replied. "Even if you weren't my father."

"Care for a drink?"

The younger man nodded.

"Whatever you're having."

Mullburn stood and walked over to the brass, mahogany, and crystal liquor cabinet behind him. He poured two glasses and handed one to Theos.

"Let's toast."

Theos rose quickly to his feet, drink in his hand, beaming at his father.

"What shall we toast to?" he asked.

Mullburn raised his glass, and so did his son.

"I propose a toast," the billionaire said, "to our global partnership—and to our family empire."

They clicked glasses.

Theos made himself comfortable on the couch as his father stood, sipping from his glass.

"I know things were not always good between us," Mullburn said. "And I'm sure your mother had some very nasty things to say."

"Well, I have to report," Theos replied, "that she would run you down...bitterly criticize you. All I heard were negative things about how you'd left her high and dry. And yet I saw with my own eyes how well you provided for her. Our Athens villa was very nice. And all of our needs were taken care of—I knew that you couldn't be the monster that she made you out to be. And so, as I got older, I decided to make up my own mind. Judge for myself."

"And?"

"And—I'm here. I'm working with you. It's obvious that I've taken a tremendous risk…"

"Of course you have," Mullburn snapped back. "We all do. How do you think I created this world for myself? By being timid and weak and fearful? If you've learned anything over the last five years, it should be this—the only world worth having is the one you create for yourself. With your own hands. By force if necessary, but always by cunning. By being smarter, better prepared, and more willing to take risks than your adversary. Leadership requires brutal choices. And it demands the courage of mind to follow through. To execute decisions, no matter what blood may be let, no matter what losses may be incurred."

Theos Petropolos smiled.

"Father, I want to make you proud of me. I want you to build in me the kind of character that has made you the man you are."

Mullburn returned to his chair behind the dining table.

"I have another job for you. President LaRouge is continuing to apply pressure to me. He's demanding more and more accountability. He's treating me like a member of his cabinet. The fact is, he has to consider himself a member of *my* cabinet—that is, if he's very lucky."

Both of them chuckled.

"I'll get some figures together later," the older man continued. "But we need to remind our island's esteemed president how very vulnerable he is. How I am his sole source of protection, domestically, internationally, economically, and most importantly—militarily. I control the Elite Guard of the Republic, not him. In an instant I can shut down all of our banks, change our currency, and orchestrate a coup. All in probably less than an hour. So as far as

Mandu LaRouge is concerned, I'll get back to you with the details on how I want you to handle him."

"Whatever you'd like me to do," Theos replied. "You can count on me, Father."

Mullburn rose, put down his glass, and strode over to his son, who was still reclining on the couch.

"Finish your drink while you head back to the helicopter," he ordered. "I want you back in the palace. I'll get some information to you then via Himlet."

The younger man quickly swallowed the last of his drink and shook hands with his father. But he hesitated at the door.

"And we will have to finish our discussion sometime," he added, "about your continuing progress regarding financial transfer."

Mullburn eyed his son carefully. "As you know," he said matter-of-factly, "I've already begun shifting control of some important assets to you. I'll continue making progress on that. I plan on regarding you as my successor. As I promised. And when the centralization of my economic structure is completed, I'll be able to have more flexibility in bringing you into some of the major global ventures. Now—you'd better be on your way."

Theos threw his father a quick wave, then disappeared up the stairs to the top deck.

After he had left, Mullburn snatched his cell phone and punched in a number. His chief personal accountant answered quickly.

"This is Mullburn."

"Yes, sir. What can I do for you?"

"It's about Mrs. Petropolos in Athens…"

"Yes, sir?"

"You know the monthly stipend I've been paying to her?"

"Yes, sir. It's been a fixed amount for as many years as I can remember."

"Stop paying it," Mullburn growled.

38

PRESIDENT HARRIET CORBIN LANDOW was seated on the couch in the Oval Office, chugging from a twenty-four-ounce bottle of French spring water and paging furiously through a report that had just been handed to her by Secretary of State Thomas Linton.

The secretary of state was seated in a chair across the coffee table from the president. His hands were folded politely in his lap, and he waited patiently for her comments.

There was a knock, and the door cracked open a few inches as her chief of staff, a middle-aged woman with short-cropped hair and a datebook in her hand, attempted to politely interrupt.

"Excuse me, Madame President. I'm sorry to interrupt, but you had asked that I let you know—"

President Landow snapped, "I don't want to be interrupted. No exceptions. Close the door, and I don't want to see you until I ask for you."

She returned to the final page of the report, studied it carefully, flipped back to a few pages in the middle, then laid the document down on the coffee table and took another slug from her bottle of water.

A few seconds passed, and the secretary of state made some initial observations.

"Madame President, this is our best information available. I regret to say that as far as the Middle East peace process is concerned—"

"Yes, let's talk about that," the president shot back. "As far as the peace process is concerned, the United States has lost control. We have been cut off at the pass by a fly-by-night, self-appointed ambassador of goodwill, Warren Mullburn, who buys himself this little banana republic somewhere in the Caribbean. And now he upstages the president of the United States. Is that what we're dealing with here? Are you saying this guy has more leverage than the leader of the free world...which I am?"

Secretary Linton chose his words carefully.

"As I often advised President Warren—and I would advise you the same thing—the mediation process over there is always fragile. And it's always subject to a changing political environment. That's what makes it so difficult. We have multiple geo-political entities claiming some interest in that process. But frankly, it all comes down to one thing—the massacre on the Temple Mount reconfigured all of the prior alliances, destroyed the fragile peace process that had been built up to that point, and basically threw everything up for grabs."

"I want you to bring me back into this process," the president replied tersely. "Go back to square one. Back to the drawing board. Get Howard Kamura back into the middle of things—in the thick of it—and get him to elbow Mullburn completely out. If it means digging up some trash on him so we reduce his credibility to a smoldering ash pile...then so be it. This guy has more hooks on him...more dirty laundry than a Chinese dry cleaner in New York."

"Well, we know about all the stories regarding Mr. Mullburn. I've seen the intelligence on him. The problem is...he has escaped any definitive proof of wrongdoing, even though there are high suspicions involving many...many questionable dealings by Mr. Mullburn. In other words, he's managed to construct a plausible avenue of deniability regarding everything that's been alleged against him. As you know, the Department of Justice finally dropped its pursuit of him."

"Maybe it's time to start up a new investigation of Mr. Mullburn," the president replied.

"I don't think that is feasible," Linton answered. "I've already talked to the attorney general. There is just nothing to go on. And at this point, if we convene yet another grand jury against Mr. Mullburn, he could make a good case for selective, discriminatory prosecution."

President Landow studied him for a moment before she continued. Linton was, of course, the selection of her predecessor, Theodore Warren. But she was stuck with him—at least for the time being. Her administration was still in its infancy, and a change in secretary of state at this early juncture would be politically disastrous.

On the other hand, although Landow knew she had to work with Linton, that didn't mean she had to like it.

"Let me just say this," Landow added. "You know what my priorities are. I want Mullburn squeezed out. I want the United States back in this process as chief negotiating agent. I want you to listen to me very carefully—I want a signing ceremony between the Palestinian prime minister and the prime minister of Israel, with me in the middle. All of us shaking hands. Right there. Clear?"

Linton smiled cautiously and nodded.

"And there is one more thing," Landow noted as she flipped through the report. "Yes, here it is. You talk about the Palestinian tribunal that's going to try the leader of that cult that blew up the Temple Mount—"

"Hassan Gilead Amahn."

"Yes. Amahn. Your report discusses the procedural aspects—the imminent trial of Mr. Amahn—the fact that the Palestinians worked hard to make sure the UN didn't take over the process because they wanted the death penalty very badly on this. Now, as you know, I take a middle road on that. Polls are still very strong about the vast majority of Americans wanting the death penalty against terrorists who kill innocent people. So I have no problem with that. But we need to get something understood..."

"Yes, Madame President?"

"Well, first of all, the United States has to have a strong presence. We have to be visibly in support of the Palestinian effort to bring this guy to justice. Do you know what I mean?"

"Yes. We have several advisors from the Department of Justice assisting the Palestinians in establishing the tribunal. Drafting the procedural laws to apply to the trial. Selection of judges and so forth. Of course, the UN and the International Criminal Court have given the primary assistance in helping to fashion the tribunal. But the United States is also very much involved—"

"No, you're just missing this, Tom," the president snapped. "We need to show that the United States helped to convict this man. We helped put him in the death chamber for his act of genocide against Muslims. That's what I'm talking about."

"Well, we can hardly put that in a report," Secretary Linton said with an air of surprise. "There has to be some semblance of a fair trial involved here. Madame President, you and I are both lawyers, and—"

"Let's not get off on the rule of law," Landow replied. "I don't need a lecture on that. I see three indisputable facts here. First of all, according to the polls I read just yesterday, about sixty-seven percent of the American people believe that this Gilead Amahn was the ringleader behind the bombings. That his religious fanaticism fueled the massacre. And then secondly, it is also pretty clear to me that Amahn was on the FBI's terrorist watch list...we've got to mitigate that issue, it could be political suicide for us if it looks like he slipped through our fingers..."

"Not exactly," Linton replied. "He was not a known terrorist. In fact, nobody had identified him as a terrorist. It's just that his ethnic background, his former Islamic ties over in Cairo, and his trips back and forth between the United States, Israel, and Jordan had some time ago raised the question about whether we needed to look at him more closely. So when he got arrested for starting a disturbance at an Islamic meeting in northern Virginia, we put a detainer on him so we could take a closer look. But the FBI and the DOJ decided he had no connections to any known terrorist organizations, so the hold was dropped."

"Well then, let me give you my third issue. And this is probably the most important," President Landow concluded. "Gilead Amahn is proof positive that what I had been saying during the campaign was absolutely true. A lot of folks...the conservative talk-show hosts—you know the same old bunch—they were going berserk when I was nominated as VP on the ticket. Especially over my comments about a conspiracy of the extreme Christian terrorist fringe. Well, all that ends up to be true, doesn't it, if you look at this Gilead Amahn. He's part of the lunatic element...this prophecy cult that thinks they can bring Jesus back to earth by blowing up half of Jerusalem. That's the kind of religious fanaticism, the kind of right-wing stuff I've been up against all my life. And now it's come home to roost. If they aren't blowing up abortion clinics, then they're blowing up Muslim sites to bring on the Second Coming. So...Amahn needs to be brought to justice for that massacre, and it has to be swift and final."

"Well, if it's any consolation," Secretary Linton replied, "the prosecution team in Ramallah has some very strong evidence. They're very dedicated to bringing Amahn to a criminal conviction."

"Tom, let's just cut to the chase," Landow said. "I know the Palestinians. I've talked to those people since the Temple Mount bombing. I know full well that they want to crucify this Gilead Amahn."

Then she put down her bottle of water, leaned forward, and looked Linton in the eye.

"So what I'm saying," the president said with the full measure of her assumed authority, "is that we need to provide them with the hammer and nails."

39

WILL CHAMBERS HAD CLEARED EVERYTHING from his calendar that day except for one case—*The International Tribunal of the Palestinian Authority v. Hassan Gilead Amahn, Accused.*

He put in several calls to Deputy Secretary of State in Charge of Middle Eastern Affairs, Bob Fuller, but each time was referred to a secretary who indicated Mr. Fuller was not available.

Finally, a call came in from the State Department. Hilda transferred it back to Will's desk.

"Mr. Chambers?"

"Yes."

"My name is Tom Fallow. I'm an assistant legal counsel over at the State Department. I know that you wanted to get through to Bob Fuller—"

"Yes," Will interrupted. "Bob Fuller and I worked together on a case I handled involving the government of Sudan. And some time ago Bob was kind enough—at least it's my speculation—he made a call to Cairo to get my client, Hassan Gilead Amahn, released from illegal detention. Now, of course, you know Mr. Amahn is being charged by an international tribunal—"

"Let me just short-cut this," Fallow broke in. "Mr. Fuller regrets to inform you that the State Department will be unable to assist you in any manner regarding your defense of Mr. Amahn. That is the formal position taken by the State Department. He also indicates that there is no point in further dialoguing with you about the Amahn case."

"Well," Will replied, "that makes it clear."

"That is my purpose," Fallow answered curtly. "The State Department wants our position to be very clear and very plain. We can lend you absolutely no assistance in your defense of your case."

Will hung up the phone, surprised that Bob Fuller had refused to even discuss the case.

He had no alternative but to shrug off the State Department's refusal to deal and turn to his other work on the case. He had just faxed and e-mailed to an Arab translator a notice of retainer he was filing with the Palestinian International Tribunal, giving notice that he had been formally retained as defense counsel for Gilead Amahn.

Now he began sketching out the broad contours of what he considered to be the foundational issues of the case. Tiny Heftland, who had just arrived in Ramallah, had not yet had a chance to interview Gilead or obtain any of the prosecution documents or pleadings, so Will was relegated to doing an Internet search of every newspaper article and government document relating to the Amahn case. He went to the official Palestinian Authority Web site and obtained a copy of several press releases that the newly created Palestinian International Tribunal had released about the procedural status of the case, along with numerous press releases from the office of the public prosecutor of the Palestinian Authority.

Will then contacted a former FBI agent, an expert in explosives, to begin schooling him on the nature of the devices and compounds used on the Temple Mount.

Will was limited to the scant information he had at that point, but his explosives expert was already faxing him some background information. The way Will viewed the issues in the case, the starting point for the prosecution's case was the forensics evidence involving the nature of the explosives and their linkage to the Knights of the Temple Mount.

But beyond that was also the ideological component. Will knew that the Palestinian Authority had to create a connection between the violent theology and apocalyptic plan of the Knights of the Temple Mount—and the belief and conduct of Gilead Amahn.

Which then brought Will to the most critical aspect of the case—what Gilead had actually known about any plans that the Knights of the Temple Mount had for the bombing—and exactly what Gilead had said, or done, to either encourage or implement that plan.

Will filled close to ten pages of his yellow legal pad with potential areas of investigation, legal research, and questions to be answered during the discovery stage of his defense.

As he looked at one of the press clippings in his file, he was reminded of the name of Attorney Mira Ashwan, the court-appointed amicus curiae for the defense of Gilead's case.

Will called his Arab translator at Georgetown and asked her if she could stand by on a conference call while he tried to connect with the law office of Attorney Ashwan in Hebron.

Will asked Hilda to put together an international call to Attorney Ashwan's office. When the call was answered, the Arab translator explained that Ashwan was on another phone call and suggested that Will try to set up a conference call ten minutes later.

The second time was a success. He was somewhat surprised, after getting past the Arabic-speaking secretary, to hear Mira Ashwan's crisp, highly intelligible English.

"You speak English very well. As a matter of fact, you speak it infinitely better than any attempt I could make at Arabic."

There was no reply at the other end.

Will dismissed the Arabic translator as unnecessary and continued his conversation directly with Attorney Ashwan.

"Ms. Ashwan, I am the newly retained defense counsel for Gilead Amahn. I wanted a chance to chat with you. I understand your role as a court-appointed amicus curiae is not exactly that of defense counsel. But in essence, the court is asking you to fashion arguments for the defense, and to that extent, we have a mutuality of interest."

"Yes," she answered cautiously. "And what would you like to discuss?"

"Well, at this stage," Will replied, "nothing in particular. I just wanted to open the lines of communication between our two offices. I'll send you a copy of the notice of retainer I just filed electronically with the Palestinian Authority and the International Palestinian Tribunal."

"I will certainly read it," Ashwan answered coldly.

"Then, I look forward to working with you toward our mutual aim of providing the most aggressive, zealous defense possible for Mr. Amahn."

"Yes. Thank you," Ashwan answered and hung up.

Will had not expected an exuberant reception from the court-appointed Palestinian counsel, and he was not disappointed.

At the end of the day, after Will glanced at his watch, he packed up some of his files, threw them into his briefcase, and drove home.

He noticed some of the cars of Fiona's recording team parked in front of the recording studio. He pulled over there and, inside, slipped into the recording booth.

"Fiona, I want you to try that again," the board engineer was saying. "That last vocal sounded a little bright. I want to soften it up at my end. So let's try it again..."

Will gave a quick wave to his wife, who was standing in front of the microphone with one hand on each headphone. She glanced up at Will, gave him a quick wave, but threw him only a half-smile.

After slipping out of the studio, he drove over to the house and trudged into the living room.

He wasn't hungry and, glancing at his watch, saw that he had two hours to kill before he had to pick up Andrew after his practice.

Will clicked on the television and flipped through the channels, finally landing on a talk show discussing Gilead's case.

A representative of the Evangelical Coalition was up against the president of the American Secular Society. The latter was arguing that the Amahn case proved one thing—that religious fanatics, and particularly Christian religious fanatics, needed to be scrutinized regarding their potential for inciting violence through their "apocalyptic and prophetic nonsense."

His opponent from the EC disagreed and tried to point out that the free exercise of religion under the First Amendment and the principle of religious tolerance should require us to be very careful before we start censuring people, even religious extremists, because of the content of their religious speech.

Will had had enough. He clicked off the television and sat in the quiet of the great room, thinking about some of the messages he had received since the announcement of his defense of Gilead Amahn had hit the news media.

He had received a raft of harassing telephone calls and e-mails accusing him of collaborating with a dangerous terrorist.

He had also had phone calls from legal counsel from several Christian evangelical and mainline denominational organizations. Each of the phone calls was courteous but highly cautious. Most were seeking information about Mr. Amahn's true theological position. Will, just as courteously, declined to discuss Mr. Amahn's case until such time as his client authorized him to make a public statement.

Will was aware also that two Christian legal organizations had offered to meet with his client to discuss the possibility of representing him. But Gilead had refused both invitations, indicating that he was waiting for contact first from the lawyer of his choice—Will Chambers.

Somewhere, Will was hearing his cell phone ring.

He strolled over to his briefcase, opened it, retrieved the phone, and checked the number on the screen. It was a call from Jack Hornby.

"Jack, how are you?" Will asked after picking up.

"So, now that you're entering into the jaws of the beast," Hornby said sardonically, "are you going to give me an exclusive on the Gilead Amahn case?"

Will chuckled.

"Sure. When the timing is right."

"Okay. Just checking to make sure you're still kicking. And you haven't forgotten me," Hornby shot back. "Keep your powder dry and your musket loaded…"

Will clicked off and began to page through some press clippings in his file. Then, glancing at his watch, he decided he needed to head out to pick up Andy.

Pulling away from the house, he saw Fiona waving to her recording staff as they climbed into their cars. As Will headed down the driveway away from the house, he could see Fiona walking toward it as he looked in his rearview mirror.

That glimpse, for Will, was sadly symbolic. He and Fiona seemed, at least for the present, to be walking in opposite directions.

40

"WILL, BUDDY," THE VOICE AT THE OTHER END of the telephone said, "this is your roving private investigator calling."

"Tiny, how are you?"

"I'm still surviving," Tiny Heftland replied. "It's been a while since I've been over here in the Middle East. Reminds me of the good old days—when I was doing security detail for the State Department."

"What do you have for me?"

"Well, let's put it this way—on the one hand I've got some bad news—and on the other hand, I've got even worse news. Which one do you want first?"

"You're always so optimistic," Will said. "Any way you want to give it to me. Hit me."

"Well, first of all, it took me a full day to work my way through the red tape at Ramallah in order to get permission to see your guy. I had your written authorization, of course. So I finally get in to see this Gilead Amahn—and the first thing the guy does is, he comes up and gives me a big hug, like I'm family or something…because he found out I was coming from your office. This guy really thinks you're the greatest thing since pizza delivery…"

"How did the interview go?"

"Well…it didn't."

"What do you mean?"

"Just like I said. I go in. The guy's all smiles. Gives me a big hug. Goes on and on about what a great guy you are. Terrific lawyer…but then he says he can't talk to me."

"What? Why?"

"He didn't give me any reason. Says he's got to talk to you in person. I try to finesse him a little—tell him I'm your eyes and ears. I'm your advance man. I'm the point man. I'm using every angle I can. And he's not buying it. He's just sitting there smiling, shaking his head saying no, no way, not going to talk until you and he are sitting across the table together. But he did say one thing…"

"And what was that?"

"He sure is happy—he's happy as a loon on a lake that you're representing him. For what that's worth…"

"How did he look? Are they treating him okay?"

"Oh…you know, at the time of his arrest, I think the Palestinians roughed him up a little. He's got a black eye. Some bruises. But all in all, it doesn't look like they're hanging him by his fingernails or anything like that. So in that regard, he ought to count himself lucky. But he didn't look too good."

"Is he sick or something?"

"I don't think so. He didn't say that. He said they're giving him three squares a day. Although he said the menu's pretty limited. I'm sure that's the understatement of the last ten thousand years. But—he just looks really whipped. I don't know what he looked like before they put him in the detention center. But, you know—circles under his eyes. Drawn. Looking nervous. That kind of thing."

"Well, I suppose if you're arrested in the Middle East for committing mass murder at an Islamic mosque that's the hottest hot spot in the world and you're facing the death penalty, it's going to take a terrible toll."

"Oh, yeah. Big time. Big time!"

"So what's the rest of your cheery news?"

"I just shipped off, via the computer at the International Palestinian Court, a huge download of electronic discovery for you that was ordered by the Court for both sides to exchange. Stuff like the investigative reports. Some of the forensic material on the device used to blow up the top of the Mount. Some of the court documents from when that English dude was representing Amahn. It should be coming into your office any second."

"You said you had worse news…"

"Yeah. Well…let me get my notes in front of me. Okay—get ready to twist and shout. First of all. This is from the office of the public prosecutor for the Palestinian Authority. They say they've got proof that Gilead Amahn previously traveled to Jerusalem and Jordan prior to the trip when the Temple Mount blew up."

"I already knew that," Will replied.

"Well, maybe. But I bet you didn't know this. That during this prior trip to Jerusalem—I guess it was last year some time—he was in the middle of a Bible study attended by several members of the Knights of the Temple Mount. So right there, you've got a prior connection going back at least a year between your guy and a group of those cult zombies."

"What else did you learn?"

"They got several statements from witnesses, including a statement from an Israeli police officer who was right there watching Gilead Amahn seconds before the explosion went off. Supposedly, your guy was doing his preaching gig…really working up a head of steam…and then, suddenly, he gives this signal—he says that the Temple Mount needs to get blown up. And then, all of a sudden, KABLOOM—bodies and buildings and everything else start flying in the air when the bombs go off."

"Do you have anything positive for me?"

"Not really. You didn't let me finish. I've got some more incoming mortar fire for you. Before the attack, did you know that Gilead had visited Cairo?"

"Yeah. As a matter of fact, he called me. I helped get him out of jail when he was rounded up there for preaching on a public street."

"Do you know why he visited Cairo?"

"Not really. That was a little bit foggy. What's the deal?"

"Well, according to a statement that they've got on file here from the Ministry of Religious Affairs for the Palestinian Authority, the Knights of the Temple Mount are kind of a splinter group from the Druze religion. Sort of a combination of a bunch of different Middle Eastern religions. Anyway, they were predicting that some kind of messiah would show up in Cairo, Egypt. And guess what? The exact day and place where these cult dudes were looking for the appearance of a messiah—that's when Gilead Amahn shows up. In this really prominent public square in Cairo. And he starts beating his chest and doing his preaching thing—and practically starts a riot there. Some coincidence, huh?"

Will, now deep in thought, didn't respond.

"You still there, buddy?" Tiny asked.

"Yeah, just thinking about something. What else did you uncover?"

"Well, last but not least—the reports from the Palestinians say that just before the bombing took place, he was walking through Jerusalem. He attracted this big mob. They're swarming around him like he's some kind of rock star, you know, and he's smiling and shaking hands and doing his thing like the high holy man, like…you know, there was this movie I saw. What was the name of it? A really, really old black-and-white movie. It was about this holy guy who sat up on the top of a mountain. And everybody's coming to him asking him when the world's going to end. That kind of stuff. He's just smiling back giving them all this good religious vibes stuff. Anyway, it's like that. You know, like the Big Kahuna. The High Yogi. I think it took place up in the Himalayas—"

"The movie was called *Lost Horizon*," Will said. "And he was called the High Lama."

"Oh yeah, yeah. Exactly. It was on about two in the morning one night I couldn't sleep. And I start watching the thing. Pretty interesting…"

"Actually, I was thinking of a different comparison," Will said. "About another entrance into Jerusalem. Two thousand years ago."

"Oh, yikes! Of course! Wow! No kidding! You know, I saw a part of that movie too. Or some of it. I think. I'm not really sure."

"Tiny," Will asked, "how long do you and I go back?"

"Wow! Oh, man. A long time."

"Well, I must have really blown it. Because I don't think I ever got you to read any of the Gospel stories in the Bible about the life of Jesus."

"I'm really more of a video guy," Tiny said. "I read stuff only when I have to. PI-type stuff. Police reports. Autopsies. Public records. Death certificates. Credit reports. Missing persons reports…"

"I get the picture," Will said with a chuckle. "Okay. What I'm going to do is one of these days I'll get you a video—an accurate portrayal of the life of Christ. But you've got to promise you'll watch it. Okay?"

"You got it, general." And then he added sarcastically, "So, general, where do I go from here? Not that I'm complaining about staying in this fleabag hotel here on the West Bank, where the only thing on TV is some dude singing and chanting…and then some angry-looking dude giving a lecture in Arabic…then some politico comes on waving his arms and yelling…and then another dude comes on the TV singing and chanting again…so, where do we go from here?"

"The last time I was in Jerusalem, working on the *Reichstad v. MacCameron* case, I developed a contact. I'm sure the guy was a member of the Mossad, though he never admitted as much. Good man. He helped me. He's got a little ancient artifacts shop in the Jewish Quarter of the Old City. His name is Nathan Goldwaithe. Look him up. See what you can find out about the Israeli side of the investigation into the bombing. See if you can get some leads within the Jerusalem police, the IDF, or even the Mossad. Find out what the unofficial Israeli take is on the bombing, the suspects, the Knights of the Temple Mount, even the forensics issue."

Shortly after Will hung up, the e-mail on his computer chimed. He opened the message and started downloading a large file of electronic documents forwarded from the Palestinian Authority by Tiny.

As he scrolled through the documents setting forth his first preview of the prosecution's case against his client, Will had one distinct impression. Not surprisingly, the Palestinian prosecutor's case had already built up a frightening level of momentum. It was as if they had tied Gilead to an anvil and thrown him off the top of a skyscraper.

Now it was entirely up to Will to see if he could reverse gravity.

41

SAMIR ZAYED WAS THE PROSECUTOR for the Palestinian International Tribunal. A Palestinian lawyer in his forties with a boyish face and close-cropped hair, clean shaven, with darting aggressive eyes, he stood before the bank of microphones in Ramallah.

He flashed a confident smile and then began addressing the bevy of reporters and television cameramen.

"Yesterday, in the late afternoon, law-enforcement agents for the Palestinian Authority secured a confession from a suspect in the so-called Temple Mount bombings. We Muslims will continue to refer to it as the 'Noble Sanctuary,' since, as you know, Muslims own and control that area which was cruelly and murderously bombed. The suspect was taken into custody shortly after the cowardly and barbaric attack took place. His name is Scott Magnit. He is an American citizen.

"Mr. Magnit is a very important person in this investigation," Zayed continued, "because he was part of the inner circle of three persons who, along with Gilead Amahn, their spiritual leader, plotted to destroy the Noble Sanctuary and murder hundreds of Muslims. Yesterday Mr. Magnit signed a confession admitting that he and his two fellow inner-circle members of the Knights of the Temple Mount planned the destruction of the al-Aqsa Mosque in the Dome of the Rock. But this is very important— Mr. Magnit also confessed that Hassan Gilead Amahn knew all of the detailed plans for the destruction of the mosque through the terrorist act of bombing. That Mr. Amahn knew the date of the destruction and knowingly gave the signal for the bombing to occur. In addition, that Mr. Amahn welcomed the support and accolades of the various members of the Knights of the Temple Mount, permitting himself to be called the High Caliph of the group and parading himself before the world as the manifestation of a messiah. All of this, Mr. Scott Magnit has admitted in writing, in his confession. I will be glad to answer your questions."

"Who were the other two members of the inner circle?" one reporter bulleted out.

"One was Mr. Louis Lorraine, a French national," Zayed replied. "Mr. Lorraine detonated the device that exploded the Dome of the Rock. The other was Mr. Yossin Ali Khalid, a Lebanese national. He detonated the bomb in the al-Aqsa Mosque. Both Mr. Lorraine and Mr. Khalid were shot to death by the Israeli Defense Force after the explosion. That was a pity. One wonders what they might have told us.

"Louis Lorraine was a former member of the French cultic religious group Solar Temple. At some unspecified time he converted to the radical and violent terrorist religion of the Knights of the Temple Mount. Mr. Yossin Ali Khalid, whose father was a caliph in the Knights of the Temple Mount, was—as his father was—a former member of the Druze religion. The Druze religion is a perverted form of Islam and is rejected by the Islamic muftis. But the Knights of the Temple Mount believed in a terrorist and violent religion that was a subcult of the Druze religion and was rejected even by the Druze leaders."

"What do you mean when you say that Amahn was the High Caliph of the Knights of the Temple Mount?"

"I mean to say," Zayed said confidently, "that he was the spiritual potentate of this very violent and terrorist religious group. He gave the orders. He gave the spiritual signal. He blasphemed the heavenly religion of Islam and the truth of Allah by leading his infidels in an attack against the Noble Sanctuary."

Another reporter yelled over the sea of voices.

"Has Scott Magnit been given a lie-detector test?"

Mr. Zayed smiled and chuckled.

"That is a very Western question, if you will permit me to say so. Here in the emerging state of Palestine, we have an ancient tradition of truth-telling and truth-seeking. We have spent much time with Mr. Magnit. We have asked him clear questions, and he has given us clear answers. And the truth he tells against Mr. Amahn is like a mosaic. Have you not seen pictures of our mosques and our beautiful historical structures? A mosaic is a picture made up of many brightly colored stones. Our case against Mr. Amahn is made up of many pieces of stone. And Mr. Magnit's confession supplies many, many stones that fit with the other stones, and the picture shows that Hassan Gilead Amahn is an evil and fanatical butcher. He has used religion and the Bible in an attempt to ignite a terrible war. So we are seeking the death penalty. And we are confident we will get it."

At that point a staff member of the Palestinian Authority's Office of the Public Prosecutor scurried out of the building and whispered something into Samir Zayed's ear.

The prosecutor smiled and waved to the cameras and shouting reporters as he turned to leave.

One question was yelled out louder than the others, and it caught his attention as he walked away.

"What about the reports that Scott Magnit was physically mistreated?"

Zayed stopped, turned quickly, and walked back to the microphones.

"It is such a pity—so unfortunate that you must deal with such lies. I am so sorry you cannot see the truth. Mr. Magnit receives regular medical attention. He receives nourishing food. He has visitors. And we are treating him with the kindness that we would our own family members."

He waved broadly, flashed one final grin, and headed to the Prosecution Building.

But another question rose above the mass of yelling reporters.

"What effect will this trial against Amahn have on the peace negotiations between Israel and the Palestinians? What happens if Amahn is found not guilty?"

The prosecutor did not turn around or acknowledge the question as he headed to the doorway behind him.

What the reporters could not see was that his expression had changed. After that final question, he was no longer smiling.

42

IN HIS OFFICE THAT MORNING, Will Chambers had been waiting for a call back from Mike Michalany, his forensics consultant. Will had shipped to Mike all of the discovery and investigative information that he had obtained from Tiny Heftland on the explosion.

Michalany had received an intensive baptism into the world of terrorist-orchestrated bombings, having helped to investigate the 1998 al-Qaeda–directed bombings of the U.S. embassies in Kenya and Tanzania. He had also been part of the investigative team for the first bombing of the World Trade Center and had helped construct a failure analysis of the Twin Towers after the 9/11 attack.

Will figured that the former FBI agent would be the perfect person to provide consultation—perhaps even testimony as an expert witness in the Amahn trial...depending, of course, on his findings.

But despite repeated calls, Will had not gotten a contact back from him.

The attorney flipped his planner open and compared it with the tentative schedule he had outlined for the next two months. The preparation of his defense of Gilead Amahn required that almost every day for the next two months be mapped out with some litigation duty: fact investigation, legal research, or consultation with experts.

And Will knew that, inevitably, the ordinary rigors of his law practice, coupled with Jacki's leave of absence for her pregnancy, would end up overburdening the office. And that, in turn, would lead to long hours, including evenings and possibly every weekend as well.

And exactly where does that leave my wife and family? Will wondered to himself. Jacki had been right. And so had Fiona. And perhaps so had Len Redgrove with his cryptic warning. And maybe even reporter Jack Hornby.

Will was seeing his life mercilessly stretched, pulled, and pummeled by this one case alone.

"Excuse me, Will," Hilda said in an exasperated voice as she poked her head into his office, "but I've got two more reporters holding asking for your reaction to the press conference that the Palestinian public prosecutor gave yesterday."

Will paused for a moment and rubbed his face. "Tell them I'll be releasing a statement. Get their e-mail addresses or fax numbers. Tell them we'll get it to them within the hour."

Will turned his attention back to his planner.

Then he had a thought. He needed to aggressively carve out some time for himself and his wife. He quickly dialed Fiona's cell phone. She had flown up to Philadelphia for a full day of meetings with the new recording executive for her label, her concert manager, her personal attorney, and her agent. After her emotional setback from Angus's death had taken her out of the loop for several concert tours, one of the owners of a performance venue had threatened to sue for breach of contract. Will knew it was going to be a long, difficult day for her.

He got her right away.

"Hey, honey," Will said. "I don't want to disturb your meeting. Do you have a second?"

"I'm just walking back into the meeting room right now. We just got through with a fifteen-minute break," Fiona said. Her voice had a world-weary tone to it.

"While I have you on the line," she went on, "Chuck Evans asked if you could do him a favor. He says he knows his role is to be my private contract attorney, but he would really appreciate it if you could take a look at the contract language that's causing the problem. He asked if I could bring it home when I fly back tonight. He just wanted to get your input…"

"No problem," Will said. "Tell Chuck I have a great deal of confidence in him. But if he wants me to second-look the documents, that's fine. When you come home tonight, honey, bring them with you."

"I appreciate it," she said. "Got to go…"

"Fiona?"

"Yes?"

"I noticed your plane's coming in about seven tonight. Why don't I pick you up at the airport and let me take you out to dinner? Somewhere nice…something fancy. We can do a little talking…"

"Well," Fiona said, hesitating, "you know I left my car in the parking structure at the airport. We'd have to take two cars."

"Fine. We'll just meet at the restaurant. I'll pick a place and leave it on your cell phone voice mail."

"On second thought," Fiona said with a subdued tone to her voice, "I'm really not feeling very well. A little under the weather. If you don't mind, I'm going to take a rain check. I'll just drive back home, get a bowl of soup, and hit the sack. I don't feel well."

"Sure. No problem. I'm sorry you don't feel good. Please take care of yourself, darling. I love you."

There was a slight pause at the other end. Fiona gave him a quick "I love you" and then said goodbye.

Will heard the intercom buzz. It was Hilda. Mike Michalany was finally on the line.

Will quickly asked Mike about his initial impressions of the forensics information on the bombing attack.

"Well, of course, the information is sketchy. But it gave me a good start," he said. "First of all, there was a pretty clear picture from the documents of the detonation device they used. It was a wireless system from two laptops in two vehicles, with a connection to the detonation devices in the explosives in the Dome of the Rock and the al-Aqsa Mosque. Something interesting about the system, though…"

"Like what?"

"Very sophisticated and difficult to intercept. Very refined setup. Last time I checked, the Israeli intelligence folks have some extremely sensitive signal detection devices all over Jerusalem and Tel Aviv. They can monitor almost every wireless connection there is. They can trace a connection from the point of origin to the receptor. Obviously, if they see any connection leading to some secure facility, or some likely target for terrorist activity, they can follow that signal to the source immediately and charge in on terrorists before they push the button. Yet it doesn't look like they knew about this one. Highly advanced tech stuff was used."

"What does that tell you?"

"Well…the typical scenario. Maybe it was terrorists with a lot of experience with explosives and electronic communications. And some of the cell groups have that capacity. They really train on that stuff. But, as far as I can see, there's nothing about the Knights of the Temple Mount having previously used explosives or having any engineering or electronics training."

"What else have you come up with?" Will asked.

"Well, the nature of the explosive, of course. They used the same one at both targets on the Temple Mount. Semtex. Sort of second cousin to C-4. Again, not the kind of stuff used by amateurs or the fainthearted. This appeared, for all the world, to be a hard-core, highly engineered attack. You know whether any of these Knights of the Temple Mount had any scientific or technical background?"

"Not that I know of," Will replied. "Of course, I'm still digging into that. But I think every one of them was an ideologue with a strong religious motivation. Whether or not they were also training as traditional terrorists, I really can't tell you…"

"Okay, well, a couple of other thoughts," Michalany continued. "And these are just random. Based on typical criminal investigation analysis." "We all know that security around the al-Aqsa Mosque was pretty high, as it normally is. It's a volatile place— probably the most sensitive place in the world in terms of the potential for violence or clashes between the Palestinians and the Israelis. Or for apocalyptic-type groups, like these Knights of the Temple Mount, to launch some kind of an attack. It all leads to one important question."

"And what would that be?" Will asked.

"Just this—how did they get access to a totally Muslim-controlled area?"

"Well, one thing I've been thinking about," Will responded. "It could have been an inside job. Someone who was a staffer with the Waqf, the Muslim trust that actually operates the Temple Mount platform. Though that seems to be unlikely. It raises the question, however, as to whether the Knights may have had special access to the area. But I'm not really sure how they could have that…"

"I've been thinking about that same thing," Michalany replied. "I'm looking into the history of some of the attacks on the Temple Mount. Of course, they've been much smaller in nature. For instance, back in 1982, a fellow by the name of Yoel Lerner was convicted of conspiring to blow up the Dome of the Rock. He was caught before anything happened and put in jail for a couple of years. Also, in the same year, an Israeli soldier by the name of Alan Harry Goodman, a U.S. immigrant, went on a shooting spree on the Mount. He was able to kill one person and wound a couple others. But there wasn't a massive loss of life. He was stopped cold before that. Which then leads me to wonder…"

"About what?"

"Well, the fact that there have been no successful large-scale attacks till now. Due, really, to two things. First of all, Israeli security. They're able to intercept most of the crazies before they get too far. And then, of course, the Arabs scrutinize everyone who gets up there. So those are the two gatekeepers that have kept anything really terrible from happening in the past. Obviously, those two gatekeepers failed."

"You have any theories on why that happened?" Will asked, now stopping his note-taking and listening intently to his consulting expert.

"Just a few thoughts."

"Such as?"

"Well, they had to evade Israeli intelligence, the Jerusalem police department, and the IDF, as well as the Mossad. Then there's the engineering of the bombing itself, as I said before—very sophisticated. They had to have money, power, technical information. Where did that come from? Then there's something else."

"Oh?"

"Yes—access to the Temple Mount, exactly as you said. Maybe the people who got into the area and planted the explosives were Arabs—maybe even Muslims, or former Muslims, themselves. Just a thought."

But it was a thought that made Will's blood run a little cold.

"And of course," Michalany continued, "your guy is an Arab."

"Yeah," Will acknowledged. "You and all the world know that. And worse is his being a former Muslim himself. A Shiite. The news media's been having a field day with that."

"I guess you got some things to ask your boy," Michalany said, trying to be casual. "Like the extent of his travels in the Jerusalem area, prior to the day that the bombing took place."

"I already know the answer to that," Will said reluctantly. "Last year he traveled to Jerusalem and spent some time there."

There was a pause on the line.

"And I'm sure you're going to ask him," Michalany added, "just what he did then…"

Michalany didn't need to say any more.

Will wondered—whether his client had traveled to the Temple Mount. Whether he had attempted to get, or had actually been granted, access. Whether he had viewed the inside of the al-Aqsa Mosque or the Dome of the Rock.

Those kinds of scouting activities were typical with every terrorist organization planning an attack.

It was clear to Will that he would soon have to pose these questions to his client, eyeball to eyeball.

And that had to be sooner rather than later.

43

IF THIS HAD BEEN A FENCING MATCH, the opponents had yet to uncork the tips of their foils.

Warren Mullburn was seated with his chief of staff at a conference table in the offices of the Israeli Foreign Ministry in Jerusalem.

The deputy foreign minister and his staff assistant, seated across the table, had been courteous enough. The Israeli minister had exchanged pleasantries with Mullburn, offering him coffee or tea. He asked about Mullburn's prior trips to Jerusalem and his work for the Republic of Maretas.

But when the Israelis brought up the rumors about Mullburn's efforts to build a global business alliance among multinational corporations, the conversation took a sharp turn.

"Rather than discuss my private interests in promoting global free trade," the billionaire said, "I would much rather get to the point of my visit."

He whispered something to his chief of staff, who then smiled, nodded, and quickly excused himself from the room.

"I've asked my assistant to give us some privacy," Mullburn said, eyeing the Israeli staff assistant, "as we have matters of great sensitivity to discuss."

The deputy minister hesitated for a moment before following suit. Mullburn had engaged in early gamesmanship. And the Israeli minister had been ordered by the prime minister, at least in the initial meeting, to play along. He motioned to his assistant, who quickly exited.

"I do thank you for meeting with me," Mullburn continued, "particularly in view of the fact—at least in some diplomatic quarters—I'm viewed as a neophyte. An interloper in the Middle East peace process. But my only concern is peace. I think perhaps that bringing a fresh, original approach may be a benefit rather than a detriment…"

The Israeli minister smiled, still simply listening.

"To be direct with you," Mullburn said, "I have been warned by some…about Israel's current posture."

"And what posture would that be?"

"Regarding the issue of the Temple Mount."

"And specifically…what aspect of the Temple Mount?"

"A report that has come to my attention—I don't give it any credence, of course—but we need to have the air cleared of any lingering questions…"

"About what?"

"Our intelligence agency has picked up a report—unconfirmed, of course—that Israel had certain information about the Knights of the Temple Mount. Information regarding that group prior to the bombings."

"I can assure you," the deputy minister replied, "that every day Israeli intelligence is the recipient of information regarding literally hundreds of organizations—terrorist groups, religious organizations, business concerns, and other entities that may or may not necessarily pose a security risk to our national interests…both within our borders and abroad."

"Certainly," Mullburn replied courteously. "The business of intelligence is to gather intelligence…to analyze the credibility of risk…to identify the most likely sources of aggression against national interests…but the information I received involved significantly more than that."

"And what did that information tell you?"

"That Israel had not only identified the Knights as an apocalyptic, religiously motivated group of radicals—but had also uncovered the fact that the Knights were planning an imminent attack on the Mount."

"I cannot, of course, speak for our intelligence agencies," the Israeli official responded calmly, "but I will be sure to pass that information on to the responsible people within our government. I'm sure there is absolutely nothing to the report you heard."

"I certainly hope not," Mullburn said slowly and deliberately, "for Israel's sake…"

"And how would you like me to interpret that statement?" The deputy minister had a slight edge of irritation in his voice.

"Simply this," came the curt reply. "I must know the parties I may be negotiating with."

"We have not yet decided that you will be the negotiator—or mediator—between Israel and the Palestinian Authority."

"Oh, I think I will be. I do believe that Israel will see the wisdom of entering into a process utilizing my services as a mediator."

"And why are you so confident of that?"

"Because, unlike the United States, or the United Nations, or the European Union, or others involved in previous failed and blundered attempts to settle the Israeli–Palestinian problem, I come from a very small island republic that has no inherent or historical loyalties—or any indelibly vested interests for that matter."

"I'm listening."

"And therefore," Mullburn concluded, "I would have no interest in portraying Israel as a complicit co-conspirator in the massacre of Muslims on the Temple Mount."

His opponent's sheer audacity stunned the deputy minister. He blinked, then leaned slightly forward toward Mullburn, carefully calculating his words before he responded.

"Your characterization…even stated as a theoretical…or as pure speculation…is outrageous. It is unacceptable. And it is unilaterally rejected by Israel. Furthermore, it presents me with a rather unpleasant scenario."

"And that would be?"

"I see someone who wants to be a negotiating partner in the peace process, but whose first step involves slandering the nation of Israel."

"You need to face up to the political realities," Mullburn snapped back. "You've got a new president in the White House. And she will not cater to Israel as past presidents have done. The United Nations is losing patience with your country. And I'm here to work out a practical solution, without escalating the stakes by exposing Israel's possible complicity in the Temple Mount incident."

"That sounds like blackmail to me."

"No. To the contrary. It is diplomatic pragmatism. I'm here to bang out an agreement. I'm telling you I have no interest in exposing any wrongdoing by Israel. In return, Israel needs to show some initial trust in my mediating capabilities. You're taking this very personally. This is not personal. This is strictly business."

"The Temple Mount incident is not a bargaining chip. It is not a part of the process. Your implications about Israel's complicity in it are very troubling, at a minimum. I reject them. And one more thing…"

"Yes?"

"If Israel has unilaterally refused over the years to negotiate with terrorists, what makes you think we would negotiate with a blackmailer?"

"Oh," Mullburn said with a slightly ironic tone, "Israel doesn't negotiate with terrorists?"

"That's what I said."

"Well—think back a few years. Your prime minister negotiates the release of a huge number of Palestinian prisoners in return for an Israeli businessman and paltry concessions. On the very day of the exchange, a Palestinian suicide bomber detonates himself, killing several Israelis. And you have the audacity to say that Israel has not negotiated with terrorists? Who's being naïve now?"

The Israeli knew this initial meeting with Warren Mullburn would have to be brought to a speedy conclusion. And as soon as the other man left the building, the deputy foreign minister would contact the defense minister, the ranking intelligence officers in the Mossad, and perhaps even the prime minister.

If Mullburn's assertions about Israel's prior knowledge of, and acquiescence in, the terrorist plans of the Knights of the Temple Mount were even remotely close to being true, an immediate decision was at hand.

In that event, Israel would have to decide whether it wished to take on just Warren Mullburn. Or whether it was willing to take on the rest of the world as well.

44

Tɪɴʏ Hᴇꜰᴛʟᴀɴᴅ ʜᴀᴅ disappointing news.

"The Israelis are simply not talking about this case," he said gloomily over the phone. "I tried everything I could. Pulled every lever. Contacted everyone I knew—I was name-dropping like I was trying to crash a Hollywood cocktail party."

"You got absolutely no information from the Israeli government about their investigation into the bombings?"

"They just told me I had to check with the Palestinian Authority—that they were the ones prosecuting the case."

"I was really banking on the Israeli government giving me access to some of their reports," Will said with disappointment in his voice.

"Well, there *was* something I got...but not really connected to your case," Tiny said.

"What was it?"

"About this Mossad agent by the name of Nathan...whatever it was. You gave me his name. I checked him out. As it turns out, he had some connection with the archaeological hoo-ha about the Deuteronomy Fragment. And this Nathan—"

"Nathan Goldwaithe," Will broke in.

"Yeah, that was him," Tiny replied. "He's the guy you knew, right?"

"I ran into him when I was in Jerusalem doing work on the *Reichstad v. MacCameron* lawsuit. He never identified himself as a member of the Mossad. But I figured he was. He seemed to have all kinds of high-level clearances. He was my personal escort over there...assigned by the Israeli government."

"Well, this guy was apparently doing some unofficial snooping in the United States," Tiny continued. "At a research center up in Maryland—the same place I located for you in the Reichstad lawsuit. Remember? Reichstad ran it, had a couple of assistants, all super-secret. Very sophisticated security protection around it. You later told me that Mr. Money-bucks...what's his name... Mullburn, had funded the operation. Of course, all that had to do with the Resurrection Fragment that was the issue in *Reichstad v. MacCameron*."

"So, why was Nathan doing surveillance there?"

"Well, this is all a number of years ago now. But it looks like he and another Mossad agent were checking out that research facility. Apparently they got some convincing surveillance—video or audio, I'm not sure which. Anyway...it apparently exposed some real questions about the origin of the Deuteronomy Fragment. So Nathan and the other agent take separate flights back to Israel. Nathan gets there first. From what I heard, he was anxious to talk to some of the folks in the government. But he took a side trip out to the Negev—why, nobody knows. Later, they found his body there. A single shot to the back of the head. His wallet, personal belongings—that kind of stuff—was all gone. Including the tapes about the Deuteronomy Fragment."

Will was silent—stunned. He reached over to a small glass box on his desk, flipped it open, and retrieved the single Byzantine-era coin it contained. It bore an ancient, worn, but still decipherable image of Jesus.

He rubbed his thumb over the contours of the visage.

"You still there?" Tiny asked.

"Yeah," Will said, his voice husky.

"I'm sorry if he was a good friend of yours."

"I didn't know him that well. But he protected me in some tough times over there. And he gave me a memento of my trip to Jerusalem—an ancient coin. It ended up meaning a lot to me...I'm very sad to hear he's gone."

"Well, sorry to be the bearer of bad tidings..."

"Did you find out the name of the other agent who was with Nathan?"

"No. I struck out on that. And they really have no idea what specifics he had about the Deuteronomy Fragment. They only know what I've just told you."

"So, do you have any other leads about the Deuteronomy thing? Any other ideas?" Will asked.

"Listen, Will boy. I'm sorry. But I think I'm all tapped out...I've got nothing else."

"Then come on home, Tiny," Will said with a tinge of resignation.

After hanging up, Will called Len Redgrove and left a message asking if he had come up with the name of the expert who might be able to assist him in the case.

Within the hour Len called back and left a message with Hilda suggesting that Will contact Dr. Daoud al-Qasr, currently on a teaching assignment in the anthropology department at NYU. Len mentioned that Dr. al-Qasr normally taught Egyptology and a subject called "Esoteric Religious Movements" at Cairo University and left a telephone number and e-mail address for him.

Will had been on the phone with Attorney Mira Ashwan.

But something had changed. In their first conversation together, the court-appointed counsel had been curt, cold, and abrasive.

But now, her voice was lively, excited, even warm.

"I've been meaning to call you, Mr. Chambers," she said exuberantly. "I was very busy when we talked the first time, and I didn't know much about you. But I have gained some information about your legal work. I very much look forward to our working together."

"That's good news," Will said. "Why don't I draw up a joint defense agreement and e-mail it to you—"

"Oh. Do you really believe that's necessary?" Ms. Ashwan asked with a little hurt in her voice. "Though I understand that you do not know me, and may be somewhat suspicious of an attorney appointed by the Palestinian Authority."

"I didn't say that…" Will replied.

"You didn't have to, Mr. Chambers. It would be a natural assumption. But you should know, first of all, that I'm Egyptian by background. It gives me an insight into Gilead Amahn's upbringing. Also, my parents are Coptic Christians. So I'm not coming from a Muslim standpoint—although I could be described as a Palestinian, politically, and I live here in Hebron. But because of the religious background of my family, I'm very sensitive to the rights of Christians."

"I certainly appreciate that," Will said. "But I would just as soon that we execute a formal joint-defense agreement. That way we are both bound to confidentiality with regard to Gilead Amahn. And we know what the ground rules are. I hope you don't mind…"

"No. Not at all. Whatever makes you comfortable," Ms. Ashwan said enthusiastically. "I think that our common defense could be very productive for Mr. Amahn. And after reviewing some information about your legal background, as I mentioned, I am thrilled and honored to be working with you on this case."

"By the way," Will was thinking back to Tiny Heftland's dismal inability to get access to the Israeli government reports, "I would very much like to get the reports from the Jerusalem police and the IDF…the Israeli reports relating to the bombing…"

"Yes. That would be wonderful. That's an excellent idea," the Egyptian attorney said brightly. "And I think I know how I might be able to obtain those. Let me work on that, please. I would very much like to get those for you."

"Ms. Ashwan—"

"Please call me Mira."

"Okay. Mira…I think you and I need to connect by telephone at least once or twice a week on a regular basis. You can be particularly helpful to me in giving me firsthand information from the Palestinian Authority. I'd like to know, for instance, when the panel of judges is going to be named."

"I expect to hear that information any day," Mira replied. "And when I do, I'll contact you with it. And when I get your joint-defense agreement, I'll sign it and send it back to you. I look forward—very much, Will—to working on this case together. I believe we can be very, very successful."

After he hung up, Will was cautiously optimistic that a good working relationship between them might well provide the extra help he so desperately needed. In addition, Mira was there in the Palestinian Authority, close to the tribunal.

On the other hand, he admittedly had some reluctance about the independence and objectivity of the Palestinian Authority-appointed amicus curiae. But he was willing, at least at this early stage, to give her the benefit of the doubt.

Considering how quickly the odds were stacking against him, he had no other choice.

45

OVER THE WEEKS SINCE Will Chambers had accepted the defense of Gilead Amahn, his trial preparation had begun to fall into a familiar routine. Although the case was extraordinary, Will was beginning to feel comfortable as he relied upon his thirty years of experience to get slow but certain control over its contours.

As Will was motoring to his office in his Corvette, he was figuring, and then refiguring, his progress thus far.

Mike Michalany had done a nice job piecing together the nature of the explosives and the manner in which they had been remotely detonated. However, he was at a loss to explain how such a sophisticated system could have been put together by the Knights of the Temple Mount, who were novices when it came to terror attacks.

Will had combed through all of the investigative reports from the Palestinian Authority and had them carefully indexed and summarized. Included were statements from eyewitnesses, who had heard Gilead Amahn make a public and inciting declaration about the destruction of the Temple Mount just seconds before the blast was detonated. There were also reports detailing how the Israeli police and the IDF had gunned down Louis Lorraine and Yossin Ali Khalid as they attempted to flee after the explosion. The only problem was, as Will clearly understood, the reports represented only the tip of the iceberg.

Tiny Heftland had exhausted his ability to gain any information and had returned to the United States. But happily, Mira Ashwan had proved to be quite helpful. Although she was still working on her promise to gain access to the reports of the Jerusalem police department and the IDF, she had been able to forward some new discovery information to Will about a Palestinian police raid on the apartments of Lorraine and Khalid.

Yet one of the sticking points of the case was Will's lack of access to his own client. He had had only four short telephone conversations with Gilead Amahn, each limited to fifteen minutes, and each time Gilead had indicated that guards were physically in his presence. Will had also assumed the phone calls were being monitored by the Palestinian Authority. Thus, whatever he had gleaned was limited to innocuous background information.

It was becoming increasingly clear to Will that he needed to travel to the Middle East and begin a series of intensive face-to-face interviews with Gilead in preparation for trial.

And he could no longer put that off. At least, though it may only have been his wishful thinking, Fiona had seemed to have softened of late regarding his participation in the case. She seemed to be bouncing back slowly but perceptibly from the death of her father. And, of course, Will was grateful for that.

Those were the things on his mind as he drove to his office. But all of that was to come to an abrupt halt.

Pulling up early, as he had ever since taking on Gilead's defense, he found the building unlocked. He made his way up the staircase to the second floor of the old, pre–Civil War building, which his law-office suite occupied. Outside the front door to the suite was a brown box lying on the floor.

Will glanced curiously at it. No return address. Apparently dropped off in person because there were no stamps or delivery markings. His name was pasted on with letters from a newspaper, and below was the word "URGENT."

He took a step back and stared at the box for at least a minute, examining all four sides. Then he clicked on his cell phone and called the Monroeville police department—slightly embarrassed, but convinced that caution was warranted.

After the desk sergeant indicated he would send someone over, Will strolled down to the top of the stairs and leaned against the railing, staring at the brown box.

Within minutes two patrol officers arrived, and seconds afterward, a plainclothes detective. Will described the appearance of the box and its strange labeling. One of the patrolmen stopped writing in his notebook, looked at Will, and after a moment asked, "You're the attorney representing the guy in the Jerusalem bombing, right?"

"That's right," Will replied.

The detective asked Will to step downstairs, and after a moment, all three joined Will on the first floor.

"We're going to have to play it safe...evacuate the building," the detective told Will. "But stay outside on the sidewalk. We're going to need some more information from you."

As the patrol officers went office to office, very quickly insurance agents, stockbrokers, and an architect all poured out onto the street.

Will stood by the front doors, which were now propped open. A few minutes later two officers arrived with a portable X-ray machine and disappeared up the stairway. Just about three minutes later he heard the scurry of feet down the stairwell as those same officers came hurrying down and ran to the front door.

"Everyone clear the area—get down to the intersection, away from the building!"

As Will and the others started running, he heard the detective on his squad phone: "We've got a device. Get the bomb squad over here immediately!"

Within half an hour a truck marked with the insignia of the Virginia State Police Bomb Squad pulled up to the scene, which had been by then cordoned off with warning ribbons and extra patrolmen.

Two technicians in padded bomb uniforms quickly exited, grabbing an extension device with numerous joints, and they disappeared into the building.

Less than half an hour later, the plainclothes detective walked over toward the group of onlookers, signaling for Will Chambers. "We've got it deactivated. Come on. We need you to take a look at something."

Will entered the building with the detective and made his way gingerly up to the second floor.

Outside of his office door he saw the box on the floor, open. The technicians were chatting on either side of the box. One of them reached down with a latex-gloved hand, and lifted something out. Will came to a halt when he saw that, but the detective smiled and told him he had nothing to worry about.

As they approached, Will could see an alarm clock and several cylindrical objects that, at a first glance, looked like sticks of dynamite. But on closer examination, he realized they were just auto flares taped together and connected with a wire to the clock.

"It's a nonbomb," one of the technicians said with a chuckle.

"This is what I want you to see." The detective held out two news clippings to Will. "We found both of these in the box with the phony device. I suppose they're self-explanatory…"

Will looked at one clipping, which contained the immense headline "MUSLIMS SLAUGHTERED IN TEMPLE MOUNT MOSQUE MASSACRE." The other was a clipping announcing that Will Chambers had been retained by Gilead Amahn with reference to the bombing.

"Any ideas," the detective asked, "who may have sent this?"

"I've been getting a lot of nasty e-mails and crank phone calls," Will said, "ever since I took Mr. Amahn's defense. So, take your pick—nobody in particular, though."

Before they parted, the detective asked Will, "Are you going to be around your office today? We're going to need some follow-up information from you."

Will assured him he was, then he made his way over to the police line where Hilda and his younger associates, Todd and Jeff, were staring wide-eyed at the activity.

"What in the world is going on, Will?" Hilda asked with panic in her voice.

Will turned around and looked at the bevy of police officers and the bomb squad truck parked in front of the building.

"Just another day at the office, Hilda."

46

"IT WAS A *THREAT*."

"Actually, I'd call it more of a prank."

"But that thing in the box—it looked like a bomb."

"Well, yes...but the point is that it wasn't a real bomb—"

"Alright. So it was a fake bomb. But someone out there wanted you and the police to think it was real. Somebody was sick enough, vicious enough to cause the whole building to be evacuated...get the bomb squad called in...the whole nine yards."

"Fiona," Will was trying to sound reasonable and calm, "what can I tell you to make you feel comfortable with all this? I need to see Gilead. There's no way around it. The trial date is rushing up. I've done everything I can remotely...from here in the States. But now I need to get over to the Middle East. To dig into the facts for myself—it's critical. I wouldn't leave you at this point if I thought it wasn't safe..."

"I've heard that before." Fiona was glaring over the kitchen table at her husband. But Will could see beyond the anger. The hurt in her eyes was obvious. Yet her last comment did make him wince a little.

"That's not fair—"

"Oh no?" she said. "It was in this house."

"I know..."

"I was asleep in my bedroom."

"That's why I had Tiny doing surveillance."

"I was just seconds from being attacked. And, my precious husband, what if Tiny had turned his back for a second...or had

244

fallen asleep? I know it was a number of years ago…but I can still remember it. Tiny shooting that man after he had slipped into the house. A man with that big, horrible knife. Long, steel, with a jagged edge. A black handle. I still remember what it looked like…"

"You know that I can't get that picture out of my mind either—"

"I thought that was all over. Those types of cases. The risks you were taking. Making the kind of enemies that come after you and your family. And now it's happening all over again…"

"Fiona," Will said, struggling against the internal conflict, "I don't know what else I can say. Tiny is going to be on guard every night. The sheriff's department will have unmarked squads posted in the area."

"And what about Andy?"

"I think you'd better take him to school and pick him up personally. No car pools for a while."

"Ahhhh…" Fiona cried out, putting her hands on the sides of her head in exasperation.

Will leaned back and studied her, trying to put his finger on it. He was being sucked down into the swirling tide. No matter which way he turned, he was feeling that his life was being swallowed up. Was out of control. That was really it—what his gut was telling him.

He looked at Fiona. Her dark hair, her deep eyes, her beautiful features. Despite the years, there seemed to be so little aging with her—just a bit of softening here and there.

"I love you," he said gently.

She wagged an angry finger directly at her husband.

"Don't you understand? It's not about me. Not at all."

Her eyes were filled with tears, and her voice was choked with emotion.

"It's you." She started to sob. "I couldn't live without you. I don't know what I would do if something happened to you. I know it sounds so faithless. The Lord must be displeased with me when I talk like this. I can sing about faith. I can live it all...except when it comes to you. I absolutely fall apart..."

Will gathered her up and held her, feeling her shoulders heave with sobs.

After several minutes, the crying stopped. Fiona wiped her eyes. For a moment or so she was silent. Then there was only the occasional sound of her taking deep, cleansing breaths.

After a little while she spoke.

"When do you leave?"

"Day after tomorrow."

Fiona paused before she spoke again.

"It's gone so fast. Our years together. Marriage. Andy. Always so busy...not enough time..."

Then she sniffed a few times, and demurely placed a finger to her upper lip.

"I need a Kleenex," she said.

They both broke into laughter.

She stepped into the bathroom to grab a tissue.

Alone in the kitchen, Will looked out the windows. He could see the treetops stretching up the mountain, and above the tops of the towering pines, the sky beyond.

Earlier it had been clear, with a bright blue and cloudless sky. But now he could see the trees starting to sway in the wind. And off in the distance, shades of billowing white and gray as the clouds were building.

Storms blow in so quickly, Will found himself thinking, *close to the mountain.*

47

ACROSS THE PLAIN WOODEN TABLE from Will Chambers, Gilead Amahn was seated in a metal folding chair, his hands resting on the surface in front of him. Down the hallway of the Palestinian police building, someone was laughing and yelling in Arabic.

Will's client looked gaunt and haggard, as if he had lost considerable weight. His face had a hollow look to it.

Will had arrived that morning and, to his surprise, clearing the red tape for his jail meeting with Gilead had taken only a few hours. Attorney Mira Ashwan had been helpful in the process.

Their conference was taking place in the police auxiliary building of the Palestinian Authority in Ramallah. The building had two large holding cells with walls on three sides and bars across the fronts. These were now the sites for imprisonment of Gilead Amahn and Scott Magnit, the American member of the Knights of the Temple Mount, who had also been charged with conspiracy to commit murder through acts of terrorism.

Will's interview with Gilead was conducted in a room about the size of a large closet. The attorney was pleased there weren't any guards present. But he also assumed that somewhere the Palestinian Authority had installed a listening device, a small remote camera, or both.

Will had paused for a moment to review a few of the notes that he had jotted down. He and Gilead had been going at it for a little more than an hour, but covering only some of the supplementary background information Will was looking for.

During the lull, Gilead spoke up.

"How are your wife and your son?" he asked, trying to manage a smile.

"They're good, thank you."

For an instant Will thought back to his departure. Before rushing off to school, Andy had given him the "shield of faith" badge he'd won at the Scripture-memory contest. He said it was so that his dad could remember him during the trial.

Fiona had driven him to Dulles airport. As he'd unloaded his multiple large briefcases and suitcase, she'd walked around to the curbside, where she kissed him goodbye.

"I love you forever," she'd said softly.

But there was that look—distant, and a little hurt.

Will had kissed her back, hard, and pulled her to himself, lingering there for a moment and kissing her—their last embrace before one of the airport police yelled to Fiona to move her car.

"I'll get back as soon as I can," he'd said. Then he'd gathered his collection of luggage and made his way clumsily inside.

Sitting there in the Palestinian police building in Ramallah, Will wished he could have said something more to Fiona.

"Where are you staying?" Gilead asked, breaking into Will's thoughts.

"In a hotel in Jerusalem," Will replied, still a little distracted.

"Okay, here it is," he said, finally remembering what he was looking for in his notes. "It's about that trip you took the year before the incident at the Islamic Center. When I represented you back then, you told me you had made a trip to Jerusalem and Jordan. But you didn't really tell me who you met with or where you went. I need to know that."

Then Will hunched forward over the table and continued in a whisper that was barely audible.

"And I want you to explain this to me very quietly—for my ears only."

Gilead nodded and leaned forward, his face only an inch or two away from Will's.

"I did some sightseeing," he whispered. "I also visited the offices of the Holy Land Institute for the Word, who did the fundraising to pay for my defense. You remember I had been giving some thought to being a missionary to the Middle East, having been raised here—"

"Yes, but your parents explained to me that you dropped out of the missionary school—the one that's affiliated with the organization that sent them over to Egypt."

"That's right. I just didn't feel it was right for me. I didn't feel the Lord's leading there. It was more like I was trying to please my parents than really find out what God's will was. That's why I was giving some thought to the Holy Land Institute, working with them over here."

"Who did you meet with?"

"With the director. I had read about the organization in a Christian magazine. So I just sort of showed up. Walked in the door and told them who I was. About my background in Egypt. The fact that I was a former Muslim. That kind of thing."

"Let me go back to something we were talking about," Will said. "About what you did in Jerusalem."

Gilead's eyes opened a little wider, and he studied Will before he answered.

"Where did you hear this?"

"I sent my private investigator here, to the Palestinian Authority, to start getting some of the pretrial discovery the court ordered them to divulge. And one of the reports we received mentions your attending a Bible study in Jerusalem. And there were Knights of the Temple Mount there with you—"

"Let me just make something very clear." Will's client was struggling to keep his composure. "I didn't even know that there *was* such an organization as the Knights of the Temple Mount. You have to believe me. So I don't know who was, or was not, part of the Knights in that Bible study. I was doing some informal witnessing, sharing the gospel here and there around Jerusalem. And I was at a café. Somebody told me about a Bible study I should go to. So I showed up."

"You know that one of the inner circle of the Knights is here in a jail cell just next to yours?"

"Right. The American. He's tried to talk to me but—"

"I hope you didn't reciprocate?"

"No. I'm smarter than that. But I recognized him. I think his name is Scott."

"Scott Magnit," Will said. "He was one of three members in the inner circle."

"Well, he was at the Bible study with me in Jerusalem when I visited there last year."

"Well, there's something else you need to know."

"What?" Gilead could see the concern on Will's face.

"Scott Magnit has struck some kind of a plea agreement with the Palestinian public prosecutor. He is now going to be testifying against you—pointing the finger—saying that you were in control of the whole operation. That you gave the signal for the detonation of the bombs. You were the mastermind, according to him."

Gilead cast his eyes down and slowly shook his head.

"Is he telling the truth?"

"Of course not," the younger man said, shaking his head vigorously.

"Tell me something. About your 'sightseeing' in Jerusalem that prior summer. Did you ever travel to the Temple Mount?"

Gilead paused. He fidgeted uncomfortably in his chair, as if he were trying to decide how to answer.

"A simple question," Will said. "Gilead—tell me straight. Did you visit the Temple Mount?"

"You know it's a highly restricted site. The Muslims jealously guard it. They say that it's sacred to them…the Haram al-Sharif. That's Arabic for the 'Noble Sanctuary'…"

"Yes, I know all about that," Will said tersely. "Did you go there?"

"I consider it nothing less than a miracle that I got in," his client said, looking at the table. "Yes, I did visit it."

"You went there?" Will asked incredulously.

"Yes. I spoke Arabic. I told them I wanted to visit the sites so holy to the Islamic religion. I told them I had been raised a Shiite. The guards let me in."

"Why did you go there? Why?"

"Curious, I guess…"

"As a former Muslim, now a Christian, you go to the most volatile place on the globe—on a whim? Because you're just curious? Come on, Gilead…"

"What do you want me to say? I'm telling you the truth. I felt called to come back to the Middle East…to be a Christian missionary here. I wanted to know all about the sites that were central to what God is doing…in unfolding His plan for the end times…"

"Did you scout out the Temple Mount plateau so explosives could be placed there? So that your friends in the Knights of the Temple Mount could know how, where, and when to place them?"

Gilead was stunned. He leaned back in his chair and lifted both hands in the air.

"I can't believe you are saying these things. No. The answer is no. Absolutely not."

Will leaned back, pushing away his notes. Now it was time to go deeper. He needed to assess not just the actions or the statements of his client…he had to go further. Beyond even his mental processes. He needed to know something about what had been going on in the soul of Gilead Amahn.

"Why did you go to the Islamic Center in northern Virginia?" He looked Gilead in the eyes. "Why did you preach to that mufti when you knew it might end up sparking a riot?"

"I felt called to do that."

"By God?"

"Yes. To preach the gospel to the people I had come from. To the religious tradition I was raised in."

"Why did you go to Cairo?"

"Same reason."

"Called by the Lord? Is that what you're saying?"

"Yes...that's it."

"When we went through the background information in our telephone conversations, you said that Louis Lorraine befriended you in Cairo. And drove you to Jerusalem."

"That's right."

"And the two of you talked about theological things? Religious theories?"

"Yes, in part."

"And he talked in some way...about the appearing of the Promised One? A great religious leader who would usher in the Golden Age?"

"Yes, we did talk about that."

The attorney waited a long time before speaking again. After a while, Gilead began shifting in his chair. He got a quizzical look on his face, waiting for his lawyer to continue.

"Do you think you're a messiah?" Will asked quietly.

Gilead's eyes widened again. He spread his open hands out and though he opened his mouth, no words came out. So Will pressed in.

"You understand my question. It's not difficult. You're an intelligent man. Do you consider yourself a messiah?"

"I can't believe you're asking me...what in the world would make you ask that question..."

"Are you?"

"Of course not. I've never called myself a messiah...ever...ridiculous...you should know that."

"But you've publicly called yourself something else, haven't you? In Jerusalem before the bombing, you called yourself a prophet?"

Gilead paused.

"I think I used that term...I was called by God...I think I said I felt called by God to fulfill a prophetic role. To do the work of a prophet."

After a dead silence fell, the younger man asked a question of his attorney.

"Is it that bad?"

"It's enough."

"Enough for what?" His lip was starting to tremble.

"Enough to send you to the death chamber."

Gilead was now covering his face with his hands. He said something low, almost a moan, but Will couldn't hear it. But after a few seconds, he spoke up.

"Everything I prayed for…what I tried to do for God…I just wanted to be the sword of the Holy Spirit. To bring people to Christ. And now…it's all gone to ruin."

Will sat motionless in his chair, waiting for the last of Gilead's emotional expiation.

"A terrible massacre…people killed…how could things have gone so wrong? My fault…all of it must be my fault…"

He was starting to weep. Just then the metal door swung open abruptly, and two Palestinian guards stepped in and ordered Will to leave the room, telling him that his conference time was up.

As he was escorted to the door, he reached out quickly and squeezed his client's shoulder.

"This is not over. You and I still have a lot to talk about."

But as one of the guards escorted his client out and slammed shut the thick metal door, Will sensed that something else was closing. Some window, or door, of understanding. Now he was on the outside looking in. Gilead's presence at the scene of the crime, or the fact that he had delivered an incendiary sermon about the Temple Mount just seconds before the blast, could not be innocently explained away. That just did not seem plausible. Not by a long stretch.

Will recognized there was much being hidden from him. And whether the forces concealing it were good or evil, he did not yet know.

48

THE NEXT DAY, WILL WAS IN THE BACKSEAT of a taxi as it zigzagged through the narrow, crowded streets, fighting the early morning traffic of Jerusalem. Ordinarily, the route from Will's hotel in downtown Jerusalem to the building which now housed the Palestinian International Tribunal should have taken only ten or fifteen minutes. But with the rush hour, Will figured it would take him close to thirty minutes.

He looked out the window of the taxi at the narrow storefronts and winding limestone walls that lined the streets, some of which were plastered with political signs and posters—some in Hebrew, some in Arabic, most now faded, torn, and flapping in the breeze.

Will was en route to his first court appearance in Gilead Amahn's case. After his initial conference with his client, Will had arranged for his driver to take him to his hotel. For the rest of the day and into the night, he had reviewed the procedural rules for the tribunal and read some background about potential judges.

Mira Ashwan had provided some limited information on the identities of the five judges that had been assigned to work with the tribunal. But the information was scant. Will was looking for anything that would give him some ideological history on them. Unfortunately, Mira had failed to provide that.

Will knew that when the UN had funded the tribunal's creation, a compromise deal had been cut. Most of the judges of the tribunal would be from other nations, but the chief judge was to be a Palestinian. The law they would apply, including the prescribed penalties, would be the recently created criminal code of the Palestinian Authority, but the procedural laws for the court had been hammered out by an international team.

The UN had appointed four of the five judges on the tribunal panel, and the chief judge had been chosen by the Palestinian Authority. Their courthouse was the Orient House, a privately owned palace in Jerusalem with a tattered history, used historically by Palestinians for political operations.

The selection of the three-judge panel for Gilead's case was supposedly random. The two non-selected judges would sit for the "motions chamber," hearing pretrial matters and attending to discovery and scheduling issues in the case.

Will had just learned the day before that his "motions judge" who was conducting the scheduling conference that day was an American, Carrie Tabir. With the help of his staff back in Monroeville, he'd been able to get some research on her. A former federal magistrate judge, she was a Michigan University law professor, currently on leave to assist in the Temple Mount trials. She was also considered, generally speaking, to be sympathetic to Palestinian complaints against Israeli "occupation." Further, she had authored a law-review article that criticized the Israeli security fence that had been erected to slow down the influx of suicide bombers and other terrorists, calling it a "human-rights violation."

Another judge assigned to the tribunal, English judge Horace Luddington, a jurist with impeccable credentials, had recently fallen ill and had to return to England, Will had learned.

That meant that he now knew, with almost absolute certainty, the identity of the three judges who would be hearing the trial of Gilead Amahn. With that information in hand, Will made a phone call to Barrister Nigel Newhouse in London. Newhouse happily took the call, and the two briefly caught each other up about their cases.

Will then explained that he needed detailed background on the three judges who would be trying Gilead's case.

Newhouse noted that the "president" of the tribunal, who would function as the chief judge, was Saad Mustafa—longtime legal advisor to the Palestinian Authority and chief counsel to its president. He had helped draft the Palestinian constitution.

Newhouse explained that after he had been retained to represent Gilead Amahn, one of his first actions had been to file a motion objecting to Mustafa sitting as a potential judge for the case, based not only on his intimate association with the Palestinian cause, but on his Muslim identification as well.

"Of course, my motion for recusal was denied," the British lawyer said sardonically. "So I'm afraid you are stuck with Mr. Mustafa. That's going to be one of your votes—and I think he will vote for conviction."

"And there's one of the two votes needed for conviction," Will noted. "No unanimous verdict like in a criminal case in the U.S."

"Which brings us to the next judge," Newhouse continued. "Alain Verdexler. He's from Belgium. Former member of the Belgian Supreme Court. He's around seventy or so by now. More bad news for you, I'm afraid—after retiring, he wrote a scathing article critical of the court's reluctance to take up a war-crimes case against several high-ranking American officers. A Belgian national had been killed in Afghanistan as part of the United States' war on terrorism, and Verdexler felt that war crimes should have been brought against the Americans."

"Lovely," Will said. "And I don't think that a motion for recusal against him is going to succeed. Particularly if you were unable to knock Mustafa off the court. I doubt that Verdexler's public pronouncements against so-called American war crimes would be seen as sufficient proof of prejudice."

"Not likely," Newhouse said, agreeing. "Though Gilead Amahn is a naturalized American citizen, that's not going to suffice to get Verdexler off your court."

Newhouse then described the third member.

"Lee Kwong-ju is a former judge on the appellate court of South Korea. A judicious man, scholarly. Good judicial temperament.

Seems to be fairly immune to political pressure, even when he was involved in some controversial South Korean cases that implicated the politics between North and South Korea. He may be your only hope. But, unfortunately—well, I'm a bit of a tennis player myself, and if we were at Wimbledon they'd say, 'You're still shy of a deuce'—even if Lee Kwong-ju votes for acquittal, you still lose unless you also get Verdexler on your side."

Newhouse's comments were still echoing in Will's mind as the taxi pulled up in front of the Orient House. A couple dozen Palestinian protestors had gathered at the ornate gates that blocked public entrance to the limestone palace, and several television cameras and reporters were interviewing some of them. As Will paid the fare and grabbed his briefcases, one of the reporters recognized him, broke from the group of protestors, and ran over.

"Mr. Chambers, as Mr. Amahn's newest lawyer, what do you expect to happen in court today?"

"Just procedural matters," Will said, then waved off any further questions.

When the protestors discovered that Will was Gilead's attorney, one of them began shouting, "Hassan Gilead Amahn is a murderer! He is a tool of the Israeli butchers! You will be crushed!"

Suddenly, a handful of Jerusalem police jumped out of their Jeeps and ran over to Will.

With an Israeli police escort, he walked quickly to the tall, ornate gate, where he was checked through Palestinian security. As the gate opened and the attorney walked up to the Orient House Palace, he mused on how ironic it was that this building would be the site of Gilead Amahn's trial.

Next to the Temple Mount itself, the Orient House had been one of the most volatile locations in the Palestinian–Israeli conflict, having been used over the years as an unofficial headquarters for the Palestinian Authority within Jerusalem. But even more importantly, it was a symbolic reminder that the Palestinians were demanding an official governmental capital in Jerusalem.

Even more ironically, numerous searches of it over the years had sometimes yielded munitions, weapons, and terrorist-related documents, particularly following Palestinian terrorist bombings.

As Will mounted the stone stairs to the palace-turned-courthouse, the site of the Temple Mount terrorism tribunal, he realized the significance of this great house of white stone. This would be the place where international polity and Palestinian vengeance would join together like the two blades of a razor-sharp pair of shears, soon to begin slicing down on Gilead Amahn.

49

"ATTORNEY CHAMBERS, YOUR DISCLOSURES of trial defenses and your listing of witnesses and evidence in support thereof are due today. That means now. And you are filing this motion for an extension of time—why?"

Motion chambers Judge Carrie Tabir, a middle-aged woman with a short haircut and a wide, expressionless face, was in no mood to grant more time.

"Your Honor," Will began respectfully, "I've only been recently retained on this case. As you know, Barrister Nigel Newhouse originally represented Mr. Amahn, but had to withdraw. I've only recently come over to interview my client—"

"And why is that our problem?" Palestinian public prosecutor Samir Zayed asked, rising to his feet at the opposing counsel table. "We cannot be burdened with this request simply because the American lawyer did not want to come over here to interview his client until yesterday."

"I'm asking for only a week, Your Honor," Will responded. "Considering the gravity of the charges and the implications of this case—"

"And I'm concerned about the implications of your not being prepared to make your disclosures today," Judge Tabir snapped. "I've heard enough," she said after a few moments of reflection.

Both Will and the Palestinian prosecutor sat down and awaited the judge's decision.

"Here's what I am going to do," Tabir said. "I'm going to give you twenty-four hours. Until the close of business tomorrow. So you have the rest of today and all of tomorrow until five o'clock. Mr. Chambers, I want those written disclosures filed at that time. This court is adjourned."

Samir Zayed wheeled around in his chair and leaned over to his two legal assistants, who were seated behind him. Zayed was smiling broadly, and his two assistants were chuckling.

Will gathered his files, closed his two oversized briefcases, and began trudging out of the small courtroom used as a makeshift motions chamber—past the scattering of armed guards and toward the back of the courtroom, where there was a lone woman seated.

A Middle Eastern woman, strikingly attractive, with dark piercing eyes, black hair, and a shapely figure, rose and walked quickly toward Will with a small hand-tooled leather briefcase in her other hand.

"Mira Ashwan," she said brightly, extending her hand and shaking Will's warmly. "A very hard beginning of the case, Mr. Chambers. But don't worry—things will get better. I'm sure of it."

"I hope so," Will said. "Thank you for the information you sent me on the background of the judges. I got some additional data from Newhouse in London. So I think we have our three-judge panel pegged—Mustafa, a Palestinian, Judge Lee from South Korea, and Verdexler from Belgium. That's a tough tribunal…"

"Yes," Ashwan agreed, walking close to Will as the two left the courtroom. "Did you see the Israeli Defense Force's reports I e-mailed to you about the shooting of Louis Lorraine and Yossin Ali Khalid?"

As the two entered the hallway, Will looked up and saw a large oil portrait of Yasser Arafat, the first president of the Palestinian Authority, on the wall.

"Yes, I did get them—I appreciate that," Will replied.

"So, what do you think? Most interesting, were they not? A possible defense?"

"In what way? Both Lorraine and Khalid were fleeing from the scene. They were given warnings to halt. Shots were fired at the tires on their vehicles. They failed to halt, and the IDF then fired at their vehicles, killing both of them. Where would you go with that?"

"Don't you see?" Mira Ashwan said, smiling. "Why would they have shot them both so quickly?"

The two attorneys were now in the front lobby, just inside the front doors of the Orient House.

Will stopped and turned to face Mira.

"Are you suggesting some kind of Israeli conspiracy? I'm not sure that makes any sense…"

"Of course it does," she replied energetically. "It seems to me that the IDF did not want Lorraine and Khalid in custody. Because then they might have given statements—could have told the world—that the bombing was actually a conspiracy between the Knights of the Temple Mount and the government of Israel."

"You really believe that?" Will asked with disbelief in his voice. "Just think about this—the third member of the inner circle of the Knights was an American kid, Scott Magnit. The Palestinian Authority has even put out a press release trumpeting his confession, in which he directly implicates Gilead as the newly appointed spiritual head of the Knights. But even the Palestinians were unable to get Magnit to point any fingers at Israel."

"Oh, I've thought about that," Mira replied quickly. "I believe Scott Magnit was not one of the masterminds. The real decision-makers were Lorraine and Khalid. They were the ones who perhaps had worked with Israel, planting the bombs. Magnit was on the outside of the circle. He didn't know about the Israeli connection."

"Do you have any other evidence? Other than your theory?"

"What evidence do you need?"

"Something," Will explained, "that would really indicate that the Israeli government was involved. Either overtly…or by implication. At least some knowledge on their part that it was going to happen. Some deliberate choice on their part that either encouraged the bombing or permitted it to occur."

"There may be something," Mira said optimistically, "the possibility that we could dig some evidence up—I will work on that. Who knows? Perhaps we'll get lucky."

"But then there's another question. Even if the Israeli government was in some way connected—and I have no reason to believe it was—how would that exonerate Gilead? It would just prove that the conspiracy to bomb the Mount was more expansive than we thought."

"Oh, I am sure it would help Gilead," she said. "Mitigation of guilty intent is very much a part of the Palestinian tradition. Remember, in the mind of the Muslim, Allah is merciful and compassionate. If we can show that Gilead was simply an unwitting pawn in the hands of the Israelis and the true insiders in the Knights, we can, perhaps, avoid the death penalty at least..."

"Speaking of the death penalty," Will commented, "I note that when the procedural rules were set up for this tribunal, there was no requirement of a separate death-penalty phase. The evidence regarding mitigation of death penalty is part and parcel of trying the issue of guilt for the crime. That's very unfortunate. That's certainly different from the American approach..."

"Don't worry, Will," Mira said warmly. "You will do your best. I know you will. That's all that can be asked of you."

The two shook hands, and Will exited the Orient House Palace. As he descended the steps, he was greeted by screams and cries from the group of protestors still assembled outside the front gates. But his mind was now fixed on Mira's theory. What if she was right? What if Israel had had some part, no matter how covert and obscure, in the massacre of several hundred Muslims—not to mention a dozen Orthodox Jews at the Western Wall?

He didn't want to believe it. And he saw little evidence for Mira's speculations.

On the other hand, he knew his duty as his client's trial advocate. It was that precise duty that weighed on his mind. When he took on Gilead's case he had pledged to himself to zealously defend him against all odds—and against all outside influences.

More than thirty years before, Will had raised his right hand in a courtroom and had been sworn into the practice of law. He remembered his oath. It had hung for years on his law office wall in Monroeville, Virginia. He knew the words by heart:

> I will never reject, from any consideration personal to myself, the cause of the defenseless or oppressed…so help me, God.

And now he wondered what price would ultimately be exacted from him before the final judgment in this case was entered.

50

BACK IN HIS HOTEL ROOM in downtown Jerusalem, Will was sitting alone at the desk. It was nine in the evening, and he had finally gotten around to eating his room-service dinner, which by then was only slightly warm.

He looked at his watch. It was mid-afternoon back in Virginia. Andy was still in school, and when Will glanced at his pocket home planner he was reminded that Fiona was supposed to be in a meeting in Washington with her concert manager, her agent, and a recording executive.

Trying to break away from his work on the case for a few minutes, Will glanced through a few English-language Jerusalem papers he had picked up. One of them had a front-page article on Gilead's case, announcing the pretrial hearing that had been scheduled for earlier that day.

But all of the headlines were zeroing in on another issue, an immensely volatile one. Debate had been raging in the Knesset over control of the Temple Mount plateau. Since the destruction of the Dome of the Rock and the al-Aqsa Mosque, some of the conservatives in the Israeli parliament, like the Temple Mount Faithful Movement Party, were calling for Israel to wrest control from the Muslim Waqf.

In response, the Arabic factions in the Knesset, like the Arab Democratic Party and the Israel Islamic Movement, were decrying that as proof of an "Israeli conspiracy behind the bombings."

Meanwhile, the moderates were fearful of any Israeli move for control, debating whether to yield to the United Nation's call for an international committee to administer the one-million-square-foot area.

And the area itself, still in ruins, was caught in nervous stalemate. IDF, UN peacekeeping troops, and the Palestinian police were jointly patrolling it in a tense standoff and were barring any entry.

Then a noise interrupted Will's reading. He glanced at the other end of the room and noticed that a plain manila envelope had been shoved under his door. He ran over, swung the door open, and looked down the hall both ways. It was empty.

After closing and relocking the door, he took a closer look at the envelope. It contained a single magazine page—from something called *International Security and Intelligence Quarterly*. On one side was a short article about a patent recently approved by the U.S. Patent Office. Will glanced again at the envelope, which did not bear a room number or any other writing. His initial impression was that it had been delivered by accident.

Then he looked more closely at the article.

The gist was that a patent had been granted for a computer-security program designed to detect attempted unauthorized entries into computers employing quantum encryption systems. That encryption process had been heralded as a virtually unbreakable type of privacy protection for computers—but after reading the article a second time, it was clear to Will that someone might have learned how to compromise the quantum-encryption process. Hence the need for a refinement—namely, the newly patented detection system.

It was an interesting diversion. But to Will, it seemed meaningless for now. He put the article back inside the envelope and tossed it aside.

He rubbed his eyes. Jet lag and fatigue were starting to set in. He poured himself a cup of coffee from the carafe, knowing he would probably have to pull an all-nighter in order to construct the discovery disclosures that were to be filed with the tribunal by the end of business the next day. He had to give a general outline of his defense, just as the prosecution already had done. If any critical elements were left out, he might well be prevented from bringing that evidence in at the trial.

But he needed to make any calls to the States now, while it was still during working hours back there.

He placed a call to the NYU anthropology department, asking to be connected to Dr. Daoud al-Qasr, the expert referred to him by Len Redgrove.

After a few transfers, Will was speaking to the Egyptian professor, who apologized that he only had a few minutes to talk before his next class.

"I did review the materials you sent to me," he remarked, "and I must say this case appears to have some issues I could address. They are—how should I say—within the general province of my expertise."

"And as I understand it," Will glanced at his notes and the biography info he had found on al-Qasr, "your field is in sociocultural anthropology of the Near East, with an emphasis on ancient religions and their current-day influence on Arab people groups—do I have that down accurately?"

"You do indeed. You have been doing your research on me," al-Qasr remarked with a little laugh. "I'm here for a short teaching assignment before I return to the University of Cairo."

Will explained his dilemma—that he had only into the next day to lay out the general contours of his defense in writing for the court and opposing counsel.

"Can you say," Will continued, "that Gilead Amahn did not share the same radical theological beliefs of the Knights—and therefore could not have been a knowing leader in their attempt to hasten the coming of their prophesied Golden Age by destroying the Temple Mount structure?"

There was silence on the other end. Will tried again.

"In other words, would it be your opinion that Gilead could not have been their ringleader—because he didn't share their religious beliefs?"

"Well, my expertise is in ancient Middle Eastern *esoteric* religions—where those religions still hold some cultural sway on present-day Arab groups."

"Exactly—like the Druze religion," Will said.

"Yes."

"And the Knights of the Temple Mount—a breakaway group from the Druze—you're one of the few experts around who can speak authoritatively about this very small subgroup..."

"While that is correct, I have to warn you," al-Qasr explained, "that I am not an expert on what you are contending is Mr. Gilead Amahn's *true* religious preference. In your cover letter to me you describe him as a 'conservative evangelical Christian, theologically'—I really cannot speak to that..."

"I understand," Will replied, "and I have another expert, Dr. Tyrone, from Southern Methodist University. He's going to address whether Gilead Amahn fits the description that you just quoted. But if we assume all that, and if Gilead was a conservative evangelical Christian on the day of the bombing—why would anyone believe he had been accepted as a leader in this secret, very esoteric cult?"

After considering the question, the professor said he had only one opinion he could give, and he gave it reluctantly.

"I can only say that given the esoteric, mystery-religion features of the theology of the Knights, and their very secret structure, they would be *very slow* to accept any hard-line Christian—someone very fixed in his belief—into their group...or at least as a *leader* of their group. They would have to verify over a long period of supervision and instruction, you know, that such a person was a *true convert* to their group..."

Dr. al-Qasr then apologized, saying he had to run. Will knew he would have to be satisfied with that.

"Will you fly over here to testify for us?" the attorney asked quickly before al-Qasr hung up.

There was a sigh at the other end.

"You know I am a Muslim."

"I know that," Will replied quickly. "Will you testify for Gilead Amahn?"

Another pause.

"I'll think about it...probably...most likely—if I can work it into my schedule."

"I did mention the trial date in my letter, and I indicated the dates I would be calling you as a witness."

"You may have written about that, but—so sorry, counselor—I really have to go." The professor hung up.

Will looked at his rough-draft listing of potential expert witnesses. Dr. al-Qasr's name was at the top—but with a question mark jotted next to his name. Will took his pen and crossed out the question mark. Time was short. And though al-Qasr might have been less than committal, Will would have to hope and pray that he would come through by the time of the trial.

His other experts were a surer bet. Dr. Edward Tyrone would testify that Gilead's theological beliefs were "mainstream evangelical," and despite his belief in a literal "end-times" scenario based on biblical prophecy, such beliefs excluded acts of terrorism by definition. Explosives expert Mike Michalany would give the opinion that Gilead, with no known experience in terrorism, could never have been the ringleader of a bombing attack that was so technologically sophisticated.

Which led to a critical question—and it came burning into Will's mind like a searing iron.

If the Knights of the Temple Mount had had no experience in terrorism—no engineering talent for destruction or mayhem—then they could have obtained the wireless detonation system and huge quantity of C-4 explosives necessary from only a very narrow range of possible outside sources.

But not from Islamic terrorists—that was certain. Then from who? Who had both the motive as well as the means to provide the material, technology, and organization for a massacre on the most contended-over piece of geography in the world?

Will jotted down on his rough-draft list of witnesses, "Joe Doe, or Jane Doe—presently undetermined and unidentified conspirators who planned, provided equipment and technology for, or provided other material support for, the bombings."

Until Will was able to answer those questions, that generic description would have to do. Back in the States, of course, a prosecutor would call that a typical defense attorney's trick—threatening to call, in favor of the defense case, the "true culprit" of the crime.

And Will knew the truth—that as a trial strategy it was like raising an impressive but little-honored flag—often run up the flagpole, but rarely if ever saluted.

As Will continued to evaluate and scrutinize the details of the case against Gilead, as well as his potential defense, he felt a growing sick feeling in the hollow of his stomach. He considered the judges who would decide the case, and the geopolitical stakes involved. And he was well aware of the wealth of circumstantial facts already lined up against Gilead. Given all of that, Will knew it would not be enough to simply argue that his client was an overzealous evangelical Christian who happened to be in the wrong place at the wrong time, saying the wrong things at exactly the right moment in history to touch off an explosion that would decimate Islam's third holiest site, along with several hundred praying Muslims.

No. That was not going to wash. From everything Will had read, Gilead seemed to fulfill the bizarre, eclectic prophecy of the Knights of the Temple Mount—the coming of a messiah to Cairo at the precisely predicted time, a messiah who also matched the characteristics of the deified Caliph al-Hakim, who had disappeared there in the year 1021. What were the odds that Gilead had simply and innocently "stumbled" into that role? No, the evidence suggested that Gilead had run headlong into playing that part.

It was clear to Will that only one thing could ultimately exonerate Gilead Amahn. Somehow, he needed to reveal *who* truly was behind the Temple Mount massacre, and even more importantly—*why*.

51

THROUGH THE EVENING WILL PORED over the multiple note-books full of documents he had collected in the case thus far. Looking for shreds of information...anything...bits or scraps... something to show him what he might be missing in his potential defense. Looking for the answers to those questions that still taunted him. Like the elusive, long-horned desert ibex, sleek and gazelle-like, that stalked the Negev Desert, the answers to those questions stayed just beyond reach, elusive to catch.

It was nearing midnight when he finished his initial document review. Before he started typing up the pretrial disclosure document on his laptop, he called home—and got the answering machine.

He tried Fiona's cell phone. But he got her voice mail.

He glanced at his home planner. Andy was in a choir concert at school. Fiona obviously had gone there after her meeting in DC. They wouldn't be home for several more hours. Will got up from the hotel-room desk, stretched, and went into the bathroom to throw some cold water on his face. He poured himself another cup of coffee...it was tepid, nearly cold, but he didn't care.

Deciding to take a break for a few minutes, he scooped up the newspapers he had not finished scanning.

And then, suddenly, as Will glanced at the familiar headlines, he was struck by a thought. It was so self-evident, he wondered why it hadn't hit him before. Outside of Gilead's family and his defense team, absolutely no one—and certainly no nation—no political entity anywhere—had any interest in vindicating Gilead's innocence. To the contrary, there appeared to be a near-universal motivation to see him convicted and executed as a terrorist.

For the United States, there was the acid-stomach embarrassment of having released its federal detainer against this "terrorist," and then later aiding his release from a Cairo jail at the request of Will Chambers, no less. But more than that, Will knew the political implications for President Harriet Landow if her administration were seen as sympathetic to someone, like Gilead, who was perceived to be an enemy not only of the Palestinian Authority, but of Muslims everywhere.

Will read the Washington papers. He had connections on the Hill. He knew that Landow, breaking from the last administration, had taken a hard line against Israel. It was clear she was bent on forcing a Middle East peace plan, whether Israel liked it or not. America would somehow, in some way, be held to account if the chief scapegoat for the Temple Mount murders—a nationalized American and a "radical" Christian "cultist"—got off. The State Department's recent refusal to talk to Will seemed to bear that out. While the Landow Administration might have only a slight political advantage if Gilead was convicted, it would suffer a truly catastrophic foreign policy injury if he was acquitted.

Then there was the Palestinian Authority and the Arab League nations. Their position in the case seemed painfully obvious.

Israel's stance was more complicated, but just as troubling. Caught in the middle, as always, the tiny nation was being hammered by accusations of showing lack of diligence by not catching the Knights of the Temple Mount before the bombings. Mira Ashwan's suggestion that its negligence went even farther—even to the point of complicity in deliberately allowing the attack— was publicly shared by several international pundits.

Thus, why would Israel have any motive to help the attorney in exonerating his client? Like the United States, its resistance to providing any intelligence information to Will seemed to substantiate all of that.

Even the international Christian community had been brutally graceless. In magazine articles, several of the mainline denominations had pointed to Gilead's "extremist" preaching as a *moral* cause of the bombings...if not a legal one. One prominent liberal Bible scholar had pointed to the case as an example of "why the preaching of Bible prophecy and other end-times nonsense is a threat to social justice, ethnic peace, and religious tolerance."

The evangelical groups were guarded at best. Concerned that Gilead might in truth have been subsumed into a dangerous religious cult, and remembering the bitter gall of abortion clinic bombings by self-proclaimed "Christian patriots," all had decried the violence—but most had taken a wait-and-see position regarding Gilead's guilt or innocence.

Will felt as if he and Gilead were together, alone, in the middle of a vast arena. All around, rising from the galleries, and the bleachers, and the box seats, was a collective cry for the conviction and death of this quiet, serious student of Scripture—this young man who seemed to have such a white-hot passion for evangelizing his own people.

In his fatigue, Will turned back to the newspaper, flipping casually to the inside pages of the article he was reading. Then something caught his eye.

On the neighboring page to the article he was reading was a photo of Warren Mullburn. He was being greeted by Israeli diplomats during his recent visit to forge a Middle East peace plan. His grin was wide—even ecstatic. His eyes were electric with an inner light of secret enthusiasm.

Will studied the picture. By now he was exhausted, and his head was spinning.

He looked at the picture again, his eyes bleary.

Then he walked to the window and drew back the curtains. It was still dark out. In the distance he saw the white limestone walls of Old City Jerusalem, washed with the golden glow of streetlights. He saw the brash neon security lamps that had been installed on top of the Temple Mount amid the ruins of the bombed-out mosques. And there were the tiny figures of Palestinian armed guards, as usual, crawling over the surface of the Mount.

At its foot he could see a few UN Jeeps and some armored personnel carriers of the IDF.

Will gazed out into the night, toward the Mount also known as Moriah. The place where, thousands upon thousands of years before, Abraham had laid his son Isaac, the son of the promise, upon a rough altar. The same place where Abraham's hand, poised to strike in one swift movement of terrible execution, was stayed at the very last second by the voice of God. For the promised Lamb of God was yet to come—and yet to die.

Here was the place where in the fullness of time, the one great sacrifice would finally be made—cruel and illegal, and yet perfectly effective...majestically triumphant...stunningly final. It would be made on a bloody, rough-hewn cross, witnessed by both the faithful and the blasphemous; by those weeping out blessings...and those shrieking out curses.

This was the city where the Messiah would declare, in His dying breath, *"It is finished."*

And then, just a short walk away from that place of execution, in a rich man's tomb carved into the Jerusalem stone—all of the forces of nature and the laws of physics and biology notwithstanding—the Messiah would sit up from bodily death and would shed His graveclothes...carefully folding His head covering and placing it with immaculate calm in one corner of the empty tomb. And then, clothed with a power never before witnessed, He would walk out into the daylight.

And within the lifetime of the Messiah's followers, the massive walls and towering columns of the Herodian Temple would be toppled and ground into shards—just as the Messiah had predicted. And it would later, all of it, be buried under the ruin of the ages and beneath the weight of empires.

And now, from his hotel window, as Will Chambers viewed the Temple Mount plateau—the epicenter of all of that astonishing history—he beheld the simple fact of it all.

The Muslim structures on the Mount, the last impediment to the reconstruction of a new Jewish Temple, had been erased by an act of swift and terrible violence—and within his seeing. Within his lifetime.

In the same fashion as He had foretold the destruction of the former one, Jesus, the Messiah, had also predicted the ultimate rise of that last Temple—before the great and terrible time. Before the end of days.

Len Redgrove, it seemed to Will, might have been correct. After all, what is there left to do but to believe, and act upon that belief, when the veil of the present is suddenly ripped away and there—standing before you—is the future, come to pass?

For Will, the time of decision was fast approaching. It was nearly here. And it was personal to him. It was a question…not just about the defense of his client. Or winning or losing. Or even the massive, almost incomprehensible political implications of the bombing of the Temple Mount. It was a matter, at once both smaller and yet larger than all of that. And it was a question for Will Chambers—seemingly for him alone.

What did he truly believe?

And what risks, *now*, was he willing to take?

History. Geopolitics. World economy. International justice. And most importantly of all, the written record of God, the King of the universe. How could he doubt that they were all converging—here, now—amid the palm trees, white limestone buildings, and crowded streets of this ancient city?

Even Jack Hornby, a skeptical news reporter with all the finesse of a rusty razor blade, had been right in something too. Back there in a restaurant in Washington, DC, Hornby's little handdrawn picture had showed it—all those arrows pointing to the circle, and right in the middle of the circle, Will Chambers.

All of that was no accident. No mere coincidence. To believe that, Will would have to believe in a random, meaningless universe where all of history was ultimately governed by chaos—colliding planets, colliding particles, and mythical explanations of origins. Will had moved away from such agnosticism more than a decade ago.

No. He was in the middle of that circle in Hornby's diagram for a reason. And alone in his hotel room, in the late hours of the night, he had to believe he been divinely called for this. He had been drawn, wooed, protected, and led to that very time and place.

So Will Chambers walked slowly over to the desk. He looked down at his notes. And at the list of his potential witnesses.

He took his pen. And he wrote the name of just one more witness.

When he had finished, he took a moment to study the name he had just written.

Then he set his alarm for two hours hence and collapsed into bed.

52

"WILL…THAT YOU, WILL BOY? Man…what time is it?"

Tiny Heftland's voice was groggy at the other end of the phone.

"Sorry," Will said. "I know it's got to be about two-thirty in the morning. I do apologize…"

"So…hey…what's up, man? You still over in Jerusalem?"

"Yes. Listen. An urgent scheduling thing—"

"Yeah…sure. What's the deal, lawyer boy?"

"I want you back over here."

"When?"

"As soon as you can get here."

Tiny was wide awake now.

"You mean, right away? Instantly? Like, you know, 'Beam me up Scotty'?"

"You can get out of your pajamas first."

"Gee, thanks. Can you tell me what I'm going to be doing over there? It'd be kinda nice to know. If it wouldn't be too much trouble…"

"Tiny, you'll probably be causing an international incident."

"Sweet. I can always count on you to keep life interesting for me."

"Oh—and Tiny…remember that brown delivery-man outfit you wore when you worked with me on the *Rogers v. Wilmington Corporation* case—gee, that was a long time ago."

"Sure—believe it or not. I still have it in my closet somewhere."

"You sure it still fits?"

"Ouch," Tiny groaned. "You know the male ego is more fragile than fine crystal—didn't you know that?"

"Look, just get over here as soon as you can. Let me know where you're staying. Better yet, stay here in the same hotel where I'm staying. Got the info?"

"Yeah, yeah. In my file somewhere. I'll give you my flight details when I get them."

Before signing off with an "adiós, amigo," Tiny assured Will he would post his best man on security detail to look after Fiona and Andy.

Will looked at his watch—it was breakfast time. He needed to get out of the room, so he walked downstairs with his notepad and his draft of his discovery disclosures. He was confident he could easily make the court-imposed deadline of day-end. The only question was the completeness of the document. He didn't want to give the Palestinian prosecutor any reason to cry surprise if he later introduced some critical but undisclosed evidence.

The café on the first floor of the hotel was lined with windows to the outside and was cheerful and bright. He ordered a light breakfast.

After finishing, he strolled past the front desk and asked for messages. The clerk gave him one. A call had come in from Mike Michalany the night before, but for some reason he had not gotten it.

Back in his room, Will continued typing up his pretrial statement.

When it was five-thirty U.S. time, he decided to return Michalany's call. He knew he was an early riser and hoped he would be up. He was right.

"I thought you might be interested in this tidbit..." Michalany said.

"I'm at the point where even a little tidbit could be great news," Will replied.

"Okay. Well, I've been doing some snooping around, jawing with some of my old pals in the Bureau. I talked to someone I know in the international unit—terrorism, that stuff. I asked whether they'd heard anything interesting on the bombing."

"And?"

"Well, they said a couple of our agents went over to Jerusalem to talk it over with some of the top Mossad people. I know you realize—because you're the one that first told me—that Israeli intelligence did a quick analysis of the computer detonation devices in the Knights' vehicles. Then they had to turn all the evidence over to the Palestinians. So...our guys heard there was some kind of feature found in both computer hard drives."

"Okay," Will said, "you said a feature common to both computers, in both vehicles. What kind of feature?"

"They didn't exactly call it that. They called it...an *anomaly*. That's the word Mossad used. An anomaly."

"Can you tell me anything else? Anything?"

"Sorry. I'm just giving you what I got. I just heard this the other day. But I assume you would like me to follow up on this?"

"Absolutely. Look, I'm making my pretrial disclosures today. Anything more you find out—get it to me immediately."

Suddenly recalling something, Will asked Michalany to hold. He dashed to the other side of the room and began fishing through stacks of papers and files.

Then he found it—the manila envelope that had been shoved under his door with the magazine article.

"Speaking of computers," Will said, back at the phone, "I'm not sure this has anything to do with anything. But—what do you know about 'quantum encryption'?"

"Not much. I've got computer guys in my company that handle that stuff. I know they think it's the most refined method to ensure computer security. But like I always say, there isn't a code out there that eventually can't be broken. Why?"

"I'm not sure. But, do me a favor will you?"

"Sure."

"Give me the name of your best computer guy. I'd like to list him as a potential witness. Just in case."

"In case what?"

"In case...in case we need some computer expertise at trial."

"Will, I've worked on several cases with you. But I've got to say, I've never known you to be so vague...maybe 'mysterious' is a better word. Though we former FBI guys don't really like that word..." Michalany chuckled. But he agreed to talk to the computer guru at his security company and obtain his approval for Will to name him as a witness. He promised to e-mail it within the hour.

Fifty minutes later, Will received an e-mail with the name and address of Kenneth Waters, a PhD in computer-science forensics.

Will was closing in on his deadline. He decided to call Tiny back.

"Tiny, one last question."

"I'm packing. I've already called the travel agent. What's the deal, man?"

"The other Mossad agent who had the Reichstad research center in Maryland under surveillance...you mentioned there was a second guy."

"Yeah...Nathan somebody..."

"No. He was the fellow I knew—the one you said was killed. I'm talking about the other agent. Nathan's partner. The one you thought might still be around."

"Yeah. Okay. Well, it's like this...I'm not always the most organized guy. I wish I'd known that you might need it. Why didn't you ask me to nail that down when I first brought it up?"

"Sorry. But Tiny, this is important. Please see if you can dig up the other guy's name, okay? Then call me on my cell."

"You've got international roaming?"

"Yes."

"Nice."

"I'll be heading over to the court building within the next hour and a half. If you can locate the name, call me."

After that, on a hunch, Will decided to call Jack Hornby. His national desk editor said he was out on an assignment.

Will called his cell phone and left a message. Then Will finished his pretrial disclosure statement for the tribunal. He left a blank line at the end of his list of witnesses, hoping to fill it in when Tiny called back. Next to the blank line he had typed, "Agent for the Israel Institute for Intelligence and Special Tasks—a.k.a. the Mossad."

On his way to the Orient House, he called Mira Ashwan. She was in Jerusalem. He asked that she meet him at the tribunal building.

By the time Will arrived at the courthouse, it was four-forty-three in the afternoon. His phone rang as he was getting out of the taxi.

It was Jack Hornby calling back.

"Sorry, Jack," Will said hurriedly, "but I'm racing to the Palestinian Tribunal to file some papers in my case. Can't really talk."

"Just calling you back."

Will stopped about a hundred feet before the front security gate. He looked at his watch. It was four-forty-four.

"In twenty words or less," Will rapped out, "have you dug up any more information that you think might help me out in the Temple Mount bombing?"

"Not really. I'm trying to wrap up this piece on Mullburn—but every time I get close to finishing it he does something more outrageous. I can't seem to put this article to bed. I think I'm going to have to head over there and do some digging for myself. About his efforts at a Middle East peace plan. Really. Can you believe the chutzpah of that guy? And the whole world seems to be buying it."

"Of course they are," Will said. "But if you don't have anything specific…"

"Not really. I'm on my way to the State Department right now. I'll look you up in Jerusalem…oh, and I wanted to tell you—I'd like my next feature article to be on Caleb Marlowe, U.S. special operations warrior, terrorist hunter, former client of Will Chambers, presumed dead, officially killed in action—"

"Not dead," Will said, panting a little as he reached the security gate.

"See, I thought there might be a story there. How do you know—"

"Just a strong hunch," Will bulleted out, hearing the click of his call-waiting. He told Jack he had to go, then took the call. It was Tiny.

"Meir. It was Mossad agent C. Meir," Tiny said loudly.

"Tiny, you're my hero," Will yelled back. Clicking off, he took his pen and printed the name in the blank lines of both the original pretrial and the copy for the prosecutor.

He looked at his watch. It was four-forty-seven.

"Please hurry," Will yelled to the guards at the gate as they checked his briefcase and cell phone.

It was four-forty-nine when Will sprinted into the tribunal building and raced to the clerk's office. There was one window open for filing court pleadings. He arrived just as an Arab man was sliding down a folding metal window cover.

"No!" Will yelled out. He grabbed the metal closure at the bottom, leaving about a handsbreadth opening.

"File this!" he ordered, and thrust his papers through the gap.

The man started yelling and tried to push the papers back.

"File these—it's your job! Do it now—do you hear me?"

Several security guards came running over toward Will, their weapons already drawn.

"I'm an American lawyer—and if this clerk does not file these papers, I will call the reporters for American television and tell them what happened here."

The guards stood motionless, their revolvers pointed at Will. The clerk, frozen on the other side of the window, still had Will's pretrial disclosure statement in his fist.

After several seconds, the senior guard waved his gun toward the clerk and said something in Arabic.

The clerk threw Will a dirty look. Then he slammed the court stamp down on the original, and also reluctantly stamped Will's copy of the papers.

Will examined his copy. The stamp bore that day's date.

When he turned, Mira was standing a few feet away, smiling.

"That was a close call," she said, laughing a little.

Will gave an exasperated sigh.

"Will, you really look tired. You work all night on this?"

He nodded.

"You poor man. You'd better take better care of yourself."

Will handed her a copy of his pretrial disclosure statement and said, "Can you serve this on the Palestinian public prosecutor's office?"

Mira nodded enthusiastically. "Is there anything else I can do?"

"Yes. Call the jail in Ramallah. Line up a meeting between me and Gilead for tomorrow. And tell them I will need several hours—and I don't want to be interrupted."

"Glad to. How about you and I both interview him? If I'm going to be effective I need to get all the information I can for his defense—"

"Listen, Mira," Will said, "as defense amicus curiae you're in a little different situation than I am as Gilead's personal defense counsel. No offense, but I think I'd better meet alone with him."

"Certainly," she said with a smile. "No problem. After I serve these papers I'll contact the jailers."

Then she pulled out one of her cards and wrote something on the back.

"Here's my cell number and my home number. It's actually my brother's apartment. I'm living with him. In case you need to contact me in an emergency."

Will took the card and nodded. They shook hands, and Will trudged out of the building and hailed a cab. Now he needed to get back to the hotel, as well as try to call Fiona. And then maybe crash for a few hours' nap before getting back to work.

53

BACK AT HIS HOTEL ROOM, Will called Fiona. Andy's solo at the concert had gone wonderfully, she reported. He was also starting baseball practice after school.

She went on to describe her meeting in DC as productive. As part of the resolution, her upcoming concert in Baltimore would be recorded—but that certainly made it much more complicated. Her agent and the concert promoter were trying to sort out the details.

"So often I wish I could just pursue this music ministry without all of the complications...all of the endless details," she said with a sigh.

"How are you doing otherwise?"

"Okay. Missing you. Terribly. I'm lonely. It's probably good I'm so busy. Keeps my mind off not having you here. And off of Da not being around anymore...I sure wish we didn't have to be separated."

"Me too. I love you, darling. So much."

"I saw you on TV."

"Oh?"

"You were walking to the courthouse building. Outside a tall gate. There were a bunch of protestors screaming at you."

"Yeah. On my way to the pretrial hearing. That was interesting."

"How did it go?"

"They're cutting me no slack at all. I have a feeling this is going to be bare-knuckle boxing all the way."

"What else is new?" Fiona said, with a little resignation in her voice. "Since when have you ever taken the easy road? That would be too obvious…too routine."

"Soon," Will said, trying to be reassuring, "I'll be home. Then it will be back to life as usual. I'm looking forward to that so much."

"'Usual,'" Fiona said, as if almost to herself. "That's not who you are. I'm beginning to wonder…did God make you that way? Or is it something else…always the steep, stony, climb for you… always the rough road. Is it something you've picked for yourself? Some need. Some hidden drive. Pushing you on. Never content."

After a moment's silence she added, "But you know…I love you so much. Sorry, I'm just rambling on here, I guess."

"No. I want you to be honest with me. Always. Listen—please pray for me—and for this case," Will said with a special urgency in his voice that Fiona detected. "And Gilead."

"You sound worried."

"Not just that. You know I've always assumed I could handle anything. Sounds awfully arrogant, doesn't it? And it probably is. I think you're right. Something is always pushing me on. Frankly, I always felt that—given enough time and energy—I could handle any case that came along, no matter how complex. But now…this is different."

"What do you mean?"

"This whole thing seems so beyond me, darling. Simple as that. I'm doing everything right. I'm preparing for the fight—just as I've done for the last thirty years. But I've never been quite so aware…so acutely aware…of my total weakness. You've always called my cases 'David against Goliath.' Good description. But this one…it's more like an ant versus Goliath."

"Grasshoppers," Fiona commented quietly.

"What?"

"Grasshoppers. Remember? The Israelite spies are sent by the Lord to check out the land of Canaan before they enter, after crossing the wilderness. They came back saying there were giants in the land, and they felt like little tiny grasshoppers in the shadow of their enemy. It took a man like Joshua to lead them in and claim victory."

Will smiled. "Maybe I should read up on it again. Thank you, dear. You're right. I have to keep a spiritual perspective on this...You know, speaking of spies, I talked to Jack Hornby earlier today. He wants to do an article on Caleb Marlowe."

"I wonder where he is," Fiona said. "You've always thought he'd survived that attack in Mexico haven't you?"

"Yes. That postcard I got later...unsigned...I've always had that feeling..."

"You know, we also got another blast from the past," Fiona added. "A note from Tex Rhoady."

"Tex? What do you know—how's he doing? I've haven't heard from him in a couple of years, ever since he left his little airplane service in Georgia and went back to Texas. What's he up to?"

"He's finally gotten married."

"No kidding. That's great."

"And he says he's running some kind of aircraft business... experimental helicopters...it didn't make a lot of sense to me."

"I'll have to get back in touch with him when this is all over."

"So, are you going to be able to come home for a few days... before you get too close to trial?"

Will's uncomfortable silence told Fiona the whole story.

"You're feeling pressed to stay over there, straight through till trial...aren't you?" she asked.

"I'm afraid so. I've already called Tiny and told him to join me here."

Fiona didn't fully succeed in hiding her disappointment. Will wanted to elaborate, to explain how *this time* it would be the last of this kind of case. But he didn't try. He was convinced it was so, that Gilead Amahn's prosecution represented a last chapter in his life. But how could he convince his wife of that? Mere words wouldn't do. He would simply have to make it happen. This would be the end of something for him, a consummation, the last act...

of that he felt unshakably certain, though he did not exactly know why.

After his call to Fiona, Will telephoned Nigel Newhouse. He had e-mailed the English barrister and very candidly revealed his concern that he might be stretched beyond his limits in mounting Gilead's defense alone. Back at the office, Todd Furgeson was totally occupied in handling Jacki's work while she was out on maternity leave, not to mention Will's other caseload. Will had assigned research, e-mail communication, and Internet information-gathering to Jeff Holden. But beyond that, the novice lawyer had little he could do to assist Will at this point.

Would Newhouse consider joining the defense team at this late hour, with the trial date only ten days away? The barrister said he would carefully consider it and get back to Will within forty-eight hours.

There was also Will's concern about a working space before and during the trial. Larry Lancer, the director of the Holy Land Institute for the Word, had a couple offices next door to the institute. He had kindly offered them to Will and anyone else helping with Gilead's defense. As promised, the institute had been paying all of the bills for the defense, which by now had become staggeringly high. Lancer had simply indicated they had a "private benefactor" who was funding it all. Will didn't pry.

Within twenty-four hours of Will's filing his pretrial disclosures, the Palestinian prosecutor filed a raft of written objections, motions, and responses. One of them—not surprisingly to Will— had to do with the name of the second-to-last witness Will had typed into his pretrial statement, the one he'd added in the middle of the night in his hotel room. After Mira had had a chance to read it over she called Will, also bringing it up.

"I was very surprised when I read your witness list," she said. "A very surprising witness name—"

"You mean the line where I added the name of Mr. Meir, the Mossad agent?"

"No, not that," Mira said. "The name before that."

"Oh. Yes." He understood her interest and the public prosecutor's interest, not to mention the media's laser-beam attention to the name. He had already received thirteen calls from the foreign press since filing his papers and could tell that the hotel's front desk was becoming exasperated. He had returned none of the calls.

"I must say, I truly admire your courage," his fellow attorney said with a titter. "I really do. To name the man who is at this moment negotiating a peace plan here in Jerusalem—Foreign Secretary Warren Mullburn—that is truly extraordinary!"

"I'll take that as a compliment, I guess…" Will said, laughing a little himself. "And, thanks, Mira, for setting up my conference with Gilead. By the way, I've secured a location for a temporary office. It's the space next to the Holy Land Institute for the Word. They're letting me use it for the case. So starting tomorrow, I'll move my files in there."

"I'd love to hear your thinking on Mullburn…and on that Mossad agent," Mira replied. "Maybe I could help you prepare for those witnesses."

After the conversation, Will checked the time. It was getting late. He would try to get four, maybe five hours of sleep. And then, tomorrow, he would meet with Gilead, move into the temporary office, and begin the final march—the last ten days of preparation before the trial.

He would be thorough, all-consumed, and focused. He would try to ignore the fact that now, at his age, the grueling process of trial preparation and sleepless nights was not as easy as it had once been. But one thing above all he would try to push out of his mind.

He would try to avoid the catastrophic distraction that kept occupying his inner moral sense. The lingering idea that threatened to tie him in knots.

The thought that his defense of Gilead Amahn, if unsuccessful, would result in Gilead's execution.

54

THE LARGEST ROOM IN THE ORIENT HOUSE had been converted into a fully functioning courtroom for the Gilead Amahn trial. Its interior had been transformed into a blandly modern space—with rows of Scandinavian-style blond wood tables, each with a computer fixed within its top, one computer screen for each seat. Each seat had a set of earphones, which were wireless and could be clipped to a belt buckle.

There were bomb-proof and soundproof panels on all the walls. At the front of the room, the high judicial bench had three red leather chairs behind it. But the bench was separated from the rest of the room by a clear, floor-to-ceiling bulletproof shield.

Off to the side was an enclosed booth, about twice the size of a telephone booth, where the witnesses would be protected during their questioning.

At the rear of the room, a one-way viewing window stretched across the entire wall. Behind it, unseen to the occupants of the courtroom, there was a bank of interpreters, who would translate the proceedings into English, Arabic, French, and Korean.

Will Chambers was at the right counsel table, at the end closest to the table of the public prosecutor. At the other end of the right table, Mira Ashwan, defense amicus curiae, was seated.

And between Will and Mira was Nigel Newhouse. The human-rights barrister had graciously cleared his schedule and agreed to appear as co-counsel. Then between Will and Nigel there was one empty chair, for the accused.

Tiny Heftland was seated in the audience section, fidgeting nervously.

Samir Zayed, the prosecutor, was flanked by two legal assistants and also had three clerks and two investigators seated in the row behind the his table.

The press was relegated to a separate viewing room down the hall, where they viewed the proceeding by closed-circuit TV. The lawyers were prohibited from giving interviews to the media during the course of the trial.

About twenty minutes after the scheduled opening of the trial, the three judges, all wearing scarlet robes with white, frilly ascots, entered the room from a side door and took their red leather seats behind the shield.

In the center was Saad Mustafa, acting as president, or chief judge, of the tribunal. The Palestinian lawyer was almost entirely bald, but with black bushy eyebrows above wire-rimmed glasses. His manner was animated and friendly. He proceeded to introduce the other two judges.

To Mustafa's left was Alain Verdexler from Belgium. He was in his late sixties, pale, with thinning sandy-white hair, worn slightly long. He had a courtly, almost bored, expression.

On the other side of the chief judge was Lee Kwong-ju, the South Korean. In his fifties, small, with a round, smooth face and dark-rimmed glasses, he nodded pleasantly when introduced, and his eyes studied the courtroom intensely, though his face was expressionless.

Zayed rose and entered his appearance. Will followed, introducing both himself and Newhouse as his co-counsel. Mira Ashwan was last to stand and introduce herself.

Zayed then stood up and raised numerous objections to the defense list of witnesses, in particular to the "obscenely absurd listing of Foreign Secretary Warren Mullburn," as well as to their proffer of legal defenses and to the addition of Nigel Newhouse as additional counsel. Judge Mustafa indicated he would handle all of the objections at the time of the defense case...except for the objection having to do with Newhouse.

"Barrister Newhouse," Mustafa said, "you withdrew once before as the attorney for the accused. Now you return—just at the final moment. The time of trial. I am concerned that the conflict of interest that prompted you to withdraw previously might still exist—who knows? Perhaps you are doing your client more damage than good..."

Newhouse gestured for an opportunity to rebut the judge's insinuations, but Mustafa ignored him and plowed ahead.

"But I will allow you to continue as co-counsel for the accused. As long as your presence does not hinder or delay these proceedings, or cause confusion or prejudice. Do you understand?"

Newhouse explained that he did.

At that point four armed Palestinian guards brought in Gilead Amahn through a side security door. He was dressed in street clothes, which now hung a little on his frame and shuffled slowly, because his ankles were manacled and his wrists were handcuffed. One guard removed the restraints, and Gilead took the seat next to Will, who patted his back reassuringly as he sat down.

Then Zayed approached the lectern to give his opening argument, immediately turning toward the left of the judge's bench, where the eye of the closed-circuit TV camera was located.

His opening was fierce, rambling, and filled with hyperbole. Gilead was a "devilish monster of epic proportions, a beast of hatred and violence." The prosecutor forecasted that they would prove he was at the very place of the crime, giving the symbolic order to destroy the "Noble Sanctuary" of Islam—that he was a known associate of the Knights of the Temple Mount cult group, and an insider of their terror-planning committee made up of Louis Lorraine, Yossin Ali Khalid, and Scott Magnit. Even more, he pointed out, swinging his arms athletically around him as he looked into the camera, the accused, that "vile murderer" Hassan Gilead Amahn, was the group's spiritual "messiah"—the supposed reincarnation of the Caliph al-Hakim. "Having posed as the resurrected person of the last and greatest Caliph," Zayed went on, "he possessed great spiritual power to further deceive and inflame his followers—the deluded Knights of the Temple Mount."

Now Will was getting the picture. This was no opening statement. It was the public prosecutor's most creative press conference yet. Barred from giving official interviews to the media, he was delivering it to them instead via closed-circuit TV from the courtroom of the tribunal itself.

Then Zayed proceeded with an even craftier tactic. He described, at great length, the history of the Druze religion. How it had begun from the mind of two preachers, a Persian Afghani and a Turk, who taught a "religion of infidels" based on the "lying belief and utter falsity that the ruler of the Fatimid Empire, Caliph al-Hakim, was the perfect manifestation of God in human form—that after al-Hakim mysteriously disappeared from Cairo in the year 1021, he would one day return, a thousand years later, and bring with him God's Golden Age."

The prosecutor pointed out how the Druze disciples had been driven out of Egypt as infidels by the "holy followers of Allah." And, Zayed asked rhetorically, how can we blame the Muslims for that? After all, the Druze religion believes in reincarnation, and had merged Christian mysticism, Judaism, Islam, and Persian Zoroastrianism "into an unholy mix of lies and false ideas." The Druze declare, he explained, that they are not of the Arabs, but are from a race of Persians, Turks, and Kurds, intermixed with the Christian Crusaders for whom, during the Middle Ages, they acted as guides in the Middle East.

"The Druze men fight in the Israeli army, the IDF, and are the enemies of the Arab nations. But after a thousand years, that false religion has given forth birth, finally, to a bastard beast of murder and mayhem—the subcult of the Knights of the Temple Mount."

Will Chambers could not help but grudgingly admire the creative and seductive story the public prosecutor was spinning. It was polemical genius with public-relations charm. According to Zayed, the Knights further twisted the heresy of the Druze, linking themselves, historically, to the Templar Knights of the Crusader period. Then they used ancient Egyptian calendars and dating systems to construct a reincarnation date for the last Caliph that was a number of years *prior* to the full thousand years after 1021, as believed by the Druze. They predicted that the Caliph messiah would have to be Egyptian—which Gilead was—and be both from Cairo and then later reappear in Cairo—again those elements satisfied by Gilead—and have to match the religious upbringing of al-Hakim, who had a Shiite Muslim background and a Christian mother. In this latter regard, the prosecutor argued, Hassan Gilead Amahn fit the bill perfectly.

But the *coup de grace* was Zayed's explanation of the motive of Gilead and the Knights for destroying the "Noble Sanctuary" structures. They had, he pointed out, selectively accepted the Gospel predictions of Jesus, who said that the end would not come until the desecration had occurred within the Jewish Temple. But was that their real motive?

Zayed asked the question, but delivered another answer. That was their theological reason—but they harbored an even darker motive. The bombing of the mosques of the Muslims was, he submitted, a "bloodthirsty payback" for the perceived persecution of their Druze ancestors by Muslims over the last thousand years.

"This," the prosecutor exclaimed in closing, "was actually an attack not just on our sacred site—nor against the Muslims slaughtered—blown to bits—while praying on their knees—it was an attack on Arabs and Muslims everywhere."

Then he strode over to the defense table, pointed at Gilead Amahn, and declared, "Behold the man, this accused—who must pay for his blasphemous, murderous acts of violent hatred."

Lastly, he turned to face the judges and add his final edict.

"He must pay with his life."

55

"MAY IT PLEASE THIS TRIBUNAL," Will Chambers said as he began his opening statement, "I will not promise you passion or rhetoric. I won't try the ill-fated tactic of trying to inflame your judgment with personal attacks, violent epithets, or tales of genocide. You've heard enough of that from my opponent.

"I promise only proof, evidence, and facts. That ought to be enough, for that is the stuff of justice. And if this tribunal cannot find my client innocent on the basis of facts we will present—facts that are cold, hard, unmistakable, and that transcend politics, perhaps much to the embarrassment of some very powerful people— if this tribunal cannot judge on the basis of the clear evidence and ignore the geopolitical implications, then we have learned nothing in the thousand years since the wars that bloodied the streets of this city, the clash between the world's three great religions as they struggled for control of Jerusalem...and the Temple Mount."

Will stepped away from the lectern, adjusted his headset slightly, and continued, gazing directly into the eyes of the three members of the tribunal, who sat silently behind the shield.

He then described the three main points that would characterize his defense. First, he said, the defense would wholeheartedly agree with the prosecution that the leadership council of the Knights of the Temple Mount was guilty of mass murder of both Jews and Muslims.

But second, Will stressed, Gilead Amahn was no follower— let alone a leader—of that secret religious cult. Even the Druze had condemned the violent breakaway subgroup—why should we believe, Will asked, that Gilead Amahn, an evangelical Christian, would, in such a short time, have been converted to the Knight's violent ideology? Gilead's mere presence at the scene, preaching the gospel of Jesus Christ and the promised signs of His coming, was no proof that he was a conspirator.

Lastly, Will promised that the defense would launch a "fearless and ruthless pursuit of truth—revealing the dark forces that lurked behind the Knights and unmasking the true culprits behind the Temple Mount massacre."

When Will concluded and turned back to the defense table, his eyes met those of Samir Zayed, who was smirking and shaking his head.

The tribunal took a two-minute break before the prosecution introduced its first witness. In the interim, Newhouse bent down next to Will at the end of the counsel table.

"When I was much younger," he began, "and a great deal more foolish, I once promised my little daughter a certain birthday present. It was a much-sought-after doll—one of those dolls that was rather all the rage at the time, I'm afraid, advertised all over the telly. But by the time I got to the stores they were all sold out. So, at her birthday party I was a bit of a cad—couldn't deliver what I promised."

Will knew where he was going, and smiled. "One of the cardinal rules of trial law, I know," he replied. "Never make promises you can't keep. So…you're wondering about my 'unmasking the true culprits' statement…"

"Yes. Have to say I was. Hope you can do it, of course. That would be rather a brilliant turnabout, wouldn't it?"

"I know you don't have the benefit of all the evidence I've turned up," Will said in a hushed voice. "Some of it you haven't yet seen for lack of time. And some of it…well, honestly…I've kept from you for your own benefit. I don't know how else to say it, Nigel. If my defense blows up—and it could—there could be some dangerous repercussions. I'll be the target here—no reason for you to catch the shrapnel."

Nigel's eyes widened only slightly, and his mouth turned up at the sides. He paused for a moment, then rose slowly, patted Will on the shoulder and returned to his seat.

Then the three judges appeared, all in the room rose to their feet, and the prosecution called its first witness.

Dr. Azur el Umal entered the witness enclosure, took the oath, and sat down. He was a middle-aged man, with black hair combed up in a kind of pompadour look and a prominent nose that was slightly crooked, as if it had once been broken but not set properly.

El Umal was a PhD in chemical engineering with a specialty in explosives. He had, he explained, received training over the years in the development of explosive devices—with Interpol and Scotland Yard. He was presently employed, as he had been for many years, in the Preventative Security Organization and the General Intelligence Service of the Palestinian Authority.

"My job is to give expert opinions on the types of explosive devices used by various persons and groups, both legal and illicit, including violent organizations and those using terrorist tactics, after an attack or counterattack takes place."

"You said 'counterattack,'" the prosecutor noted. "What do you mean?"

"Sometimes Palestinian freedom fighters must...and occasionally do...use explosive devices in response to insurgent, excessive invasions by the Israeli forces. And there are accusations made, and an inquiry must be conducted relating to the nature of the counterattack, that kind of thing..."

El Umal went on to explain that he had been asked by the Palestinian Authority to conduct an analysis of the ballistics and properties of the explosives used to "decimate the Noble Sanctuary mosque structures and the Dome of the Rock, the place Muslims hold dear because it was the site of the ascension of the great prophet Muhammad."

He painstakingly described his initial view of the site less than one hour after the explosions—the emergency personnel scrambling to the scene, the wreckage, the screams of survivors and the dying who lay under the collapsed stones...and the body parts strewn over the plateau of the Temple Mount.

"It was horrific—more gruesome, more awful than words can describe," el Umal said softly. All of the judges seemed to be visibly moved by his description of the carnage.

He then explained how, over the course of the next two months, he had collected chemical samples from each of the two sites of the original blasts. He was able to determine, with a high degree of scientific certainty, the nature of the explosives used.

"The blasts were accomplished through the detonation of several hundred pounds of Composition-4, commonly known as C-4, explosives. They are often used by terror groups of all kinds."

"What advantage did the Knights of the Temple Mount gain by using this kind of explosives?" Zayed asked.

"First, they are the most energetic of all agents, outside of nuclear materials. Second, they are safe to handle. Until properly detonated with a blasting-cap-type device, you can set a C-4 on fire, even shoot a bullet into it, and it will still not explode."

"So," the prosecutor noted, "C-4 can be placed in a subfloor, as it was in the al-Aqsa Mosque or the Dome, left there for days or weeks, and protected until just the right moment—such as when hundreds of innocent Muslims are kneeling and peacefully praying—and then it can be exploded remotely as a tool of deadly surprise and utter genocide?"

Will rose to object to the argumentative and leading question. Judge Mustafa shifted his head from side to side.

"Objection noted. But overruled. Continue, Mr. Prosecutor." Zayed asked how the explosives had been detonated.

"Remotely—by the use of portable computers in two vehicles, each sending a wireless signal to a triggering device at the site of each of the payloads of C-4."

El Umal then identified the photographs of the two vehicles that had been captured and impounded after the blasts, noting that the computers and keyboards in the VW van and panel truck operated by Louis Lorraine and Yossin Ali Khalid had also been taken into evidence and analyzed.

"Those two vehicles were less than one-quarter mile," the prosecutor asked, "from where the prosecution's diagram, admitted into evidence by stipulation of both parties, places the presence of Hassan Gilead Amahn, who was preaching at the time, calling loudly for the destruction of the Temple Mount?"

"Yes. The vehicles that contained the computer detonation devices were within a quick walk from where Amahn was preaching."

"So, when the accused had given the command by referring to the obliteration of the Mount, then Mr. Lorraine and Mr. Khalid had time to run to their vehicles, detonate that massive store of C-4, and commit mass murder?"

Will again objected, this time to the reference to his client's "command," but again he was overruled.

El Umal answered, ending his direct examination concisely and dramatically.

"The plan was very effective—they obviously were able to run to their vehicles after Amahn's command and then key in the code for the detonation and send all of those praying Muslims to their death, all in a matter of minutes."

Zayed sat down, and Will wasted no time.

He asked el Umal about the benefits of C-4 explosives—"One of them being that they are not as easily accidentally detonated as, say, dynamite or nitroglycerin."

The prosecution expert agreed, then chuckled a bit, and explained that he had, as a young man, tried an experiment with nitroglycerin. "It succeeded. Unfortunately, I almost didn't. It sent me flying—I broke my nose in the fall."

Belgian Judge Verdexler smiled broadly and also chuckled.

"So, C-4 would be a good choice for a religious group bent on destroying the Temple Mount—but a group with no real prior experience handling explosives?"

El Umal was still thinking when Will clarified his question in a rapid-fire sequence of follow-up.

"In other words, C-4 can be effective in the hands of novices?"

"In a manner of speaking. Yes. But novices can rarely obtain it—"

"Which is why hardened terrorist groups often use it—but others can't often get hold of it?"

"Governments highly restrict the transfer and sale of it, yes…"

"True or false—terror groups can often be recognized by the 'explosives signature' or the 'technical fingerprint' of the type of explosion?"

"Sometimes. Not always."

"For instance, Hamas is known to use tri-acetone combinations in its bombs?"

"Sometimes…"

"Terrorists from Gaza often use nitric-acid components?"

"I've seen that, yes. But it has nothing to do with this case—"

"And the IRA—they were known to use Semtex, a variant of C-4, coupled with a detonation device using a Japanese-made miniature receiver?"

"Oh yes, I've seen that in my training with the Europeans."

"But the Knights of the Temple Mount—they had no prior history with explosives?"

"That we know of…that is true."

"And the explosive system used in this case—a huge amount of very refined C-4, coupled with a wireless-computer detonation method—have you ever seen that before?"

El Umal paused to reflect.

"Not to my knowledge."

"Is it possible, then," Will continued, "that the reason for that is exactly this—that we have, behind this bombing, the first-time appearance of a new entity—an entirely new kind of terror mastermind at work?"

The prosecution's expert could see where Will was going, and he sat up straight in the booth, then shifted a little before answering.

"Just because the engineering system appeared to be unique doesn't exclude the possibility that a prior, experienced terror group had refined its older techniques," but then he quickly added, "but as you say, the Knights of the Temple Mount and Mr. Amahn could be properly described as a new terror group using this new system."

Will decided to let the last comment go, at least for now.

"Now the exact form of C-4 used for the attack in this case—do you agree it was actually Semtex?"

"Well, yes. True. But not significant—"

"And of course no one is alleging, are they, that the Irish Republican Army was in any way involved in supplying those explosives?"

El Umal smiled. "Of course not."

"So where did the Knights get it?"

"What?"

"The Semtex."

"I have no idea."

"Was either Louis Lorraine, or Yossin Ali Khalid, or Scott Magnit for that matter—were any of them chemists? Or engineers? Or trained in any way with explosives?"

"Not that we know of—"

"So it's not only possible, but *probable,* that *someone else* provided both the explosives and the computerized detonation system to them?"

"These terror groups all have a custom of working together... networking..."

"So your answer is *yes?*"

"My answer is that someone in their terror network, whatever that was, did provide the explosives and the very sophisticated detonation system to the Knights."

"You did say 'sophisticated'?"

"Yes."

"Is it your opinion, Dr. Umal, that the more sophisticated the explosives and the detonation system, the more likely we are looking at the possibility of a state-sponsored terror attack?"

The witness shook his head violently at that.

"I see no such evidence—certainly, of any Arab League nation involved in this…if that is what you are insinuating…that would be preposterous. Of course, some have speculated that Israel might be behind the bombings…but we just don't know—"

"Of course—but didn't you make that exact point at the forensics conference in Paris last year—that extreme technical sophistication in explosives could mean state-sponsored terrorism?"

"I said it *could be* evidence of state-sponsored terrorism—one possibility. If you read my speech, which I presume you did, then you also noted that I mentioned other explanations."

"Yes, I did," Will replied. "And I did note another explanation. I will now read it—and tell me if you said this—'Overwhelming quantities of C-4 explosives coupled with technically advanced detonation systems can also point to terror-planning entities, or persons, with *powerful international connections and substantial financing capacity, or both.*'"

"Those sound like my comments."

The chemical engineer began to rise, but Will motioned for him to be seated.

"Just one more question. If you don't mind. After you disassembled the hard drives of the computers used as detonation devices—tell the tribunal—did you become sick?"

El Umal narrowed his eyes, studying Will. He finally gave his answer.

"I had the flu, I suppose. It must have been going around."

Then the prosecution's expert smiled, assured in his own mind that both the question—and the answer—were meaningless.

And Will Chambers smiled back.

But for a much different reason.

56

As HE CLIMBED INTO THE WITNESS BOOTH, Pastor Ralph Wyman of the Rolling River Bible Tabernacle looked uncommonly uncomfortable.

For the senior pastor of the small church that was tucked deep within the mountains of West Virginia—and as the former ministry superior to Gilead Amahn during the time he had served as the assistant pastor—making difficult decisions about his former subordinate's conduct was one thing. But being forced to testify against Gilead—to be called as a witness for the prosecution in an international terrorism trial—was quite another.

The Palestinian public prosecutor had subpoenaed Pastor Wyman to attend the trial. Wyman had consulted a lawyer, who wondered if the Palestinian Authority even had jurisdiction to require the pastor's appearance in Jerusalem. The matter might have ended there, except that the Landow administration decided to use the full measure of the power of the U.S. Department of Justice to transport Pastor Wyman to the trial before the Palestinian International Tribunal.

That single fact had represented the strongest sign yet that the U.S. government was weighing in on one particular side of the prosecution of Gilead Amahn. And it certainly wasn't on the defense side.

The pastor tugged a little at his necktie as he related the "troubling" things he had begun to notice about Gilead Amahn's "spiritual progress…and his ministry leadership."

"What kind of troubling things? How was your heart troubled by the accused?" Samir Zayed asked, with a well-varnished veneer of sympathy.

"Things he said."

"Things like 'God has called me for a prophetic calling'?"

"Not so much that..." the pastor replied.

"When he said he was going into the West Virginia wilderness for forty days and forty nights—that troubled you?"

"Well, we're a small church...I needed his help. He was actually sort of taking a leave of absence without prior notice to me...or to the board of elders for that matter."

"He was thirty years old at that time?"

"Yes. We actually had a little birthday party for him."

"How old does the Bible say Jesus was when He began His preaching?"

Pastor Wyman sighed.

"Thirty."

"And it was at the birthday party that Mr. Amahn announced he felt that God was calling him to 'have a wilderness experience.' Those were his words?"

"Yes," Pastor Wyman replied. "That is what he said. Don't know exactly what his meaning was."

"Did he explain in some fashion?"

"Well, not fully. But it had something to do, he said, with what he saw as his mission—to go to his own people first..."

"The Arab people—the Muslim Arabs?"

"Yes. To preach the gospel to them...which is fine by us. We are a gospel-preaching, missionary-supporting church, you understand...and so that wasn't really the problem...it just was that he hit us with this—no discussion—just out of the blue."

"And some of your church people, they said that Mr. Amahn was talking and acting as if he believed he was a kind of messiah for his Arab people?"

Will was on his feet.

"Objection. Hearsay."

"As you know," Judge Mustafa noted with a smile, "the rules of evidence adopted for this tribunal are not the American rules of law. They are international in origin. We respect American law, but it is not the last word—nor even the first word here, for that matter. Hearsay can be admitted here unless there is a substantial prejudice—"

"The prejudice is severe," Will countered, "because this is the linchpin of the prosecution's case—that Gilead Amahn believed in his own spiritual messiahship and thus knowingly served as a kind of religious guru for the Knights of the Temple Mount. If they are going to try to prove his criminal intent through this 'messiah' theory, then let them call witnesses directly."

"Oh, we will," Zayed said, rising confidently. "Perhaps the American lawyer has not read our pretrial list of witnesses. We will call a witness who will testify to that exact fact, which is why there is no real prejudice in our bringing this out indirectly through hearsay now. What harm can it cause? How can you honored judges possibly be misled by this testimony?"

Will looked to the panel, and noticed Judge Lee Kwong-ju nodding in agreement.

Judge Mustafa wasted no further time and overruled the objection. And he accompanied it with a look that was universal in any language. Will got the message. If he continued objecting, it would be at his own peril.

Ralph Wyman was shaking his head, as if he didn't want to answer.

The prosecutor asked the question again.

"Some of the folks in the church…a few of them…they said that…that Gilead acted like he had some kind of messiah complex—but I sure didn't ever see it. And I just want to say for the record here, for what it's worth, I never saw anything in his behavior or his walk with the Lord that in any way indicated he would ever hurt a single person…he was just not a violent person…he was as gentle as a dove."

Zayed moved that the tribunal strike the last part of Wyman's answer, and Judge Mustafa ordered it stricken. The prosecution rested.

Will Chambers' examination would be succinct.

"Does the New Testament speak of prophetic gifts—'Christ gave some to be prophets'—that's what it says of the gifting of the church of Jesus Christ?"

"Yes. It certainly does."

"And there is some difference of opinion among Bible-believing, born-again Christians about what that means, is there not?"

"Yes. That's true, Mr. Chambers."

"So when Gilead said he was called to fulfill a prophetic role, you didn't believe that he was necessarily departing from the doctrine of the Christian faith?"

"No, sir. I did not."

"Did Gilead preach on a few Sundays when you were away on church business—like at a pastor's conference, for instance?"

"Yes. He did."

"Were his messages recorded?"

"They were."

"Did you review them on your return?"

"I sure did."

"Anything objectionable about his teaching or preaching?"

"None whatsoever."

"Nothing bizarre or unbiblical?"

"Absolutely not."

"Did he ever preach violence or the condoning of violence?"

"Just the opposite. One of his messages was on the Beatitudes—'Blessed are the peacemakers.'"

Will sat down. Samir Zayed strode up to the podium with two pieces of paper in his hand.

"You had Mr. Amahn's Bible preaching recorded, didn't you?"

"Yes. I already said that."

"And won't you tell our esteemed judges why that was? Was it because a Mr. and Mrs..." and with that Zayed glanced down at one of the papers, "because a Mr. and Mrs. Cornwalls and a Mr. Goodie, from your church, said they suspected Hassan Gilead Amahn of believing some things that were not the truth from God—and so you decided to record his preaching to check him out for yourself?"

"What you are reading is probably from our church minutes that got subpoenaed. And of course, we objected to having to produce that…"

Then the pastor turned to the judges.

"We thought that the First Amendment of the U.S. Constitution, which protects the free exercise of religion of everybody, including churches—we thought that should mean that the government doesn't have the right to make a church open up its private board of elders meetings for everybody to look at—"

"Mr. Pastor Wyman," Judge Mustafa broke in, with a measure of irritation in his voice, "please don't lecture this tribunal. Attorney Chambers already filed arguments making the very same point you just made…and this tribunal has rejected those arguments. Please try to remember, sir—you're not in West Virginia now."

The look the witness in the booth gave the chief judge made it clear to everyone, that he was painfully aware of that last fact.

Prosecutor Zayed then pulled out the second piece of paper he had in front of him.

"And in another meeting of your church elders board," the prosecutor said, "several people said that Hassan Gilead Amahn seemed to be pretending to be some kind of 'special agent of God' rather than a regular preacher, is that right?"

"Well, that's what the minutes say…but that's not what the discussion was really about—"

But before the witness could continue, Zayed cut him off and sat down.

Will Chambers rose for recross-examination.

"The real discussion," Will said, "reflected in those minutes had to do with what, Pastor?"

"Had to do with the fact they thought Gilead was acting too autonomous…didn't check in enough with the board of elders. It had nothing to do with their believing that Gilead thought he was some kind of messiah. There is only one true Messiah, one mediator between God and man, as Scripture says, and that's the Lord Jesus Christ! And I'm sure Gilead is in agreement with that."

"Amen," Gilead said quietly from his seat at the counsel table.

Will sat down.

But Samir Zayed jumped up and walked quickly back to the podium for his final examination.

"Your church minutes say this, do they not Mr. Wyman— 'Gilead Amahn seems to be acting as if he reports directly to God only. He's acting like he has the role of a prophet or special apostle, but only Christ Himself was able to account directly to God without a structure of church authority. Does Gilead think he's equal to the authority of Christ?' The minutes of your own church say that, correct?"

Pastor Wyman's eyes were searching. Then they found Gilead Amahn. After a few seconds, he answered.

"They do say that. One of the deacons was making that point. And it got written down. But sir, I know what I remember about that meeting…and it was different than what that piece of paper makes it appear."

The prosecutor smiled. He lifted the copy of the church minutes high over his head.

"You choose your own mind about this rather than *what is written?*"

"I guess I do."

"Do you have your Bible with you, Pastor Wyman?"

The pastor smiled, retrieved his pocket Bible out of his suitcoat, and held it up.

Then Samir Zayed went in for the kidney punch.

"Now will you tell this tribunal, Pastor Wyman, do you believe, more, what is in your mind—or do you believe the Bible, *that which is written?*"

"If I can clarify one thing, you're a little bit confused on something...comparing church minutes to the Word of—"

"Answer, please, the question that I put to you!" Zayed exclaimed.

"You know what my answer is going to be—"

"Answer the question now."

"Of course," the witness said with exasperation, "I believe the written record, the written Word of God."

"That which is written?"

"Yes. What is written."

As Wyman slowly and awkwardly made his way out of the booth, Will understood something.

It had of course dawned on him, from the very beginning, that this criminal trial would inevitably and slowly constrict—like a powerful gravitational force, imploding to the core issue of what Gilead believed about himself, about his calling, and about God.

Will wondered how far it would go—the extent to which the public prosecutor would attempt to have those theological issues swallow this criminal case whole—like some massive, constricting anaconda consuming it in a slow and merciless digestion.

As the next prosecution witness mounted the stand inside the enclosure, Will knew he was about to find out.

57

"WHEN THE ACCUSED, HASSAN GILEAD AMAHN, appeared at the Islamic Conference in Virginia, America, what did he do?"

"He stood at the microphone on the floor of the hall and proceeded to insult all of those of us present—to hurl violent statements."

"What violent insults did he cast upon you personally?"

"That I have led millions of Muslims astray. He accused me of idolatry…that I was a teacher of false religion…that I was vain, and of a fleshly mind…that Jesus would judge me and all those who follow the heavenly religion of Islam…and that when Jesus returns—and he was yelling and screaming this—there would be judgment in store for us."

"Did the accused say when this judgment was coming?"

"He screamed at me, and at all of the clerics of Islam, that Jesus' coming was very, very soon—as if it were just around the corner. That judgment was about to begin."

"What happened then as a result of the insulting, disruptive behavior of the accused?"

"A riot broke out, caused by the violent rantings of the accused, this Hassan Gilead Amahn, and many people were injured, and many were very upset. It was a terrible thing."

Will Chambers rose to object. He had anticipated that the prosecution, in calling Sheikh Mudahmid, a mufti of Islamic terrorists, would use him to describe the Islamic Center riot. Thus they could paint Gilead as an agitator, a provoker of violence, and a hater of Islam.

"I move to strike the sheikh's last answer. Mr. Amahn was tried in a court of the Commonwealth of Virginia regarding that incident. He was found not guilty of any wrongdoing and declared innocent of provoking a public disturbance. Thus, the judgment of that court constitutes 'collateral estoppel' and precludes the issue from being retried."

Judge Lee Kwong-ju motioned to the chief judge, asking permission to engage defense counsel.

"For that doctrine to apply," Lee inquired, "there must be a common identity of issues and parties—here, comparing your opponent in Virginia in that case to your opponent here. That is true?"

"That is true, Your Honor," Will replied. "And I would suggest that the Commonwealth Attorney's office sought in that case—very aggressively, I might add—to prove my client guilty. The same motivation Mr. Zayed has in this case."

"But different crimes?"

"Yes."

"And different jurisdictions—one, a state court within a given nation—and here, an international court reviewing international crimes against humanity. Do you not agree?"

"True, but the underlying intent of the prosecution," Will continued to press, "is the same in both cases—to show that the accused, Mr. Amahn, provoked violence—"

"I believe we can accept the reciting of facts from this witness without being bound by the Virginia judgment in the other case," Judge Lee said matter-of-factly.

Judge Mustafa nodded vigorously. "Motion to strike is denied. Your objection is—*again*—overruled, Mr. Chambers."

"One last question," the prosecutor Zayed said. "Within just a few weeks of the statements of the accused, threatening judgment against Muslims, what terrible thing happened?"

Sheikh Mudahmid leaned forward in his chair. He stroked his long beard, carefully considering the question.

"Within just weeks of the accused...threatening Islam with judgment and destruction...the sacred site of the Noble Sanctuary, our holy mosques and the Dome of the Rock—our Muslim people—were blown up, destroyed, in a bloody act of vengeance by Mr. Hassan Gilead Amahn and his infidel followers, these Knights of the Temple Mount."

Zayed strode back to the prosecution's table with a look of consummate satisfaction.

As Will made his way to the podium he knew two things. First, he was forbidden from challenging the mufti about his own terrorist connections. That avenue of inquiry had already been barred by the prosecution's *motion in limine*, which had been granted by the tribunal in a pretrial ruling.

And secondly, he would have to be as cautious in handling this witness as a snake charmer lifting a cobra out of a basket.

"Sheikh Mudahmid," Will said in a confident greeting.

"Attorney Chambers," the witness said, nodding his head slightly but never taking his gaze off Will.

"Sheikh, you say that Gilead Amahn was insulting to you and to the other Muslim clerics. True?"

"Of course this is true. I have explained this very clearly."

"The insult came from Mr. Amahn's words?"

"His very presence in the Hall of the Prophet that day was an insult."

"So then, his *words* were neither insulting nor threatening—just his *presence?*"

"I did not say that. His words were an insult. And a clear threat."

"Then let's talk about his words. Why would you—a very powerful mufti, a religious leader who has many bodyguards protecting him wherever he goes, who issues religious fatwahs to thousands of his followers—why would you have felt insulted by the mere words of this young preacher?"

"He was insolent and blasphemous."

"Because he elevated Jesus the Christ, the Messiah, the Son of God, above the prophet Muhammad?"

"No one can elevate Jesus above Muhammad. Only Allah himself, may his name be praised, decides who rises and who falls. And that includes you, Mr. Chambers."

"So, did you agree with Gilead that Jesus is the Son of God?"

The sheikh was sending Will Chambers a scorching, withering gaze.

"Such things are for Allah to declare—and he has declared it in his holy book, the Quran. I would recommend that you read it."

"I have," Will shot back. "Let's take this section of the Quran, Sura 17:111—it says, 'Praise to God who took not a son...'—did I read that correctly?"

"You did."

"God has no son, then?"

"Allah has spoken."

"But Gilead Amahn preached to you that Jesus was indeed the Son of God and that He has the power to judge both the living and the dead?"

"The accused sitting there," and with that the sheikh pointed through the glass booth to Gilead Amahn, "said we were to be judged by Jesus, and he said, 'Woe to you false teachers of the law'—that is what he said."

"But he also said that Jesus has the power to forgive and to save?"

"What is this you are saying to me? Do you provoke me?"

"Gilead came to you and preached Jesus the Christ, who died on the cross to cleanse us, all of us, from the stain of sin, the perfect Lamb to the slaughter. But you, as a Muslim, do not believe that. And so you were insulted—not threatened with destruction or violence—but your heart was troubled because of the preaching of this young man, like a sword into your soul. Right?"

The sheikh was silent, seething.

"For the Quran teaches that Jesus did not die on the cross—is that not correct?"

"The Quran teaches that Jesus the prophet did not die on the cross. But such sayings are only for the wise who can accept them. Not for the fools who cannot."

"What were Gilead's last words to you that day, sheikh? What were they?"

"He condemned me to judgment and destruction!"

"Were those his last words?"

"Did I not already answer you?"

"Be very careful, sheikh," Will now raised his hand up, holding a sheaf of papers. "I have the verbatim transcript from the recording of the meeting at the Islamic Center that day—do you need me to show you what Gilead Amahn actually said?"

Sheikh Mudahmid glared, his rage now barely contained.

"Are you threatening me, Mr. Chambers?"

"Only with the truth," Will replied. "It is the only weapon I have."

"And what truth would that be?"

"That Gilead said to you, and I quote—'If you embrace Jesus the Messiah, His love is great enough to save you, Sheikh Mudahmid.'"

The sheikh paused and raised his head, his gaze still locked onto Will's.

"It was said. You have read it. What more must we discuss? Why didn't this infidel go to those who wanted to hear such rantings? Go where he was welcomed...rather than where he was not?"

"Perhaps," Will said calmly and quietly, collecting his papers from the podium, "because he felt that the sheep who have wandered are the ones most in need of being guided to the Great Shepherd."

Samir Zayed leaped up and objected, moving to strike Will's last comment.

Judge Mustafa hastened to grant the objection, and then issued a stern warning to Will to "cease from any further intolerant religious sermonizing during this trial."

Will, unperturbed, smiled, nodded in acknowledgment, and sat down.

Mira Ashwan rose and asked permission to question the witness as defense amicus curiae. The tribunal quickly granted her request.

"Sheikh Mudahmid," she began, "you were not present at the destruction of the Noble Sanctuary on the so-called Temple Mount, were you?"

"No, I was spared having to witness that slaughter of my people."

"You did not see, or hear, what Hassan Gilead Amahn did or said that day?"

"That is true."

"Are you a scholar who has studied the history of the so-called Temple Mount in Jerusalem?"

"Yes."

"On June 7, 1967, when the Israeli army forced its way into Jerusalem during the Six-Day War, was there a Jewish army rabbi who was with that army during its takeover of the so-called Temple Mount?"

"Yes, the history is very clear on that. I believe his name was Shlomo Goren. He was a general in the Israeli army and a rabbi."

"What was his recommendation?"

"That the so-called Temple Mount area—the Muslim mosques, the Dome of the Rock—*that they all should be bombed and exploded to make way for the appearing of the Jewish Messiah.*"

The sheikh's voice boomed throughout the courtroom.

"And did the military do that?"

"No...that one time the Israeli army did the correct thing. But, it does point out the obvious..."

"What is that?"

"That there has been a longstanding Jewish conspiracy to destroy the Muslim presence on what they claim is the Temple Mount."

"Why do you say, 'What they claim is the Temple Mount'?"

"Because I know there is no evidence of this mount being the site of the Jewish Temple of Solomon, which was rebuilt by Herod. No evidence—simply Jewish fables."

"And in regard to this Jewish conspiracy to destroy the Muslim structures on top of the mount—Gilead Amahn is Arab, is he not—not a Jew?"

"That is correct, as I understand it."

"So perhaps there was a Jewish conspiracy to destroy the Noble Sanctuary, but Gilead was simply not part of it?"

Will and Nigel Newhouse exchanged nervous glances. They both knew the dilemma they were facing. They did not want to divide the defense team by objecting to the questions of defense amicus curiae. On the other hand, Mira was venturing onto dangerous, speculative, and unproven ground.

"That is a possibility," Sheikh Mudahmid said, "but there is another explanation."

"What is that?"

"That such a conspiracy was larger than Mr. Amahn even knew himself—but he willingly allowed himself to be swept away in it."

Mira sat down. Will jumped up to do damage control.

"What proof do you have—facts, witnesses, documents, names, dates—of any Jewish conspiracy to blow up the Temple Mount, other than what you have already said?"

The sheikh paused for only an instant.

"Sixty-seven years living on this earth, in this land, watching the persecution of my people by the nation of Israel."

"In your sermons, you have said that 'America is the beast of unrighteousness...and Israel is its whore.' Have you not?"

"I'm sure you have copies of my words...to try to trick me."

"Other than your hatred for Israel, do have a single fact that establishes such a Jewish conspiracy?"

"I would have no hatred for Israel…if they would simply stop occupying our land and cease oppressing our people."

"I will take that as a 'no' to my question," Will said, and then launched his final question.

"And as for your statement that the Temple Mount has no historical claim to be the site of the Jewish Temple, rather than boring this tribunal with hours of proof and thousands of historical records showing the contrary, let me simply end with this. Is it correct that even the Supreme Muslim Council, which controlled the Temple Mount plateau in the 1930s, issued a written description of that area attesting that 'its identity with the site of Solomon's Temple is beyond dispute' and footnoting that with a reference to Second Samuel twenty-six, verse twenty-five?"

The sheikh was in no mood for further debate. So he glanced over at the judges, looked back at Will Chambers, and then answered diplomatically in a sudden exercise of restraint.

"They were mistaken."

58

IN THE ARTIFICIAL ENVIRONMENT of an extended trial, Will had gained, through his years of trial practice, the knack of becoming comfortable in uncomfortable surroundings. He had been in the Middle East for weeks now. And the trial had been grinding on for days. The nights in his hotel room were never very long, and he was always short on sleep. The days were filled by droning hours of testimony, argument, and inevitable delays while waiting for a witness to arrive, some document to be located, or the personal schedules of the three judges to be accommodated.

At the end of each day in court, he had developed a familiar routine. He would get about an hour alone with his client in a small side room before the guards would whisk Gilead back to the jail. Will had learned the names of the guards, and Gilead was teaching him a few Arabic words, which he would use when he greeted them. They would usually laugh at his bad pronunciation, and that would break the tension a little bit.

Will's discussions with Gilead were more for his client's benefit than for the strategy of the case. Of course Will planned on calling his client during the defense case, and they often touched on that. But Will had decided that proving Gilead's lack of guilt would have to rest on more than simply the force of his client's insistence on his own innocence. It would have to rest on other facts, and other witnesses.

In the final minutes of each of those end-of-the day meetings, Gilead usually asked that his lawyer pray with him. And so they would. The last time they were together, Will had closed in prayer and had found himself choking back emotion as he prayed for justice and protection for his client. It had just seemed to sweep over him suddenly, out of nowhere, and he was displeased that he had almost lost control with Gilead. He saw it as his job to be strong for his client—not to let his emotional attachment for this young man cloud his objectivity.

But with Will, the thought that this was not just a legal case but a life-and-death struggle would always rise to the top—like a desperate swimmer breaking to the surface, gasping for air.

One morning he was perusing one of the daily newspapers before dashing down to catch a cab to court, when a headline caught his eye. It said that the Palestinian Authority had finally decided on the form of death for Gilead Amahn in the event of his conviction. Under "great international pressure," they had reluctantly decided to utilize lethal injection rather than the other proposed methods, which included beheading, shooting by firing squad, and hanging.

He had not had the heart to raise that issue with his client yet.

After his daily post-trial testimony conference with Gilead, Will would meet with Nigel, Tiny Heftland, and Mira Ashwan for dinner. The four of them would then dine together at one of the four restaurants they frequented in Jerusalem. Will's favorite was a steakhouse specializing in Argentinian beef, the others were Indian, Hunan, and Italian.

The four dinner companions would usually start out with small talk or personal things about friends, family, or pastimes. But the conversation would always drift back to the case. Will mildly scolded Mira for her examination of the sheikh, saying it laid "more potholes in the road than asphalt," but Mira disarmed him by simply laughing at his illustration—forcing him, to the amusement of the others, to explain the process of asphalting roads.

Then, she turned the joke around against Will, noting that Westerners—and in particular Americans—automatically assume that Arabs in the Middle East know nothing of paved roads, modern transportation, or contemporary technology.

After the laughter had died down, Will reiterated his warning—that Mira needed to abandon her "Jewish conspiracy" theory. Mira accepted the admonition with a tolerant smile but said that she was still an independent amicus curiae in the case and was bound to argue those things that she thought best for the defense, whether the rest of the team agreed or not.

In the end, Will chalked up the Egyptian attorney's position to the strange and tortuous maze that was the Middle Eastern mind-set. With a thousands-of-years-old history of entrenched beliefs about people and land and conflict, he concluded that she probably believed she was actually being objective in her attack on Israel's position about the Temple Mount.

Nigel Newhouse had proved to be an invaluable asset. He had ably handled the cross-examination of a number of lesser supporting characters in the prosecution's legal drama.

For instance, on one day the Cairo police captain who had interrogated Gilead after his arrest in that city for illegal preaching was called by Samir Zayed. He described the melee caused by Gilead's appearance and his "religious disruption" near the entrance of the revered Muslim Citadel. That played into the prosecution's theory that Gilead was on a self-designed path to Armageddon—starting with his "spiritual preparation" in the "wilderness" of West Virginia, then causing a riot at the Islamic Conference in Virginia, following that with a minor religious war in Cairo, then heading off to Jerusalem for the "great battle" for the Temple Mount.

But on cross-examination, Newhouse adroitly undermined the police captain's explanation that he released Gilead from police custody only on the "insistence of the United States State Department who called me...and demanded his release."

"Captain," Newhouse asked, "you are in charge of the police barracks, are you not?"

"Of course."

"And being so close to the great Citadel," the barrister continued, "I assume that your police jurisdiction is considered a rather important one."

"I would think so," he answered with a smile.

"You make the decisions about who to arrest, who to charge with criminal offenses, and who to release?"

"That is my position—to make those decisions."

"You are to protect the property and the welfare of the citizens of Cairo, and to enforce the laws of Egypt?"

"Yes, yes, of course."

"You would never release a suspect who you know to be a threat to the safety of the people of Egypt?"

"I've never been known to have done that."

"And so, I would put to you," Newhouse concluded, "that the request from the American State Department notwithstanding, you ultimately released Gilead Amahn because you had no reason to conclude that he was a terrorist, or had terrorist connections, or posed a threat of terror to anyone—except to the sensibilities of Muslims and a few Europeans on vacation in Cairo who didn't wish to hear his message?"

After a short round of the captain's trying to challenge Newhouse's use of the term "terrorist," he finally capitulated. He had to admit he had had no reason at the time to believe that Gilead was a terrorist, and so he had released him.

But the prosecution's presentation of the testimony of several Israeli police at the scene of the bombings was a bumpier ride. They confirmed that Gilead Amahn had been preaching to a large crowd in the Old City of Jerusalem, under the shadow of the Temple Mount itself, and had then shouted out, "The Muslim buildings you now see atop the Mount—what will become of them? Can there be any question that God Himself must remove them first?"

And at that very instant, death and destruction had rained down from the bone-jarring fireball on the top of the plateau.

They also described how Louis Lorraine and Yossin Ali Khalid had both tried to flee in their vehicles and had been shot dead.

The prosecution made much of the fact that the two leaders of the Knights of the Temple Mount had not been firing back…merely fleeing. "Isn't it regrettable," Zayed noted in one of his questions, "that the world never received the benefit of an interrogation of these two men? Who knows what they might have told us? Perhaps much about other conspirators who helped plan this barbaric attack…"

To Will's disappointment, Mira followed up along the same lines also in questioning the Israeli police, still doggedly pursuing her "Jewish conspiracy" theory.

At Will's suggestion, Nigel Newhouse, nailed down one small, discrete line of testimony from the police at the scene. They confirmed what Will knew—that Israeli intelligence officials had impounded the two escape vehicles and the computer detonation systems inside them and had evaluated them quickly before being ordered to turn the evidence over to the Palestinian Authority.

Samir Zayed did not seem to understand the significance of this. Will hoped that, eventually, the full weight of that evidence would collapse down on the prosecution. But it was a gamble, and Will knew it. Only time would tell whether he would be able to pull it off.

The remaining witnesses called by the public prosecutor were part of what Will called the "emotional piling-on." Several emergency personnel testified to the carnage at the scene—the dead, the dying, and the disfigured. The horror of combing through rubble and rock and dust and body remnants.

Relatives of the victims were called to show pictures of their loved ones and to cry for justice for the dead and the maimed. After several days of such testimony the effect was emotionally and morally fatiguing.

For Will, and certainly for the rest of the defense team, one thing was brutally clear. A horrendous crime against humanity had been committed. And the inner circle of the Knights of the

Temple Mount was clearly responsible. The only remaining issue was a chillingly simple one: Was Gilead Amahn a knowing and willing part of that inner circle?

That evening after dinner, Will and Nigel and Tiny worked for several hours at the makeshift offices next to the Holy Land Institute for the Word, preparing for the next day of trial. After Nigel had headed to bed, Will and Tiny continued to work together. Tiny's subpoenas had been accomplished, and now the two were discussing the other project the big investigator was working on.

It had to do with his contacts inside the Mossad and a lead that Mike Michalany had turned up. It was still too early to determine whether that was going to bear fruit. Will tried not to ponder what would happen if his outrageously audacious plan did not work.

After returning to his hotel room that night, around one in the morning he called home. Fiona's concert was coming up, but all the details had finally been ironed out. Then Will talked to Andy.

"You know what I take to court every day with me?"

"What?" Andy asked.

"That faith badge you gave me—"

"No way! Really?"

"Yep. Keep it in my shirt pocket during trial so I can think of you when I'm in court. Oh, and one other thing…"

"What?"

"I think I'm going to talk to a former client of mine. He runs that summer baseball program down in North Carolina, at Baseball Island—remember I told you about that? How about we sign you up for this summer?"

"All right! That is so cool!"

"Let's talk it over with Mom, see what she says. Okay?"

"Sure thing. Wow, that's so great…"

After a little pause, Andy asked, "When are you coming home, Dad? We miss you…"

"I miss you too. I love you, Andy. Sorry we've been separated. This trial still has a ways to go. I'll come back as soon as I can."

"Mom wants to talk to you again…Love you, Dad—'bye…"

"So," Fiona said, "who's in the dock tomorrow?"

"Scott Magnit. The prosecution's star witness."

"I'll be praying for you, darling."

"I'll need it."

"How's Gilead holding up?"

"Very average…"

"That poor man…so…This house is awfully empty without you. Help Gilead. Then hurry home to me. Are you keeping safe?"

"Sure."

"I had a nightmare last night," Fiona said. "Da was in the dream, along with you. You were both talking. I had something I had to warn you both about…but I couldn't get to you in time. You both just faded away before I reached you…"

"I'm not going anywhere, sweetheart. The Lord will get me back to you—and then we can do some talking about the rest of our lives…"

After their final goodbyes, Will hung up and gazed around his hotel room littered with files and papers from Gilead's case, coffee pots, and trays of half-eaten room-service food. Then he felt the full weight of the realization. He still had a long way to go in the Gilead Amahn trial before he could once again see the Blue Ridge Mountains from his front porch and hold his wife in his arms.

59

"AND SO, MR. MAGNIT, AS YOU TOLD US THEN, you were religiously confused and were searching for, in your own words, a 'greater spiritual truth,' and that is when you met Yossin Ali Khalid in Jerusalem?"

As Scott Magnit considered the prosecutor's question, he was not the same man he had been at the time he'd met Khalid. Or at least he didn't *look* like the same man.

After his capture and his agreement to cooperate with the Palestinian public prosecutor, the twenty-nine-year-old American had been cleaned up. Gone were the tattered clothes and the Knights of the Temple Mount T-shirt that, despite Khalid's warnings, Magnit had worn anyway underneath a dirty sweatshirt on the day of the bombings.

Now, as he sat in the witness chair within the booth in the Orient House courtroom, he was clean shaven, his formerly long, straggly hair was neatly trimmed, and he was wearing a dark green suit with a white shirt and red tie—the colors of the Palestinian flag—conveniently supplied by the public prosecutor. The suit was a little too big. He also was sporting a new pair of glasses.

Under direct examination by the prosecutor, Magnit had described how he was raised by divorced parents in northern California. His father was a member of a Unitarian church, his mother a follower of a "new age" kind of religious movement. He had graduated from a small local college with barely passing grades. He took peyote, dabbling in Native American religion, and later in Westernized versions of Buddhism and Hinduism.

He eventually made his way into the Peace Corps and was assigned to Africa. Discussing religion with another Corps volunteer, he had heard about the strange and little-known religious colony of the Druze, who worked and lived in the remote agricultural areas of northern Israel, near the Golan.

Magnit had been particularly intrigued when he'd heard that the Druze were looking for the imminent appearance of a "Messiah" figure—the reincarnation of the Caliph al-Hakim, who had mysteriously disappeared a thousand years before.

So after leaving the Peace Corps, he had worked a few odd jobs, saved up some money, and traveled to Israel, landing in Tel Aviv. He had traveled first to Jerusalem in search of a guide who could introduce him to the Druze community—which is where he'd met Khalid.

"Back then," Magnit recounted, "Yossin's father, Caliph Omar Ali Khalid, was still alive, but he was—you know—really sick. But even so, Omar was sort of running things."

Zayed had Magnit describe in great detail how he had never reached the Druze community. He had just stayed with Yossin, his wife, and Omar in their dingy little apartment in the eastern section of Jerusalem. They would just "sit around and drink tea, and read the Quran and compare it with the Old Testament and the teachings of the Caliphs and the writings of some Christian mystics who lived out in the desert."

The American explained how he learned that the Knights of the Temple Mount started as members of the Druze but had broken away and formed their own secret group as the time for the appearing of the "last and greatest Caliph" approached—the "messiah who would bring with him God's Golden Age," as he described him.

"We—the Knights—felt we had discovered some stuff the Druze missed." There was an air of superiority in Magnit's voice.

"Like what?"

"Well, like the fact that Yossin and Omar said they could trace their lineage directly back to the intermarrying of Druze with some of the Templar Knights, you know…the guys in the Crusades. There was a lot of talk about the hidden secrets and treasures of the Templars, and the search for the Holy Grail, which was, like, the cup supposedly used by Christ in the Last Supper and all of that…"

"What other things did you believe you had discovered that the Druze had not? Anything about the time of the appearing of the messiah—the reincarnation of the Caliph al-Hakim?"

"Louis and Yossin had figured out when he would appear—and it was sooner than the Druze had counted on."

"And their calculation would mean that this so-called messiah, the reincarnation of the Caliph al-Hakim, was supposed to appear when?" Zayed asked.

"Earlier this year—just before the bombings took place," Magnit replied.

"Now, we will get back later to the timing of this so-called appearing," the prosecutor noted, "but tell this honorable tribunal—tell us, what were the signs to be of the coming of this last prophesied Caliph, according to what the Knights believed?"

"Well, first, he had to be, like, an Arab, and from Cairo, and have a Shiite Muslim background but with a Christian mother—because that was all stuff that was true of Caliph al-Hakim."

"And further," Zayed probed, getting excited, "where was the site he was to appear?"

Scott Magnit knew the importance of this series of questions and answers. So he took his time, first taking a sip of water from the glass next to his seat.

"In Cairo, Egypt. That's where the original Caliph disappeared, ascending directly to God in the year 1021."

"Now," Zayed lowered his voice almost to a whisper, bending toward the microphone at the podium, "tell us this—did someone actually appear in Cairo, Egypt, earlier this year, preaching publicly the coming of the new kingdom of God—someone who arrived at the exact time predicted by the calculations of the Knights of the Temple Mount, and who fulfilled all the prophesies about the new Caliph al-Hakim, the supposed messiah?"

This was Magnit's moment. He knew it. He nodded slowly, turning to the three judges in their red robes behind the wall of glass. Then he offered his answer.

"Yeah—Mr. Hassan Gilead Amahn there, he arrived in Cairo right on the money. And he seemed to fulfill every one of those things—from Cairo originally...a Shiite Muslim background... mother a Christian...the whole nine yards. It was like, you know, a home run, bases loaded."

"But Mr. Magnit," Zayed allowed a tinge of skepticism to creep into his voice, "was this information about the reincarnated Caliph—the exact date of his predicted arrival, his required background, the fact he was to make a dramatic appearance in Cairo and not somewhere else—was this kept a secret, or was it allowed to be leaked to the public?"

"Well, not exactly leaked to the public," Magnit said, bobbing his head a little from side to side. "It was supposed to be kept a really tight secret among just a few of us in the inner circle."

"Who?"

"Louis Lorraine...and then Yossin, of course, and his dad, Omar, knew about it too but he died...and then there was me. That was it."

"How many followers did the Knights have on the day of the bombings?"

"Couple dozen regulars and maybe a hundred hangers-on."

"Were they ever told the details of the anticipated appearing of the Caliph?"

"Not really...not the particulars...just real general stuff. See, this stuff was what they called the 'esoteric mysteries.' They were to belong only to a small group that went through the initiation and hung in there for a long time and could be trusted. That sort of thing. The small inner circle."

"So," Zayed said, his voice building now, "you were to have kept these details very secret?"

Magnit paused and looked down.

"Yeah. I was."

"Did you?"

Again, Magnit looked down dramatically, then turned to address the tribunal directly.

"Not really."

"How many others did you tell?"

"Just one person."

"And who was that?"

Magnit took a deep breath, then exhaled. And then he replied.

"Hassan Gilead Amahn. The accused right over there."

Will Chambers had his attention laser-beamed on the faces of the judges. Mustafa was alternately nodding and shaking his head vigorously. Judge Verdexler had his head leaning a little against his hand, which was supported by an elbow on the bench, but he was entirely unmoving, transfixed by the testimony.

Judge Lee had no expression, but his eyes were flitting from Scott Magnit to Gilead Amahn at the defense table, then back to Magnit in the booth.

"And when did you share this information with the accused?"

"The year before the bombing. In Jerusalem. The Knights would hold these Bible studies…sort of religious discussions…to get new members. And the accused, Mr. Amahn over there, he showed up last year. Talked some. Seemed friendly. We took a break during the Bible-study meeting and I introduced myself. We talked a little."

"How did you get on the subject of the coming Caliph—the supposed messiah of the Knights of the Temple Mount?"

"Well, he's the one…Gilead Amahn…he sort of brought it up. He says to me, 'You know He's coming again.' I say to him, 'Oh yeah?' Amahn says, 'Yeah, the Messiah is on His way here…to the Middle East. We need to get ready. The signs are coming together.' And I'm thinking, *Maybe he's in the know…maybe we ought to think about him to be part of the circle…*"

"So, what did you tell him at that point in the discussion?"

"I'm sorry…what was the question?" Magnit was shifting a little in his chair.

"What did you tell him?"

"Well, about the details…"

"Which ones?"

"About, you know, all of the stuff we just talked about—the appearing of the Caliph and all that…"

"Did you tell him about how the Knights had calculated the date, and what the date was?"

"Yeah."

Will rose to his feet, straining not to overreact, but objecting to the "clear attempt of the prosecution to lead this very critical witness down the primrose path—"

Mustafa shook his head.

"And what primrose path would that be?" he asked with an amused smile. "We do not have many primroses here in the Middle East, Mr. Chambers. I am sure Barrister Newhouse would tell you that they have many of that species where he comes from, but not over here in the desert…"

Judge Verdexler smiled and leaned back in his chair.

"Leading and suggestive questioning," Will said tersely, "is never permissible in the prosecution's direct examination of a witness. But it's particularly outrageous in the examination of a witness like this—someone so integral to the prosecution's theory."

Mustafa smiled and glanced over at Samir Zayed.

"Mr. Public Prosecutor, try to let the witness answer the questions himself—in his own way. Let's hear what he has to say."

Zayed bowed slightly and resumed his questions, but with little correction.

"So, you told Mr. Amahn when, this year, the supposed Caliph-messiah was to appear?"

"Yes."

"And where? In Cairo?"

"Yeah, that too."

"And what of the personal characteristics of the Caliph...did you also tell him these?"

"Well, sure. I didn't think in a million years he had that kind of background. Shiite Muslim, Christian mother, born in Cairo. I mean, what were the odds of that? Like one in a zillion?"

"Did you tell Mr. Lorraine or Mr. Khalid you had shared that information with Mr. Amahn?"

"No."

"Why not?"

"They would have got really teed off at me. It was secret stuff. Not for public consumption."

"In retrospect, have you now concluded anything about how Hassan Gilead Amahn used that information?"

Scott Magnit squinted and half-tilted his head, scrunching up his face at the question.

So Zayed repeated the question again, this time much slower, and emphasized the words 'used that information.'

"Oh, right," Magnit said, the lightbulb going on. "Yeah. I think that Mr. Amahn there just...you know, like, took the information I gave him that I wasn't supposed to, and then he just made sure he was in Cairo at the right time to make it look like he was the reincarnation of the Caliph..."

Will objected to the answer as "improper opinion evidence, and commenting on the state of mind of the accused."

This time Judge Verdexler asked permission to weigh in.

"Counsel," he said, "opinion evidence, even under the federal rules in the United States, can come in from a lay witness like Mr. Magnit, as long as it is reasonably based on the perception of the witness."

"But what perception is being conjured here?" Will asked, his voice strained with frustration. "Mr. Magnit wasn't in Cairo when Mr. Amahn arrived there. This is unabashed, wild speculation on the part of this witness."

"And what is your theory, Mr. Chambers," Verdexler snapped back, "your alternative as to why the accused showed up in Cairo when he did? That he *really was* the reincarnation of the Caliph al-Hakim come back from the dead after a thousand years? Is that what you are planning to argue?"

Mustafa and Verdexler were both chuckling.

"Not at all," Will said in a controlled but impassioned tone, "rather, that Gilead Amahn's arrival in Cairo just happened to coincide with the wild calculations of a small religious cult—and that this witness, Scott Magnit, is fabricating his story. Lying to this tribunal."

There was a momentary hush in the courtroom. Then Verdexler responded in a calm but pointed fashion.

"You are free to conduct your defense any way you want," the Belgian judge said, speaking slowly enough to ensure that the translators were getting it to Will, "but you have a very high hill to climb in order to prove that theory," he concluded. Judge Mustafa nodded along with him.

Lee Kwong-ju was simply staring at the defense attorney.

Zayed, empowered by the last interchange between the bench and Will Chambers, brought his direct examination to a close by asking Scott Magnit whether Gilead Amahn attended any "inner circle" meetings in the weeks just prior to the bombings.

"Yes. Many."

"Meetings where you, and Mr. Lorraine, and Mr. Khalid, were actually planning the bombing of the Temple Mount?"

"Yes. That's right."

"What was your understanding," Zayed asked with an air of triumph in his voice, "of what Mr. Amahn's role would be on the day of the bombings?"

With only a moment's hesitation, Magnit answered.

"He was to give the signal—in his preaching down along the streets of the Old City—when the bombs were to be detonated."

"And did he?"

"Oh yeah," Scott Magnit replied, "he did. He sure did."

60

"Scott, I want you to look at these documents," Will Chambers said, handing several marked exhibits to the armed bailiff, who in turn slipped them in to the witness through a small tray mounted in the glass booth. Will was now homing in on the specifics of the several statements given by Magnit to the Palestinians following his arrest.

"Look at your first statement, given to the Palestinian Authority police on day two of your arrest. Here is all you say about Gilead Amahn:

> Hassan Gilead Amahn was at a Bible study held by the Knights of the Temple Mount last year. I met him then. On the day of the bombings, Mr. Amahn was on the streets of the Old City of Jerusalem. He was preaching to a crowd of people. At a certain point, when Mr. Amahn spoke about the Temple Mount in his preaching, then Yossin Ali Khalid gave the signal to Louis Lorraine, who went to his vehicle to detonate a bomb. And Khalid ran to his vehicle to do the same. I got a cab driver, one of our group, who got Mr. Amahn into his cab and was to drive him around, in a hurry, to the walls of the Old City that face the Mount of Olives. At the point where the "Golden Gate" was located, the bricked-over wall was to be blown up, and Mr. Amahn was supposed to be told to run in through the opening, just like the Messiah.

"And that is the *sum total* of everything you said at that point, about Gilead Amahn, isn't it?"

"That's what this paper says. Right."

"But in the rest of that twenty-two-page statement, you give a detailed account of your own involvement in the plot to destroy the Muslim structures on the Mount, right?"

"Well…yeah. I said I was involved."

"You confessed to knowing about the bombs…about the detonation devices in the two vehicles…to knowing that Lorraine would set one explosion off and Khalid the other. That you met with them and planned all of it out in advance. You admitted that in this statement given on day two after your arrest. Correct?"

"Yeah. I said I did—"

"But tell me, where in this twenty-two-page statement do you ever say that Hassan Gilead Amahn was involved in the planning of the bombing—or even that he knew about the plan to explode the Temple Mount?"

The witness fumbled through the multipaged exhibit in his lap.

"Take your time," Will said.

After several minutes of deafening silence Magnit spoke up.

"I guess I never said anything like that in this statement."

"So, let's go to the second statement you gave to the Palestinian police," Will said, his voice rising slightly now. "Day four of being in police custody. Earlier that day you were injured. After you get hurt, suddenly you decide to sign a second confession. Now that injury—it must have happened while the police were right next to you. You said you were going down some stairs, right?"

"Yeah. Down a stairway. Stone stairs."

"A couple of Palestinian police next to you—obviously—because they would not have allowed you to walk around freely. Correct?"

"I think there were three of the Palestinian cops with me."

"And—what was it—you tripped on a loose shoelace and tumbled down the stairs?"

"I can't remember all the details. I hit my head. Sort of blacked out."

"You can't remember whether it was a loose shoelace that you tripped on?"

"I'm a little fuzzy on the whole falling-down deal."

"I thought a few minutes ago you said you tripped because you were wearing jail slippers. I have it right here in my notes. Didn't you say that in your testimony?"

Samir Zayed rose quickly and objected that Will was "pestering Mr. Magnit. Harassing the prosecution's witness." The prosecutor had one hand behind his back and was gesturing athletically toward Will Chambers with the other.

Judge Mustafa was nodding in agreement, but Judge Lee was raising his hand discreetly, motioning to be heard. Mustafa nodded in his direction, and the Korean spoke up.

"The purpose of cross-examination is to put the prosecution's case to the test. Challenge the credibility of the witness—test memory. The defense should be given some leeway, I think."

Mustafa and Lee both looked at Judge Verdexler, who was between them. Verdexler glanced over at Scott Magnit in the booth. And then at Will. Then he gave a kind of reluctant shrug in agreement with Judge Lee's position.

"Mr. Chambers," Mustafa warned, "be careful not to harass the witness. This tribunal will not tolerate that. But...you may proceed with your question."

Will asked that the last question be reread to the witness. Behind the one-way wall of dark glass at the back of the courtroom, the English-speaking translator repeated the question. Magnit listened in his earphones and then looked up at Will.

"I'm not sure how it happened."

"That wasn't my question. I was asking, do you agree that a few minutes ago you said you fell because of the jail slippers you were wearing?"

"Maybe I did."

"But now you don't know why you fell?"

"Not really. I said I can't really remember."

"So—you don't recall whether it was a loose shoelace…or the jail slippers…or maybe being pushed by the police officers down the stairs—"

Zayed leaped up and waved his arms frantically.

"This cannot be allowed! The defense attorney is asking illegal and improper questions—attacking the honesty and legality of the Palestinian police. This is nothing but a dirty political trick to slander the Palestinian Authority, and I object!"

Mustafa was not inclined to listen to argument or comments from the other judges.

"I have warned you, Mr. Chambers—and these appear to be nothing but unfounded and wild accusations concealed as cross-examination questions."

Will waved a photograph in front of him, then motioned for the bailiff to take it to the witness booth.

"Please, Your Honor, before you rule on this," he countered quickly, "I've handed what has already been marked and stipulated into evidence as a photograph taken by the International Red Cross when they paid an unannounced visit to the jail facility shortly after Mr. Magnit's injury. Let the witness look at it and see if it will refresh his memory."

Judge Lee was nodding but Mustafa was not convinced.

Judge Verdexler's brow was wrinkled. Then he broke his silence.

"Your Honors, I think refreshing the witness's memory is appropriate—given his own testimony that he can't fully recall the incident." Mustafa slowly yielded and permitted the witness to view the photo.

"Look at the photo," Will continued, "blackened eye…what seems to be a broken nose…cut lip…and bruising on—well, the photo seems to show bruising on *both sides* of your face—isn't that correct?"

Magnit was staring at the photo. Now his face had the look of barely camouflaged internal misery.

"How were you able to fall down the stairs and beat up *both sides* of your face?"

Magnit was unresponsive in his quiet torment.

"No answer to that?"

Magnit shook his head.

"Let the record reflect," Will announced, "that the witness has no answer."

"And also on this photo," Will's voice now quickened, driving home the point, "a red streak across your cheek—as if someone had whipped your face with a belt or a rope—you do see that?"

"Yes," Magnit muttered, barely audible. Now, Lee and Verdexler were leaning forward to get a better look at the witness's demeanor.

"Do you have any explanation for how those marks could have occurred from a fall down some stone steps?"

"Not really."

"Tell the truth," Will said in a penetrating voice that made one of the prosecution assistants jump a little. "Did someone cause you to fall that day?"

"I said I can't remember what happened."

"Push you down the stairs?"

"Can't remember."

"Strike you in the face?"

Now Magnit was silent, but he was shifting back and forth in his chair.

"Whip your face?"

Magnit was still nonresponsive, and so Will asked the tribunal to order the witness to answer the question. But before Mustafa and the other judges could consider the request, Magnit blurted something out.

"Can't remember. That's my answer. I said I can't remember."

"But the fact is—that after getting these injuries," Will continued pressing in, "then, and only then, is when you decide to give a second confession, and at that time you implicate Gilead Amahn in this bombing for the first time—by saying that he had attended planning sessions with your group before the bombing. Right?"

"You could say that."

Now Will relaxed a bit, and he moved back to the podium and then picked up another document.

"Look at the *third* confession you gave," Will said. "This was on day ninety of your imprisonment by the Palestinian police. Now this last confession was given after your meeting with the public prosecutor, Mr. Zayed here. Right?"

"After we met, yes."

"And you gave it after you signed a document called a 'plea agreement'—a contract with the prosecution where you agreed to say certain things about Gilead Amahn. That he not only attended planning sessions, but that he knew about the plan to blow up the Temple Mount, and that he willingly agreed to give the signal for the detonation of the explosives—is all of that true?"

"Sure."

"And the public prosecutor also agreed to do something for you in return, according to this agreement. True?"

"Don't know what you're getting at..."

"Well, didn't the public prosecutor agree, in the plea agreement, that in return for your testimony against Gilead Amahn, he would not seek the death penalty against you, but ask only for a life sentence?"

Magnit looked over at Samir Zayed, who was staring back.

"I guess that's what the agreement says...but everything I said against Mr. Amahn was true."

"All of it—absolutely true?"

"Sure."

"In that plea agreement did you also agree to confirm in court that your accusations against Gilead Amahn are all true, and agree to the stipulation that, if you admit to lying, then the prosecutor can retract the agreement, and seek the death penalty against you?"

"Something like that."

"So if you were to say today, 'I only gave that second statement against Gilead because I was beaten up, and I only gave that third statement to save my life, but those accusations I made against Gilead are actually false'—if you did that, then the public prosecutor would seek to put you to death. That's the real situation—correct?"

Scott Magnit had enough. His eyes were closed. His lips were pursed together and working and his face was tensed, as if he were being forced to chew something indigestible and disgusting.

"Look—all I know is what I put in those confessions."

"Are you willing to tell this tribunal the truth about Gilead Amahn?"

Magnit's eyes were still closed. But his lips parted.

"All I know is what I put in those statements…"

Will announced the end of his cross-examination. Zayed then scurried to the podium, asking Magnit several times, in several different ways, whether the "third statement was the most complete and accurate of all your statements, because only then did you have the opportunity to think back clearly about the accused, and the bombing, and get in all the facts, and for no other reason."

Magnit quickly agreed to that, hoping to be relieved from the witness booth.

But Will stepped back up for re-cross.

"One last area," Will said quietly. "You were very scared when you were told by the public prosecutor that, unless you pointed the finger at Gilead Amahn, you'd get the death penalty, right?"

"I was pretty scared all during the time I was in jail. Not just that time."

"But you were the most scared on day ninety, when you were told that, unless you gave a third confession and actually accused Gilead of being a co-conspirator, on conviction you'd be put to death?"

"I can't say that. I was nervous all the time," Magnit answered, trying to muster a last vestige of bravado.

"Oh? Is that true?"

"Yeah."

Will then placed some transparencies on the scanner for the exhibit viewer, which displayed the images on the screen in the courtroom wall. Two signatures of Scott Magnit were shown.

"Farthest to the left—your normal signature, written on the first confession. Correct?"

"Yeah."

"Middle signature—that's your signature on the second confession, after your serious injuries—a little unsteady, but pretty normal?"

"Yeah. I guess."

Then Will put the third transparency on the scanner. A third signature appeared on the courtroom viewing screen.

"Third signature...were you on any drugs that day?"

"No."

"I ask because—well, just look at that signature, Scott. It's very zig-zaggy—looks like it was written when your hand was shaking considerably. Like it was shaking uncontrollably. Was your hand in fact shaking like that when you signed the plea agreement and your third confession statement, wherein you made your most serious accusations against Gilead Amahn?"

Magnit saw no way out. There it was—his signature zoomed up by a power of ten, displayed on the screen for all three judges to see. It was written in a jagged and sharply erratic hand, almost comical in its bizarre appearance...were it not for the tragic import of the document he had been signing. But now, sitting in the glass witness booth, Scott Magnit had little choice.

"Was your hand shaking from fear?" Will asked again, his voice ringing out.

"I guess so," Magnit replied, and then he took a deep breath and exhaled slowly, like a swimmer filling his lungs before plunging into the deep.

61

AFTER WILL'S CROSS-EXAMINATION of Scott Magnit, the witness was excused. He exited the glass-enclosed site of his inquisition and was escorted out by several Palestinian police. Then Samir Zayed approached the podium. He paused dramatically, then announced that the prosecution was resting its case.

Will immediately moved that the court dismiss the case. He argued that the Palestinian public prosecutor had failed to make out a prima facie case that Gilead had willingly and knowingly participated in the conspiracy of the Knights to carry out the bombing attack on the Mount. He pointed out, further, that the Ninth Circuit of the United States Court of Appeals had struck down portions of America's antiterrorism law that had outlawed "the providing of material support" for terrorism—on the grounds that the law didn't sufficiently require that the accused *actually know* he was assisting a terrorist conspiracy. And because the Palestinian International Tribunal had based its criminal law for Gilead's case on the American model, "we should be very diligent," Will submitted, "to require the prosecution to prove that Gilead actually knew he was aiding the murder and mayhem of the Knights."

But Judge Verdexler, after pointing out that even he knew that the Ninth Circuit was more often overruled by the U.S. Supreme Court than any other federal circuit, noted, "This tribunal is not bound, in any event, by United States law. We are an international body." Both Judge Lee and Judge Mustafa nodded at that.

Will's final point was also quickly rejected by the judges. He directed the tribunal's attention to the fact that the criminal law specifically exempted "the providing of religious materials" from its reach. "Gilead's preaching therefore cannot be deemed a terrorist act or part of a criminal plot," he contended.

But Judge Lee responded that the exemption was intended to cover the providing of written religious literature, not an act of preaching that—under the prosecution's theory—was a signal for the detonation of explosives.

After the court denied Will's motion for dismissal, the tribunal adjourned for the day. Nigel Newhouse tried to be optimistic, focusing on what had been achieved in the cross-examination of Scott Magnit.

"Well, as we both know," Nigel said to Will in a hushed voice, since the public prosecutor was still lingering at his counsel table, "it's rarely a matter of getting a complete obliteration of the key prosecution witness. But I think, at a minimum, you neutralized Scott Magnit in your cross. Good show, Will."

The two shook hands. Then Mira Ashwan came over and shook hands too, smiling and congratulating Will on a "truly excellent examination" of Magnit. During that interrogation she had sat quietly at counsel table, taking copious notes but asking no questions.

The three lawyers chatted briefly about the schedule for the next day. Both Nigel and Mira, and even the Palestinian prosecutor, knew who Will's first defense witness would be. The prosecution had announced there would be strenuous objections raised on that issue. And they all knew there was likely to be a frenzy of legal fireworks. But what Will hoped to accomplish with his first, controversial witness was still a mystery to everyone except Will himself.

The trio also talked a little about the headlines of the day, something they had not had time to discuss during the lunch break. The newspapers were all reporting that Warren Mullburn's negotiations with the Israelis seemed to be temporarily stalled.

At the last moment, Israel was balking at ceding control of the eastern half of Jerusalem to the Palestinians. That had sent the Palestinian Authority into a rage. Hamas leaders were promising to send a new wave of suicide bombers into Jerusalem to "break the back of Israel's oppressive reluctance."

The parties were going to break for several days and then resume talks. President Harriet Landow, ever anxious to put her administration back into the limelight, had offered to send U.S. special envoy Howard Kamura to break the impasse, but her suggestion had been politely rejected by both sides.

During one of the breaks earlier that day, Mira had suggested a dinner meeting with Will. She said there were some defense strategies they needed to discuss, particularly dealing with the witness Will had subpoenaed for the next day. And she didn't feel comfortable sharing some of her concerns in front of the others. Her brother, a local chef, would prepare an Indian meal at their apartment. She and Will could then discuss the case while her brother was doing the dishes.

The two attorneys took a taxi to the apartment, which was located a few blocks away from the Damascus Gate of the Old City. En route, traffic was congested. The cars snaked along very slowly. The taxi then came to a complete stop along with the other traffic. Seeing a way to squeeze out, their cab driver wheeled his taxi sharply to the right and began nudging into the opposite lane. That was when they saw it.

There was a man wearing a heavy coat in the middle of the intersection behind them—four cars away, next to a bus stop. As the driver pulled into the opposite lane, he started saying something excitedly in Hebrew, motioning backward.

Instinctively, Will and Mira glanced back. An Israeli policewoman started running away from the man, waving to the cars and shouting in Hebrew, "Suicide! Suicide!"

Then, as they left the intersection behind them, it exploded in a deafening blast that rattled the cab windows. Mira shrieked and began crying. She buried her face in Will's coat.

Within seconds, the cab driver's cell phone went off. He snapped it on. Speaking Hebrew, he was talking to someone at the other end in calm, reassuring tones. After a few minutes he finished, sighed, and asked in English, "Everyone okay back there?"

Will was still numb, trying to process what had just happened. "We're all right," he muttered.

Mira's face was still in Will's chest, her shoulders were shuddering. She stayed there until she was able to regain her composure. Then she looked up at Will, wiping the tears away, and cursed softly in Arabic.

As they took an alternate route, Mira talked about the weariness of living in the midst of violence. How she hated groups like Hamas, and how she was "tired of 'Israeli intransigence.' Why doesn't Israel simply let the Palestinian Authority have the eastern half of Jerusalem?" she asked forcefully. "Is a little piece of land so important that people have to die in the streets?"

The two lawyers were still in shock from the suicide bombing. They talked about it in the cab and were still talking about it as they walked up the narrow corridor of the apartment building.

Mira unlocked the door to the apartment, and Will followed her, smelling the aroma of Indian food. Taking her suit jacket off, Mira headed into the kitchen. There she found several covered dishes on restaurant warming plates along with a note from her brother.

"He was called into work at the restaurant," she said, reading it. "I hope you are hungry. There's so much food here. You'll be plenty full when I get through with you."

Will looked around the apartment, trying to cope with an increasingly uneasy feeling. He was still in shock from the suicide bombing. *Perhaps*, he thought, *that was it*. But he still had the lingering feeling it was something else.

Mira seemed to have shaken off the incident. She ran her hands through her hair, letting out an exasperated groan.

"I am in such a mess," she said. "I just need to freshen up real quick. That's okay, isn't it?"

Will started to say something, but she interrupted him as she ducked into the bathroom, which was just off the living room.

"Just make yourself at home," she shouted. "Take some of the food. Start eating. I'll only be a minute."

Will sauntered into the kitchen. As he took the top off one of the dishes, something caught the corner of his eye and he glanced over.

Mira had left the bathroom door open at least six inches. She had started the shower and was now standing, poised and naked, in front of the open door, tying her hair back. She called out to him.

"Will, sometimes it's so nice just to wash the worries of the day off your body."

He had caught only one inadvertent look. Now he was quickly walking out of the kitchen and away from line of sight into the bathroom. Shame and anger were pulsing through him.

How could he have gotten himself into this dangerous position with Mira? At first, standing in the living room, he tried to dismiss the incident as simply a cultural difference.

That's ridiculous, he concluded. *Some things are universal—like sex. I've got to get out of here now.*

As he started toward the door, on the table by the front door he noticed Mira's purse, which she had left there upon entering the apartment. There was a colored plane-ticket envelope inside. Something told him to pull it out. He did.

Will stared at the ticket inside.

That was when he realized the full extent of the betrayal.

And he would still be trying to come to grips with it when, down on the street, he hailed a cab, ducked in, and gave the cabbie the directions to his hotel.

62

A SMALL ARMY OF LAWYERS HAD ASSEMBLED in the main courtroom of the Orient House building, where Gilead's trial was progressing. The legal contingent was gathered at the prosecution table, and they had come to object, in the loudest and most persuasive fashion possible, to Will Chambers' controversial tactic.

And, more to the point, they had come to protect their internationally celebrated client.

The three judges were seated, as were Will, Nigel, and Gilead. Mira Ashwan scurried in slightly late, apologized to the judges, and threw Will a confused, distressed look as she sat down.

A well-dressed Palestinian lawyer rose and introduced himself as local counsel for a New York law firm specializing in international law, which had been retained by a prominent client who had been served with a subpoena by Will Chambers. The subpoena had commanded that client to appear and give testimony at Gilead Amahn's trial. The Palestinian lawyer then yielded to one of the four lawyers from the New York firm.

The one with a little gray in his sideburns and the custom-tailored Italian suit strode confidently to the podium and introduced himself. He jumped right into the event that had sparked the court hearing that day.

"My client, Foreign Minister Warren Mullburn, was served with a subpoena to appear today in this prosecution against the accused, Hassan Gilead Amahn. Minister Mullburn has been called as a witness by the defense. We object, in the strongest possible terms, to our client—who is, as this tribunal knows, the

Foreign Minister of the Republic of Maretas—being forced to take time away from his involvement in delicate and highly critical international negotiations. After all, he is here in Jerusalem to help forge a peace agreement between Israel and the Palestinian Authority, not be dragged into a criminal case. Minister Mullburn is entitled to the protections of diplomatic immunity as well as foreign sovereign immunity. And we demand that this outrageous subpoena be quashed by this tribunal immediately."

Judge Mustafa asked for a quick recital of how Mullburn had happened to be served.

The New York lawyer proceeded to explain that Mullburn, his chief of staff, and several of his security detail were dining at the American Colony in Jerusalem. "A very large man dressed in a brown express-delivery outfit and carrying a box wrapped as a birthday present entered the restaurant, got past the maître d' and past one of Mr. Mullburn's personal security guards. Then he walked right up to the table and said the box was an urgent gift to Mr. Mullburn. One of the security agents at the table reached out, but before the delivery man could be stopped—by the way, he is seated behind the defense table there—he lifted the top off the box and tossed the subpoena at Minister Mullburn."

Tiny leaned forward and whispered to Will with a grin, "I couldn't believe they fell for it."

Judge Lee's usual tabula-rasa facial expression of controlled non-emotion had now changed slightly. He raised his hand to ask a question. As he did, his face was registering something, perhaps mild amusement.

"Did Minister Mullburn catch the subpoena?"

"Ah…as a matter of fact he did," the New York lawyer replied.

"Then it appears," Judge Lee concluded with a smile, "that Minister Mullburn was effectively served."

The lawyer was nonplussed. He proceeded to argue eloquently that, because Mullburn was in Jerusalem on "an urgent diplomatic peace mission," he was entitled to diplomatic immunity.

Further, he said, "because Minister Mullburn is an official with the government of the Republic of Maretas, he is entitled to foreign sovereign immunity."

His last point went to the reasons listed by Will Chambers in his brief to the court as to why Mullburn was being sought as a witness in the first place. "Minister Mullburn knows absolutely nothing—I repeat, *nothing*—about the matters regarding which attorney Chambers proposes to question him."

When the New York lawyer sat down, Will strode up. He paused, not just to collect his thoughts, but to ponder, just for an instant, exactly how high the stakes were at that very minute.

Will understood that if Mullburn's attorneys prevailed, the oil tycoon would be deemed immune from questioning. If that happened, then the central core of Will's defense would probably collapse. The final piece in Will's theory of Gilead's innocence relied on the circumstantial proof showing that Mullburn had some connection to the Temple Mount bombings. If Mullburn couldn't be forced to testify, then Zayed would move that the court exclude the defense's attempt to go down that route. He knew that the Palestinian prosecutor would object to any of the Mullburn-related defense evidence on the grounds that it would be unfair to impugn Mullburn, or to tie him into the massacre, without hearing *directly* from the notorious billionaire and current international diplomat himself. And if Mullburn were immune from testifying, the tribunal would have little choice— the court would likely have to bar that portion of Will's defense.

Will spoke first to the diplomatic immunity issue.

"In truth," he argued, "Mr. Mullburn was not in the course of diplomatic activities when he was served. And as we all know, Mr. Mullburn's negotiations between Israel and the Palestinian Authority are currently on a temporary hiatus. Therefore, his testimony here will not interfere with that process.

"And as far as foreign sovereign immunity is concerned," Will continued, "there is a well-known exception to the protections of such immunity. A tribunal can exercise jurisdiction over an official of a foreign state as long as the purpose of that jurisdiction has to do with acts that *were not done* in the official capacity of such person's government position. That was the ruling in the *Estate of Ferdinand Marcos* case that I cited to this tribunal. In that case the court rejected sovereign immunity for President Marcos for alleged acts of torture and murder—ones that were done more for his own personal benefit than as an official act of his position as president of the Philippines…"

But Judge Lee was having a problem with that.

"I'm looking at your proffered reasons for questioning Minister Mullburn," Lee said, "and—well, counsel, frankly, I am shocked. Very shocked. But more than that, you say you want to obtain evidence from Minister Mullburn about Israeli intelligence, what its computer logs showed about the Knights of the Temple Mount, and whether its computer system was possibly tampered with. And secondly, you actually propose to suggest that Minister Mullburn knows something about the source of the explosives and detonation system used to blow up the Temple Mount. You actually want to question Minister Mullburn about that?"

"I do," Will said. "I have only two areas of inquiry for Mr. Mullburn. First, his knowledge about entries into the computer logs of the Israeli Mossad relating to the Knights of the Temple Mount. And secondly—" And with that, Will paused and took a quick breath. All three of the judges were leaning forward, wide-eyed.

"Secondly, his knowledge about—and possible complicity in—the providing of computer equipment and explosives materials used by the Knights in the Temple Mount bombings."

This was the first time Nigel Newhouse had heard the true intent behind Will's subpoena to Mullburn. The barrister maintained a cool exterior, but inside he was wilting. Will Chambers, lead trial counsel for the defense, had in effect launched an official indictment of conspiracy to commit mass murder against the foreign minister of another nation—and not just any foreign minister, but against Warren Mullburn, the man who appeared to be on the verge of achieving a major Middle East peace settlement.

Will scanned the faces of the three judges. Judge Lee Kwongju was staring at the table of New York lawyers. In spite of his expressed shock at the audacity of Will's intended questions to Mullburn, Will was counting on one thing—Lee had written in an international law journal about the need for jurisdiction by international tribunals over reluctant witnesses from other nations. In consideration of that, Will added another comment.

"Of course, the rules of this tribunal give it jurisdiction over witnesses from other nations," Will said, "and in fact, the procedures adopted for this case were based on Rule 54 of the Rules of the International Tribunal for the Former Yugoslavia—namely, that 'The Trial Chamber may issue...such subpoenas...as may be necessary...for the conduct of trial...'"

Lee leaned back in his chair.

Then Will looked at Judge Verdexler, who was sweeping his long gray hair back from his forehead. The attorney was counting on the Belgian's previously expressed position that his own supreme court should have been more aggressive in going after heads of state in war crimes cases. But Will didn't want to risk antagonizing him by appealing directly to that. Verdexler, he concluded, was the kind that should be left to form his own conclusion, rather than being backed into a corner.

That left only Judge Mustafa. Will knew he could not make a direct appeal to Mustafa's background as one of the framers of the Palestinian Constitution and an ardent supporter of the Palestinian Authority, as well as his background as a Muslim. That would be too obvious.

"The ultimate question here," Will said, making his final point another way, "is whether this tribunal has the real authority it purports to have. Mr. Mullburn is here in Jerusalem and is available. My proffer of evidence shows a likelihood that he—and he alone—is the best one to give an answer regarding these profound issues. Mr. Mullburn's attorneys are saying that this tribunal is impotent—incapable of bringing him to the witness booth and forcing him tell the truth of what he knows about the murder of hundreds of Muslims. But if they are right, that means that we and the Palestinian Authority may never know why the Temple Mount exploded, and why all those Muslims died that day."

Judge Mustafa was eyeing Will closely. Then he reached over and turned off the microphone to the judges' bench so that the panel could deliberate in secrecy. All three turned their backs to the courtroom and began their discussion.

Gilead had a confused look on his face, and he bent over to his attorney and simply asked, "What do you think?" But Will shrugged. It was simply too close to call.

Nigel looked sympathetic, but Will could still decipher the real meaning behind the barrister's expression. It was the kind of look the passengers who were safely tucked in the lifeboats must have given to those left behind on the *Titanic*. Nigel and Will had developed a warm professional friendship, and the barrister simply didn't want to see Will, desperate to prove his client's innocence, committing professional suicide.

As for Mira, she studiously avoided Will's gaze during the arguments and the ensuing deliberations.

After some fifteen minutes, all three judges swung their chairs around. Judge Mustafa clicked on the microphone.

The small gang of New York lawyers, who had been milling around in the courtroom, scrambled back to their seats at the prosecution's counsel table.

Judge Mustafa cleared his throat.

"In the matter of the motion to quash the subpoena," he said, "that motion is denied. Gentlemen, please bring Minister Mullburn into the courtroom and escort him into the witness booth."

Then Mustafa turned to Will. "We will allow Foreign Minister Mullburn to be asked only a very few questions by you, Mr. Chambers. So you had better make them good."

Nigel pushed his notepad over to Will.

It read simply, "Out of the skillet, but into the fire?"

63

WARREN MULLBURN, BILLIONAIRE, genius by anyone's standard of measurement, and Foreign Minister of the Republic of Maretas, was sitting in the glass witness booth. He was wearing a perfectly tailored dark-blue suit, a light-blue silk shirt, and a tie with an abstract geometric floral pattern. The tie had been personally designed for Mullburn by artist José de Vargos, a cubist painter.

Mullburn was tan, and as he sat in the stand he smiled pleasantly, appearing rested and at ease. The global financial titan had reason to look confident. In breaks during his shuttle diplomacy between Israel and the Palestinians, he had managed to host an international economic summit in Singapore. His move toward forging the Global Economic Alliance, linking together transnational corporations, had been fabulously successful. Mullburn had successfully sold the idea of an alliance as a necessary defensive reaction to the attempts by the United Nation and the European Union attempt to impose operating standards on all international businesses.

The cartel of megacorporations, loosely headed up now by Mullburn, currently spanned the areas of transportation, communications, computer, satellite, and aerospace technology, international banking, mining, and of course, petroleum products. His own share of the world oil market now seemed secure since the Republic of Maretas had recently been permitted a seat in OPEC. But after all, the little island republic's oil interests were simply a front for Mullburn's now well-established Mexico oil bonanza, and his more recent successful bid for oil production in the Black Sea and in Siberia.

In the two hours before Mullburn had walked into the courtroom, there had been a flurry of legal maneuvers from his New York lawyers. First they tried to delay his testimony, though he was admittedly in the witness waiting room just down the hall. Then they moved for the panel to reconsider their ruling that Mullburn must give some limited testimony. Their last effort was to request that Mullburn testify in the open courtroom rather than in the witness booth, arguing that "his high official position as Foreign Minister would be demeaned by giving testimony in such a cramped little venue."

But the judges, all wanting to move the trial along, denied the requests.

Now Will was at the podium in the courtroom, gazing at Warren Mullburn, ready to begin his questioning. The Virginia trial lawyer's first task was to put aside all of the tortured history between the two men and focus on the task at hand. To disregard what Will believed had been Mullburn's hidden conspiracy to destroy, first Will, and then his wife, Fiona, in the past. He needed to ignore the all-too-coincidental attacks on his family that had happened during two of his cases—two different lawsuits. But in both cases Will's pursuit of justice had produced evidence that had tainted the billionaire and frustrated some of his economic schemes. For Will, knowing Mullburn as he did, the cause-and-effect relationship was too close to be coincidental.

He glanced down at his outline of questions, then looked Mullburn in the eye.

"Mr. Mullburn, we meet again," he said calmly.

Mullburn gave a smile but did not respond.

"I know your time is valuable," Will continued, "and so I intend to be brief."

His eyes quickly glanced over two papers on the podium. First, the intelligence-research memo generated from Mike Michalany's contacts with the FBI. And second, the corresponding memo from Tiny Heftland, outlining his meeting with Israel's Mossad. Michalany and Tiny had painstakingly scouted out the opposing team.

Now it was Will's time to put the ball into play. He would start with a number of fastballs.

"Within the past year you have purchased a controlling share in oil production companies in Russia—Yukos and Sibneft—correct?"

"You are correct," Mullburn said in a booming and deliberate cadence.

"The *World Financial Times* says you have had many personal telephone contacts with Secretary Lazenko in the Russian Federation—have you?"

"That is also correct."

"In your dealings with the former Soviet-bloc countries, you have come to learn that there is an ongoing problem over there with criminal syndicates?"

"Yes. And there is also an ongoing problem with criminal syndicates in New York, Baghdad, and Mexico City, Mr. Chambers. And I would imagine you may even have criminal elements in the pastoral hills of the Commonwealth of Virginia, where you come from."

Judges Verdexler and Mustafa smiled at that.

"Secretary Lazenko, in a statement given to a Moscow newspaper, mentioned the problem with contraband weapons and explosives being smuggled out of the Russian Federation countries by criminal elements and sold on the black market. Would you dispute that?"

"I would have nothing to contradict that. It's a sad fact."

"One of your degrees was in mechanical engineering, with an emphasis on geophysical location of petroleum?"

"Yes," Mullburn said with a sigh.

"Do you know what Semtex is?"

Mullburn paused for only the briefest millisecond and then bulleted his answer out.

"No."

"If I told you it was a substance made in Slovakia, would that assist in refreshing your memory?"

"No. I would still have no idea what it is."

"In its uncolored form it has a whitish appearance. That doesn't help?"

"No," Mullburn said showing only the slightest irritation.

"But in light of your engineering degree and your considerable knowledge in international matters, can you explain why you would not know what Semtex is?"

"How can I explain why I don't know what I don't know?" He chuckled to himself at that.

Zayed was on his feet, objecting to the last question as "badgering the witness." Judge Mustafa sustained it.

"Ever present in a meeting or discussion of any kind where Semtex was mentioned?"

"No."

"Well, don't engineers use explosives in both construction and demolition projects?"

"Occasionally. Yes. Fine. They do. So?"

"Well, given that engineering is your background, and that you own oil companies and vast exploration projects, I would think that the use of explosives—Semtex in particular—would have come up in certain conversations among your engineers."

"Plastic explosives may be the force majeure in terrorist attacks, Mr. Chambers, such as in this case," Mullburn said with a smug smile, "but civil engineers have much more conventional means of demolition. So to answer your question, no, I cannot recall the mention of Semtex in recent conversations—"

Will paused. The three judges had all caught that, Will was sure of it. But to make sure he asked the court reporter to read back the answer and have all of the translators repeat it too.

They began to repeat Mullburn's answer, starting with "Plastic explosives may be the force majeure—" And at that point Will asked them to stop.

"*Plastic* explosives," Will said, staring at Mullburn.

"Yes?"

"You said *plastic* explosives. Who said anything about Semtex being a form of *plastic* explosive?"

"You were clearly talking about explosives—"

"Yes, I was. But I *never* delineated nor described the fact that Semtex was a kind of *plastic* explosive—a cousin of C-4—nor did I indicate in any question that it also happens to be the precise type of plastic explosive used in the bombing of the Temple Mount. But you said that it was. So, how did you know that?"

Mullburn was not going to let this minor irritant of a trial lawyer have his way with the cross-examination. He snapped his answer back like a rifle shot.

"In the newspapers, Mr. Chambers. On the television. The whole world is talking about the bombings. It is the singular event that has made my diplomatic efforts at peace-building much more difficult. Perhaps I've even heard it in the course of my negotiations between the Israelis and the Palestinians. So I'm sure I've read or heard somewhere the fact that the plastic explosive Semtex was the substance used."

Will paused again. Then he decided to throw a knuckleball.

"But Mr. Mullburn, you testified under oath just a few minutes ago that you had no idea what Semtex was. Those were your words—I noted them on my notepad—you said '*I would still have no idea what it is.*' Isn't that what your testimony was?"

"This is ridiculous," Mullburn protested.

Zayed was up again, objecting. Again, Judge Mustafa sustained the objection, this time with agitation in his voice.

But Will noticed that both Lee and Verdexler were leaning forward ever so slightly, their eyes on Warren Mullburn in his glass booth.

"Let's change gears," Will said nonchalantly. "In the government of the Republic of Maretas, you have a department of computer intelligence. Yes?"

Zayed jumped up, but Judge Mustafa didn't need to hear an objection.

"Mr. Chambers, you are getting dangerously close to areas of government secrets and matters of national security regarding Minister Mullburn's nation. I will not let you enter those areas—"

"I will not enter any area," Will replied, "that has anything to do with a legitimate national interest of the republic. My questions will go only to subversive activities accomplished for *personal benefit*—not for any official or governmental goal."

The word "subversive" rang like a fire bell through the courtroom.

"This is outrageous," Mullburn fumed.

Will was locked in on the witness now, watching his every move, even the smallest movements and nuances. And he noticed that Mullburn quickly thrust his tongue into the side of his check with that last question. And there was also something else.

In the last few seconds, the billionaire started glancing around the witness booth—looking to the sides, down at the floor, up at the ceiling. Little glances, mere fleeting motions. But to Will they were significant.

He had the distinct feeling that Warren Mullburn was claustrophobic. That was probably why his lawyers hadn't wanted him testifying in that enclosed area.

So Will's next question was preceded by a long pause. Then he delivered it in a plodding, overarticulate fashion.

"Do you have a person…in charge of the computer intelligence department…of your republic…a person by the name of…*Orville Putrie?*"

Mullburn—just momentarily—lost his sense of presence, allowing his torso to jerk forward, as if he'd been shoved in the back by someone.

Will noticed that too.

And so did the judges.

Mullburn's soaring intelligence kicked in. He knew the implications and the various scenarios. The fact that Putrie's name had come up was a huge problem, if not a potential disaster. Mullburn was certain that the little computer geek's identity had been buried in the lead-lined computer lab on the island. Only a handful of people knew about Putrie—and President Mandu La Rouge didn't even know that Mullburn had formed the department of which Putrie had been made the chief researcher.

There was no question now, the billionaire quickly concluded, that Will Chambers had retrieved some critical information. But he could be bluffing. The only question was the extent of the lawyer's apparent penetration into the secret network that Mullburn had established on his island empire.

"And before you answer," Will added about three seconds into the pause that Mullburn was taking before attempting to reply, "we have secured the service of a subpoena on your personal secretary in the palace on your island, the personal assistant with the desk on the second floor—an ornate desk, I understand…Italian design—and we've also subpoenaed her diary of appointments, to the extent that they may show any meetings between you and Mr. Orville Putrie."

The witness tried to smile.

"Your recital of those facts was a waste of time," he said. "Yes, I know we have a person by that name in the current-research branch of the administration."

"And do you know," Will said deliberately and painstakingly, "that Mr. Putrie has developed a program…a program to detect how and when…an unlawful entry is attempted into a computer system—one that's protected by a process called quantum encryption?"

Mullburn was moving slightly in his chair, glancing quickly from side to side as if he were on the lookout for an errant wasp that was loose in the glass booth with him. But his mind was busy scheming—and this much he had decided. It was time to deny everything, stonewall Will Chambers, and then get out.

"No. I did not know that."

"Well, I am holding in my hand," Will announced oratorically with a document in his right hand, "an application for a patent— one made to the United States Patent Department—for that very system. This application was made by an individual named Orville Putrie…"

Then Will added as an aside, "Strange that someone with an open arrest warrant for him would apply for a public patent. I guess he didn't think that one through, did he?"

Mullburn was struggling to conceal his volcanic rage, first at Will Chambers for, once again, defiling and disrupting his well-orchestrated symphony dedicated to self-aggrandizement—his pretensions to global achievement and personal empire. But his napalm-like hate burned deeper still…at the bizarre little computer genius who had apparently blundered so ineptly as to drag Warren Mullburn down with him.

"Well, let me get right to it, Mr. Mullburn."

Will was now picking up the pace, trying to burn each question into the strike zone.

"Did you, or anyone at your command, instruct Orville Putrie to unlawfully enter the quantum-encryption-protected computer system of the Israeli intelligence department—the agency known as the Mossad—to manipulate data in that system referring to the Knights of the Temple Mount, so as to make it appear that the Israeli government had willfully permitted that religious cult to blow up the Temple Mount?"

Three of the New York lawyers leaped to their feet and began shouting out objections. The lead partner, the one in the expensive Italian suit, dashed toward the podium so quickly that he tripped over his briefcase on the floor and had to catch his balance on the run, like a halfback who had slipped out of a tackle.

"We claim the privilege under the rules of this tribunal," he called out, "for our client to refuse to answer on the grounds of the appearance of self-incrimination…as I hasten to add, *appearance,* because Minister Mullburn is entirely innocent of these scandalous, slanderous, malicious lies—"

"If he's innocent," Will interjected, "then how can you claim that his answering my question would incriminate him?"

"I deny it—all of it!" Mullburn was now shouting from the inside of the glass booth.

"Next question," Will bulleted out. "Did you order Orville Putrie to construct the computer hardware for the detonation system used in the bombing of the Temple Mount?"

The lead New York attorney was still at the podium, just inches from Will, leaning toward him and eyeing him like a pet owner who was trying to prevent a house cat from scampering through the front door.

"Same objection. Instruct the witness not to answer!" he shouted out.

"Next question," Will said, hammering it out. "Did you provide, through your network of connections in the former Soviet-bloc countries, a sufficient quantity of Semtex to the Knights of the Temple Mount to decimate the structures on the mount and kill the hundreds of people who were in or near them at the time?"

Mullburn was shouting indecipherably inside the glass booth. His lawyer was yelling even louder, that they would not permit their client to answer "these mindless, criminal, absurd accusations…"

Finally, Will reached into his briefcase and quickly pulled something out. Then he went for the last pitch.

"Did you arrange a meeting with defense amicus curiae Mira Ashwan in order to covertly obtain intelligence on our strategy for the legal defense of Gilead Amahn?"

"I don't even have any idea who that person is, you fool!" Mullburn cried out.

"Well, then perhaps Ms. Ashwan can explain," Will held up a colored envelope, "why she flew to the Republic of Maretas just before the start of this trial—and why she has an open-ended, one-way ticket back to Maretas—I have the ticket stub and the ticket right here—"

Mira was on her feet.

"You went in my purse!"

"You bet," Will snapped back. "Mira—how could you?"

Judge Mustafa, sensing a loss of control over the trajectory of the trial, quickly and loudly gaveled the hearing to an adjournment for the day, instructing Mullburn and his entourage to leave the courtroom, and all of the participants to exit immediately.

Mullburn's security detail rushed to the glass booth and, followed by his dazed lawyers, led him quickly out of the courtroom—out of the Orient House to the back of a waiting limousine.

Only Mr. Himlet was in the backseat. He raised the privacy glass behind the driver.

Then Mullburn exploded in a molten rage of threats—against Himlet for ever finding Orville Putrie in the first place, and then against Putrie, who Mullburn vowed to personally execute, but only after a prolonged session of unimaginable torture to find out the sum total of the information the computer genius had allowed to leak out.

"Call the island!" Mullburn screamed. "Find out where Putrie is this very moment and have him put in chains in a locked room in the basement of the palace, till I can get to him myself!"

Himlet had something to say. He paused, his expression still blank, and in his calm voice he answered.

"I'm afraid that may not be possible."

"Why not?" Mullburn shrieked, now red-faced.

"Because it appears," Himlet continued, "that Mr. Putrie has disappeared."

64

Will was looking at a picture that was indexed within the section of his trial notebook containing his anticipated direct examination of Dr. Daoud al-Qasr. The picture was a photocopy of an ancient Egyptian mural. It depicted several mythological characters gathered around a large weighing scale.

After Will had led Dr. al-Qasr through questioning about his professional and educational credentials and his writing and teaching experience, the witness had easily been qualified as an expert in the fields of Egyptology and cultural anthropology by the tribunal. And he had also been certified as an expert in the current esoteric religions of the Middle East—the "mystery cults" that professed secret knowledge based on ancient, long-dead religions.

In the witness booth, al-Qasr was now waiting for the next series of questions. He was a large, tall man in his forties, with a broad, pleasant face and a balding head.

"Now, I would represent to you," Will continued, "that the parties to this criminal case have stipulated that the handwritten documents, notes, and journals we will discuss, were all in Yossin Ali Khalid's handwriting and found in his apartment. So you can assume that to be true in giving us your opinions."

"Very well," he said.

"How did the Knights, and in particular Khalid, calculate the date of the appearing of the last Caliph, the supposed reincarnation of al-Hakim—their religious messiah?"

"Well, the Druze, the group from which the Knights broke away, believed that he will reappear literally one thousand years from al-Hakim's disappearance in Cairo in 1021—which means the appearing is supposed to be in the year 2021. But Yossin and his father, Omar—actually going all the way back to Omar's grandfather—calculated it differently. They believed that the calendars were different back in 1021. Further, they were convinced that the Caliph was influenced by the ancient Egyptians. As a result, the Knights had always believed in a sooner return than the Druze. But they had been unable to agree on a precise calculation. Then Louis Lorraine, who had an extensive background in ancient Egyptian religion, joined their group. Lorraine and Yossin Ali Khalid worked together to finish the determination of the year of the appearing of the Caliph al-Hakim."

Will led Dr. al-Qasr through questioning that established, in precise detail, the convoluted system of logic and ancient historical research used by the pair to recalculate the "true date of appearing" of the last Caliph. Khalid's journals had laid it all out.

In them it was explained how the ancient Egyptians, in their calendars, would exclude five days per year. Those days were considered to be yielded up to the first five of the Egyptian gods—Atum, Shu, Tefnut, Geb, and Nut.

The ancient Egyptians also excluded, every third year, a sixth day—in honor of the god Thoth. But the Knights decided not to deduct that day because, in their thinking, Thoth, the god of wisdom, secrets, and writings, was actually the pre-incarnation of the Caliph al-Hakim.

"Therefore, the Knights figured the appearing of the Caliph–messiah would be calculated by starting with the year 2021, then subtracting five days multiplied by a thousand years—or in other words, a total deduction of five thousand days."

"And that date just happened to fall around the same date that Gilead Amahn landed in Cairo from the United States?"

"As it turns out, that is correct."

"In any of Khalid's journals, is Gilead Amahn ever discussed?"

"Well—not directly."

"His name does appear on one document?"

"Yes."

"We'll return to that in a moment," Will noted. "Now these date calculations you mentioned appear to be very complex, requiring a great deal of historical knowledge. Do Khalid's journals ever indicate that anyone other than he and Louis Lorraine ever discussed those calculations?"

"No."

"Now Scott Magnit, a member of the Knights, has testified for the prosecution that he was told, by Lorraine and Khalid, the date that had been calculated for the appearing of the Caliph–messiah. And he then tried to paint Gilead Amahn as the impersonator of the messiah by saying that Gilead knew the exact date to present himself in Cairo because Magnit had divulged that date to him when the two had met at a Bible study in Jerusalem last year. Now Dr. al-Qasr, in all of the records and writings of Khalid, coupled with your knowledge of the Knights, is there anything to suggest that Scott Magnit was ever privy to the secret doctrine dealing with the date of the appearing of the last Caliph?"

"I saw nothing to that effect. Khalid's papers only suggest that the date was known to him and to Louis Lorraine."

"Would the date of that predicted appearing have been a critical element of their secret cult?"

"It would have been of utmost importance—very tightly guarded information."

"Scott Magnit also described the initiation ritual of the group—fasting in the desert. Was this group quick to accept people into leadership?"

"Clearly not," the witness said with assurance. "In fact, they would screen people for months before they would let them know that the group was something other than a 'nondenominational Bible-study group,' which is how they would usually introduce themselves to new members. But from my research, only four members ever made it into the inner circle of leadership. Scott

Magnit—and he was a little on the outside of the circle—along with the taxi driver who drove the accused over to the Golden Gate after the bombing…but he was slightly below Magnit in authority. And then there were Lorraine and Khalid—they were at the top."

"What are the odds that Gilead would have received entrée into the inner circle of the Knights in just a matter of weeks…as the prosecution would have us believe?"

"The odds would be heavily against that," al-Qasr replied.

"Lastly, you said that Gilead's name did appear on one of Khalid's papers. Which one was that?"

"It was a photocopy of an image of an ancient Egyptian mural, typical of those found etched on the walls of the tombs of the pharaohs. We Egyptologists call it the *psychostasia*—the weighing of the conscience of the dead. You Westerners would probably refer to it as the last judgment. The Egyptians believed that, after death, the heart of the deceased, along with all of its good deeds is balanced on the great scales of justice—against the weight of a feather. If it fails, the person goes into condemnation and destruction. If it passes the test, the deceased enters paradise."

"And this particular mural is of an ancient Egyptian named Ani—he died, and this picture represents his last judgment?"

"Yes. The characters in the mural are well-known figures in ancient religion. Off to the right side of the great balance scales we see the man with the head of a hawk, called Thoth—he is writing down the results of the divine weighing process."

"Did Khalid write down a note underneath that figure?"

"He did. He wrote the name 'Louis Lorraine.'"

"And what is the figure crouching underneath the center post of the great scales—the one that looks like a man with the head of a jackal?"

"That is Anubis, the mythological character who is actually doing the weighing of the heart."

"What did Khalid write on the picture under Anubis?"

"He wrote his own name—Yossin Ali Khalid."

"And where is Gilead's name mentioned on this picture?"

With that, Will clicked on the computer, and an enlarged image of the mural appeared on the screen of the courtroom.

"Khalid jotted Gilead's name," al-Qasr was raising his voice slightly to emphasize the importance of the point, "underneath the oblong container sitting in the tray of the balance scale—the jar containing the heart of the deceased."

"Based on your expertise in understanding the theology of the Knights of the Temple Mount and your review of this document, what is your opinion as to the religious significance of the placement of Gilead's name on this picture?"

"It seems clear that Gilead Amahn was considered a person who would be put to the ultimate test—weighed in the balance. That if he were the true Caliph–messiah, he would survive the test. If not—he would be destroyed. But it is clear that Khalid was not convinced himself that Gilead was the messiah they were looking for—the outcome had not yet been determined. Gilead's heart, so to speak, had not yet been weighed. It was about to be weighed."

"And would Khalid's notes written on that picture, suggest that Gilead was a decision-maker within the Knights of the Temple Mount?"

"To the contrary—they would suggest that Gilead was the one about whom decisions were being made. And that Khalid and Lorraine were the decision-makers in charge of that process."

Will rested, and Zayed hastened to the podium. He looked confident.

"In the original mural Ani was having his heart weighed by the gods. Who was Ani in ancient Egyptian history?"

"He was the chancellor for a pharaoh. He was in charge of the revenues for the temples at Thebes and Abydos. Lived around 1500 BCE. Give me a minute and I can try to remember the precise date of his death..."

"Don't bother," Zayed said with a smile. "The point is, the accused, Hassan Gilead Amahn, was associated with the ancient person of Ani, as indicated by Khalid. Is that true?"

"Yes."

"The inner circle of the Knights of the Temple Mount linked Gilead with Ani?"

"In a manner of speaking."

"And Ani was a 'chancellor,' a high-ranking ruler in the court of the pharaoh?"

"That is true."

"So the inner circle of the Knights must have considered the accused part of their leadership structure—right?"

Dr. al-Qasr saw the dire implications of the question.

"I am afraid that would be a logical deduction from the picture, yes."

Zayed did a little wave with his hands and left the podium. Will had anticipated the question and the witness's answer. It had been a calculated risk. But the expressions on the faces of the three judges indicated that his ploy in having al-Qasr refer to the picture might have backfired. In the next few minutes he was about to find out.

"In the picture, the character Anubis, who is crouching under the scales," Will began, "he is reaching up and touching something in the center of the scales. What is he doing?"

"He is manipulating the adjusting screw at the center of the balance scales."

"What happens if the adjustment is set improperly?"

"You get a false balance."

"And Yossin Ali Khalid is the one in this picture doing the adjusting—determining, in effect, the outcome?"

"Yes. That would be correct."

"The part played by Khalid in the picture indicates he is the one who can tip the scales—make the heart of Gilead Amahn come out looking one way or another. In other words, Khalid had the power to create the illusion that Gilead was even the reincarnation of the last Caliph, the promised messiah of the Knights' secret theology—and without Gilead even knowing it. Doesn't this picture, through Khalid's own notes, show us that?"

But there was no way that the prosecutor would let that stand, and he jumped up and objected that the question assumed a knowledge of the state of mind of Khalid, and also improperly sought an opinion as to the ultimate issues in the case.

Mustafa granted the objection. Judges Lee and Verdexler, in their silence, concurred.

Zayed returned for a short re-cross.

"Are you a Muslim?"

"Yes, I am."

"Are you a good Muslim?"

Before Will could raise an objection, Zayed clarified.

"By that I mean—have you, in your scholarly writings, criticized some of the muftis and other teachers of Islam regarding the importance of Muslims retaining complete control of the Noble Sanctuary—regarding certain rulings of the Waqf, the Muslim Trust that has authority over the so-called Temple Mount. And as a result, you have been barred from the Noble Sanctuary and have been excluded from certain Islamic conferences—all of that is true?"

Al-Qasr, visibly uncomfortable, was trying to manage a smile.

"Yes…all of what you say is correct. But there are other Islamic scholars who have taken up my side of this…"

"You have been called an infidel by many Islamic leaders?"

"Yes. I am no infidel…but they have called me that."

"And so, having been called an infidel, an enemy to Islam, you take up the defense of Hassan Gilead Amahn, accused of conspiring to destroy the holy place and holy people of Islam?"

The witness was no longer smiling. He glanced down and answered in a quiet voice, nearly inaudible.

"I have been called as a witness for the defense. That much is true…"

Will tried to read the faces of the judges, but only one of them was obvious.

Judge Mustafa was visibly scowling at al-Qasr as he walked out of the witness booth.

65

In the judgment of Will Chambers and Nigel Newhouse, Dr. al-Qasr's testimony had been close to a zero-sum game. On one hand, they were thankful that his expert opinions had likely raised more questions in the minds of the judges about Scott Magnit's credibility and about whether Gilead had actually been an unwitting pawn in Yossin Ali Khalid's barbaric theology of destruction. Yet they also realized his testimony was less than compelling—particularly because he had admitted that Khalid's jottings on the ancient Egyptian picture could be interpreted as proof that Gilead was within the leadership circle of the Knights.

The two attorneys, joined by Tiny, discussed that and other issues over a carry-out Italian dinner they ate in their temporary office. Mira had been barred from their meetings—and for his part, Tiny had no doubt that Will's deductions were correct—that Mira had been recruited by Mullburn to spy on Gilead's defense team. But Nigel was less sure, wondering what the billionaire had to gain by such an audacious act of legal espionage.

Will's only explanation was that Mullburn wanted to find out how close they were getting to the golden vein underneath all those layers of rock and soil—to the buried "mother lode"—the evidence that Mullburn had personally orchestrated the bombings to create massive instability in the peace negotiations. Then, Will contended, Mullburn could step in as a supposedly neutral "mediator." What no one else understood, Will continued, was that Mullburn alone possessed the politically damaging information he would try to use to blackmail Israel.

"Information...like what?" Nigel asked, taking a few last bites of his *rigatoni al profumo di mare.*

"He had Orville Putrie break in to the Mossad computer logs. There were surveillance records showing that Israeli intelligence was keeping an eye on the Knights prior to the bombings."

"A bit politically embarrassing, perhaps," Nigel remarked, "but not enough to force major concessions from Israel in return for Mullburn's keeping it quiet."

"That's why he needed to up the ante," Will continued. "He had Putrie add some incriminating text, making it look like the Mossad was deliberately standing down in order to permit the Knights to attack the Mount."

The barrister was deep in thought, but remained unconvinced.

"The kind of plot you are describing is contemptible...so complex and so brilliantly arrogant that I find it hard to believe. Mullburn may be a genius of sorts—bold, aggressive, perhaps even ruthless—but if I'm finding it a rather bitter pill to swallow, then how are you ever going to convince the tribunal? Really, are you able to present unimpeachable evidence substantiating all of this?"

Will glanced over at Tiny, who was smiling to himself.

"I hope so," Will replied.

Nigel could see he was being excluded. As an accomplished barrister, this was the first case where his lead trial counsel had deliberately kept him out of the loop. The American attorney had assured him it had to be that way. The fact that the barrister accepted it in good faith was a testament not only to Will's leadership but to Nigel's teamsmanship as well.

But as they concluded for the night, all three of them agreed on one thing. They had all observed Gilead's demeanor during the trial. He was deteriorating, looking increasingly forlorn and abandoned. No amount of encouragement from the defense team seemed to buoy him.

It was as if he had already begun visualizing himself on the table, strapped down, IVs connected...with nothing to do but count the minutes before the lethal injection was administered. It was heartbreaking—and from a strategic standpoint it could be a crippling problem. Gilead had yet to testify. He needed to tell his story incisively and with bold confidence. Whether he would be able to do that now seemed to be in grave doubt.

Will only hoped that the fact that Bill and Esther Collingwood had finally arrived and waded through the paperwork and background checks so they could sit in the courtroom would lift Gilead's spirits. Will had shared that with his client, but the young man had managed only a weak smile in response.

Now, Will and Nigel could only look to the next day for some solid signs that the course of the trial was turning their way. They were cautiously optimistic that they would win several central points during the upcoming testimony.

But they were to be bitterly disappointed.

They had subpoenaed Farousha Ali Khalid, the submissive wife of Yossin Ali Khalid, to testify. She was to be questioned on the many covert meetings in their apartment between her husband, Louis Lorraine, and Scott Magnit, where the attack on the Temple Mount was discussed. Will fully expected Farousha to deny that Gilead had been present at any of those meetings.

But she never uttered a word on that subject. She answered only a qualifying question, put to her by the prosecution in an attempt to block her testimony.

"You understand that under our rules of procedure," Zayed asked, "you have the right of marital privilege to refrain from giving any testimony that might be considered offensive to the interests of your late husband?"

"I do," she answered quietly in Arabic.

"Do you claim that privilege—and do you refuse to testify?"

She looked down. "I do refuse."

Will objected to the ploy by the Palestinian prosecutor, arguing that he "had stretched the marital privilege beyond the point of any legal recognition," particularly because it was Gilead—not Farousha's husband—who was on trial. Judge Lee seemed mildly inclined toward Will's position, but in the end Judge Verdexler and Mustafa forged a majority to overrule his objection, effortlessly sidestepping the fifteen pages of argument Will had filed that morning on that exact point of evidence.

Farousha Ali Khalid, the only living witness to the meetings of the inner circle of the Knights other than Scott Magnit, was excused by the tribunal. She quickly exited the glass booth and scurried out of the courtroom, having never commented on the conspiracy that lay at the heart of Gilead's trial.

As his next witness, Will called Dr. Edward Tyrone, a history and religion professor at Southern Methodist University. With a PhD in history and an MDiv in theology, Tyrone was an undisputed expert on the history of evangelical Protestantism, having written numerous articles and books on the subject. He had reviewed the record in the case and interviewed those who knew Gilead's theological beliefs before he left for Cairo, including members of the Rolling River Bible Tabernacle in West Virginia. He had also reviewed the records of the Israeli police, which described much of Gilead's final sermon in Jerusalem just seconds before the blast shook the Temple Mount. Tyrone was prepared to testify that Gilead's theological leanings were perfectly consistent with mainline evangelicalism—and dramatically at odds with the theological position of the Knights of the Temple Mount.

And that is exactly what he would have indicated to the tribunal—had he been permitted to give his opinions. But immediately after Will had had Tyrone describe his educational and professional credentials, Samir Zayed rose to his feet and moved the court to bar the professor from testifying.

"What the accused may have believed in his mind about religion," the prosecutor argued, "prior to his trip to Cairo, where he chose to play the part of the Caliph al-Hakim—or prior to the bombing—these things are irrelevant to this case. The accused is not being charged with religious heresy—he is charged with being part of a plan to commit mass murder against Muslims. His actions, not his beliefs, are on trial."

It was difficult for Will to maintain his composure during counterargument. "This is absurd," he stated forcefully. "The prosecution wants it both ways. They want to try my client for being part of a religiously motivated bombing—yet they would deny me the right to show what my client's religious beliefs really were. As a believer in Jesus Christ, Gilead Amahn would never deliberately destroy innocent human life. And as a Bible-believing Christian, he simply would never have knowingly joined this dangerous, theologically confused religious cult—if they had clearly explained what they really believed. Mr. Zayed's argument insults the intelligence—and the judicial integrity—of this tribunal."

Judge Verdexler lashed out first, suggesting that Will Chambers was the one who was insulting the integrity of the court, not the prosecutor. "You are telling us, Mr. Chambers, that if we don't see things your way, we are either fools or we are corrupt."

But before the attorney could respond, Judge Mustafa joined in the fray, adding his admonition and reminding Will that he had been "previously warned against your self-righteous Christian preaching to this tribunal."

With an uncharacteristic degree of emotion in his voice, Judge Lee voiced concern about the fairness of the majority's ruling. But Verdexler and Mustafa were not swayed. The positions of the judges were now falling into a recognizable pattern. And as Will saw it, he was consistently one vote short.

Larry Lancer next testified as a fact witness, and was mildly helpful to the defense. Under Nigel Newhouse's questioning, he described how, in the year prior to the bombing, Gilead had visited his office at the headquarters of the Holy Land Institute for the Word. Lancer had known of Gilead's adoptive parents and their mission work in Egypt and had discussed the evangelistic mission of his institute with the young man. Gilead had taken some literature, but had never returned and never called back. The impression Lancer had was "that Gilead was a normal evangelical

Christian man, who was considering doing some evangelistic work in Israel…there was nothing in our conversation that gave me any concern about the orthodoxy of his theology."

With that last comment, both Will and Nigel felt they had recovered some small amount of ground that had been lost when Dr. Tyrone had been prevented from testifying.

However, in cross-examination, Lancer admitted a deep sympathy toward Gilead's plight—and he admitted that a wealthy supporter of his ministry had been paying, through his institute, all of Gilead's legal fees and expenses. Further, Lancer had to concede that his institute was providing free office space to Gilead's defense team. As the two attorneys sized it up, if the tribunal wanted to look for reasons to discredit Lancer for obvious bias in favor of Gilead, it wouldn't have to look very far.

The last defense witness of the day was a young woman with long blond hair named Susan Solomon. Will led her through the questioning. Solomon's parents, who lived in a religious community outside of Jerusalem, were orthodox Jews. However, she had found herself searching for her own individual spiritual road. So when she heard about a "nondenominational Bible-study group" that was meeting just beyond the Damascus Gate in Jerusalem, she decided to attend.

Solomon recalled meeting Gilead in a crowded upper room in an empty apartment…and how she had asked him questions about the Old Testament versus the New Testament.

"What did he tell you?" Will asked.

"That a relationship with God wasn't about rules, exactly. It was about God's grace. And he went on to say he felt God had led me to that meeting."

"I have shown you pictures of Yossin Ali Khalid and Louis Lorraine. Did you see them there that night?"

"I did. At one point they left and went downstairs."

"Did they take Gilead with them?"

"No. Mr. Amahn was still answering some questions I had."

"When did you leave the room?"

"A few minutes later, I decided to take a break…go outside and smoke a cigarette. When I got to the top of the stairway to go down, I saw them—that Lorraine guy talking with Mr. Khalid. They were just outside on the street level… the door where they were was sort of half-open."

"As you stood at the top of the stairs, could you hear them?"

"Sort of…I did hear Khalid say they shouldn't force some question to Mr. Amahn. Lorraine wanted to ask Mr. Amahn something about himself, but Khalid said no, not to do that…"

"Did they say anything else?"

"Well, that Khalid guy said he was keeping his eye on a girl with a backpack—and I was sure he was talking about me. It was a little creepy, because all of a sudden I got the feeling he was trying to recruit me for some religious group—and I really wasn't into that. So I hurried down the stairs and walked right past them. Khalid saw me hit the street, and he called after me…but I just kind of kept walking."

"Did Gilead Amahn, in any of his statements to you, talk about the Knights of the Temple Mount?"

"No. Never heard of them till after the bombing."

"Were Gilead's statements about God—did they strike you as being Christian in nature?"

After a moment's reflection, Solomon said, "I'm not sure. I'm not that much into Christianity per se. I did think that some of the things he said made some sense…you know, got me thinking. But then I was totally bummed out by what I overheard from Khalid about his trying to target me for his group."

Zayed was friendly and warm as he questioned the witness.

"In response to Mr. Chambers' questions, you said that you 'sort of' heard Khalid and Lorraine—those were your words—'sort of' heard them."

"Yeah."

"But didn't hear very well?"

"Some things I heard. The things I described already."

"Good. Thank you. That's what I meant. Okay—but some things they were discussing you didn't hear. Right?"

"I guess."

"Right before you left the room and got to the top of the stairs—whatever they were discussing then down on the street you could not have heard. True?"

"That's probably right."

"And if they were saying, for instance, that Gilead Amahn was part of a plan to destroy the Temple Mount…that his job would be to give the signal for the bombing—"

"Hey, wait a minute—"

Will looked up from his notes. There was a look of surprised recollection on Solomon's face. Then she explained.

"I just remembered. Khalid did mention a *signal*."

"Did he say that the accused, Mr. Amahn, would give the signal?"

"He may have…I'm not sure."

"You must be sure. Didn't he say that the accused would give the signal for the bombing—"

"No—nothing about a bombing. Believe me, I would have remembered that. He just said, like, 'he will give us the signal'… something like that."

"Hassan Gilead Amahn would give the signal…"

"I'm not sure who he was talking about…"

"He must have meant the accused because you said they had just been talking about Mr. Amahn."

"I'm just not sure who, or what, he meant…"

"You must be sure about this—you will not leave this courtroom until you are very sure—"

Will was up on his feet, objecting loudly that the prosecution was "harassing the witness, and engaging in repetitive questions in an apparent attempt to wear down Miss Solomon."

Judge Mustafa intervened. But rather than sustain Will's objections, he launched into his own questions of the witness, asking her in several different ways whether Khalid seemed to be saying that Gilead Amahn would be giving some kind of signal.

In the end, Susan Solomon admitted confusion about the whole incident. Whether the prosecution had really gained ground with their cross-examination was unclear to Will and Nigel. But Samir Zayed's grinning exhuberance at the end of the day left no doubt how he was feeling about his capital case against Gilead Amahn.

The two lawyers then met with Bill and Esther Collingwood, who had attended the day's proceedings. Having missed the prosecution's case and Will's cross-examinations, they were confused about the evidence. But it was not confusion that their faces expressed. It was grief. They were stunned that the case was still progressing against their son...and from what they had seen in court, the prosecution's case seemed to be gaining momentum.

Nigel urged them not to judge the whole case by one day's testimony. And Will stressed that the defense still had crucial evidence to present—particularly Gilead's.

"He looks just awful," Esther lamented, ignoring what the two lawyers had just said. "Doesn't he, Bill? He looks just miserable. He's lost weight. There are dark circles under his eyes, and no spark in them."

Her husband had to agree. Then he said he knew Will and Nigel were doing their best, and they would leave them alone to prepare for the next day's testimony.

They worked late. Then Will caught a cab back to the hotel and trudged up to his room. He lay down on the bed for just a moment, but fell asleep in his clothes. Court was to convene at one in the afternoon the next day, which would leave him free to travel over to the jail and spend the morning with his client, going over his anticipated testimony.

The bright Jerusalem sunlight would break into Will's room far too soon the next morning. The end of the case was approaching. He had to keep pushing. Keep praying. Not give up.

And somehow, he needed to convince Gilead Amahn of the same thing.

66

WILL SPENT SEVERAL HOURS in the tiny jail conference room, preparing Gilead for his testimony. His client was hesitant and tired, and was having problems focusing his thoughts. The stress of the months of imprisonment and his concern over the trial and the looming possibility of a death sentence had been wearing him down.

"One thing I wanted to clear up." Will glanced down at his notes. "When you visited Jerusalem last year, you said you took a side trip to Jordan. Exactly where did you go?"

Gilead looked at his lawyer blankly. "What did you say?"

"Gilead, I know you're under a lot of pressure, but you're going to have to focus."

Will repeated the question.

"Well...I visited my namesake."

"What do you mean?"

"The Gilead region on the east side of the Jordan River...my mother named me after it."

"That's interesting. Tell me about that."

"My mother visited there with her family when she was a teenager. She said, having grown up in a flat, desert part of Egypt, she found the Gilead region so beautiful...mountains and trees and streams. She always remembered that trip—wanted to return some day—but...well...never got the chance..."

His voice trailed off as he remembered his mother.

"You know," Will said gently, "it must have been hard for you—no that's not the right word. Horrendous—devastating—to see your mother burned to death in front of your own eyes—and you, being just a boy. My Andy...I think what it would be like for him to see that...I can't imagine it."

Gilead nodded, took a deep breath, and continued.

"It was...I was just numb for so long—then the hate and anger started building up. I was a handful for my father. Then we moved to America and he came to Christ, and we started going to church together, and then I accepted Jesus into my heart—and things started changing. Slowly...and then faster and more decidedly, I had this feeling that my mother's death could not have been in vain. Her martyrdom for the Lord Jesus at the hands of the Muslims there in Cairo had to have been for something. I felt that God was picking me to deliver the message to the same people who killed her."

"I can understand that—"

"Only—I felt that I was to be bold. No matter what the cost...or the risk."

"Do you think you were right?"

Gilead's face was troubled.

"I believe I was called to preach the gospel to the Muslims. I believe God loves me and saved me through Christ. And that His Word is powerful and perfect. But...beyond that...I have so many questions now..."

He couldn't speak for a few seconds. So Will gently intervened.

"You were telling me about how your mother named you after the Gilead region..."

Gilead nodded.

"When I went there last year, I went up on one of the mountains—a quiet place with a beautiful vista. I sat under a tree, and I had my Bible with me. I read Jeremiah—I think it was chapter eight—God is giving his message to Israel through His prophet. And the Lord is quoting the people who are saying, 'The harvest is past, the summer is ended, and we are not saved!' Then God replies, 'Is there no balm in Gilead, is there no physician there?' The Gilead area had this famous medicine—this special balm that could heal all kinds of sickness. But the people just wouldn't go there to get healed. So I thought to myself...*If people won't go, then I will go and bring the healing balm of Jesus to them...*"

His voice cracked a little. "When I was up there on that mountain I thought of my mother, and I just cried like a baby."

"You said you are dealing with some questions now," Will prompted quietly.

The young man lifted his head and looked deeply into Will's eyes.

"Maybe it's lack of faith. Or because I had so little discernment. I let myself get surrounded by members of a cult...they urged me on...meanwhile, I didn't realize they were just using me as a front for their plans...to murder all those people...so much death and destruction..."

"And you're blaming yourself?"

"I'm now doubting almost everything about my ministry. Maybe none of this would have happened if I hadn't decided to fly to Cairo...to try to reach the city for Christ...the same people that had persecuted my mother. Maybe things would have been different. And if that's true—then everything I tried to do is turning to dust..."

Gilead had his face buried in his hands.

Will leaned forward and grabbed his client's arm, speaking to him in a voice filled with quiet intensity.

"I'm thinking about this one particular prophet of God—for a while, fabulously successful. And then one day he found himself arrested and thrown into this dank, foul dungeon. He probably looked back at his life, much as you have. At one time his preaching along the Jordan River had attracted huge crowds. Everybody came. Peasants. Royalty. Soldiers. You know who I'm talking about—John the Baptist. He had spoken powerfully, pointing the way to the appearing of Jesus, the Promised One. Throngs of disciples had followed him.

"But then one day Jesus publicly appears. And they all start following Jesus. And John turns around, and the next thing he knows, his followers have dwindled down to nothing. And then King Herod throws him into prison. So, before they execute him—remember how it goes?"

Gilead looked up into Will's face.

"John in the dungeon, and he starts questioning," Will continued, "whether Jesus is the One—and John's disciples carry his doubts from his prison cell to where Jesus is preaching. And Jesus gives him the answer and tells them to take the message back. And the message for John is very simple—that the blind are seeing, the lame are walking, and the poor are having the gospel preached to them. That's the message. God's plan is being carried out. He is in control. His love is at work."

Then Will looked into Gilead's eyes and asked his last two questions of the day.

"So, what you have to ask yourself is this. Has the saving message of Christ been preached through you? And if it has—then are you willing to trust the rest to God?"

67

GILEAD'S DIRECT EXAMINATION WENT WELL. He looked rested and confident as he answered Will's questions. He vehemently denied any knowledge about the true theological agenda of Louis Lorraine, Yossin Ali Khalid, or any of the others who had befriended him in Jerusalem.

He was, he said, guilty only of naïveté in trusting those who turned out to be fiends rather than friends.

But Samir Zayed's cross-examination was cutthroat.

"Do you mean to say that you were just a poor, naïve little boy who got caught up with the wrong bunch?"

"I lacked discernment," Gilead answered, "but I had no intent to be part of their awful plot—"

"But you admit to visiting the al-Aqsa Mosque the year before..."

"Yes."

"And then it is bombed."

"Yes."

"You hold these so-called Bible-study meetings with the Knights of the Temple Mount—and they end up being terrorists and murderers?"

"I did not know that—but my answer to your question is yes."

"You preach on the streets of Jerusalem about Jesus predicting the rebuilding of the Temple of the Jews as a sign of His Second Coming—and you add that the Muslims will have to be removed from the Temple Mount for that to happen—and then—BANG! Explosions rock the Temple Mount at your very signal."

"I did not intend to give any such signal—"

"But the Knights of the Temple Mount took it to be a signal…"

"I could not read their minds."

"No, but you knew their plans…"

"No, never."

"Why did you accept their adulation as their promised messiah, the reincarnated Caliph al-Hakim?"

"I never believed I was any such thing—"

"Then why, after the explosions, did you hop in a cab and go to the famous Golden Gate and enter the city through that newly opened gate—the gate through which the promised messiah—as everyone knows—is supposed to enter Jerusalem upon his return?"

"I was driven there…there was gunfire…I was simply running for my life."

"But you got into the taxicab driven by a member of the Knights of the Temple Mount, who drove you directly to the Golden Gate."

"It seems planned, I know…but I was just running for my life…"

"Coincidence…after coincidence…after coincidence—Mr. Amahn, how many coincidences do you believe that this tribunal will accept before they find you guilty and sentence you to death?"

Gilead paused only an instant before he answered.

"Just as many as God allows."

Zayed waved his hand, scoffing and dismissing Gilead's testimony with contempt.

Will returned to the podium.

"About the Golden Gate—you are a student of Scripture—where does it say that Jesus will enter the city through that gate?"

"It doesn't," Gilead answered. "I talked to several Bible scholars and some very learned rabbis when I visited Jerusalem last year.

About the walls of the city, and the various gates and so forth, and their history. I was told that the business about the messiah returning through the Golden Gate is not mentioned in the Torah or the Midrash either, or in any other of the Jewish writings… apparently it is more of a legend, I guess."

Will sat down.

Zayed returned once more to the podium.

"You consulted with Christian scholars about the Golden Gate?"

"Yes."

"And consulted with Jewish rabbis about the Golden Gate?"

"Yes, I did."

"You showed a very great interest in that gate for someone who says he was not planning to enter through it himself, pretending to be some kind of messiah."

"Just a historical interest, nothing more than that."

"Then why," the prosecutor demanded, "did you not put the same question to a *Muslim* cleric as well?"

Gilead thought for a moment, then answered hesitantly.

"I'm not sure…I don't know…"

"Well, I know," Zayed said scornfully, "and I think that the members of this tribunal know the answer to that as well."

As the Palestinian prosecutor finished his examination, Will surveyed the judges for some glimmer of sympathy for Gilead's side of the story.

But scanning their faces, he found none.

68

"WHILE AT THE FBI, I SPECIALIZED in what you might call domestic terrorism…both homegrown groups that used violence, like white-supremacy groups, and cells in the United States that were suspected of being part of international terror networks."

"You investigated the use of explosives in crimes of violence?"

"I did. Prior to my work at the Bureau, I was in the bomb squad of the Boston police. When I joined the FBI, they naturally tapped into that experience. Later, I taught explosives-investigation techniques at their training school at Quantico, Virginia. After I left the Bureau, I also worked on a private-contract basis with the Israeli police in trying to construct a strategy to foil suicide bombers."

Mike Michalany was a stocky, red-haired man with a friendly manner—but an underlying no-nonsense approach to bombs and those who would use them. With experience in hundreds of criminal cases involving explosives, he looked comfortable as he sat in the witness booth.

"And presently," Will continued, "you are president and CEO of Intellitek, an international security firm?"

"Yes. We specialize in providing intelligence data and safety systems to global corporations and multinational companies. We help business folk stay safe as they expand operations in foreign sites."

Will led Michalany through a series of questions about his investigation, as an expert for the defense, into the Temple Mount attack, including his visit to the site, his meetings with Israeli officials, his review of both Israeli and Palestinian police reports about the incident, and his "contacts with acquaintances within the FBI, and some foreign law-enforcement agencies regarding the bombing."

The witness described his conclusions about the material used for the bombing.

"The explosives used were a species of C-4 plastic explosives, with the operative agent being something called RDX. But the particular type of plastic explosive used was Semtex. That is a harder-to-obtain variety—it originated in the former Czechoslovakia. Terrorists like the stuff because it is higher grade and packs a more lethal punch. It's the most powerful non-nuclear explosive in the world."

"How would a terrorist group—or anyone for that matter—obtain Semtex?"

"Two primary ways. First, you could try to get it from either a terror group or a rogue state that deals in terror, like Libya—but that's difficult if you don't have the terrorist credentials. The other way is to go directly to the source. That would require that you have some entrée into the criminal syndicates operating within the Russian Federation. And, of course, you need a whole lot of cash to buy that amount of Semtex."

"Did you utilize FBI contacts within the Russian Federation to find out whether a large quantity of Semtex had exchanged hands within the months prior to the bombings?"

"I did."

"We'll return to that issue in a minute. Changing gears, did the United States formally participate in the investigation into the Temple Mount attack?"

"Well…the federal government made a policy decision to send FBI agents merely as 'consultants'—primarily to the Palestinian Authority…"

"How about sending FBI agents over to assist Israel's Mossad in investigating the bombing, as well—since a number of Jewish citizens were also killed?"

"There was...a high-level policy decision from our government not to do that...it was a somewhat controversial decision."

"A decision at how high a level?"

"At the very highest level in Washington."

"Did you evaluate the detonation apparatus used in the two vehicles—the one manned by Louis Lorraine and the one by Yossin Ali Khalid?"

"I did. It was a very sophisticated wireless computer and keyboard system sending a signal to remote switches, which then ignited blasting caps, which ignited the Semtex plastic explosive."

"Exactly how sophisticated was that system?"

"So advanced that, when I reviewed the Israeli police and Mossad data which described it, I was immediately convinced that the Knights—remember that they had no technical experience in explosives—must have had the system rigged for them by some outside provider."

"A minute ago I said we would return to the issue of the Semtex—whether your FBI contacts within the Russian Federation were aware of any large purchases of that plastic explosive just prior to the bombings. What did you learn?"

Michalany glanced down at his notes. Then he looked up at Will, smiling.

"That there was a bulk delivery through the Russian criminal syndicate—to some outside entity."

"Which entity?"

Samir Zayed's torso was stretched forward over the prosecution table, tensed like a guitar string.

All three of the judges had their eyes riveted on Michalany.

In the crammed media room down the hall from the courtroom, Jack Hornby was now standing up, bouncing on the balls of his feet. When he had heard, some days before that Warren Mullburn might be called to testify, he had caught the next flight to Jerusalem. The journalist figured that the deadline for his almost-completed article on the billionaire would have to wait. He intended to catch the last act of this drama in person.

"Which entity received the explosive?" Will asked again.

"The Russians were unable to determine that."

Prosecutor Zayed slowly eased back in his chair.

"Were they able to determine anything about the delivery?"

"Yes—they were."

"Like what?"

"Like who paid for it."

"And—who paid for it?"

Now Zayed was leaning forward again in tortured anticipation, his feet barely on the floor.

Back in the media room, Jack Hornby stopped bouncing. No one was breathing.

"The Russian police followed the money trail—" Michalany continued, but then stopped. He glanced at his notes. Then he finished his answer.

"And the money trail led to an account in Rome—and the account belonged to a foreign state."

"Which foreign state?" Will asked from the podium, almost in a whisper.

"The Republic of Maretas."

Hornby was muttering to himself and shaking his head, "He's going to do it. Will—you're going to do this…. you're bringing this right to Mullburn…"

Judge Mustafa had a disoriented look on his face, as if he were refusing to process the answer to the last question. But Alain Verdexler, seated next to him, was already calculating the implications. And for him, there now seemed to be no easy way out of this yawning geopolitical abyss.

But in a moment that abyss would crack open even wider.

"And have you been able to trace the source of the computer hardware that was used to detonate the explosion?"

Zayed stood up. He wanted to object. But he was caught in an intractable dilemma. To object any further would make it appear as if he were attempting to cover up the true identity of the killers of his fellow Muslims.

"What is it?" Judge Mustafa asked, in a voice reflecting fatigue from the unraveling of the prosecution's case before him.

"Nothing." Zayed slowly sat down.

"Please continue," Will said to his expert.

"We did trace the computer hard drive—"

"How?"

"When the Israelis had possession of the hard drive and computer keyboards before the Palestinian Authority demanded they be turned over, they disassembled the equipment and did a quick forensic evaluation."

"What did they find?"

"Nothing, really. There were no serial numbers. No identifying components that would point to any one source—"

"Was there something else?"

"Oh, yes. There was," Michalany glanced over at the judges, who were transfixed.

"There was a sort of…anomaly. You see, the forensic specialist with the Israelis became ill after examining the computer components. You, Mr. Chambers, told me that you had read in the Palestinian reports that Dr. el Umal, their expert, who had also examined the components, had also fallen ill. You suggested I follow up on the nature of the specialist's illness."

"Did you?"

"Yes. It was a rare form of botanical poisoning—caused by exposure to resins from a plant that had found their way into the inner components of the computer…probably from the hands of the computer designer."

"What kind of plant?"

"Something called—" Michalany looked down at his notes, "called *cicuta maculata*—otherwise known as 'water hemlock.' It can look deceptively like the kind of greens you could put in a salad. It's indigenous to the swampy areas of North Carolina, among other places. But if ingested, it can cause respiratory distress, followed by foaming at the mouth and a very unpleasant death. Happily, the residue picked up by the computer specialist was quite minimal."

"Did you do any research regarding recent use of this plant?"

"Yes. The FBI botanical section verified only one recent incident. A real-estate salesman from North Carolina died on an airplane flight en route back to the United States. The cause of death was poisoning by ingestion of the *cicuta maculata* plant."

"You said this unfortunate man was flying back to America. Where had he been just prior to his death by poisoning?"

In the media room, several dozen reporters were frozen in disbelief, hardly daring to think they would witness the unveiling of the real plot behind the Temple Mount massacre.

"The real estate agent," Michalany replied, "had just left the large island of the Republic of Maretas."

"Will Chambers—you are doing it! You are doing it!" Jack Hornby was yelling as the other reporters knocked over chairs in a scramble to reach their laptops and cell phones.

"Of course," Michalany continued, "we knew that Mr. Orville Putrie was now living on the islands of that republic and was employed by its government, and was a former resident of North Carolina and an avid amateur botanist. So that naturally led us to the conclusion that someone in the government of that republic had sponsored the Temple Mount attack—and that Khalid and Lorraine were simply a couple of religious cultists used as the front for the real conspiracy."

Then Will asked the final series of questions, which dealt with the Mossad's detection of someone's unlawful entry by remote computer access and the manipulation of its encrypted surveillance logs concerning the Knights of the Temple Mount—all, apparently, to make it look as if Israel had deliberately neglected to stop the plans of the Knights. It was the final link exposing Warren Mullburn's convoluted plot.

Will Chambers had intended to use Michalany to tie that computer hacking to Orville Putrie, computer intelligence chief for Mullburn's island republic.

But here, Zayed objected, wanting to exclude any evidence that would exonerate Israel from the incident.

Judge Mustafa quickly sustained the objection, characterizing Will's inquiry as "beyond the scope of the knowledge or expertise of this witness."

But Will simply smiled and said quietly to himself, "It doesn't matter."

"Did you say something?" Mustafa asked in a bewildered voice.

Will shook his head. *Soon enough*, he thought, *it would all be clear*.

Zayed tried a half-hearted cross-examination, focusing on the fact that Michalany was relying on the equipment evaluation done by the Israelis, rather than his own personal observation. But the witness quickly replied that he had had his own computer consultant at Intellitek independently review the work of the Israelis and verify their findings—and he further pointed out that his computer expert was there in Jerusalem, ready to testify if needed.

Mira Ashwan, who had been silent during the last few days, rose for some limited questioning—mainly impugning the motives of the Israeli military and police in so quickly confiscating the computer evidence before finally turning it over to the Palestinian police. She was no match for Michalany's deft answers.

"Does the defense rest?" Mustafa asked hopefully as Mira sat down.

"No," Will declared. "One more witness."

Just then noise erupted in the hallway outside. Voices were yelling. First, warnings in Arabic. Then responses in Hebrew. The shouts were getting louder. It sounded as if a fight were about to break out just outside the courtroom.

"I believe my last witness has just arrived," Will said with a smile.

69

A SMALL SQUADRON OF ISRAELI OFFICERS with sidearms burst into the courtroom. In their midst, clothing disheveled, hair uncombed, Orville Putrie was in custody, peering out of the thick lenses of his glasses as he was hastened to the front. Leading the contingent was a large, thick-necked man in a black suit and black turtleneck, sporting a completely bald head. Putrie was wearing handcuffs, but the man in the black suit unlocked them and gave him a little shove in the direction of the witness booth.

"Orville Putrie," Will announced, "the last defense witness."

In the doorway of the courtroom, several Palestinian police were loudly murmuring in protest against the presence of the Israeli military inside the Orient House.

"Quiet!" Judge Mustafa cried out.

Putrie slowly shuffled toward the booth, giving one last, resentful look at his captors before he entered and closed the door.

Then Will began. He questioned Putrie on his area of responsibility within the island republic controlled by Mullburn...on Mullburn's face-to-face meeting with him and his boss's personal reliance on his expertise in breaking through the encryption system of a foreign state...and how later Putrie discovered he was to hack into the Mossad computer system and manipulate intelligence data regarding their surveillance of the Knights of the Temple Mount. Once he had accomplished that, Putrie reported, he had decided to apply for a U.S. patent for a program designed to detect the precise kind of decoding he had just done on Israel's quantum-encryption system. Lastly, the computer genius recounted how, in the month prior to the bombing, he had been instructed by Mullburn's assistant, Mr. Himlet, to design and then construct a remote detonation system capable of setting off a large quantity of plastic explosives.

"Do you know of any involvement of the Israeli government in planning or encouraging the attack on the Temple Mount—or in deliberately permitting it to be carried out?"

"No. Those guys were not involved."

"Do you know of any involvement whatsoever of Gilead Amahn in any part of this plot?"

Putrie paused for only an instant. Then he simply said, "No. Not him either."

"And do you, Mr. Putrie," Will asked, "have an interest in botany?"

Putrie gave a little grimace.

"Oh yes."

"Including the deadly *cicuta maculata* plant, cuttings of which you brought to the Republic of Maretas from North Carolina?"

"Yes. Matter of fact, I have a fine collection now in my greenhouse..."

"Did you happen to work on the aforementioned computer detonation system after cutting some of those plants in your greenhouse?"

"I believe I did. Caught—green-handed, I guess."

With that, the witness started mumbling something, half-smiling in a twisted grimace as if he were telling himself his own private, tortured joke.

When Will rested, Putrie perked up.

"Aren't you going to tell everybody how we first met?" he asked.

Will rose and faced the tribunal.

"The witness is referring to an encounter we had in North Carolina when I was working on an unrelated case."

Then he concluded by adding, "But that is a different story altogether."

Samir Zayed stepped quickly up to the podium. He asked Putrie how he happened to be in Jerusalem.

"I was kidnapped off the main island of Maretas...in the middle of the night...by these Israeli goons..."

The prosecutor then howled out several objections to the defense "obtaining a witness by an illegal seizure in violation of international human-rights standards."

Mustafa, trying to contain the legal melee unfolding in front of him, said the tribunal would defer ruling on that until later.

Then Zayed asked what plea bargain the Israelis had made with Putrie to get him to testify.

"No death penalty."

"Outrageous!" Zayed yelled.

"No more outrageous than your plea bargain with Scott Magnit," Will countered loudly.

"The government of Israel can make no such promise to bind us!" Zayed went on. "The Palestinian Authority is not bound by that plea bargain. Mr. Putrie, we will arrest you here and now, and we will then prosecute you, and we will obtain a death penalty. Now, Mr. Putrie—do you wish to retract your testimony in light of what I have just said?"

The bald man in the black suit rose to his feet and stepped briskly forward to face the panel.

"Mr. Zayed—and Judges of this tribunal," he said solemnly in a thick accent, "I am authorized by the government of Israel to announce that the Israeli police and the IDF have this building entirely surrounded and secured. Mr. Putrie is in the lawful detention of the nation of Israel. Any attempt by the Palestinian public prosecutor or the Palestinian Authority or their police to interfere with our custody of Mr. Putrie, will result in my ordering an immediate military intervention against this facility."

There was a stunned silence in the courtroom.

In the media room, reporters were motionless, as stiff as stone artifacts, some holding cell phones, some with fingers poised over keyboards. They were waiting, eyes fixed on the television monitor.

But Samir Zayed had played his last card. The catastrophic revelations in the final phase of Will's defense had left his prosecution dazed and dismayed. He raised his hands up in frustration, then dropped into his seat at the table.

Orville Putrie was quietly escorted out of the glass booth by the Israeli agents, out of the courtroom, and into an armored personnel carrier waiting outside the building. The Israeli police and IDF troops then rapidly retreated from the Orient House with their prisoner.

"The defense rests," Will announced.

Then he renewed his motion for dismissal of the criminal case against Gilead Amahn.

"This tribunal will take the motion under advisement," Mustafa said with an overwhelmed look on his face. He then declared the proceedings adjourned for three hours and slammed his gavel down on the bench.

In the media room, Jack Hornby was still standing in the same position. But his mouth had dropped slightly open. And his eyes were unblinking as he stared at the television monitor, shaking his head.

70

As THE COURTROOM CLEARED, Will and Nigel tried to explain the significance of the day's roller-coaster developments to Bill and Esther Collingwood. While there was no guarantee that Gilead would be acquitted, they said, the testimony of Michalany and Putrie did establish a positive link to Warren Mullburn. That meant that the real plot had been hatched between Mullburn— for his geopolitical purposes—and Khalid and Lorraine—who had sought to fulfill the prophecy of their religious cult. For his part, Will figured that the oil tycoon must have used a highly trusted middleman to connect with the Knights and supply the deadly hardware, but his identity was still unknown.

As a result, that placed Gilead one full step removed from the real conspiracy. And it distanced him even further from the real players in the murder-and-mayhem plot. Coupling that with the other evidence of his innocence, the lawyers felt a real confidence that justice might be done after all.

Esther looked upset and pale, so Bill decided to take her back to the hotel. As Will, Tiny, and Nigel strode down the hallway to catch some fresh air, Jack Hornby dashed out of the pressroom in a frenzy to get a few quotes from the defense team, not only for his magazine article, but for the story he was now sending out over the wires.

"So, 'man meets grizzly bear,'" Hornby said, calling out a mock newspaper headline to Will, "'and man eats bear!'"

The trio caught a taxi and found a nearby café. It was a clear bright day, and they found an outdoor table, where they ordered some coffee and untwisted the defense of Gilead that had just rested.

Will explained to his bewildered co-counsel how it had all started with a magazine article that had been shoved under his hotel-room door. It was about the patent application Putrie had filed.

"Who on earth fed the information to you?" Nigel asked.

"A former Mossad agent in Jerusalem. And a good friend— Nathan Goldwaithe."

"I thought he was dead," Nigel exclaimed.

"No. That was actually his partner," Will explained. "To protect him, the Mossad treated the death as if it were Nathan's— and he in turn has been living under an assumed identity ever since. Tiny and I finally pieced this all together when Michalany connected the dots on the plant toxin found in the computer components. We finally got a sit-down with the Israelis—who decided it was time to lift the cover on Nathan and start working with us to zero in on Mullburn. The only way to do that was to literally grab Putrie. When we convinced the Mossad it was in Israel's best interest to completely clear its name in the bombings, they decided to send in a group of special ops guys to seize Putrie and offer him a deal in return for his testimony."

"Which is why," Tiny said to Nigel, "Will here thought you ought to be protected from any involvement—in case things went bad, you know, allegations of kidnapping Putrie and that stuff. No sense putting two heads on the chopping block when only one will do."

"Well, I must say," Nigel said, still laughing a little at Tiny's sardonic comment, "your cases are hugely more exciting than the criminal suits I handle down at the Old Bailey back in London."

When Nigel glanced over at Will, he noticed that his lead counsel had a strange look on his face.

"What is it?" Nigel asked, slightly alarmed. "You look like you've seen a ghost."

"I just remembered why there was something familiar about you. I had this lingering feeling we had met. And I don't mean just last year at that legal conference—I mean way back, years ago."

"I don't understand…"

"Your name. Newhouse. I just remembered. I had this case down near Cape Hatteras about ten years ago. An inheritance case, a contested probate of a will. That's where I had this run-in with Putrie, by the way. Anyway, I had to do quite a bit of historical research into a related case handled under the English court system all the way back in the 1700s…I read these old court transcripts. The arguments of counsel from three hundred years before. And there was this English barrister by the name of—"

"Oliver Newhouse," Nigel said quickly.

"Exactly. That's the one."

"Right you are. He was a rather famous barrister of his day. Actually, I am his direct descendant. His oil portrait hangs in our law rooms…in our offices there in Fleet Street. Where the old Inns of Court used to be."

Will was shaking his head and laughing. Tiny and Nigel were now chuckling at him.

"You'll have to forgive me. But…Oliver Newhouse…that is amazing. You see, I sort of developed this connection with him during that case—bridging the centuries—a lawyer-to-lawyer thing. In a strange way, I felt it was almost as if Oliver had been my co-counsel in that case. I relied on his cross-examination questions from that ancient transcript—his arguments. It's hard to explain…"

After a moment of silence, Nigel raised his coffee cup and offered a toast.

"Here's to lawyers from all the ages," he said.

"And to their private investigators!" Tiny added with gusto.

After more joking, the three of them started thinking about their return to the courtroom. And the solemnity of the moment started setting in once more. Despite rocking the prosecution's case with their revelations of the Mullburn connection, they still had no way to predict the outcome. They simply did not know whether they had succeeded in sparing Gilead's life or not. And that uncertainty had all the terrible crushing force of a pile driver.

By the time the three of them cabbed back to the Orient House, the Collingwoods were already in the courtroom. Palestinian police were nervously stalking the hallways. Then Zayed and his entourage filed in and sat down. Lastly, Gilead was led into the courtroom, flanked by his guards.

Gilead threw a quick kiss to his mother, nodded to Bill, and sat down. Will patted his client on the back and said a few things to reassure him as they awaited the entrance of the judges.

Minutes later, Judge Lee Kwong-ju, followed by Judges Alain Verdexler and Saad Mustafa, each in their crimson judicial gown, filed into the courtroom, seating themselves behind the wall of glass.

Lee glanced over at Gilead. Verdexler was looking aimlessly around the room. And Mustafa was nervously tapping and re-shuffling the papers in front of him.

"The matter of the Palestinian International Tribunal versus Gilead Amahn, Case Number PA-ICRT-001...will all counsel and the accused re-stand, please."

There was a shuffle of feet as Samir Zayed, Will Chambers, Gilead Amahn, Nigel Newhouse, and Mira Ashwan stood up.

"This tribunal has considered, first, the defense motion to dismiss this case."

Mustafa glanced sideways at Lee Kwong-ju. Then he continued.

"The votes on this motion are as follows—Judge Mustafa votes against dismissing the prosecution."

Esther Collingwood gave a pitiful groan and closed her eyes.

"Judge Lee," Mustafa continued, "votes for dismissal of the prosecution. And lastly, Judge Verdexler—"

Mustafa scratched the side of his face, and then gave his head half a shake.

"Judge Verdexler votes—to abstain."

"It's a tie," Nigel Newhouse shot out in a strained whisper.

"A deadlocked court," Will snapped.

Gilead was looking at one attorney and then at the other in total confusion.

"What's going on?" he asked hoarsely. "What…what's going to happen now?"

Judge Mustafa would answer that question immediately.

"It is my authority as president of this tribunal and chief judge of the trial chamber, to enter the final judgment in this case. Which is—that the prosecution shall be *dismissed*…but *without prejudice*. This leaves the Palestinian public prosecutor free to refile charges against the accused in the light of the new evidence that was presented during this trial by the defense—but only if the prosecutor so chooses."

Bill and Esther Collingwood, who were holding onto one another, were now starting to summon up some hope—guarded—but hope nonetheless.

"Release of the accused—" Will announced. "The tribunal must address that issue as well."

Samir Zayed, who seemed strangely unsurprised by the dismissal, smiled and then completely surprised the defense team.

"We do not oppose the immediate release of the accused into the custody of his attorney," Zayed declared.

"So ordered," Mustafa answered.

Two Palestinian guards swept over to Gilead's side as the three judges rose and quickly exited the courtroom.

Zayed ushered Will and Gilead to a different side door than the one he'd entered through, instructing them to go immediately to the processing office to file the paperwork for Gilead's release.

Will and Gilead stepped through the door and into a dim hallway. Nigel was about to follow, but Zayed stopped him abruptly, closing the door behind Will and Gilead.

"Only one lawyer," he told the barrister firmly.

Will and his client made their way down a flight of stairs toward a heavy metal door. When Will pushed it open, their eyes were momentarily blinded by the bright Jerusalem afternoon sun. They stepped out and found themselves in the narrow side alley outside of the Orient House.

That is when they both knew something was terribly wrong.

A black European-model van was parked by the door.

Then the doors of the van burst open. Three gunmen jumped out, bearing automatic weapons and wearing black hoods with ragged eye-holes.

Screaming in Arabic, they pointed their weapons at Will and Gilead, grabbed them and wildly shoved them into the back of the van. The doors slammed shut and the vehicle raced off.

Will could not understand what they were screaming.

But Gilead could.

They were shouting, "Allah is great! Allah is good! Allah is great! Allah is good!"

The van sped out of the city and onto the Dead Sea Road. They were now rapidly moving away from Jerusalem and toward the desert regions of the south.

71

IT WAS SHORTLY AFTER DAWN when Fiona awoke. Something had startled her, though she could not remember what. Perhaps a dream. Or a sound. Or a vague sense that on this day in particular, she needed to rise, and rise quickly. And so she got out of bed.

Intuitively, she checked on Andrew. He was slumbering deeply, his young body wrapped in a confusing tangle of sheets, his arm dangling over the side of the bed. On the floor, directly below his hand, was a Heroes of the Bible comic book. She quietly picked it up and read the page where Andrew had placed a Baltimore Oriole's baseball card as a bookmark.

It was entitled "Abram the Warrior." The chapter started out,

> Abram (later named "Abraham" by the Lord) used a small band of trusted friends, in a daring nighttime raid, in an effort to try to save his nephew, Lot. The Kings of the East had captured Lot. Now Abram is in pursuit. Read what happens!

The text was accompanied by a cartoon drawing of Abram on horseback, sword raised, leading his men as they galloped to the north of Damascus for battle.

Fiona put the comic book on his dresser and slipped downstairs. Then she poured herself a cup of coffee, grabbed her Bible, and went out onto the porch. She usually started her day that way. But this morning she couldn't focus. Her mind was racing. She knew that Will's trial should be ending soon. And now she needed to have him with her.

Soon you'll be home, darling—we'll be together. Oh, Will, I feel so useless without you, she was thinking. Then something Will had said once—a small, insignificant, and silly joke—suddenly came into her mind, and she found herself laughing out loud. She put her Bible down and spent some time praying.

When she opened her eyes, she took in the view of the mountaintops off at the horizon. It was a mild day. In the distance, a few clouds were sailing across the Blue Ridge.

Andrew had the day off school because of a teacher's convention, so Fiona decided to take him with her to Baltimore, where she was going to do an early run-through at the pavilion where her concert was to be held that night.

It was mid-morning in the United States when the news hit. Fiona was already at the concert hall near Baltimore's Inner Harbor when she found out.

It was the auditorium where Will had first heard Fiona sing. They had barely known each other back then. But, off in the wings, he had watched her in concert. And he had seen this beautiful woman who sang like something from heaven. And had felt himself drawn to her in an irresistible way.

Fiona was up on the stage now, and the concert manager was asking her to go through one more sound check.

"Sing anything for me," he shouted out, his voice echoing.

Andrew was sitting in the front row reading his comic book, a little bored. In the middle of the empty hall, a burly bodyguard hired by Will and Tiny was sitting quietly, studying all the corners of the space.

Then Fiona started to sing in a slow, lilting, ethereal soprano, almost as slow as a dirge,

> *Jesus loves me! This I know,*
> *For the Bible tells me so.*
> *Little ones to Him belong;*
> *They are weak, but He is strong.*

Just then Fiona's agent came running full speed down the center aisle. The bodyguard, sensing something wrong, jumped up and followed him up the stairway to the stage.

Andrew somehow knew that his mother needed him, and he followed up the side stairs to the stage platform as well.

Fiona's agent was saying something to her in an urgent voice. She cried out, then put her hands over her mouth. As she faltered for just a step, the agent reached out and steadied her.

"Mom, what's wrong?" Andrew asked, pushing his way through the grown-ups.

"It's your dad…he's in trouble."

"Trouble?" Andy cried out, his face a reflection of boyhood suddenly being overwhelmed by the juggernaut forces of life.

"Yes, darling," Fiona said, composing herself, "very bad trouble. You must pray for him…pray hard. Very hard. God, protect my precious husband…"

Then she turned to the agent.

"I need phones. As many as you can get."

The agent and the bodyguard both pulled out their cell phones.

"And I've got one!" the lighting technician up in the catwalk yelled down to the group.

"Bring it down!" Fiona called up. "I've got mine. That's four. I'll call over to…what's his name…oh…the general at the Pentagon. Will and I met him. Worked with Will on the ICC case in The Hague. His daughter likes my music. Tucker—General Tucker. I'll call. Someone has to contact the State Department. Someone has to track down Tiny Heftland in Jerusalem—"

"I'll do that!" the bodyguard said and started calling his office to make the international connection.

"Hurry—we have to hurry!" Fiona cried out as she started madly punching numbers for Washington, DC, information into her phone.

72

DAKKAR WAS LISTENING TO THE NEWS on the radio in the horse barn on the Dupree farm. It was announced that a Hamas splinter group had kidnapped Virginia lawyer Will Chambers and his client, Hassan Gilead Amahn, in Jerusalem immediately following their court victory, in which the criminal charges relating to the Temple Mount attack had been dismissed.

Muttering to himself and with a lump in his throat, Dakkar picked up the phone on Bill Collingwood's desk and began calling his cousin Akbar, who lived in Hebron and was a Hamas sympathizer.

"Akbar—the son of my friend here in the States, Bill Collingwood, and the son's lawyer, Mr. Will Chambers...they were kidnapped. I heard it on the news...have you heard about this?"

On the other end Akbar chuckled. "Heard about it?"

"Yes. Heard anything?"

"Heard! I just got a call from Yaheed. He's one of the courageous ones in on the operation!"

"No. No. They can't do that—"

"They've done it. Allah be praised. You're becoming like the soft American infidels. Now get off the phone. I have to keep this line free."

Then his cousin hung up.

Dakkar was still holding the receiver. His hand was quivering.

He felt the vise grip of tribe and religion, reinforced by the weight of the centuries, crushing down on him...why should he believe that he could do anything against such imponderable forces as those?

Tears began to trickle down his face. He was still weeping as he slowly stood up—and then put one foot in front of the other, walking out of the barn.

Roland Dupree was climbing into his Land Cruiser when he saw Dakkar coming up the long driveway from the barn. And by now he was at a full run, and he was yelling something.

73

FIONA WAS TALKING ON THE PHONE with General Tucker when her call-waiting flashed that an international call was coming in. She apologized to General Tucker—could he wait? Then she took the call.

Jack Hornby was on the other end, talking a mile a minute. He had just talked to Bob Fuller at the State Department, asking him what the U.S. government was going to do about the kidnapping.

"On the record," Fuller had said, "we're deeply shocked that two American citizens are victims of what appears—at this point—to be a terrorist-orchestrated kidnapping. We are working with Israel's government and the Palestinian Authority, as well as the UN peacekeeping force already in Jerusalem, to locate the captives and return them safely."

"And off the record?" Hornby had asked forcefully.

"Well, look, Jack—you know the administration's policy on Israel. So…we're mainly relying on the UN forces and the Palestinian police to track them down."

"Then those two guys are dead meat," Hornby replied brutally. "Why doesn't President Landow authorize our American guys to go in there and get Chambers and Amahn right now?"

"Not going to happen, Jack," Fuller said. "The timing is too tricky right now. Too risky. Maybe in a few days…after we see whether the golf ball is lying on the fairway or—"

Hornby had hung up on the State Department secretary in mid-sentence.

"Tell General Tucker," he told Fiona, "that he's got to use his black-ops authority—I've heard about it—he can put together something very quick. President Landow is simply not going to officially authorize a search and rescue. End of statement. Tucker has to do some kind of end run. He just has to."

Fiona immediately relayed the information to the general. He paused for less than ten seconds.

"Got to go, Mrs. Chambers," he said with a confident tone. "I'll see what I can do. We'll try to get your husband safely home by the time of your concert tonight—though that may be pushing it a bit."

Tucker immediately dialed an international number. A man's voice answeered in a marked West Virginia accent. "CM Pest Control."

"At least you're creative," Tucker said. "Look, Caleb, I've got a situation here—"

"Is it about Will Chambers and Gilead Amahn?"

"Yeah. You've heard?"

"I'm already on it. As you know, General, I'm not too far from the region right now."

Just then an aide rushed in with a message.

"Colonel Marlowe," Tucker said with an official tone to his voice, "I've got some additional intel on this. Some Middle Eastern fellow in Virginia has a cousin who is apparently in on this deal. It looks like credible information. We've got a landline number in Hebron that is receiving calls from the cell phone of the kidnappers."

"Can we do a SIGINT on the number of the bad guys?" Marlowe asked immediately.

Tucker looked at his watch.

"Possibly. I'll have to order that the Orion satellite be tasked to intercept—but the request has to come from some other country. The president would not like me very much if we did this American-style—maybe the Brits will do it for us. Put an official request into us because we jointly share the satellite. I'll work on it."

"I'll get to Jerusalem ASAP," Marlowe said. "I'll just figure you'll get me a location by the time I'm there. Let me work on putting together a team."

"You have to understand," Tucker said, "that this cannot be viewed as an operation of the U.S. government."

"Sure. Lone Ranger. That's me all over."

Up at the Syrian border, Caleb Marlowe, sporting a black beard, darkened skin, and traditional Arab dress, clicked off his phone.

Then he immediately began wondering where he was going to get his white horse.

74

GENERAL TUCKER PUT A CALL IN to Rear Admiral Reggie Chittenden at MI6, Britain's foreign-intelligence service. He explained his delicate dilemma—the United States could not be seen as taking the initiative in using its own spy satellite to track the terrorists, even though they had kidnapped two American citizens. President Harriet Landow was committed not to do anything that could be perceived as disrupting the peace process, particularly because she was now hoping, in light of Warren Mullburn's rapid geopolitical disintegration, that the United States could again take over the position as chief peace mediator.

It was clear, the two agreed, that the request could come from England, who shared satellite time on Orion. The U.S. could then rapidly permit the satellite to be tasked.

"I will have to put a call in to the prime minister," Chittenden noted. "Because a British barrister may be, hypothetically, in jeopardy in this kidnapping incident, that will give us a certain degree of political cover."

Tucker's next call was to the National Security Agency, the mammoth American surveillance and intelligence organization outside Annapolis Junction, Maryland.

"You're going to be getting a request from the British government to task Orion for a cell-phone number and to track the originating phone. Somewhere in Israel proper, but possibly including Syria to the north, Jordan to the west, and Egypt to the south. I want you to prioritize that request—I already know about it, and I've cleared it for the Pentagon."

Twenty-five minutes later approval had been granted. A coded message was received at Menwith Hill, the U.S. military satellite installation in North Yorkshire, England.

In Maryland, the NSA processed the order to task the satellite for all transmissions received via cell phone by the number of Dakkar's cousin in Hebron.

Responding to the NSA directive, two technicians in the satellite-tracking facility in Pine Gap, Australia, quickly calibrated the Orion.

And then, the listening began.

Minutes went by. Then ten minutes. Twenty minutes passed, with no cell-phone call connecting to the only telephone number they knew had any connection to the kidnapping.

At forty-seven minutes, the phone rang in Hebron. Akbar, Dakkar's cousin, answered. It was his cell-phone contact with the Hamas group that had snatched Will and Gilead.

Back in the U.S., in the tactical-operations office of the National Geospatial Intelligence Agency, two men and one woman sat in front of a computer screen. Then suddenly, a line of numbers rolled on to it.

"We've got it!" the senior official called out.

"Operation Paul Revere," so dubbed by General Tucker himself, was now underway.

In the computer-map room, a large grid of southern Israel was displayed in quarter-mile quadrants.

Then they calibrated the satellite for a closer look.

Rows of houses, streets, and blurred images of persons in a densely populated area.

Then a closer look.

A large rectangular object in a street. Surrounded by buildings. Suddenly four human thermal images rushed out of the van and pulled out two more human images from the back. Then all of them disappeared into the adjoining building.

"Get me map coordinates *stat!*" one of the map officials ordered.

Fifteen minutes later, General Tucker was on the phone with Caleb Marlowe.

"Speak louder," Caleb said. "I'm inside a Blackhawk helicopter. I caught a ride with the IDF. We're practically at Tel Aviv."

"You better keep flying...farther south..."

"How far?"

"We've got the coordinates," the general said. "And a fairly precise location. But it's not good news."

"Where do the kidnappers have our guys?"

"In the Gaza Strip. The place where, since we kicked the Taliban out of Afghanistan, there's probably more terrorists per square mile than any other part of the planet. We've located them on a street in a little rathole of a city called Rafiah. It's known for having a lot of tunnels that connect over the border to Egypt. And the terrorists scamper back and forth from Egypt to Gaza through those tunnels like a bunch of rats..."

"Are they in an apartment building?"

"Yes, our guys said they saw several armed figures in proximity to the location of the number we tracked, getting out of what looks like a van with two captives—and then they rushed them inside a building."

"Well, the Israelis said they can give me one Blackhawk helicopter and a handful of commandos, but that just isn't going to cut the mustard."

"No, I don't think so. A Blackhawk is way too big for a snatch and run. One of them comes in to that crowded street in Gaza and our guys are going to be dead in a minute."

"Do we have anything smaller? Some way to drop us in to that site with less noise—a minimal amount of fuss and bluster?"

Tucker thought for a few seconds.

"Let me call down to the R&D boys and see what we've got. I'll be back to you in less than five."

But the news that General Tucker received from the head of R&D for small military aircraft was not good.

"We've got one project, but I'm not sure if we're ready to go on it. We've got a contract with a former military aviator who has been working with an aeronautics engineer outside of Houston. But we haven't committed to production yet because we haven't test-proven this thing."

"Try to get the contractor on the line—I'll wait."

General Tucker was put on hold, and a few minutes later, he got his answer.

"I'm sorry, General," the voice at the other end said, "but Mr. Rhoady says he's not quite sure that the PUMA is ready to go into an actual tactical operation yet. He's test-flown it a lot but said there still need to be a lot of adjustments."

"PUMA?" Tucker asked.

"Yes, Personnel Ultralight Military Aircraft—but we've sort of nicknamed it 'the Mosquito.' It's designed for one pilot and can carry only a handful of men—it's on the plan of a helicopter with two small fixed wings for stability. It can zip in and zip out of areas like—well, sort of like a mosquito. Highly manageable, incredible response—very quick and very quiet."

"Patch me in directly to this Mr. Rhoady…is he still on the line?"

"He sure is, General—hang on."

In a private aircraft hangar on a flat stretch of land twenty miles outside of Houston, a tall, lanky ex-military aviator, stunt flyer, and now would-be military aircraft entrepreneur was holding the phone in his left hand and waving to a gray-haired man at the other end of the building.

"Bud—hey, Bud!" Rhoady yelled. "Come on over here. I've got somebody from the Pentagon asking about the Mosquito. They want to put it into some kind of actual military operation. I told them we're not there yet. What do you think?"

The gray-haired man, in blue jeans and a work shirt, calculator sticking out of his pocket, sauntered over to Rhoady.

"Way too early," the man said. "Remember—we still got that problem. Increased air speed with the requirement for erratic maneuvering, you get just too much instability. We're still working on that—"

"Yeah, but Bud—I'm the guy who's flown this thing," Rhoady said. "I've felt what you talked about. I think it might be manageable—I'm not saying I want to sell this thing to the government quite yet. We got to work out the kinks. But the question is, can we put it into actual operation—you know, as a test flight—"

Then a voice on the phone caught his attention.

"Mr. Rhoady, the next voice you hear will be that of General Tucker from the Pentagon."

"Mr. Rhoady…"

"General Tucker, it's an honor," Rhoady replied. "But everybody calls me Tex. So can you."

"All right, Tex. We need to put the Mosquito into an actual combat operation. We've got to do this stat. I just need to know whether this thing can be flown or not."

"Well, honestly, it can be flown…because I'm the guy who's flown it…but we've still got some adjustments—"

"We have to take this into a serious nest of terrorists—into a location I'll disclose to you later—but it's in the Middle East. It'd have to be brought into a very narrow street outside an apartment, drop a few special ops guys into a building, pick up some cargo, and take off—all in a very short period of time, while probably dodging some missiles and mortar fire."

After a few seconds of thought, Tex answered.

"I suppose you'd need a pilot?"

"Tex, I got a brief look at your military record. As far as I know, you're the only guy who has flown this—'Mosquito'…"

"I was afraid you'd suggest that," Tex said gloomily. "No offense, General, but I'm not a spring chicken anymore. I'm married…married for a number of years. Happily, I might add. I'm settled down. I just don't know…"

"I can understand," Tucker responded. "This is a high-risk situation. Everybody involved already knows that. We've got two American citizens, a lawyer and his client, who were kidnapped in Jerusalem by Hamas. If we wait too long there's going to be a double execution. It's been all over the news…"

"I haven't been hearing anything in the last three days," Tex said. "We've been pushing on this contract…ah…did you say it was a lawyer?"

"Yes," Tucker quickly replied. "A Virginia lawyer named Will Chambers. I had the opportunity to see him in action when he successfully defended one of our special operations guys a number of years ago."

"I can't believe it…Will Chambers…"

"You know him?"

"Yep. I did private-charter flying for him on some of his cases. We got to be pretty good friends. Flew him through a bad tropical storm once in an old double-winged Boeing PT-17 Stearman. So, General, looks like he's back in the thick of it…"

"Tex, we can have a small transport landing at your airstrip there in Texas within the hour. If you're willing to do this thing, you'll have to have the Mosquito fueled, primed, and ready to go. Load it on board, hop on, and they'll take you to the staging site in southern Israel."

There was a pause of a few seconds before Tex gave his answer.

"Okay, General—let's saddle up."

"One other thing. When this is all over, I'd be glad to set up a demonstration of your aircraft before the Joint Chiefs. And assuming everything goes well there, I'd probably be inclined to give a strong recommendation for some kind of production contract."

"With all due respect, General," Tex replied, "there's one thing you need to know."

"What's that?"

"I won't be doing this for the contract."

75

Caleb Marlowe had been briefed on the city layout of Rafiah in the Tel Aviv office of the Mossad. Tiny Heftland had been picked up and quickly transported to the meeting to give background on the day of the kidnapping.

Then Caleb Marlowe, Tiny Heftland, and the special-operations volunteer from the Mossad loaded into the lead Blackhawk helicopter, which was followed by two other choppers. They sped off to the south, toward the Gaza Strip.

Tiny continued to explain the events of the day that had led up to the seizure of Will and Gilead. He had already spoken to the Israeli police, who had a description of the van and an estimate of the number of gunmen involved.

Seated in the helicopter next to Caleb Marlowe was the only man the Israelis said they could afford to let join Marlowe's miniature special-ops team.

Because of geopolitical tensions, Israel could not formally enter the Gaza Strip in an offensive operation—though they could respond to a request for assistance from American citizens at risk in that region.

As a result, the immediate strike at the terrorists had to be something other than an Israeli military operation.

Nathan Goldwaithe, ex-Mossad member and no longer officially on the Israeli government payroll, fit the bill—except, of course, for the fact that he was now forty-five years old. The operation would require speed, strength, agility…and youth.

"So, Nathan," Caleb Marlowe said with a wry smile, "you think you can still rappel down a rope?"

"Colonel Marlowe, my friend," Nathan zinged back as Tiny Heftland grinned, "you're no spring chicken yourself."

When the squadron arrived at the staging area in the desert outside of the Gaza Strip, the high-speed transport bearing Tex Rhoady and his experimental helicopter had not yet arrived from the States. The sun was setting, and the cover of darkness would give them some slight advantage as they entered a Palestinian city known to be a nest of terrorists.

Two hours later, the transport jet set down on the abandoned strip of highway they were using as a makeshift landing strip.

Within forty minutes the Mosquito had been unloaded, Tex was at the controls, and Caleb Marlowe and Nathan Goldwaithe, supplied with automatic weapons, a variety of grenades, and night-vision glasses, were climbing in.

"I'm going along!" Tiny yelled. "There's no way you can leave me behind."

Caleb Marlowe shook his head.

"Sorry, Tiny," he yelled out of the open door of the strange-looking ultralight helicopter. "We've got two more people to pick up. One more man would make us too heavy."

As the Mosquito took off, Tiny ran briefly alongside the little helicopter, yelling up to Tex, Caleb, and Nathan.

"You guys make sure you get my boy, Will Chambers," he was yelling. "You bring him back safe!"

Marlowe threw a short salute to Tiny as the Mosquito sprang up into the air and then whisked off into the distance.

76

Night was falling in Rafiah. Outside, from the minaret a few blocks away—the one with the little green light at its peak, prayers were being droned out from a loudspeaker.

Will Chambers could see out the window of the third-story of the building they were in that the day was slipping away. Neither he nor Gilead had been blindfolded. He took that as a very bad sign.

Apparently the Hamas captors didn't care whether he and Gilead remembered where they had been taken or by whom. The three gunmen had pulled off their hoods and in addition to the driver, they had been joined by another man with an automatic weapon.

The two Americans sat cross-legged in the corner of the squalid, empty apartment that smelled of human waste and heat and dust, their hands tied behind their backs. The gunmen were checking their watches, pacing and looking like they were waiting for someone.

"A sheikh is coming...they're talking about a mufti...they're waiting for him," Gilead whispered to Will. "The rest...I can't make out."

One of the gunmen saw Gilead whispering. He strode over to him and with a stick he was carrying, beat the younger man across the face until his nose started bleeding profusely. The other men trained their guns on Will, who was forced to watch helplessly.

At first the attorney thought Gilead had been knocked unconscious. But after a few minutes he groaned—and finally, clumsily, jerked himself up to a sitting position.

"I think they broke my nose."

"Don't talk," Will said, barely audible, "unless I tell you."

Then the terrorist who had been using his cell phone during the trip pulled it out and made another call.

That cell phone was the only solace Will had found in their nightmare drive from Jerusalem to their final destination, the heart of Palestinian terrorism within the Gaza Strip. He could only hope that someone had witnessed their being seized outside the Orient House. If so, he knew the U.S. had the satellite capacity to track cell-phone calls. But only if they had a cell-phone number to track in the first place.

As Will sat in the sweltering, airless heat of the abandoned rooms, the odds of a rescue seemed infinitesimally small.

Then he whispered over to his companion.

"Pray…pray for a plan. I've got to figure this out…"

But for Will, there in the night, in that dismal room in Rafiah, there seemed to be little that could be figured out.

He prayed. For Fiona. That she would be comforted and protected in the aftermath of the news. *Lord, please let her know that my last thoughts were of her. How I want to hold her just once more…*And for young Andrew. He would be without a father… *Oh God, be the Father to him when I am gone…he's so young…*

Then they heard a commotion. Voices, coming up the stairs.

In less than a minute, two imams, worship advisors to Hamas, appeared in the room. Then the men stepped to the side and a third man entered the room. As he did, the two imams and the gunmen all bowed low.

Will looked up.

In the middle of the room was Sheikh Mudahmid.

He nodded, smiling grimly, to Will and Gilead, then waved his hand vaguely to the corner of the room. The men hastened over to the chairs that were there, ran them over to the sheikh, and set them down for him and the two imams.

"The Council of Eid al-Adha is commenced," the sheikh began when he was seated.

"What's that?" Will whispered to Gilead.

"The judgment of sacrifice…as in the sacrifice of the goat…slitting its throat…"

"Stand up!" one of the imams commanded. Two of the gunmen laid down their arms and produced a long, razor-sharp knife.

As Will and Gilead awkwardly struggled to their feet, Will whispered, "Is the sheikh their highest spiritual leader?"

When they were finally standing, Gilead whispered back.

"No. Sheikh Yassiheim, very old, he's the top—"

"Silence, pigs!" one of the imams yelled.

"Allah commands justice," Sheikh Mudahmid said calmly. "You, Mr. Chambers—you profess to know what that word means. But today, you will *feel* what it means—you will sense the cold steel of the blade and feel the blood running from you as your life ebbs away."

Then he turned to Gilead.

"And as for you—you were raised in the truth of Islam…you were taught the truths of the heavenly religion…I do understand that you were poisoned by your mother, who became a ranting Christian, an infidel…and even your father turned to the lies of the Christians when he went to America…but you are without excuse. Allah is not merciful to those who will not acknowledge him. And it shall be even worse for those who slaughter Allah's children as they kneel in worship—"

"You say this is a council," Will cried out. "You, Sheikh, are a man of great authority. Yet you were given the chance to testify against Gilead before the Palestinian International Tribunal—and they dismissed Gilead from any responsibility for the murder of your people in the Noble Sanctuary—"

"That tribunal?" Mudahmid roared back. "A mockery! Judges from Korea and Belgium deciding justice for the slaughtered souls of Muslims? Even Mustafa acted like a coward."

"Are you allowing us to present evidence, at least?" Will said, frantically struggling for some way to put off the inevitable.

"No," Mudahmid scoffed. "We have all the evidence we need." Then he nodded to the two men with the knives, and they walked toward Will and Gilead.

Will looked over at the approaching men. Then something caught his eye. Outside the window...in the dark...he saw a red laser light, and a flashing glint of metal, perhaps a reflection...and the shape of a large, oblong object suspended silently in the air outside, containing within it the red beams and human shapes. And then it was gone, like some great, flitting insect.

And that is when Angus MacCameron's words were there, burning far brighter in Will's memory than the red of the laser lights and the white glinting reflections.

"Like the apostle Paul before King Agrippa..."

He could almost hear the old Scot asking him, as he would often, *"Do you remember your Bible, son?"*

"Yes, I do."

"And what does it say?"

"That Paul preached to Agrippa..."

"And when he was done preaching, then?"

"Then...then he appealed...to Caesar..."

"Stop!" Will cried out.

The knives were already at their throats. Sheikh Mudahmid leaned forward slightly.

"I appeal to Sheikh Yassiheim—to the highest mufti—the greatest spiritual advisor to this group."

"You have no right to any appeal," Mudahmid said, laughing contemptuously.

"No—but my client does. An Arab—and a former Muslim— he has come to know that Jesus, whom you call a prophet, is also Jesus the Savior, the only one who shed the purest blood for our vilest sins. Shouldn't Hassan Gilead Amahn's case be heard before Sheikh Yassiheim, the highest mufti? So that he may explain the truth of his heart, and that his hands are innocent of the blood of your people?"

"*I* am the highest mufti!" Mudahmid yelled.

But one of the imams whispered something to him. Mudahmid replied loudly, angrily.

The imam then rose and said something in Arabic, waving his arms.

Mudahmid also got up, raising his voice in reply and shaking his finger.

The men with the knives were waiting nervously, their blades poised near the throats of Will and Gilead.

But the delay had worked.

As Sheikh Mudahmid turned to the men to order the execution, he moved away from the window. And did not see the approaching assault.

The window glass smashed, shards flying, as Caleb Marlowe and Nathan Goldwaithe rappelled into the room, firing at the gunmen as they somersaulted in.

Two of the gunmen fell immediately. The third one shot back, clipping Nathan in the arm and knocking him to the floor, from where he still managed to return fire, killing the terrorist.

Caleb was yelling for Will and Gilead to lie down as he fired at the two executioners, who were scrambling for their guns.

As he downed both of them, for just a fleeting instant, Gilead had a shock of recognition…and that is when he knew he had seen him before…that Marlowe had been the bearded man who had shoved him out to safety at the Islamic Center riot. "Thank you, thank you," Gilead was trying to say yet could not quite get out in all the confusion and shooting.

But Caleb's back was turned to the sheikh, who had stayed back when the two imams had scrambled out of the room. His face contorted with fury, he pulled a revolver out of his robe and fired directly at Caleb Marlowe, hitting him in the back. Then he turned the weapon toward Gilead and fired, sending a bullet into his head.

Gilead blinked, and with a look of confused calm, collapsed to the floor.

Mudahmid then began to fire at Will. As his target tried to scramble away, the sheikh, who was walking toward him while firing, pointed the barrel directly at his chest.

The gun fired, and the bullet struck Will in the upper left quadrant of his chest, a perfect shot to the heart, sending him to the floor with the impact.

Nathan, struggling up from where he lay fired the rest of his clip into the sheikh, who crumpled to the ground as one final terrorist appeared in the doorway.

He tossed a grenade into the middle of the room and ran out. The grenade landed only a few feet away from Will, who was lying on his side, his eyes still processing the last images…of Gilead laying stone-still…and Caleb, bleeding profusely, rising on his hands and knees turning to Will…just for a millisecond…but long enough to lock eyes with him and send him a last look that went beyond language. And then Caleb Marlowe fell on the grenade as it exploded.

When the smoke cleared a little, Nathan Goldwaithe screamed into his walkie-talkie, "American citizens hit and down—request immediate assistance!"

A group of Israeli-operated Blackhawks, containing IDF forces, already in the air just outside of the Gaza Strip, bolted forward in formation toward Rafiah.

In the darkness, they entered the town, dodging ground fire and sniper fire from rooftops. As the Blackhawks came into sight over the streets, now filled with hordes of people pointing, yelling, and shooting guns, the signal was given to Tex Rhoady, who had been hovering over the building. Now he could speed off and leave the rest to the big choppers.

As Tex whirled out of the area ducking ground-to-air missiles and random gunshots, the Israeli Defense Forces landed in the street and on the roof of the apartment building.

They had come to rescue the living, collect the fallen, and gather the dead.

THERE WAS A MILD, WARM BREEZE blowing that day in Jerusalem, and the sky was clear. A group had gathered at a small cemetery on a hill overlooking the Kidron Valley and the Old City of Jerusalem that lay just beyond it. The Temple Mount plateau still rose up in the midst of it all, as it had for thousands of years.

In the past centuries, the sunlight would sparkle off the golden Dome of the Rock, which had dominated the Mount. But since the devastation of the bombings and the international tensions following them, those days were gone.

As the caskets of the dead were lowered down into the two graves, Fiona stood by, weeping. Tiny Heftland was at her side, and next to him, Tex Rhoady. She was holding hands with young Andrew. Nigel Newhouse was there too, trying to make sense of it all. Behind him, Jack Hornby—a man who was rarely at a loss for words—stood wordlessly.

General Cal Tucker and his aides, as well as several special-operations veterans who had served together, snapped to a sharp salute as the American flag-draped coffin of Caleb Marlowe was lowered into the ground.

And then the second coffin, containing the body of Gilead Amahn, was lowered. It was draped with a white flag that, at its center, displayed a cross, and in its background, a green outline of the mountains of the Gilead region. Bill and Esther Colling-wood, who were struggling now for composure, thought their adopted son would have appreciated that.

But someone else was there at the graveside service.

In the very front, just inches away from the edge of Marlow's grave, stood Will Chambers. He was fingering the metal "shield of faith" that his son had given him. His son's badge now had a bullet-tip indentation in it—created by a forty-five-caliber round fired from the revolver of Sheikh Mudahmid. The heavy brass badge had stopped it from striking Will's heart.

Will had a bandage, covered by a black patch over his left eye. He had been hit by some shrapnel from the grenade explosion that Caleb had blocked with his body. The doctors told him he had lost the eye. But somewhere in all of what had happened, Will figured, he had actually gained some additional sight.

A Bible verse—the one about there being "no greater love" than that someone should lay down his life for another—that was what was going through Will's mind as he stood by the grave of Caleb Marlowe.

And Will also was thinking about the life of Gilead Amahn as well. About his passion to tell the greatest story that could ever be told…whether it was told in peace or, as seemed to typify Gilead's short life, preached in the maelstrom of a violent world spinning toward its final destination.

With the kaleidoscope of events that had occurred during the last few days, and the urgency, hope, relief, and sorrow that had followed, few in that assembly had been following the news.

But if they had been, they would have learned of a strange transfer of power that had just taken place away in the Caribbean, in the tiny island nation of the Republic of Maretas. The body of Warren Mullburn had been found, stretched out in convulsed posture, in the stateroom of his great yacht *Epiphany*. Having finished a huge lobster, squid, and artichoke salad brimming with plenty of greens, he was suddenly taken ill. Almost immediately incapacitated, in less than an hour he was dead. The island coroner ruled it was death by accidental poisoning…ingestion of the deadly *cicuta maculata* plant that somehow had found its way into his salad.

It was rumored that President Mandu La Rouge might have been behind the death. Or perhaps even Mullburn's illegitimate son, Theos, who had inherited his father's global fortune and who was showing himself to be, in his own way, even more ruthless than his father. After all, there were suspicious circumstances. Mullburn could not have asked for help even if he wanted to. The door lock to his stateroom had been glued shut with a high-strength industrial epoxy. The phone lines had been disconnected. And his cell phone was missing.

But only the billionaire's personal chef, whose cuisine had been constantly and viciously criticized by the oil tycoon and who had shared Orville Putrie's interest in botany and greenhouses, probably knew the whole truth. And he had been permitted to leave the island for parts unknown.

Scott Magnit was given a life sentence in prison. As was Orville Putrie.

Judge Lee Kwong-ju returned to South Korea. And Alain Verdexler, on reaching his home in Belgium, was flooded with media requests from around the world, asking that he explain his vote to "abstain" in the last judgment of Hassan Gilead Amahn. But he declined to break his silence.

As for Saad Mustafa, as a result of mounting international pressure, he launched an investigation into Palestinian public prosecutor Samir Zayed, in order to determine whether he had conspired in the kidnapping of Gilead Amahn and Will Chambers.

So, on that hill in Jerusalem, Will Chambers stepped back from the graves, placing himself close to Fiona and Andy.

Reaching out, he pulled Andy to him and squeezed him tight. On the other side, he wrapped his hand around Fiona's, and then wrapped his little finger around her little finger, and squeezed. She squeezed back—in that secret communication of joined intimacy, the kind that is spoken silently in a wedded pair's own private language.

When they returned to the United States, Will would meet with his law-office associates, display his black leather eye patch, and announce his "informal retirement." And then he and Fiona would figure out exactly how they could best celebrate the sweet blessings of the rest of their life together.

Now, the graveside service was almost finished.

Pastor Wyman, who had stayed in Jerusalem to fulfill his longtime dream of touring the Holy Land, had been asked to lead the service. So he gave a short message. It was based on the one-hundred-fourth psalm, verses ten through twelve—the picture of God giving water to the beasts of the desert and sending springs of water through the dry valleys.

On that hill overlooking Jerusalem, he quietly explained how God provides the "springs" of living waters for our souls when we are spiritually parched and feel ourselves surrounded by the lonely desolation of the desert all around. How Jesus Christ is the source of that living water. And how only He can make us sing, even though our hearts are broken and our heads are bowed low. And then he read the final verse again:

> By them the birds of the heavens have their home;
> They sing among the branches.

Bill and Esther had requested that Fiona sing at the graveside. After composing herself, she took a step forward, glancing out at the ancient city spread out before her, and then began to sing.

> *There is a balm in Gilead*
> *To make the wounded whole;*
> *There is a balm in Gilead*
> *To heal the sin sick soul.*
>
> *Sometimes I feel discouraged,*
> *And think my work's in vain,*
> *But then the Holy Spirit*
> *Revives my soul again.*

If you can't preach like Peter,
If you can't pray like Paul,
Just tell the love of Jesus,
and say He died for all.

When she was done singing, there was quiet. Though the quiet would not last. Weeks later, massive violence would erupt in Jerusalem, caused by several Palestinian groups in retaliation for the Israeli troops' daring to enter the Gaza Strip during the rescue operation. The Israeli Defense Force would strike back, driving out the Palestinian police and the UN troops that had encircled the Temple Mount.

After two millennia of waiting, the nation of Israel would finally be in exclusive possession of the Mount. The long-awaited rebuilding of the ancient Jewish Temple would then begin.

And more wars, and the rumors of them, would also begin—and then the march toward the last judgment of history...and of God.

But in that brief moment of reflection, as Will and Fiona and Andy, and the small group of mourners, cast one last look over Jerusalem, it was peaceful.

And there was no sound, except for the sound of the breeze whispering through the leaves of an ancient, spreading olive tree nearby, and the warbling song of the birds who were safely nested in its branches.

About the Author

CRAIG PARSHALL is a highly successful lawyer from the Washington, DC, area who specializes in cases involving civil liberties and religious freedom. He is also the frequent spokesperson for conservative values in mainstream and Christian media. *The Last Judgment* is the final installment in the Chambers of Justice series, following four other novels—the powerful *Resurrection File,* the harrowing *Custody of the State,* the gripping *The Accused,* and the suspenseful *Missing Witness.*

THE CHAMBERS OF JUSTICE SERIES
by Craig Parshall

The Resurrection File

When Reverend Angus MacCameron asks attorney Will Chambers to defend him against accusations that could discredit the Gospels, Will's unbelieving heart says "run." But conspiracy and intrigue—and the presence of MacCameron's lovely and successful daughter, Fiona—draw him deep into the case...toward a destination he could never have imagined.

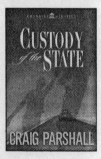

Custody of the State

Attorney Will Chambers reluctantly agrees to defend a young mother from Georgia and her farmer husband, suspected of committing the unthinkable against their own child. Encountering small-town secrets, big-time corruption, and a government system that's destroying the little family, Chambers himself is thrown into the custody of the state.

The Accused

Enjoying a Cancún honeymoon with his wife, Fiona, attorney Will Chambers is ambushed by two unexpected events: a terrorist kidnapping of a U.S. official...and the news that a link has been found to the previously unidentified murderer of Will's first wife. The kidnapping pulls him into the case of Marine colonel Caleb Marlowe. When treachery drags both Will and his client toward vengeance, they must ask—*Is forgiveness real?*

Missing Witness

A relaxing North Carolina vacation for attorney Will Chambers? Not likely. When Will investigates a local inheritance case, the long arm of the law reaches out of the distant past to cast a shadow over his client's life...and the life of his own family. As the attorney's legal battle uncovers corruption, piracy, the deadly grip of greed, and the haunting sins of a man's past, the true question must be faced—*Can a person ever really run away from God?*

The Last Judgment

A mysterious religious cult plans to spark an "Armageddon" in the Middle East. Suddenly, a huge explosion blasts the top of the Jerusalem Temple Mount into rubble, with hundreds of Muslim casualities. And attorney Will Chambers' client, Gilead Amahn, a convert to Christianity from Islam, becomes the prime suspect. In his harrowing pursuit of the truth, Will must face the greatest threat yet to his marriage, his family, and his faith, while cataclysmic events plunge the world closer to the Last Judgment.

FORGIVING SOLOMON LONG
by Chris Well

Kansas City—home of the *Star,* the Chiefs, and the blues. Visit. Have the time of your life. Just don't lose it if you meet one of these players at the wrong end of his piece...

Crime boss Frank "Fat Cat" Catalano—a man with a vision. With dreams of building a legacy, Fat Cat has his fingers into nearly every business sector, legal or otherwise. But a coalition of local store owners and clergy has gotten it into their heads to band together and try to break Catalano's stranglehold.

Detective Tom Griggs—a man with a mission. He and his small task force have been shadowing Fat Cat's operations, looking for cracks in the wall. Griggs will give it all he has until the whole house comes down. No matter the cost. Even if that cost is neglecting—and losing—his own wife.

Hit man Solomon "Solo" Long—a man with a job. Fat Cat's about to make important changes in the family business...and doesn't need troublemakers rocking the boat. Solo is a "cleaner" flown in from the coast to make sure the locals get the message.

It all adds up to a thriller that crackles with wit and unexpected heart—that smokes you with machine-gun action and hits you in the gut with a powerful message of forgiveness.